CW01217738

DEAD MAN TALKING

MARK STIBBE

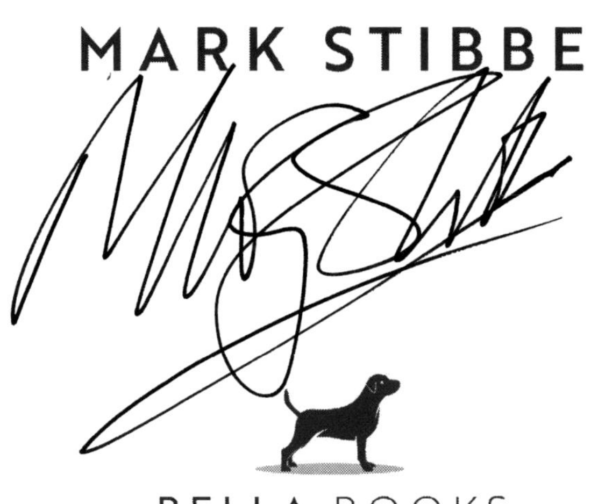

BELLA BOOKS

First published 2024 by Bella Books UK, a Pawprint/Imprint of BookLab

www.thebooklab.co.uk

British Library Cataloguing in Publication Data. A catalogue record for this book is available from the British Library.

ISBN: 979-8-3384-8190-5

Cover design by Esther Kotecha

DEDICATION

This story is dedicated with gratitude and love to my Northern Irish family and friends, and to my African American spiritual family and friends

I will arise and go now, for always night and day
I hear lake water lapping with low sounds by the shore;
While I stand on the roadway, or on the pavements grey,
I hear it in the deep heart's core.

W.B. Yeats
The Lake Isle of Innisfree

It has always been difficult for white people to empathize fully with the experience of black people. But it has never been impossible.

James H. Cone,
The Cross and the Lynching Tree

CONTENTS

1

THE PHOTOGRAPH

As an academic, Cameron Stone was something of a sceptic when it came to the supernatural - until, that is, he saw the photograph. Three years before, he had been given the chair of history at his university. Once installed, he had made it clear to his more speculative students that he preferred to deal with the seen rather than the unseen, with the physical not the metaphysical. When he saw the photograph, however, the rigid plates protecting his core began to shift.

At 9pm on a Monday evening in February, Professor Stone walked from Old Portsmouth, where he lived, to the university library fifteen minutes away. When he arrived upstairs at the collection room, the archivist – an elegant man with dark hair, a three-piece suit and tie, just north of sixty – was waiting for him.

"Here it is, Professor," he said, his accent a fusion of the east coast of America and the west coast of Ireland. "This is the photograph album you requested."

When the archivist left, Stone began to turn its cardboard

pages. Halfway through, he paused at two photographs. The first showed the port side of a seaplane resting at anchor. It had RAF markings on the fuselage and its large, curved tail. Underneath, it said, "Lough Erne, County Fermanagh, 1943." Stone withdrew a magnifying glass. Studying the bow of the flying boat, he made out the words, 'Lady of the Night.' He frowned at the bewitching name.

Pulling himself together, Professor Stone looked at the second photograph which depicted a group of nine airmen. Five were standing. Four were kneeling in front of them. Underneath were the words, "The Destroyers of two U-Boats in one mission. RAF Castle Archdale, 1944." Each of the men was clothed in flying suits and life vests, and they wore their goggles over their foreheads rather than eyes. They stood in front of a Georgian mansion situated on the crest of a hill. Stone noticed Ionic pilasters at the entrance. He counted the windows - eighteen of them, six on each of its three floors.

In Stone's eyes, one of the crewmembers stood out from the rest – a black airman standing in the centre of the second row. The others were as pale as the seaplane in the first photograph. This airman, however, had ebony skin and was a young man of extraordinary personal beauty. Just as striking, his dark hands were wrapped around a small white dog – a Westie - trying to lick his chin. Stone imagined he could hear the deep and distant boom of his sonorous laugh.

And then it hit him.

He wasn't imagining it.

He was hearing it.

The professor wiped his eyes. The airman seemed not only to be alive but laughing. His lips were broadening and his eyes shining. While his comrades beside and in front of him were all motionless, frozen in time, this man's shoulders were juddering at the antics of the canine companion he was cradling.

Stone shook his head.

He pressed his fingers to his eardrums.

Still the tall man laughed.

The professor looked at his watch.

9.45pm.

Surely, he was at home and in bed.

Fast asleep.

He pinched his arm so hard that the nails produced a thin red line on his skin.

He was not dreaming.

The man and his dog had somehow been revivified.

Just then, the archivist reappeared. He leant into the room, his dark eyes scanning the table.

"Everything all right, Professor?"

Stone looked up from the album. He sighed and asked, "Could you come here a moment?"

Stone could hear the airman's laugh.

The man approached the table.

"What is it?"

"Here," Stone said, pointing at the second picture. "My eyes are tired tonight. Could you tell me what you see?"

The archivist studied the image.

"I see a Catalina if I'm not mistaken. Played a vital role in the Battle of the Atlantic."

Stone nodded.

"And the second picture?"

"The crew," he said. "It looks like they've just returned

from a successful mission. From the description below, it seems they'd sunk a couple of U-Boats. No small feat."

As Stone stared at the same image, the airman continued to laugh, and his little white dog continued to stretch its tiny tongue towards his stubbly chin. They were very much alive.

"Anything strange?"

"Only that the tallest man on the back row seems to be a black airman while the rest are not."

"Nothing else?"

"The Westie, I suppose."

"You mean the dog?"

He nodded.

Stone waited a few more seconds.

The archivist continued. "I suppose there's the fact that they're Royal Canadian Airforce men, and they're wearing standard RAF combat uniforms. But that's not all that strange. There were Canadians flying Catalinas in the RAF."

Stone mumbled a yes.

When he realised that the archivist appeared not to be seeing what he saw, he thanked him, and the man walked from the room. Stone returned to the picture. As soon as he did, the airman stopped laughing. During the time it took for Stone to register this, the pilot's expression changed to one of anguish. His dog, sensing this, was now shaking, emitting a low and heartbreaking whine. The creature was no longer trying to lick him. He was cowering, burrowing his head as far as he could beneath his master's arm.

As Stone rubbed his eyes again, the man and his dog began to fade. But before they disappeared, the airman stared at the historian. He uttered a cry. And in that cry, which seemed to come from the deepest place in his soul, the historian heard two words.

"Find me!"

With that, the man and his dog were gone.

"Are you still studying that picture?"

The voice belonged to the archivist who had returned to retrieve the precious album.

Stone nodded.

"Something troubling you?"

"See for yourself."

"What am I supposed to be looking at?"

"The black airman and his dog."

"What about them?" he asked.

The professor turned back to the image. The airman was not there, and neither was his dog. The archivist, however, seemed unimpressed. He did not seem to note the surprising lacuna.

Stone thanked the man and made his way back through the open-plan library. As he passed through the glass doors into the cold night, he tried to comprehend what he had just seen.

What did it all mean?

Stone headed back to his apartment, stopping only to look out to sea. He could just make out the lights of a ship in the distance, although its contours were invisible to the naked eye. He thought of the Catalina lying moored on the lough in Fermanagh and imagined it flying low across the water, gaining altitude, heading to its cruising height of around two thousand feet. He thought of the handsome airman on duty somewhere in its ghostly fuselage.

What was it like flying out at night across the Atlantic, searching for the silent and invisible wolfpacks harassing the allied merchant ships? What challenges did the airman face from those who thought less of him because of the colour of his skin? And what forces had engineered the strange apparition he had just witnessed? And why to him, a professor wary of such phenomena?

As he turned to walk the cobbled street to his apartment, a gust of icy wind blew in from the ocean. As it stung his ears, he swore he heard the airman cry to him again.

"Find me!"

2

THE GRANDDAUGHTER

The following evening, Professor Cameron Stone could still sense the trembling in his spine as he sat on the stage of the Guild Hall waiting to receive his award. The memory of the airman had clung to him all night. Worse still, he had developed since awakening the nagging feeling that he had seen the man's face before, but he could not remember where. It was still bothering him as he turned to his research assistant. Bret was a 23-year-old postgrad student with long, wavy brown hair. He was sitting next to him on the stage.

"Did you manage to find some visuals?" Stone asked.

Bret's blue eyes glowed beneath his high forehead. He replied, "They'll sync well with your talk."

"How will I see them?"

"There's a TV monitor at the front of the stage facing you. You should be able to follow them on there."

"And you'll be operating the slide show?"

Bret produced a small remote.

"With this," he said.

Stone nodded.

Just then a man in red corduroy trousers left one of the seats and headed to the front of the stage.

"My publisher, Greg," Stone whispered.

In a smooth English accent, Greg welcomed those watching online before addressing the audience in the hall.

"Ladies, gentlemen, distinguished guests, we are here to hand out the Wolfson History Prize and a cheque for £50,000 for this highly acclaimed, bestselling book."

Greg lifted Stone's book which the cameras amplified. The central image on its cover showed a black-and-white photograph of two Tuskegee airmen in front of a P51C Mustang. The title was in a strident red font, which Stone knew – because he had chosen it – was the same colour as the Mustang's tail. It read, *The Jostlers*.

The publisher continued. "Tonight, the author will also receive the prestigious Howard Prize for historical research dedicated to the eradication of racial injustice."

When the clapping subsided, the speaker concluded. "The author will now give a summary of his thesis before taking questions. Please welcome Professor Cameron Stone."

Stone stood as the audience applauded again. At the podium, there was a hush as he made to begin. "I'm sure most of you haven't read my book, and, if you're anything like I am in situations like these, I'm also sure many of you never will..."

A ripple of laughter.

"So, let me be brief. *The Jostlers* is about what happened to many Tuskegee airmen after the end of World War Two. Many know of these brave souls who flew the famous Red Tails."

Black-and-white footage appeared behind and above the professor - American bombers guarded by the black airmen in their Mustangs. Stone could make out the same images on the monitor facing him at a small distance in front of the podium.

"The mostly white US bomber crews always breathed a sigh of relief whenever they were being escorted by the courageous Tuskegee pilots. No one had a better record than the Red Tails at protecting these heavy aircraft as they conducted dangerous missions in the European and Pacific theatres of operation."

The screen now showed African American airmen in WW2 combat flying uniform, some on their own and others sitting or standing in groups near their aircraft.

The sequence finished with a photograph Stone had seen before in one of the books he had read while researching for his own. It showed a tall, clean-shaven airman in front of his training aircraft at Tuskegee. Something looked familiar. Stone shook his head. Surely, he was imagining things. Then it struck him. He was staring at the same man he had seen the night before - the man who had laughed and then cried, the mystery man with the little dog.

The professor froze.

The image remained for two more seconds.

But during the time it was there, the man in the picture mouthed again the words, "Find me!"

Stone shook his head and wiped his eyes.

Everyone was staring at him now.

He heard a woman on the front row mumble, "Is he having a stroke or something?"

Stone apologised, then continued his summary.

"Sadly, the outstanding young men who survived these sorties discovered after the war that these were not the only battles that they had to face. They now had the terrible evil of segregation to contend with once again. In the wake of such ingratitude for what they had given by way of service to their country, they could have chosen to act violently against their oppressors. But they did not."

On the screens, an image appeared of an officer's club with a notice outside the entrance. 'Instructors Only.'

"In the Spring of 1945, over 100 servicemen of the all-black 477th Bombardment Group engaged in a protest at Freeman Field Base in Indiana. Tired of discrimination, they refused to sign an agreement that would have led to them agreeing to two officer's messes, one for blacks – trainees - and the other for whites - instructors."

There was murmuring in the audience.

"These brave men had trained at the Tuskegee airfield in Alabama and were in no mood to back down."

A ripple of approval.

Stone took a sip of water before adding, "Their refusal became known as the Freeman Field Mutiny."

The ripple turned to a wave.

"This was not welcomed by white officers. In fact, the opposition to their protest came right from the top. Major General Frank Hunter, the man who commanded the same 477th Bombardment Group, proclaimed that America was not ready to accept white officers and coloured officers at the same social level. He added that he based his view on the past 125 years of American history."

There were gasps in the audience.

"You can read in my book a full account of what happened

next. But let me summarise by stating that a few black officers started getting arrested on a charge of 'jostling.' They entered whites-only clubs and made their presence felt. At least one officer, Roger 'Bill' Terry, was court-martialled on a charge of 'jostling'."

There were sounds of disdain in the audience.

"In my book, I explore how these actions became a template for the tactics employed by the leaders of the civil rights movement during the 1960s and following."

Stone took a deep breath as a photograph of the murder of George Floyd appeared on the screens.

"The world is still racially divided. Hatred, as Dr King taught us, simply breeds more violence. I therefore commend to you the example of the jostlers in the pursuit of just causes in our world, especially in the context of civil rights."

Applause.

The publisher returned to the podium. After thanking Stone, he invited questions from the audience.

The first came from an elderly man with a knitted hat. He spoke in a soft, measured tone.

"My father, after arriving on the Windrush, travelled here to work in the docks. I was born in this city and, along with others, have suffered discrimination because of the colour of my skin. So, I'd like to ask, what is the real motive for your research? What is in your story to make you so opposed to segregation?"

Someone in the audience whispered, "cultural appropriation", and the professor winced.

"It's a very fair question," Stone said.

A few people shifted in their seats.

The professor took a deep breath. "I've not shared my

own story publicly before, but perhaps I should now. I was brought up by my mother. It won't come as a surprise to learn she was white. She died when I was twelve."

He took a sip of water.

"I was then looked after by the man who meant more to me than any other; the man who looked after my mother when she was orphaned; the man who became an adoptive father to her, and an adoptive grandfather to me."

Everyone was still now.

"He was a Jamaican gentleman, and he too was on the Windrush. He too worked in the docks here. Perhaps your father and my adoptive grandfather knew each other. Maybe later, we can find out. But let me just say this. It was my grandfather who lit the fire for racial integration that you'll find in my book."

Stone looked out at the audience.

"I research these topics because I want to honour his memory and continue his legacy. But most of all, I do what I do because I loved him, and will always love him."

The old man who had asked the question nodded. He thanked Stone before taking his seat again.

Stone responded to five more comments before Greg stepped up again to ask him one final question.

"Tell us, Professor, what's your next project?"

"I'm currently interested in the use of Lough Erne as an RAF base during the Battle of the Atlantic. I'm especially interested in black US service personnel in Northern Ireland during that time. I'm taking a sabbatical to research the topic."

Applause.

"And now," Greg said, "It's time to present the professor

with his cheque for £50,000."

More applause.

The rest of the night was a blur, at least until Bret bundled the professor into a car.

"Were you all right up there tonight?" Bret asked.

"What do you mean?"

"You seemed to get stage fright."

"I just felt a bit tired, that's all."

Bret sighed.

"What is it?" Stone asked.

"I'm afraid there's something else before you can sleep."

"Not a party."

"No. It's an email."

"Can't it wait till tomorrow?"

Bret shook his head and passed his phone.

Stone began to read. It was from a woman in Boston who had leaped onto the livestream earlier that evening. She said she needed to meet him. She wanted to find out about an airman in World War 2. He had been stationed in Northern Ireland. Was a second pilot on a Catalina. The plane was nicknamed 'Lady of the Night'.

The hairs on Stone's neck began to bristle.

She wrote that he flew with the Royal Canadian Airforce, but he was an African American. Trained at Tuskegee. He disappeared from all records in 1944 and she couldn't find out why. His name was George Hailey. "I am his granddaughter, Maya Hailey. We have one photograph of him. I've attached it this email."

Stone opened it.

He gasped. It was the same airman he had seen in the album in the archives room.

3

THE WATCHER

As Robert Miller waited at the junction, he glanced in the rear-view mirror. For a 70-year-old, he was aging well. He was entirely bald, and he ensured he remained that way by shaving any new flecks of grey hair. This helped to sustain an aura of indefinability. When people ventured a guess, they always put him in his fifties, at worst early sixties. The fact that he did not wear glasses, nor needed them, helped. He had been blessed with extraordinary vision considering he had now lived out his three score years and ten. His eyes had not failed at all, but had retained their ability, like an eagle in high flight, to watch over large landscapes and discern minute movements. As he prepared to turn onto the main road, he smiled. His eyes were perhaps his best asset, not just in terms of his appearance, but also his profession.

Miller joined the A59 towards the spa town of Harrogate and headed past drenched sheep towards his place of work on Menwith Hill. No attempt had been made to conceal this military base. It was visible for miles around on account of its huge white, golf-ball-shaped domes. Outwardly, it presented itself to the world as an RAF base, but those in the know understood it had another purpose. It functioned as the primary listening post for America's National Security Agency and National Reconnaissance Office in Great Britain. From this hub, American personnel watched for any signs of threat to homeland security posed by members of the British Pakistani community. Or at least that was its stated purpose. In fact, this remit had expanded to almost any and every perceived nuisance.

Miller stopped at the gates.

A guard approached.

Miller opened the driver's window.

"Morning, sir," the guard said.

"Is it?"

The soldier smiled. Scanning Miller's badge, he said, "You still under the weather, sir?"

"That's the problem. The weather. Nothing but grey skies, cold winds, and hard rain. So, yes, I'm under it."

"I'm sorry to hear that, sir."

"Don't feel too sorry. I'm retiring soon. Then it'll be back to fishing in the Everglades."

The guard said, "No Yorkshire rain there, sir."

Miller forced a smile, nodded at the guard, and drove to his parking space. As he walked through the doors, he presented his badge at reception and navigated his way through two sets of metal detectors before entering his office two floors below.

Removing his thick navy-blue overcoat, he set his leather briefcase beside his office chair. He was about to get up and make himself a strong coffee when the door opened, and a young woman entered. She stopped just short of the desk.

"Your morning briefing, sir."

She handed Miller a beige file.

Miller skim-read the two pages.

"Get me a secure line to the Pentagon," he said.

"I already have it ready for you, sir."

Miller nodded. He had now managed two smiles on the same day. Something of a record.

Miller picked up the phone and beckoned for the young officer to leave, mouthing the words 'thank you.'

When the door was shut, he heard a familiar voice at the other end. "What can I do for you, Miller?"

"We may have a problem, Ma'am."

The woman waited.

"One of our signals intelligence officers has picked up communications between an African American woman in Boston, Massachusetts and an academic at Portsmouth University, a professor of history called Cameron Stone."

Miller could sense his superior's indifference.

"The academic has just picked up the scent of a story about an airman from World War 2."

"Which airman?"

"An African American airman in Northern Ireland."

"Are we talking about the person I think?"

Miller replied, "George Hailey, Ma'am."

The woman cussed.

"It gets worse, Ma'am."

"Really?"

"The woman who's talking with him is George Hailey's granddaughter, Maya Hailey, the former pastor of a church in Boston. She heard Stone speaking about African

American airmen in World War 2 at an awards ceremony. She contacted him. She's arrived in the UK on a red-eye flight this morning."

Another expletive.

When she had recovered her equilibrium, the woman in the Pentagon spoke again. "You must be under no illusions, Agent Miller. If the story about what happened to George Hailey gets into the public domain here in the States, it could make the reactions we have seen recently look tame in comparison."

"I know Ma'am."

"Things are like dry tinder," she continued. "Something like this could be incendiary. It's the last thing we need right now. The country is already on the edge."

Miller nodded.

He raised his head.

"What are your orders, Ma'am?"

"You're retiring soon?"

"In three months."

"Then this will be your swansong. Head down to Portsmouth. Have eyes on them both. Don't allow either to access any sensitive data. Obstruct them, Miller, but try not to destabilise the special relationship between our two countries."

"What are the limits of my remit, Ma'am?"

"Give me a moment."

Miller heard typing.

"This history professor," she said.

"Ma'am?"

"According to what I'm seeing, he teaches about the civil rights movement and the history of slavery, and he's about to start a year-long sabbatical, conducting research into the flying boats of Lough Erne during World War 2."

"That's right,"

"Is he single?"

"Yes."

"Any family."

"He's an only child. His mother's deceased."

"Father?"

"There's nothing on file. Seems to have come and gone... if you'll pardon the expression."

"He's a loner then."

"He is, but he's also becoming more visible due to his book. And he's popular with students and staff."

"Then keep an eye on him, and Hailey's granddaughter. I'll authorise whatever inventory you need after we hang up. But I need to stress. This is an off-the-grid mission."

"Understood."

"Nothing can be traced Stateside."

"Yes, Ma'am."

"And one more thing."

"Ma'am?"

"I know about the trauma you suffered in the past. Don't let that affect your judgment."

"Ma'am?"

"I'm talking about your parents."

"Ancient history, Ma'am."

"Good, because we can't afford any mistakes. Your station is constantly being investigated by the British Press, and it's under review by the British government."

"It's always under review."

"This time it's serious. Some members of the press, not to

mention conspiratorial members of the public, are digging for anything incriminating about surveillance."

"I'll be discrete."

"And try to be restrained."

Miller ended the call and headed to the armoury. There he withdrew and signed for a pistol, a silencer, some ammunition, and an assortment of surveillance gadgets.

He walked back to his office, donned his coat, headed to his car, and sat looking at the radomes. These huge spherical enclosures were designed to hide the electric equipment inside, including the radio antennae, and protect it from harsh weather. As he gazed at the gates and thought about heading back onto the A59, Miller decided to wait until the rain stopped. But it didn't. And as the downpour intensified, the front windscreen began to run outside and steam inside, sending him into a trance-like state.

In a heartbeat, Miller was a boy again, away at a summer Bible camp in the hills of the deep south back home. His youth leader was sitting next to him on a fallen tree trunk, his arm around his shoulder. He had just shared the news that his parents had been shot dead by a black drug dealer in a gas station. A primal rage had been born at that moment, an eternal hatred. His whole life had been dictated and defined by it. He had tried to push down the volcanic lust for revenge, but it had always threatened to erupt.

One time he had placed a hangman's noose outside the motel room where a black NSA agent called Harper was sleeping. The whole service had felt the repercussions. Miller had remained undetected but had been forced to duck and weave in the glare of suspicious minds. He had decided to refrain from similar actions.

Until now.

He made up his mind there and then. If Hailey's granddaughter posed any threat to what was left of the status quo back home, he would threaten her. And as for the academic, if he had to be persuaded to stop meddling, then persuaded he would be.

The rain stopped.

A gap formed in the dark grey clouds, revealing a patch of blue sky and a hint of sunlight. Miller shook himself out of his dissociative state and switched on the engine. He headed through the gates and away from Harrogate on the A59.

He was on his way to Portsmouth and to better weather.

If this was his final mission, Agent Robert Miller would make sure he would succeed.

4

THE LETTERS

Cameron Stone looked at his watch. Maya was late. Fifteen minutes late, to be precise. Yes, she had just recently flown in on the overnight flight from Logan International Airport, and yes, her body clock had to be all over the place, but the one thing Stone resented more than anything was waiting. He hated being late, and he hated when he was the one waiting, tapping his toes on the floor in frustration.

The venue he chose for their meeting was a café at the Portsmouth Museum and Art Gallery - a four-storeyed, red-brick building near his apartment. This grand edifice was 250 years old and had originally been a barracks accommodating up to 1000 soldiers. Most of the barracks had now gone, but the officer's quarters had remained, providing a home for some of Portsmouth's most treasured historical artefacts. The front entrance was flanked by two towers, both with conical turrets. Stone hoped she would be impressed.

When Maya Hailey entered, Stone forgot that she was twenty minutes past the hour they had agreed. The professor estimated, rightly as it turned out, that she was about thirty years of age. Her skin was not as dark as George Hailey's; it was more like sand than earth, closer to honey than to bronze. Her jet-black hair, parted in the centre, had long box braids descending as far as the front and back of her white polar-necked jumper and her short black jacket. Even though she was tired, her skin was smooth and her eyes alert.

Stone stood as she looked around the crowded café. He waved. She nodded and approached the table.

"Maya Hailey, I presume."

"That's me," she replied.

"Hungry?" he asked.

"Just coffee."

She cleared her throat.

Everyone heard it.

"Sorry," she said. "Must have picked up something on the plane." As she sat, Stone pushed her chair towards the table. Maya said, "Let me give you some money for that."

"You're my guest," he replied.

She looked up at him, her dark brown eyes studying his.

When Stone returned with the two coffees, Maya was leaning her head on her right fist, her elbow acting as a support. As he placed her cup and saucer on the table, she rallied.

"Thanks for seeing me, Professor. You must be a busy man."

"I'm on sabbatical, and please call me Cameron."

"All the same, I'm sure you've got plans and those didn't involve seeing a jet-lagged woman from Boston."

As she said Boston, her accent betrayed her.

"Was that where you were born?"

"My father is the pastor of a large church northside. A mainly African American congregation. He's called 'Bishop' outside our family. To me and my six brothers, he's Daddy."

"Six brothers!" Stone exclaimed.

"It taught me to be independent, which was what Mamma wanted. She named me after Maya Angelou. She often repeated something the great woman said. 'I love to see a young girl go out and grab the world by the lapels... You've got to go out and kick ass!'"

The professor could not hide his surprise. "I thought you said your father was a pastor."

"A bishop, yes."

"Isn't 'ass' a rude word."

"Mamma is a free spirit. She isn't shy of using words like 'ass.' In fact, that's her favourite word for my ex-husband. His name always makes Mamma cuss."

There was a sideways glance as she mentioned him. A synapse of memory. A hint of grief.

"You married, Professor?"

"Single."

"Divorced?"

"No."

"Gay?"

Stone coughed as a gulp of coffee went down the wrong way. Unable to vocalise his reply, he simply waved his hand as he recovered his breathing.

She said, "Bostonians can be blunt."

Stone used his napkin to daub a stray drop of coffee from the sleeve of his woollen sweater.

"Let me get to the point," Maya said, pulling her briefcase from the floor to her lap. She withdrew an A4 folder before returning her case to the side of the table. “I’m here about my Granddaddy, and I’m here because you’re the only one who can help me.”

Stone watched her expression change as she said the word ‘help’. Like she was biting her pretty lips as she said it.

“If it’s okay, I’ll tell you what I know.”

Stone nodded.

“His name was George Hailey. After Pearl Harbour, he was desperate to join the United States Army Air Force as it was called, so he went to Tuskegee and trained as a pilot. But he was one of the men who got washed out even though he passed.”

“That sounds familiar,” Stone said. “Something to do with too many applicants, not enough places.”

She nodded.

“Anyway, Granddaddy was disappointed but not deterred. He travelled to Ontario and joined the Royal Canadian Airforce after training there. He was then posted to Northern Ireland to join an RAF squadron in County Fermanagh.”

“The Catalinas,” Stone said.

“That’s right. He was the only black airman in his nine-man crew, in his entire squadron. He trained to be a second pilot and flew out into the Atlantic to fight the Nazis.”

Stone started jotting down a few notes on his phone.

“This was in 1943 and 1944,” Maya continued. “And during that time, he met a local girl in Fermanagh. A pretty, white girl. An Irish Catholic called Myra. They fell in love. Sometime after Christmas or New Year 1943, they must have conceived a child, because in late August 1944, Myra gave birth to a baby.”

"Your father?" Stone asked.

"My daddy."

Maya finished her coffee.

"But here's one of the mysteries," she said, her voice softer now. "Myra travelled alone to Boston to have her child. She died after my daddy was born. No one knew where she'd come from, or her family name. All they knew she was called Myra. I think that's another reason Mamma called me Maya. It sounded like her."

Stone glanced up from his notetaking. There was a faraway look on Maya's face.

"I presume your family adopted the baby?"

She nodded. "When he grew up, Daddy tried to find out where Myra was from in Northern Ireland, and who her family was, but it's as if she didn't exist at all." She shook her head. "And she's not the only one in our story you could say that about."

"Let me guess," Stone said. "George?"

Maya withdrew a bundle of hand-written letters from a folder. They were tied together by string.

"These are the letters George Hailey sent home to his father, my great grandfather."

She passed them over the table.

"I would like you to study them."

Stone took them in his hands. "Originals?"

"They are."

"Wouldn't it be safer to give me copies?"

"No, Professor. There may be things that a historian like you can only see in the form you have them."

"What do you want me to find out?"

"What happened to my granddaddy."

"What don't you know?"

Maya looked at the bundle. "There are just twelve letters there. The last one was posted to George's father the night before he and his crewmen disappeared."

"Disappeared?"

"On the night of the 15th of March 1944, George's flying boat was returning from a mission. It had passed through the Donegal Corridor and was flying back to Lough Erne. That's the last anyone knew of its position. Like I said, it disappeared."

"Maybe it crashed in the lake," Stone said. "It's an enormous stretch of water. There's both an upper and a lower part to it. There are many islands. It would have been challenging at night."

"Maybe," she admitted. "But there's something not quite right with that explanation. In the 1970s, Daddy contacted all the families of the other crewmembers. Each one had been informed by the base commander at RAF Castle Archdale that their loved one was MIA, presumed KIA. Each one accepted the report."

"So, what's the mystery?"

"My family was the only one they didn't contact."

"Maybe it was an oversight," Stone said. "Or perhaps, I'm sorry to say, an example of military racism."

"I don't think so, Professor."

"Why not?"

Stone knew the answer before she offered it.

"Because in every other situation we have found where an African American sailor, soldier, or airman was either MIA or KIA in World War 2, the authorities informed their families."

Stone took a sip of coffee.

"So, what are you suggesting?"

"None of us in my family is susceptible to conspiracy theories. Black people don't get excitable around them. But we do smell a cover up. Something's not right."

"But what if there's an innocent explanation?"

"Listen, Professor. If you tell me that you've found proof that my Granddaddy was MIA or KIA like his eight other comrades, then I'll tell my family and that'll be the end of it. But if you find a different story, then we'll want to make sure we tell it."

"Then I accept," he said.

"Thank you, Professor."

"Cameron," he reminded her.

As they left the table, he asked where she was staying.

"The Marriott."

"I can contact you there?"

"For the next seven days."

They walked into the crisp, cold afternoon air. Maya stopped outside the entrance. As she waved for her taxi, she turned to him. "I know it may be because I've come all this way, and you therefore feel a little obligated, but I need to ask why. Why are you agreeing to help me? I don't understand?"

"You won't believe me."

"Faith is my area of expertise," she said. "So, let me ask you again. Why are you helping me find my grandfather?"

Stone lowered his voice. "Because he asked me to."

LETTER 1

October 20th, 1943

Dear Dad,

I have arrived safely at Londonderry. The voyage across the Atlantic was much easier than I expected. Not too rough. Unfortunately, I now have a cold. It's not as heavy as it was at the start of the journey, but it may be a while before I shake it. It's raining hard. The skies are as grey as the USS Mason. There's not a hint of the blue skies and sunshine I enjoyed in New York. I will need to wrap up here.

The Irish seem to be a warm-hearted people. All the locals I have met since I got off the ship couldn't have been more welcoming. They refer to me as a Yank. They make no reference to the color of my skin. No talk of being a "tanned" Yank, or a Negro. They treat me as an American fighting man, as they do with all the white boys. It's refreshing. Maybe a foretaste of what one day will happen back home.

I was driven to my new base by an Irishman who kept talking all the way to County Fermanagh and made me laugh every other sentence. He used many strange phrases that I had to ask him to translate. He said at one point that something was – and I'm writing this as it sounded – a "quare handling", meaning an unpleasant situation, and he ended many of his sentences with the word "so".

When at last we entered Fermanagh, he stopped, insisting we went and had something to drink at his cousin's house. I was given three cups of tea and as many rounds of sandwiches. As we were about to leave, his aunt said, "You'll take a wee cup of tea in your hand." Tea seems to be the national drink. It would be wrong to refuse!

By the time we arrived at Lough Erne, my sides were aching. There's no humor like Irish humor. My driver told me that he had once been at a wake after the death of an elderly uncle. The dead man had recently been on holiday somewhere a lot warmer than Northern Ireland. My driver overheard two of his aunts as they looked down at the tanned face of the corpse. One turned to the other and remarked, "I've never seen him look so well."

That brings me to the weather, which seems to be bad much of the time. In fact, I asked my driver whether he ever enjoyed sunshine in Northern Ireland. He replied, "I think we had summer on a Thursday last year." I laughed again but groaned inside.

When we arrived at my base, the first thing that caught my eye was the headquarters - a proud old mansion that stands watch over an enormous lough. Over 2000 souls are stationed here. Don't be fooled. I'm not living in the house! I'm billeted in one of the Nissan huts in the grounds. I share this with the other eight members of my crew. I'm the only Yank, and the only Negro. But I'm not looked at any differently. They treat me as an equal, as the Irish do.

I think you'd be impressed by the lake. There are many islands, some of them with ancient pagan and Christian monuments. I feel a sense of mystery lingering over the water.

I can't think of very much more to say right now. I'm dog tired. I'll write again in a few days.

God bless you, Dad.

I hope to hear from you soon.

Your son, George
VV

PS. Please send copies of the Pittsburgh Courier whenever you can, and some hair tonic too.

5

THE ANOMALY

Jack Gallagher was sitting in his armchair when he heard the postman. He rose to his feet in slow and careful movements, grasped his gnarled stick, and walked from the sitting room to the front door. The moment he saw the official envelope on the doormat he knew what it was. He had been expecting it for three days.

"Orla," he called. "It's arrived."

His wife followed in a hurry from the kitchen, wiping her hands on her apron. She came and stood alongside her husband as he ran his thumb through the top of the envelope and liberated the letter. He pressed his glasses to his eyes.

"It's the O.B.E," he said, enunciating each letter. He read on, one eye betraying the hint of a tear. "For a lifetime of research into the flying boats of Fermanagh during World War 2."

Their embrace was interrupted by the doorbell. Orla opened the front door to a man with greying hair. He smiled at Jack and pointed to his old green Land Rover.

Orla said, "Take care on the lough."

In under an hour, Jack was on board a vessel with two friends who were a quarter of a century younger than him. Rory O'Neill, his hair ginger but greying, was ex-military. Birgit Dahl was a tall, strong woman with a Nordic jumper beneath her raincoat.

"Congratulations on the O.B.E., Jack," Rory said.

"Other Bugger's Efforts," Jack muttered.

Rory and Birgit laughed.

When they had recovered, Rory said, "Ach, Jack, you deserve it. You've helped many grieving families."

"I like what you've done to the boat," Jack said, changing the subject, and observing the new equipment on board. "It must have cost you a wild amount of money."

"It did," Birgit said. "But I think you're going to think it's worth it when we show you what we've found."

"And what have you found?"

"You'll see," Birgit said, untying the mooring ropes.

The boat, which was now pulling out into upper Lough Erne, had once been a fishing rig. The two friends who now maintained and operated it were members of a special interest group and had turned it into a research vessel in which they scoured the vast stretches of water in lower and upper Lough Erne. Their boat was kitted out with the latest equipment - including radar, a sonar for searching the waters of the lough, and a 3-D scanner designed to present images of the wrecks at the bottom. Both were intent on prising every secret from the arms of the mysterious and elusive Erne.

As the boat motored out into the lough, Jack took out his binoculars and observed a bevy of Whooper swans feeding on the grasslands near the shore on one of the islands. As the vessel drew nearer, he could see one of the swans raising its neck and issuing a trumpet call. He thought of the long crossing these birds had made from Iceland to Ireland the previous October. Ever since he was a boy, he had loved these large waterbirds with their black-and-yellow bills. One time, when he was seven, he and his father had stumbled upon a nest in a low-lying marsh near Devenish Island. Guarded by a male and female adult, the nest had five eggs. His Da had explained that these Whooper swans were very faithful birds. He pointed to one of them and told Jack she had been injured. Her right wing had been torn, perhaps from a collision with a telegraph wire.

"He won't ever leave her," his father had said. "They pair for life." He had paused and taken Jack by the arm. "We humans could learn a thing or two from them, to be sure."

As Jack recalled these words, he said a silent prayer of thanks for Orla. Only the previous week they had celebrated their sixtieth wedding anniversary. They were loyal Whoopers who had produced two sons. They, in turn, had given them six grandchildren – hungry cygnets who fed from the rich arable field of his heart.

Jack continued to reminisce until the engines of the boat slowed and the smell of diesel filled the cabin. Looking out the window, he saw a bright-red buoy bobbing up and down in the choppy water of the lough. Birgit put the engine to idle while Rory readied an inflatable dinghy at the stern of the vessel.

"We're here," Birgit said.

The two explorers seemed excited.

"Well, what's the craic now?" Jack asked.

"You'll see," Birgit replied as she walked out of the cabin and helped Rory lower the dinghy.

When it was secured to the side of the larger vessel, Rory checked his life vest before climbing down and pulling at the outboard motor. The engine started first time.

Birgit withdrew a long, thin gadget from a black case in the cabin. Jack had never seen such a thing before. It was over 100cms long and about 9cm in diameter. Shaped like a miniature submarine, it had yellow and black markings, and on its side was printed the make and number followed by the words 'Search and Recovery.'

"What's that?"

Birgit lifted it. "It's heavy, that's what it is. Weighs about the same as a fully grown Labrador."

"I mean, what's it for?"

"It's our new toy. A digital sonar. High resolution. It's what we used to locate the anomaly."

"What anomaly?"

"That's what we wanted you to see," she replied, passing the object down to her companion.

Jack could now hear the dinghy moving away, carrying Rory and the slim sonar with its phosphorescent finish. They were ploughing through the wavelets towards the buoy.

"Come with me," Birgit said as she entered the cabin.

Jack followed and stood behind her as she sat at a small pull-down desk and opened a custom-configured laptop. Before long, the camera was transmitting images from its camera onto the laptop screen. Within two minutes, the sleek sonar was scanning the bottom of the lough, surveying the mud 150 feet beneath.

"There it is!" Birgit cried.

Jack rubbed his eyes.

"What do you make of it, Jack?"

Embedded in the silt far below was a white object resting on the brown-and-orange bed. It was the wreck of an aircraft. The large tail fins, the fuselage, the transparent blister on its port side, the forward section of the aircraft, were all intact. Only the large single wing once fixed to the top of the plane seemed to have been damaged. Although Jack could see a stump where the portside part of the wing should have been, both it and the engine it once bore were nowhere to be seen. As soon as he set eyes on it, he knew what it was. Its colour – the same as the Whooper swans – gave it away.

"It's a Catalina," he said.

"That's why we wanted you to see it," Birgit said. "We thought it might be, but we needed you to confirm it."

"Who knows about this?"

"We've contacted the Department of Agriculture, Environment and Rural Affairs at Stormont and simply told them we've found an anomaly. Nothing more than that. But now you've identified what it is, we'll have to be more specific."

"DAERA will declare this a war grave," Jack said. "There'll most likely be human remains."

Birgit nodded.

Jack chuckled.

"What?"

"Well, we always knew," Jack said.

"Knew what?"

"That there'd be more to find."

"Aye, I suppose we did."

The door opened.

As Rory entered the cabin, Birgit turned to him. "Jack says it's definitely a Catalina."

"Any idea which one?"

"There were two that went missing during the Battle of the Atlantic," Jack said. "One was believed to have crashed somewhere between Donegal and the Black Gap."

Rory interrupted. "Black Gap?"

"The 300-mile stretch of sea halfway between here and America. An area where the U-Boats made hay. One Catalina just disappeared. No one knows what happened. They simply failed to return from a patrol. 17th May 1942, if memory serves."

"And the other?"

"That one was presumed to have crashed here."

"Had it been damaged by enemy fire?" Rory asked.

"Not necessarily," Jack replied. "The pilots could have been confused by something called 'night effect', which affected the direction finder. Or, it could have been strong winds, or a faulty altimeter, caused by changes in barometric pressure."

Jack paused to stare at the frozen image of the ghostly Catlina on the still-opened laptop.

He was almost whispering now. "The last anyone heard from the radio operator was at the RAF radio station at Dernacross, southwest of Belleek. The American station at Magheramena also picked up the message. There was nothing to give any cause for alarm. The crew were not far from home. It's always been a mystery. No one has ever discovered what happened to them."

"Until now," Birgit said.

"Ach, it's still a mystery," Jack muttered.

"But we've found it," she protested.

"Unless we can take a closer look," Jack said, "We're unlikely to know if it is our missing plane, or what caused it to crash." He pointed to the laptop. "Thon gadget is all very well and good, but it would take a very skilled diver to get inside the fuselage."

"No diver would ever agree to it," Rory said. "A local fisherman told me there are pike here the size of sharks."

Jack laughed. "I think that might be an example of a fisherman's tale," he said.

"There's also unexploded bombs." Rory added.

"That wouldn't be an issue," Jack interrupted. "We know from their radio messages from the Atlantic the crew discharged their full complement of explosives."

"So, it wouldn't be dangerous?" Rory asked.

"It would, but not from the depth charges. The currents here are lethal, and the amount of peat in the water makes the visibility poor. You'd need a drone to get inside that wreck. But who, besides the Royal Navy, would own such a thing?"

Birgit opened a long wooden chest along the starboard side of the cabin. She began to pull at something covered in transparent polythene – something large and curved at the edges.

"We would," she said.

"You're codding me!" Jack exclaimed.

LETTER 2

October 27th, 1943

Dear Dad,

I have just spent my first night onboard our Catalina. We have a guard roster and all nine of us in the crew – even the skipper - take it in turns to sleep onboard, making sure enemy spies and saboteurs don't steal or sink it. The Germans know about us and refer to our white Catalinas as "the swans of Lough Erne." That is not such a bad metaphor. When I was taken out to ours, I could see her pale outline in the darkness. She was resting at anchor near one of the many islands.

I boarded the plane after saying farewell to the ferryman. I took a good look around. I started at the rear. I stood on a metal walkway and looked out of both the port and starboard sides through two blisters with mounted machine guns. These blisters are like glass bubbles. There is also a toilet. It looks like a metal bucket.

I then walked through a bulkhead to where there are three, fold-up beds. Here the boys have time to sleep when flying to and from the Black Gap of the Atlantic where the U-Boats like to hunt. I slept that night on one of these bunks. It wasn't easy. I am the tallest member of the crew. The beds are too short for me.

Then it was through another bulkhead into the engineer's area, filled with engine and fuel controls. Our engineer keeps an eye on those when we're in the air. We have 1500 gallons of fuel, so we can fly for about twenty hours. There's also a primus cooker with two stoves. I cooked eggs and bacon for dinner.

Through the next bulkhead and I was into the area manned by the wireless operator, the navigator, and the radar lookout. It's very cramped. There's a table on one side for the navigator to study charts, and a desk opposite where the two huge radios are situated. There's also a chair for the radar operator.

After that, I passed through the fourth and final bulkhead into the cockpit where there are two seats for the first and second pilot. There are a lot of controls in front of and above the first seat on your left as you look out the front, as well as a wheel the skipper uses to steer. Beyond that is the bow machine gunner's post, separated by a curtain. This crewman acts as bombardier too.

It may not have the glamour of the Spitfires flown by our British friends, but the Catalina has a charm of its own. The skipper is a keen gardener. His favorite flower is called the Lady of the Night – a white orchid that blossoms once a year. He has nicknamed our plane the 'Lady of the Night' - 'Lady' for short.

And that brings me to my dream. After my meal, I checked everything on my list. There was no cause for any alarm, so I settled on one of the beds.

I took out *Native Son*. Yes, I know, Dad. Fourth time! I bumped into some brothers in Cookstown the other day. One of them was reading it too. We agreed that every colored man has lived something of Bigger's story. We sense a strange affinity with him.

I slept well until the sun began to rise. I looked outside at a rolling mist making its way towards us. It seemed to have a mesmerizing effect because I drifted off again. I fell into that space between sleeping and waking, that strange landscape we've spoken about often. My dreams are at their most vivid when I wander there.

In my dream, I observed a strange and startling figure walking on the water, emerging from the mist. She was more ghostly than human; tall and slender, with long blonde hair, she wore a long dress that covered her pale body from neck to knee. She had a garland made of the flowers I had seen beside the lough. To my eyes, she looked like the model John Whitehouse – the pre-Raphaelite artist - used for the Lady of Shallot. Her eyes were full of yearning.

This strange figure passed through the frame of the fuselage as if it didn't exist. She stood beside my bed. I was unable to move or speak as she bent down. "Don't follow me," she whispered.

I woke suddenly, beads of sweat on my forehead. When I looked out the rear blisters, the fog was gone, the sun was up, and some swans were flying in formation over the islands.

I wondered if the woman was Erin, a Celtic lady said to have drowned in the lake while fleeing from a giant. Maybe she was telling me not to become fascinated by the old pagan ways whose traces are still visible here. Some of us have just visited an island called Boa. We saw a strange and ancient statue that the locals believe represents a Celtic goddess older than Christianity. Her large eyes seemed to follow me around the cemetery.

What do you think it means, Dad? I wish we could sit on our deck, drink some cold beer, and talk about it. I miss your reassuring and wise words. I'm sure you'd know what to say.

Other than that, it was an untroubled night. No German spies or saboteurs. I checked each part of the aircraft before making breakfast on the stove. Then I waited for the ferryman.

I love you, Dad.

Your son,
George
VV

6

THE BUGGING

Agent Miller guided his hired car into a parking space off the high street. As he closed the door, he turned to check the vehicle. He had lived in England for a decade, but still found small cars and roads a challenge. His parking, however, was on point; there was no reason to worry about drawing attention to himself. The car itself was a nondescript hatchback, as beige as his nondescript raincoat.

Miller held his briefcase in his right hand. His left hand was tucked into the pocket of his coat. In recent months, he'd sensed arthritic discomfort in his fingers. Low temperatures exacerbated the pain. He winced and cursed the debilitations of age. He remembered the days of his youth when no mission or task seemed burdensome. He had sprinted beside long canals and climbed over high walls with ease. The days of chasing prey were coming to an end.

But there was still one more target. Two to be precise. Professor Cameron Stone and his new friend from Boston, Maya Hailey. He could not allow them to access any information about her grandfather, George Hailey. The threat to Homeland Security if they did was to his mind unimaginable. The race riots and marches of the 1960s were threatening to ignite again. He had to stop these two people from pouring fuel onto the coals burning in the national grate.

Entering the old part of the city, Miller walked down a cobbled street towards a yellow house that overlooked the sea. He withdrew a miniature camera no larger than a thimble and hid it opposite the entrance to the house. The professor, his target, occupied the top floor. Several of his windows looked out onto the sea.

He turned and headed back to a bespoke café and ordered a flat white. He placed his spectacles over the bridge of his nose, activating a switch in one of the temple tips. The inside of both lenses showed the entrance to the yellow house. The images appeared in a small square in the centre of each lens, allowing him to see his immediate surroundings through the spaces around them.

Miller took two sips from his coffee before detecting signs of activity in the pictures transmitted from the camera. His target emerged from the house. The professor had wrapped a mustard-coloured scarf around his neck and pushed it under an olive Barbour jacket that had seen better days. He wore russet corduroy trousers and a pair of jaded chocolate brogues. Sweeping back his brown hair with his right hand, he placed a cap on his head and strode up the same street towards the café. Miller had positioned himself so that he could see but not be seen. As he removed his glasses, he observed his target passing the front window. Seconds later Miller paid his bill, pocketed his glasses, pulled his beanie down to his eyebrows, and exited.

He glanced to his left. Stone was way up the street now. Miller hurried in the opposite direction.

Withdrawing an electric multi-pick device - German engineered – he opened the front door of the professor's house. On tiptoes he climbed one flight of stairs and then another to the top-floor apartment. The door yielded to his pick. He passed over the threshold and paused, listening out for any signs of life. There were none.

Miller sized up the layout in seconds. In under two minutes, he had decided on four locations for his eavesdropping devices. The first was a large spare bedroom the professor had turned into a study. Miller had imagined it full of clutter, with books and pamphlets strewn everywhere. But even as he entered, he realized how wrong he was. The study was immaculate. There were books on the shelves, yes, but they were positioned so that the tallest were at one end and the shortest at the other. Apart from five framed pictures – certificates of writing awards and academic prizes – there were no pictures or photographs on the walls. There were two armchairs in the space opposite the desk. These were as tidy as the coffee table between them, on which a healthy-looking parlour palm was busy purifying the air.

And the air needed purifying. The professor's one vice seemed to be smoking, something he'd clearly done before leaving the apartment. There was a small Rasta pipe resting in an ashtray on the spacious glass desk. A tin of tobacco next to it had the words, "Jamaican Flake," on the top, and a ghostly wisp of smoke lingered beneath the fake chandelier in the centre of the ceiling.

The only other object on the glass desk was a closed

laptop. Miller took a moment to memorise the position of the computer in relation to its surroundings. Then, donning a pair of gloves, he opened it. The screen lit up and the password box appeared.

Miller reached into his briefcase and withdrew another gadget. He plugged a lead into a USB port on the laptop and waited until the glass digital display on the decoder gave a prompt. In under one minute, the password had been cracked.

He now set to work accessing the computer's microphone and camera, reconfiguring both so that they could function as an open window onto the professor's world. Next, he pulled a portable hard drive from his briefcase and copied every file from the professor's computer. When the last documents had been exported, he made sure to leave no trace of his handiwork, covering his tracks with the efficiency of one who had performed many such undetected intrusions.

After scanning the room, Miller exited the study and headed for the TV in the living room area. This was a large, flat screen model that covered most of the wall above the mantlepiece. There he noticed a framed photo of the professor when he was about ten, leaning his head on a young woman's shoulder. She was trying to look happy, but her eyes were sad. Miller guessed this was the boy's mother. He also observed that this was the only photograph in the apartment.

Miller planted a camera and microphone in the back of the TV before using a small electric drill and returning the screen to the exact same position. He then proceeded to the kitchen and planted a voice-activated camera and bug within the Alexa.

The final space he wanted to watch was the professor's bedroom. This was again devoid of any clutter. There was a king-sized bed and a bedside table. On it there was a small touch-sensitive lamp and a book. The fountain pen next to it gave its genre away; it was a journal. Picking it up, Miller skim-read the contents at speed, pausing at several entries, reading more closely, sometimes taking pictures on his camera, before returning it to the same place.

The only other feature of the room was a huge oil painting hanging on the wall opposite the head of the bed. It depicted an old man whom Miller inferred from his hat, skin, and dreadlocks was West Indian. His face was frozen in a perpetual smile and yet there was a look in his tired eyes that hinted at long years of suffering. He looked like a weary philosopher – a Stoic perhaps – who had seen many traumas in his life, yet never lost his wit or joy. Contributing even more to this sage-like disposition, the man had an impressive beard which was black around his mouth, then white as the feathers of a snowy owl the further it extended from his creased lips. From the furrows in the man's forehead and the lines beneath his eyes, Miller guessed the painted gentleman was in his mid to late seventies.

As he contemplated installing the device in the painting, Miller caught the old man's eyes again. They seemed to have changed, no longer looking resilient but questioning. Miller couldn't endure the accusatorial stare. Instead, he glanced at the ceiling and reached for the single, hanging light.

It was just as he was finishing the installation of the device that Miller heard something.

The turning of a lock.

The door to the apartment was opening.

He heard someone placing keys on a marble work surface in the kitchen. When the person headed from there to the study at the end of the corridor, Miller decided to look at him through a crack between the door and the wall. The newcomer was a man. He was standing outside the study at the far end of the apartment and carrying a box of books. He was Caucasian, young, wavy-haired, and nimble. He wore a thin black tie over a white shirt covered in red-petaled flowers. He had draped a velvet jacket over his shoulders.

As the young man entered the study, Miller slipped out of the apartment and headed down the stairs, out onto the cobbled street. After gathering the tiny camera from its hiding place opposite the house, he marched up the sidewalk and returned to his car. Sliding into the front seat, he turned on the ignition and drove out of the city. After stopping in a small carpark overlooking the ocean, he reached under the passenger seat and withdrew a tablet. When he opened it, four cameras activated, revealing the professor's private world – his bedroom, living room, kitchen, and study. The picture was high definition. The sound quality was impeccable. Miller could hear the young man still whistling. It was as if he was next to him in the car.

Miller attached the hard drive to his tablet and accessed the professor's documents. These were all organised in folders with clear headings. Most were niche subjects connected with his lectures, writing, and research. A swift scan betrayed no subterfuge, no secrecy, no smokescreens. The professor didn't seem to have anything to hide. His history was clean. His only unhealthy habit appeared to be a liking for Jamaican tobacco which he had ordered from the same website on a regular basis. It quickly became clear to him that if Miller was going to dig out some dirt on his prey, he'd have to bury it somewhere himself. The academic seemed to have a blinkered obsession for historical study. Even his financial accounts were unsuspicious. They were healthy, and the sources of his income all looked legitimate.

Before he shut the tablet down, Miller found his way into the professor's emails. Once again, the predilection for tidying everything into folders was evident. The inbox of recent messages was almost empty. Everything had been moved to dedicated files. Miller conducted a swift search of each, setting aside in his mind two folders that demanded further attention at the end of his sweep.

The first read Bret.

The second, Maya.

In Bret's file, Miller located the twelve letters sent by George Hailey to his father during World War 2. These were attached to an email to Bret, with a message from the professor asking him to study each one and pass on anything important.

"Focus on anything that might give us clues about what happened to George Hailey. Did he die with the rest of his crew in a terrible accident? Or did he suffer some other fate, disconnected from his missions on board the Catalina?"

Miller cursed. He closed Bret's file and opened Maya's. There were five emails, three of which dealt with the practicalities of her visit to Portsmouth. Flight times. Hotel suggestions. Even down to details about weather and clothing.

The other two emails drew more interest. There was one in which Maya asked the professor to help her find her grandfather. His response piqued Miller's curiosity. "Your message is timely. I have been prompted to do some research on your grandfather's story. I can understand why you feel moved to discover what happened. If it was my grandfather, I would be taking such steps too."

Miller studied the message a second time. What was it that bothered him? It wasn't so much the fact that the professor was so obviously motivated to help. It was more the reason for his motivation. What was it that "prompted" him? What had caused him to take a sudden interest in George Hailey's death?

The next email irked Miller even more. There was an even greater sense of enigma about the communication. Maya had written very early that morning asking to meet. She wanted to know what he'd meant when they said goodbye at the museum.

Miller found the professor's reply.

"I'll pick you up at 7pm tonight if that works. There's a restaurant with your name here. I'll explain what I meant about your grandfather when we meet."

Miller cursed.

Usually, reading other people's emails was a case of too much information. This was the opposite.

Miller read the final sentence.

"I'm sorry I didn't explain what happened. I'm not used to a dead man talking."

Miller shook his head.

"What the hell does that mean?" he said out loud.

There was nothing else for it.

Miller used his phone to search for restaurants in Portsmouth. He found nothing with the name Hailey. But he did have success with Maya. There was a restaurant with that name in Southsea, specialising in Latin-American cuisine.

Miller smiled.

Using the booking engine on the website, he chose a time – 6.45pm – and secured a table for one. As he drove back in the direction of his hotel, he couldn't help thinking of the old man's eyes in the bedroom. He swore he had seen them change.

At the beginning, they had been weary.

Then questioning.

Before settling in anger.

Rage, even.

Miller had seen a fire in the old man's pupils.

He sighed.

Shook his head.

As he grasped the manual gear stick in his left hand, the pain flared up again.

"I'm getting too old for this," he muttered.

LETTER 3

November 3rd, 1943

Dear Dad,

Thank you for your thoughts about my dream. I guess you're right. We sometimes only know the meaning later.

I've just returned from an exhausting mission. We took off in beautiful weather conditions and almost forgot that we had a serious job to do. It all felt so peaceful and carefree. Halfway into our flight, we descended through some clouds and discovered what we thought were two U-Boats, one large and one small. But as we flew lower, the crew at action stations, we saw that it was several Blue Whales – a mother and her offspring – swimming side by side. It was a sight as breathtaking as it was surprising. We had our depth charges all set, but fortunately the Skipper realized in time.

On our way back towards Ireland, one of our two engines started to sound uneasy, like it wasn't striking all the cylinders. We waited to see if it would correct itself, but it didn't. As we drew near to the west coast, the engine caught fire and the wireless officer was ordered to send a May Day to Castle Archdale. Our commanding officer there, the group captain, ordered us to dump our depth charges. The carefree atmosphere of the start of the mission departed with them.

As black smoke poured out of our starboard engine, we flew over the little town of Belleek and then over some fields, trying to get rid of two thousand gallons of fuel as we went. I soon saw that our fuel was pouring out near the burning engine, so I told the Skipper and shut off the fuel dump valve. As if this wasn't bad enough, the track we use for releasing the depth charges stuck, so the boys had to defuse them and then get them out of the plane by hand.

The next thing that happened was that the burning engine froze. Its propeller shot off the shaft and did some damage to the starboard wing and float. With only one engine working, the Skipper did an excellent job of guiding us down to the lough. All the crew braced for impact, but the Skipper managed to slow Lady down, right her for the landing, and then put us down on the water.

Thanks to his skills, no one was injured.

We caused quite a stir.

The Irish Army had to blow up the jettisoned depth charges the next day, overseen by officers from Castle Archdale.

Of course, the Erks back at base had many repairs to make. The engine needed to be completely repaired and the propeller replaced. There are also quite a few holes and scars in the wing and the fuselage that will need to be patched up before we can fly again. The poor ground crew have their work cut out over at RAF Killadeas.

I had quite an experience several nights later. I saw a

notice about a 'Dance for the Black Men.' This aroused my curiosity. I was keen to enjoy an evening of Guinness and fun with some of my brothers from Cookstown, so we commandeered a jeep and headed to Bessbrook in County Armagh. Imagine my shock when I walked in and found about sixty men and women, not one like us. Every one of them was white skinned. It was like one of those old Western movies when the gunslinger enters the saloon and the piano stops playing. The place fell silent. Everyone stared at us.

As I stared back, I noticed something else. The men were wearing a predominantly black sash over their black jackets. Even though they warmly welcomed us, it soon became clear that I had been guilty of a misunderstanding. The Protestants here have an exclusively religious organization called the Royal Black Institution. The word "royal" is a reference to the royal priesthood mentioned in the New Testament, and the word black is a reference to death and mortality, so you'll probably guess the atmosphere was sober and serious. The men referred to each other, though not to me, as "Sir Knight." Apparently, there are quite a few preceptories of this club within County Fermanagh, so it's not a great surprise we ran into one.

All of which is to say that the Black Men referred to in the notice that I had seen in Irvinestown turned out to be these elite Christian gentlemen, not men of color. They were friendly though. They patted our backs and said we must be 'clean scundered' – a phrase that probably needs no translation. Feeling, yes, embarrassed, we retreated from the hall and drove back to our respective bases.

So, all in all, it's been a week for misinterpretations.

Firstly, there were the two Blue Whales in the Atlantic.

And then there were the Black Men of Bessbrook.
Things are not always what they seem!
God bless you, Dad.
I miss you.

Your son,
George.
VV

7

THE TAPAS

Stone was aware that Maya was staring at him. Very aware. It was over 24 hours since he had mentioned why he was helping her find her grandfather. The words "he asked me" had intrigued her. Stone knew she was waiting for an explanation.

"So?" she said.

"So what?"

"How did my grandfather ask you?"

Just as he was about to answer, the waiter arrived carrying a large tray with six tapas dishes. These he placed around a candle burning in the centre of the table. The same young man had escorted them downstairs to a booth that could accommodate four. Stone and Maya had occupied the seats next to the wall.

When he left, Stone lowered his voice. "Before I explain my remark from yesterday, I want you to know that I'm sound of mind, and I don't have hallucinations or visions."

"I believe you, Professor."

"A few nights ago, I went to the university library. The archivist, at my request, brought out some World War 2 photographs in an album. Your grandfather's Catalina was in one of the pictures I studied. The seaplane was called..."

Maya interrupted, "Lady of the Night."

"That's right." Stone sipped some water. "The second photo was the one that ... well... unsettled me."

Not even the tapas could divert Maya's gaze.

"It showed the crew of the Lady. All nine of them. Including your grandfather. He was standing in the back row, with his dog reaching up to lick his chin. From the stubble, I'm guessing he had just returned from a long mission in the Atlantic."

Maya nodded.

"It was then that something very odd occurred." Stone shook his head at what he was about to say. "Your grandfather came alive. His little dog did too. He was laughing as the dog..."

"Scratch," Maya interrupted.

"Yes, Scratch was playing with him. They were the only two in the photo who were ... well, animated."

Maya seemed more curious than shocked.

Stone continued. "Your grandfather smiled for a few seconds, but then his expression changed. He looked alert and alarmed. So did Scratch. It was then that he spoke." Stone took another sip. "He just uttered two words. *Find me*."

Maya's eyes watered.

"What do you make of it?" Stone asked.

Maya composed herself. "I know what some of my fellow Pentecostals would make of it. They'd cite Deuteronomy 18 and tell you that this is dark, devilish, and deceptive, and that you are risking God's anger for consulting the dead."

"But that's the whole point!" Stone cried. "I didn't consult the dead. The dead consulted me. Twice!"

"Precisely," Maya said, nodding. "On both occasions that you saw and heard my grandfather, you were not seeking contact with him, as a medium would."

"But then what's your explanation, Maya? You're the former pastor. The supernatural, paranormal, mystical... whatever word you'd use ... that's your province not mine."

"There's something I learned from one of the Matrix films," she said, her tone more pastoral. Stone, who had been expecting her to quote a passage from the Bible, or an esteemed theologian, was caught off guard. Maya allowed herself a smile. "Your comprehension is not a prerequisite for your cooperation."

Stone sighed. "So, I may never understand."

"I'm not saying that. What I am saying is that we can only determine the nature and the source of an experience like this over time... as we pursue its meaning and purpose."

Both leaned back in their seats.

Stone muttered, "The truth is out there."

Maya laughed. "Yes, it is," she said. "But don't go comparing me to Dana Scully, or yourself to Fox Mulder!"

"Shame," Stone said. "That was my favourite TV programme in my twenties. Probably still is."

"I loved it too," Maya said.

Just then, Bret entered. "You must be Maya Hailey," he said, reaching out his hand.

Maya offered her hand and smiled. She looked him up and down and said, "Nice shirt."

Underneath his blazer, Bret was wearing a white shirt festooned with red flowers.

"Thanks," he said. He turned to his boss. "I've left a box of books in your study at home. In the corner, out of sight." He winked at Maya. "He likes everything just so, does the Prof."

"I haven't ordered for you," Stone said.

Bret looked around the dimly lit basement. The waiter was clearing a table near the stairs. Bret smiled at him and nodded. Within several moments, the young man was at the table, opening a menu and placing it in Bret's hands.

"I'll have two dishes, please," Bret said.

"Any particular ones?"

"Surprise me, darling," Bret said, closing the menu.

Bret turned to Stone. "Was I interrupting something? You both looked very serious."

Maya replied first. "He was telling me that my grandfather spoke to him four nights ago."

Bret chuckled. "That would be highly unlikely, given he's been most likely dead for eighty years."

"Apparently, my granddaddy spoke to him through a photograph in the university library."

Bret swivelled around to stare at Stone.

"I'm going to have to confess it's true," Stone said. "I saw something. Heard something too."

"Pray tell!" Bret exclaimed.

"George Hailey came alive in the photograph. So did his little dog. He asked me to find him."

Bret's eyes bulged. "So, that's why you froze on stage! He did it again, didn't he?"

"What's he talking about?" Maya asked.

"It was the talk you listened to via live stream," Stone explained. "The one where I received those awards for my book. Your grandfather was in one of the photos in the slideshow Bret organised. He spoke to me. Said the same thing as before."

Maya shook her head.

"How very Dorian Gray!" Bret squealed.

"Say what?" Maya exclaimed.

"It's a Gothic novel by Oscar Wilde," Bret explained, "about a young man who has his portrait painted. He sells his soul for the love of pleasure. He remains youthful, but his image in the portrait grows older and uglier, both physically and morally."

"And here's an interesting little coincidence," Stone said. "Oscar Wilde went to school in Northern Ireland – a school on the edge of an enormous body of water..."

"Not Lough Erne?" Bret asked.

"The same."

He squealed again. When he calmed himself, he said, "Speaking of talented writers, I've been studying the first three letters your grandfather wrote." He withdrew some folded photocopies from his shoulder bag. "There are two things that interest me, and I'm wondering if either of you can help me."

Bret spread out the three sheets.

"Great handwriting," Stone noted.

"His letters are beautiful," Maya said.

"Here," Bret said, pointing to a paragraph in the third letter. He had used a yellow highlighter to spotlight certain phrases. "Your grandfather talks about his favourite book. He says he's been rereading it. A novel called *Native Son*."

Maya smiled. "He took it everywhere with him," she said. "He was obsessed with the story. It was published in 1940 to a mixture of great acclaim and consternation. Acclaim in the black community. Consternation among many whites."

"Why?" Bret asked.

"The story was about a young black man, a chauffeur called Bigger Thomas, who drove a white girl home. She had got blind drunk. He couldn't leave her on the doorstep. So, he took her up to her room and laid her on the bed."

"Sounds like a good guy," Bret said.

"A good guy caught in a bad situation," she said. "Her blind mother came upstairs and asked what was going on. Bigger became afraid. He covered the girl's face with a pillow so she wouldn't give him away. I'm afraid he just panicked."

Bret sighed. "What is it you guys say? He was caught between a rock and a hard place."

"Exactly."

"So, what happened?" Bret asked.

"He killed her. It was an accident. As soon as he realised, he knew he was in trouble, so he went on the run. In the end, he was caught, tried, and executed. It's a tragic story, but it became a sensation, selling a quarter of a million copies in three weeks."

Bret took one of the letters. "Every coloured man has lived something of Bigger's story," he read. "Since I first opened *Native Son*, I have felt a strange affinity with the man."

The three diners fell silent for a moment, joined together by an unspoken reverence when they heard George Hailey's words. They were only broken out of it by Maya, who reached down into her handbag and fetched out a hardback novel. She laid it over the photocopied letters, coverside up.

It read, *The Man who Lived Underground*. The author was the same Richard Wright.

"You may be interested in this," she said. "It was thought too radical to publish in Wright's lifetime. It's another protest novel – a graphic description of white police brutality against black Americans. It was published a few years ago. 2021 to be precise. Nearly sixty years after Richard Wright had passed. It came out in the same week Derek Chauvin's trial came to an end."

"That name rings a bell," Bret said.

Maya refreshed his memory. "George Floyd's killer. A white cop. He was found guilty."

"Do you think anything's really improved since Richard Wright's time," Bret asked.

"No," Maya said.

That single word was like the crack of a breaking bone. It seemed to hush the whole room. When conversations kickstarted, Stone – who had not spoken during the entire discussion about Richard Wright – began to mutter some words from memory.

"The white folks like for us to be religious, then they can do what they want to with us."

"What's that?" Bret asked.

"He's quoting from *Native Son*," Maya said.

"That's because I'm surprised," Stone said.

"What at?"

"At the fact that you are a former pastor, and yet you, like your grandfather, are a fan of a writer who seems to be trenchantly opposed to your Christian religion."

"But is it my religion?" Maya asked.

"It's Christianity," Stone said.

"There's no such thing as Christianity, at least in America. There's Christianities, plural. The religion of most white Americans is different from the Pentecostal faith that has sustained my brothers and sisters through four centuries."

Stone could have continued, but the conversation was now beginning to feel like a verbal duel after one of his lectures. Besides which, the tapas dishes were getting cold.

As Maya took a spoonful, the waiter returned with Bret's order. "Mayan mash," he said. "And this is my personal favourite. Aubergine topped with harissa, bravas, mozzarella and kale."

Bret rubbed his flat stomach.

"Did I choose poorly?" the waiter asked.

Bret, recognising the film reference, smiled at him. "No, Indy. You chose wisely."

As Bret tasted the red mash, he shook his head. "Divine," he whispered. "Simply divine!"

The three of them were quiet for what seemed like many minutes. The food was just too good to interrupt.

When the plates were at last removed, they ordered cocktails. Stone asked for a mocktail; he was driving. Brett ordered a Raspberry Sting, Maya a Passion Victim.

When Maya took her first sip, it was as if it awakened a synapse of memory. "The second thing!" she cried.

"I'm sorry," Stone said.

"What was the second thing about my grandfather's letters? Bret, you said there were two things."

"Oh yes, what a dozy thing I am. Here. Look at this." Bret pointed to the bottom of the three letters. George Hailey had ended each the same way. He had written what looked like a capital W.

"What's with this W?" Bret asked.

"It's not a W," Stone answered.

"Come again?"

"The professor's right," Maya said. "It's two Vs, very close together. It was granddaddy's way of signing off his letters back home to his father. The V stands for Victory."

"But why two of them?" Bret asked.

"Because he wanted to see victory on two fronts," Stone said. "In the war against the Nazis abroad, and the war against racism back home. Hence the double V."

Bret leaned back against the booth. He said, "So, that's why you wrote *The Jostlers*."

"Partly, yes. I wanted to highlight the courage of all the black service personnel fighting a war across the ocean, then returning home to continue fighting another war. I don't think it's possible for us to imagine what that was like."

"Unless you're black," Maya said.

Those three words, like a vortex, swallowed up every other conversation in the room.

After a brief silence, the three diners were roused by a text alert from Stone's phone.

"Excuse me," he said.

He read a few lines.

"This is significant. Very significant indeed."

Bret cried, "Don't keep us in suspense!"

"It's from Northern Ireland. It seems that some intrepid wreck hunters have found a World War 2 plane at the bottom of Lough Erne. A Catalina. Well preserved."

"Is it Lady?" Maya asked.

"They haven't identified it yet, but they do give the name of one of the men who confirmed what it was. Jack

Gallagher. He's interviewed in this news report."

"Can we get hold of him?" Maya asked.

Stone forwarded to Bret the article with the man's name. Within two minutes, Bret had located his contact details and Stone had sent a message explaining who he was, what he and Maya were doing, and why he would like to speak.

Stone paid the bill.

"Thank you, Professor," Maya said.

"Yes, thanks, Prof," Bret added, before hurrying after the waiter, speaking with him, then giving him some money.

"I've already given him a tip," Stone said.

"He's an undergraduate," Bret said. "Earning a bit of extra cash to pay the bills. I think he did us proud tonight."

"I agree," Maya said, slipping him some more cash as they headed up the stairs towards the ground floor of the restaurant. As Stone stepped into the room, his phone rang. He didn't recognise the number, but his phone suggested Northern Ireland as the source.

"That would be perfect," Stone said.

When they were outside, Stone turned and looked at Maya. "When are you due to go back to the States?"

"Saturday."

"That's just long enough for us to make a trip."

"What trip?"

"To County Fermanagh. Jack Gallagher, the man who identified the Catalina, is keen to meet you. He says he's got something important to show you. But it will have to be in person."

"Fine with me," Maya said.

"And there's one more thing. He's asked that we keep the trip and all details pertaining to it, including what they share with us, a secret. He said we'd understand why when we've met with them."

Maya nodded. "When do we go?" she asked.

Stone looked at Bret who was already typing into his phone. Bret provided the answer.

"Tomorrow morning at 10:25 from Southampton airport. EasyJet. Arriving Belfast International. I'll book you a return flight when you tell me to. I can pick you up at Eastleigh."

Stone looked at Maya. "All right with you?"

"I'll be good to go," she said.

LETTER 4

November 22nd, 1943

Dear Dad,

All the boys are downcast. A week ago, one of our Cats was sent on an OFE, an Operational Flying Exercise, and sent to drop two DCs (live depth charges) in the Atlantic. This was a routine training exercise. The crew followed normal procedure and transmitted a wireless code just before discharging their load. That was the last anyone heard from them. No one knew what had happened.

The next day, the CO ordered two Cats to repeat the same exercise. One of the aircraft was to carry two live DCs, just as the lost one had done. This was piloted by a Canadian, Ted Muffitt, one of the nicest guys you could meet. He had been an airman before the war, flying over the sparsely populated regions of the Canadian Arctic as a bush pilot in the RCMP (Royal Canadian Mounted Police). To say he was experienced would be an understatement.

Anyway, Ted's Cat (FP120) was tasked to follow the same

mission pattern as the lost plane and drop two DCs. With the other Cat observing at a safe distance, and the wireless code duly sent, Ted dropped both depth charges. Instead of sinking into the ocean and detonating twenty-five feet below, both DCs exploded on impact with the water fifty feet beneath Ted's Cat, rupturing the aluminum skin of his aircraft. The two DCs destroyed Ted's plane, killing everyone on board. The other skipper, seeing this horrifying spectacle, descended to look for survivors. Seeing none, he radioed back to base, informing the CO that Ted, his Cat, and his crew had been lost.

The crew members of the companion Cat were enraged when they returned. It was clear the pistols of both DCs had been incorrectly set, resulting in the two Torpex explosives causing catastrophic damage to the aircraft. These fuses were supposed to be set so that they would explode when the water pressure beneath the waves triggered them. It turns out there was a design fault with the entire batch of DCs sent to our squadron. Everyone is mad about that.

We are all distraught by the loss of Ted and his comrades, and by the loss of the original crew, although we are all also very grateful that Ted and his boys gave their lives for us. Imagine the carnage if a whole squadron had taken off for the Atlantic with these faulty fuses in the DCs. The consequences are unimaginable. We have already lost too many aircraft and crew defending the Merchant Navy. This would have been a completely senseless waste.

It's obvious to all of us that someone somewhere made a catastrophic mistake with these DCs. Some of the boys are claiming that German spies got to them at the factory. Most of us think it was human error. An investigation has begun, but no one is holding out much hope. These things tend to be swept under the carpet.

This incident has unsettled us. Up until now, we've felt relatively safe. We have put our trust in Coastal Command, our suppliers, fitters, comrades at the base at Castle Archdale, and above all our fellow crewmembers. No one, until the needless loss of these two Cats, has had any real cause for concern. Our missions over the Atlantic may be long and often arduous, but they are most often uneventful, with very low levels of risk to the crews. Now, everyone's nerves are on edge. We cannot help seeing the faces of the lost crews. I knew Ted's second pilot, Doug Disney. He was a good man.

The good news is that the Erks are now checking everything even more carefully than before, especially the DCs and their fuses. They are all giving a new and special hand signal to the skippers of each Cat, indicating that the pistols have been set right. This is helping to ease the 'jitters', but I would be lying if I denied that we are all still worried about other unseen faults.

That said, I don't suffer from fear. Ted and his crew would have known nothing. Their deaths would have been instant. And they died not only doing what they love, but more importantly in the service of others, saving potentially many lives.

When I was training in Canada, everyone was talking about a young pilot officer called John Magee. He was an American who ended up flying in the RCAF, like me. In fact, he'd trained at the same place I did, although he went to England to fly Spitfires, not to Northern Ireland to fly Cats. This was in 1941. Like our comrades, he also died in a tragic training accident. Three months before his death he wrote a sonnet with the title 'High Flight.' Seeing that he was an American pilot, this was published in a Pittsburgh newspaper, which is how I got to hear about it. It made a very deep impression on me then, and does so still, especially in the wake of our own losses.

I can't remember all of it, but it's a celebration of what it felt like to the poet being in a Spitfire high above the 'tumbling mirth of sun-split clouds,' wheeling, soaring, swinging through 'footless halls' of air in the silence of the heavens. It is a most exhilarating sonnet, ending with a fine line about rising high above where even eagles cannot fly, stretching out his hand, and touching the face of God. The Canadian padre read it at the service for our lost friends. There were few eyes dry.

He also told a tale about Ted. A week or so before the crash, the padre, a keen horse rider, had gone with Ted and Doug – the two pilots - to Dublin. The two RCAF airmen had a day's leave and wanted to go horse riding. The horse given to Ted turned out to be skittish and wild. To any other rider, this could have proven dangerous, but Ted's experiences in the Royal Canadian Mounted Police came in handy and he reined the stallion in, calming him first, then coaxing him to walk, trot, canter, and gallop with discipline. Everyone was impressed by Ted's horsemanship, including the locals.

The padre told us that we could all learn from Ted, reign in the wildness of our fears, enjoy a new calm, and fly with discipline, enjoying our own experience of high flight.

I was struck by that thought, as were many others. And since hearing his words, I've felt only the still small voice of calm we sang about at the memorial service.

So, I don't want you to worry about me, Dad. The crew and I have put our trust in each other and in our Lady. They're a great team and she's a great aircraft.

I love you.

Your Son,
George.
VV

8

THE FATHER

Maya sat at a table in her hotel room. She bowed her head and uttered a whispered prayer before opening her laptop. Within seconds her father's face was on the screen. Even though it was late afternoon in Boston, he was in his pyjamas and dressing gown, sitting in an armchair in a hospital sideward. His skin looked paler than she remembered, and to Maya's eyes his full head of hair was growing greyer by the day. A nasogastric tube hung from the little column of his nose.

"Hello, daughter," he said. His bloodshot eyes brightened a little as he saw her face.

"How's it gone, Daddy?"

"They finished an hour ago."

"Is that the last course?"

He nodded.

"There's nothing more they can offer?"

"I'm afraid not."

"Not even something experimental?"

"My oncologist says they've run out of road. That's it now. I'm sorry to be the bearer of bad news."

Maya held herself together.

Her father, seeing the struggle in her eyes, said, "Don't be despondent. Faith does not buckle in the face of sickness. Prayer can destroy cancer. I've seen it. So have you."

Maya nodded.

"I know, Daddy. It's just that... when it's your own flesh and blood... it all feels so..."

"Different?" he interrupted.

"I was going to say impossible."

Her father smiled. "Remember what I've always taught you. The word 'impossible' ... isn't in heaven's dictionary." Maya completed the sentence with him.

"How's things going over there?" he asked.

"We've made progress," Maya said, rallying. "I've met the professor and his assistant Bret a few times. They are now studying granddaddy's letters. And then there's the wreck."

"The wreck?"

"A World War 2 wreck has just been discovered at the bottom of Lough Erne, the lake that Granddaddy used to fly from when he was patrolling the Atlantic."

Maya could see the curiosity returning to her father's eyes, like a pilot light of life.

"Is it my father's plane?"

"We don't know, yet."

"Does it look like a Catalina?"

"There's no mistake. It is a Catalina."

"Can they examine it?"

"We don't know how much of the wreck has been explored yet, but I'm heading over to Northern Ireland tomorrow with the professor. We're meeting the guy who identified it."

"That's exciting," he said.

"And concerning," Maya added.

"Why do you say that?"

"Because it'll be sad if we find it is your father's seaplane, sadder still if his remains are inside."

"That's true, but it will mean we can lay his soul to rest and honour his service. These are good things."

Maya nodded.

Her father tilted his head both ways, looking at her with eyes that burrowed deep into her heart.

"What's going on in that sweet soul of yours?" As he looked at her, his eyes were filling.

"There's something strange about all this, Daddy."

"Strange?"

He waited.

"The night I emailed the professor..."

She took a deep breath.

"He was showing World War 2 photographs during a talk he was giving. Including one of Granddaddy. Apparently, Granddaddy came alive and spoke to him."

Her father shook his head.

"Say what?"

"I know! And that wasn't the first time, either. The same thing happened a few evenings before, when the professor was studying a photo of your father in the library."

The sick man shook his head.

"What do you think, Daddy?"

"I thought you said this professor was an academic."

"He is!"

"Are you sure he's not some kind of medium?"

"He says he's never had any experience like it. He seems quite a cerebral guy. Intellectual. He's baffled by the whole thing. He's even been asking me what it means."

"I still think you need to be careful, daughter. Theologians in our tradition would see darkness here."

"But what if the theologians are wrong? What if this experience isn't either dark or bright? What if it's just something that occupies a space between the two."

"You're saying there's a grey area?"

"I don't know. Maybe Granddaddy's spirit is restless and needs our help if he's to enter his peace?"

Winking, her father said, "That sounds a bit more Catholic than Pentecostal, daughter."

"Well, didn't Granddaddy love a Catholic girl?"

"He did."

"So, it's appropriate," she said, winking back.

"Just so long as you don't come back home preaching all about purgatory, saints, and what not."

Maya smiled again. "Daddy, you forget that one of Northern Ireland's greatest spiritual giants believed in purgatory. C.S. Lewis. Your favourite author. Remember?"

Her father braced himself. His face suggested that he knew from years of conversations what was about to come.

Maya prepared her thoughts and then spoke.

"Many American Protestants worship C.S. Lewis, making him a little less than a member of the Trinity. But they conveniently forget that he embraced some quite Catholic views too, like Purgatory. He liked the idea that there's a place where souls can be purified and prepared for their final journey into God's presence."

Maya's father sighed. "And where in Scripture do you find justification for this?"

"Where in Scripture do you find the doctrine of the Trinity, father? It's implied, not explicit. So is Purgatory."

"I'm not so sure about that, and in any case, aren't you confusing Purgatory with Limbo?"

Maya laughed. "No, I'm not. Look, let me try out an analogy with you. We know that Granddaddy lived to fly, right?"

He nodded.

"One of his favourite poems was *High Flight* by John Gillespie MacGee. He quotes it in a letter. He wanted nothing more than to slip the surly bonds of Earth, to fling his eager craft through footless halls of air. We know that. He wanted to fly high in the sunlit silence, reach out his hand, and touch the face of God."

More tears were now congregating in her father's eyes.

"But to do that, he had to go to boot camp, didn't he? He trained at Tuskegee. Then in Canada. Finally, at RAF Killadeas in Northern Ireland. He needed preparation."

Her father smiled as he recognised her logic.

"Bootcamp was like purgatory. Flying was like heaven. It's quite simple really."

She smiled as she rested her case.

"You were always good at thinking on your feet," he said. "That was a good analogy, daughter. I'll give you that."

As he spoke, it seemed to Maya as if a wave of weariness broke upon her father's heart.

"Okay, Daddy. You look exhausted. I'm going to love you and leave you before you drop your phone. Give my love to Mom, and to my brothers, and we'll speak again soon."

Her father lifted the phone so close to his face she could detect the stubble growing on his chin and cheeks.

"Keep me posted," he said.

"I will."

"And keep the faith, daughter."

"You too, Daddy."

When Maya clicked on the red button and her father disappeared, she closed the laptop and fell on its cover, as if its edges were her father's skeletal shoulders. There, in the privacy of her room, she at last allowed the tears to fall. And somewhere, from deep within her reservoir of resilience, she found the energy to pray a prayer.

"Heal Daddy, O God!"

LETTER 5

December 3rd, 1943

Dear Dad,

I received five letters from you today, along with your Thanksgiving greeting card. They all came at once, tied up in a small bundle with a piece of string. That's the way sometimes here - no letters for a few weeks, then a lot at once. This will be the first holiday I've not been with you, but at least we have our letters. And I'm luckier than some. Many brothers overseas hardly ever get to hear from home.

I don't want you to worry about me, Dad. I am not lonesome. In fact, I have found a new friend. The other day, I came across a stray dog. He's got white matted hair and dark brown eyes that shine like the buttons on my uniform. I petted him for a while and gave him a biscuit. He took a liking to me, and I to him.

Three weeks ago, well after lights out, he came to the Nissan hut where I am billeted. He pawed the door until the WO (Wireless Operator) opened to let him in. The little dog headed straight for my camp bed and slept on my feet all night. That turned out to be a blessing. It's mighty cold here. We all sleep with our high-necked sweaters underneath our nightclothes.

So, I have a new friend. I call him 'Scratch' because that's what he does every night at the door. Scratch is going to come up with us in the Catalina. The skipper has granted permission. He's a good man. A Canadian. An animal lover, like us.

The boys spoil Scratch because they think he's good luck. They've set up a small bed for him behind my seat in the cockpit. Mine's the second pilot's chair on the righthand side as you look forward through the window at the front.

When I'm out walking with Scratch, he struts with his head high next to me. No one knows where he's come from or who's his owner. Everyone thinks he's cute. As for me, I think he's a sign and a wonder. When we are together, we are black and white, never segregated, at one with each other and the world.

Perhaps one day we will all be like that.

There is a lot of racial reconciliation needed even here in Northern Ireland. Yes, the Irish treat men like me very differently. They are kind, respectful, hospitable, and polite. But I'm coming to ask what the real reason might be for this.

I can hear you muttering, what's changed your tune? A local Catholic priest, Father O'Riley, opens his doors and his Irish whiskey to us 'Yanks'. The other evening, I was on my own with him. Most of the time, his room is full of thirsty comrades. This time, it was just him and me. And we got talking about race.

"How do you find the Irish?" he asked.

"Very accepting of us black folks," I answered.

"Are you used to that?"

"Not really." I revised my answer. "Not at all. Our politicians want to persuade your politicians to impose Jim Crow on us black servicemen while we're here."

"You mean segregation."

"Do you think they'll succeed?" I asked.

"No, I don't. There's already segregation here in Northern Ireland, don't forget. It's a very sensitive subject. I think it's very unlikely that they'll agree to more of the same at Stormont."

"Stormont?"

"Our parliament," the priest said.

"Well, then, I'm grateful."

"Don't be too grateful," he said. Finishing his tumbler of golden liquid, he added, "I know you think we're being friendly and welcoming, but I'm not sure how genuine this is."

I must have looked confused.

"There are growing signs of prejudice here as well. Let me fill your glass and give you two examples."

I drained the last sip of my shot of Bushmills whiskey. As he filled my glass, the liquor seemed to glow in the warm light.

"The first is the fact that some people have overheard the insults of your white comrades and are starting to use them too. Perhaps you've heard them doing this."

"What insults?"

"Words like 'Negro' and 'darky'."

"I've only heard those from white GIs."

The priest frowned.

"I'm afraid it's not restricted to them. I've had to reprimand some of my own parishioners for parroting the language of those who seem to despise you. And I've reminded them as Catholics that we too have endured such degradation from those who hold power over us. So, we ought to know better."

I frowned and took another sip.

"The second is this. Behind the scenes, some of our politicians are sounding very damning of black servicemen. One has roundly condemned Catholic girls for walking out with black soldiers, warning of the danger of what they call 'brown babies.' And here I believe we see peoples' real feelings break cover."

"I'm not sure I understand," I said.

"Then, let me explain. In the New Testament, there are two Greek words that are translated "reside". One has the connotation of longevity. The other, transience."

"You're talking about the difference between being a temporary visitor and a permanent resident."

"I am indeed. And I'm proposing that many of my countrymen may be giving you respect and welcome only because they see you as passing through as opposed to staying. If they felt you were going to be here long after the war, then they would almost certainly be less friendly, unless of course they are the Catholic girls that some politicians regard as the lowest of the low."

"So, that's why there's all these warnings behind closed doors about brown babies," I said.

He nodded. "Brown babies would most likely mean that black fathers are here to stay."

I finished my glass. "Then Northern Ireland may end up

being little different from what it's like back home."

"I'm afraid so."

The priest poured a third glass.

"Ask yourself this question," he said, sitting back in his armchair next to the fire. "How do the Irish in America treat people like you and your family?"

"Not very well," I admitted. "In fact, my father told me that growing up in Boston he experienced the worst racist abuse from Irish Americans on his street."

Just then, there was a knock on the door. When the priest opened it, he ushered four white boys, all GIs, into the living room. The visitors looked strangely at me - half-suspicious, on account of the color of my skin, and half confused, on account of my Canadian uniform. I guess if I'd been dressed in US uniform, they'd have called me a dusky doughboy, or some such thing.

I turned to the priest, thanked him, and left.

That priest has given me much food for thought. What are your thoughts about all this, Dad? I look forward to hearing what you have to say about it all.

Write to me soon.

I love you.

Your son, George.

VV.

9

THE FLIGHT

Agent Miller was not in a positive mood. His scrutinization of the professor's computer had yielded only the fact that the young academic had been planning for several years his research into the role played by Lough Erne in the Battle of the Atlantic. There were copious notes from academic books, journal articles, and seminar papers, each one part of a growing database in support of the professor's thesis about the centrality and significance of County Fermanagh in World War 2. Reading this, Miller conceded to himself that he found the research interesting. His own father had fought as an airman in the same war. Donald Miller had flown from England on multiple missions as a gunner on board a B17. The professor's desire to honour the places and people that had supported these young airmen was something Miller would have found compelling in alternative circumstances.

But these were not alternative circumstances, and in Miller's eyes the professor was a threat. None of this research, however much it connected with his own past, was enough to dilute the strength of his resolve. That resolve had taken him to a restaurant the previous evening. He had not foreseen that there were two floors and had booked a table upstairs. His two targets, meanwhile, had been seated downstairs, in a refurbished cellar accessed by only one set of stairs. Miller had thought of asking for another table near them, but he had assessed the risk and determined it was not worth taking. This meant he had failed to eavesdrop on any of their conversations.

Later that night, he observed the professor returning to his apartment alone with a small overnight bag. He watched and listened on his laptop using the four devices he had planted. The professor had not spoken during the time it took for him to head to bed and fall asleep. Something else, however, had piqued Miller's curiosity. The professor had packed a passport into his bag.

Before he went to sleep, Miller conjectured that the professor was heading to Northern Ireland – a trip motivated most likely by the need to do some research for his new book, or to investigate the circumstances surrounding George Hailey's disappearance, or both. He therefore accessed flights to Belfast International and, in under two minutes, had found the professor and the pastor.

Easy Jet.

Southampton to Belfast International.

1025.

Miller bought a ticket for the same flight. He repeated the same actions as the professor, finding a carry-on bag, packing his passport. He added a tracking and a listening device, hiding them inside a fountain pen and an electric toothbrush.

Sure enough, at 0930 the next morning, Miller breezed through security and into the departure hall. He never let the professor or the pastor out of his sight, while never permitting himself to enter theirs. Without them knowing, he navigated a path to a position just behind the professor in the boarding line. Miller saw his chance and took it. The professor had draped his tweed sports jacket over his arm. Made of pure Helsinki wool, this high-end jacket had a breast pocket whose sole function was to accommodate a silk handkerchief. This was the ideal location for a listening device. No man ever thrust his hand into a breast pocket in the same way he did a side pocket. Miller could insert the bug there and it would never be found.

Having secured the device, Miller relaxed. He no longer cared if he was sitting behind the two targets on the plane. In fact, it would be advantageous if he put some distance between them and him, thereby lessening if not destroying the possibility of being spotted. In the end, he found himself in front of them, sitting in the second row, while they were seated together towards the rear of the plane.

Miller leaned his head against the window, making it seem as if he was going to sleep, and switched on the device. He adjusted his earpiece. The professor was speaking.

"You mentioned that there are different kinds of Christianity in America these days."

"Uh huh."

"What kind do you believe?"

"My hero is Harriet Tubman."

"As in the underground railway?"

"The same."

"Why her?"

"She combined two things that are usually separated, not just by individuals, but by entire religious systems."

The professor waited.

"Mysticism and justice."

"You'll have to explain."

"Harriet had mystical experiences. There were many times when she was given visions about where to go and where not to go when she was helping slaves to escape. On no occasion did these deceive her. She was always listening. And she heard the voice of God speaking to her with remarkable accuracy. Every time."

Miller allowed a sardonic smile.

"But she didn't seek after such things. Her mission was to end slavery, not to have visions. It was justice – God's justice – that drove her. She knew God was enraged by what wealthy whites were doing to my African ancestors. She risked her life rescuing scores of slaves from their oppressive masters."

Miller snorted.

"So, what you're saying is that Harriet Tubman was unusual because she combined something very private, her mysticism, with something very public, her social activism."

"That's exactly what I'm saying, Professor. This fusion just doesn't happen often today. There are whole religious movements who love visions but ignore justice, and there are equally entire churches and denominations that prioritise the social but neglect the mystical. Harriet was a both-and girl. I try to be the same."

"That's interesting," the professor said as the plane taxied from their gate towards the runway.

"Why do you say that?"

"My adoptive grandfather was called Harold King. He was a black West Indian, and a devout Christian. His hero was Howard Thurman, and his favourite book *Jesus and the Disinherited*. I got the impression from my grandfather that unlike Harriet Tubman, Howard Thurman was more social than mystical."

"First of all, that's amazing!" the pastor exclaimed. "I didn't know about your grandfather. But also, it's neat that we've been influenced by two black activists with the same initials."

"You're right! Harriet Tubman..."

The pastor finished the sentence.

"And Howard Thurman!"

There was a pause as the engines revved.

"Maybe," the pastor said, "we have more in common, you and I, than I first realised!"

"We both have grandfathers we miss," the professor said, his voice softer now, almost lost by the thrust of the engines as the plane accelerated down the tarmac.

There was a period of silence as Miller continued to listen, right up to the point when the plane reached its cruising altitude, and the fasten-seatbelts sign was disengaged.

The conversation then restarted.

"Do you think we'll find him?" Maya asked.

There was a pause before the professor spoke.

"Yes, I do."

Miller pressed his earpiece deeper into his drum, making sure he didn't miss a word.

Stone said, "It might be good for you to prepare yourself."

"I've been doing that all night."

"I'm sure. It can't be easy. If it was my grandfather

potentially at the bottom of the lough, I'd be anxious too."

Miller shook his head. What were they talking about? Had he missed something?

Miller continued to listen to the professor trying to reassure the pastor while, ignoring the airline protocols, he went online and conducted a search on his phone.

He stumbled on a news headline in an Irish online newspaper, the Belfast Times. *World War 2 Seaplane Found at the Bottom of Lough Erne*. The aircraft was a Catalina. The site had been declared a war grave. Members of a specialist interest group had discovered it. There was a photograph of the ghostly fuselage 150 deep. A man called Jack, who seemed to be an expert, was talking about it. He said that its whereabouts had been a mystery since 1944.

Miller winced.

Meanwhile, his two targets were still talking.

"It could be your grandfather's plane."

"How do you know?"

"Jack emailed me. He thinks it is."

Miller scanned the article. There was no mention of the name or number of the Catalina on the bottom of the lough. How could the professor be so sure? And who was Jack? Was he the same person being interviewed in the newspaper?

Miller began to shake, as if passing through a turbulence that affected no one else on the flight.

"Jack says he'll tell us everything when we arrive at his house. He is very relieved you've come too, Maya. His life's mission is to help the surviving relatives of the lost airmen of Lough Erne."

"He sounds like a good man."

Stone's answer was lost within the announcement over

the cabin speakers that they had started their descent and the preparations for landing had now begun.

Miller made some notes on his phone – the bare bones of what he intended to share with his boss at the Pentagon.

- WW2 seaplane found at the bottom of Lough Erne.
- Local expert, Jack Gallagher, believes it is a Catalina.
- It could be the Catalina we didn't want found.
- Gallagher was part of a group that identified it.
- The professor and pastor are now flying to Belfast.
- As am I, and I'm listening to them.
- They are going to meet the local expert.
- He seems to have vital intel about the wreck.
- Has he seen inside?
- Pictures so far are of the outside of the plane only.

Miller ended his summary and looked out of the window. Everything appeared to him so much greener here than back home. There was every shade, from light to emerald. The verdant landscape below looked to him to be wet with rain and overflowing with vegetation. There were so many fields and so many farms. And then there was the vast saltwater expanse of Strangford Lough, with lone fishermen casting lines from their motorboats. How he envied them. Not long until retirement; then it would be his turn.

The jet landed and the passengers deplaned. Miller headed in a taxi to the General Consulate's offices in Belfast where he was granted a secure line for submitting his report. Having been given a pickup, he drove towards Belleek in County Fermanagh to spy on the man whom the news reporters referred to as Jack. The device in the professor's jacket was working well.

The article in the papers had stated that the site of the wreck was now protected by law. Under the Protection of Military Remains Act 1986, anyone touching, moving, damaging, or unearthing any of the contents of the Catalina would be prosecuted. Unless they had a licence granted to them by the marine and fisheries division at Stormont, they would be arrested.

But what if Jack and his team had seen more than they had let on when they first located the wreck?

Miller was suspicious.

Not just by profession, but by nature.

And as it turned out, he had every right to be.

10

THE WRECK

When Stone and Maya arrived at Jack's bungalow in Belleek, they noticed the curtains were closed even though it was midday. When Jack ushered them into his living room, they saw a laptop set up on a coffee table in front of the open fire. It had been connected using Wi-Fi to a TV in the corner beneath the window.

"I apologise for the closed curtains," Jack said. "We don't want any prying eyes looking into our home. Besides which, you'll be able to see what's on the screen a lot better. The picture is grainy and dark in places, so you'll welcome the darkness."

Just then his wife entered bearing a plate of sandwiches. "Ach, sure, everyone knows everyone in Northern Ireland," Orla said as she passed around a China plate with floral patterns. "People will already be talking about your visit!"

Stone took a sandwich bursting with sliced chicken and mixed green salad. Maya declined. Mary was about to insist when Jack gave her a look that told her to stop.

"I'll love and leave you, so," Orla said before hurrying out of the room and closing the door.

"Thank you for doing this," Maya said.

Jack looked at her with concerned eyes. "You're George Hailey's granddaughter, then?"

She nodded.

"I think you'll see in a few minutes why you needed to be here in person, you and the professor."

Jack switched to the media player on his laptop, activating play mode. He reached behind the sofa to two switches on the wall and doused the lights. The room was now in darkness, except for the freckled images on the TV screen.

"This was filmed a few days ago at a location on Lough Erne now protected by law." Lowering his voice, Jack continued, "What you're seeing now are images from the camera of a drone owned by one of the two people who discovered the wreck. As you can see, the pictures are clear enough in this light."

"What kind of drone is this?" Stone asked, adding, "It looks as if it's quite sophisticated."

Jack tapped his nose. "I'll just tell you that it was formerly owned by the Royal Navy."

"So, it's a good one."

"Top of its class."

Stone followed the drone's-eye view as it descended. Before it had travelled far, there was a jerk as the tiny submersible seemed to bump into something large in the water.

"What was that?" Maya asked as a shadow passed in front of the drone's cameras.

The tiny forward lights in the drone's curved front arms revealed the answer before Jack responded. Stone saw the distinctive jelly-bean pattern of the creature's lateral spots, its forked caudal fin, and above all its ugly jaws and sharp, needle-like teeth. He knew what it was - a pike, and no ordinary specimen either.

"That thing's about four feet long!" Stone said.

"Five," Jack muttered.

The drone continued its descent until it arrived at the bottom, 150 feet below the surface.

"We're approaching the wreck."

Stone and Maya saw something white illuminated by the penetrating lights of the submersible. At first, both thought it was the soft underbelly of another large fish. But then it became clear what it was – the remains of a Catalina's fuselage.

"I want you to see this first," Jack said.

The Catalina was lying on its side at an angle of 45 degrees. One side was half buried in the silt. The other revealed the full flank of the seaplane as well as most of the hull. As the drone drew closer, it homed in on a space just behind and below the cockpit. There were four words painted there: 'Lady of the Night'.

"It's your grandfather's plane," Jack said, his voice so soft it was almost a whisper.

Maya took a deep breath.

The camera proceeded to a position in front of the aircraft. The bow gunner's turret was a terrible mess. The machine gun had been rammed backwards into the cockpit. The nose section was crumpled, the metal torn and depressed.

"Make a note of what you see there," Jack said as the drone left the front section and returned to the side of the fuselage. As it hovered right next to the pasty flank of the Catalina, both Stone and Maya could see it. There was a catastrophic tear in the hull of the aircraft, from the front right back to the tailplane.

"I think it's obvious what happened," Jack said, his tone grave. "During its landing on the lough, Lady must have struck some uncharted rocks. She lurched forwards at unimaginable speed, breaking the wing into many pieces, sending the fuselage straight down like a torpedo. None of the crew stood a chance. The devastation caused to the front gunner's body just confirms this theory."

Maya covered her mouth with both hands.

"Would you like me to pause?" Jack asked.

She shook her head.

"Watch now as the drone heads to the largest fissure at the tail end of the plane."

The drone passed through a crack where a machine gun had been positioned in the underbelly. The glass of the one large blister still visible was gone, as was the 50mm calibre machine gun that had once protruded like a porcupine's spine from the bubble-like structure. There were ammo cans and flare tubes strewn on the silt that lay above what had once been a metal walkway through the aircraft's bulkheads. But that wasn't all there was. Three bodies were slumped in the seats into which they had been strapped on impact.

"The two aft gunners and the rigger," Jack explained.

"Rigger?" Maya asked.

"The man responsible for doing running repairs to the airframe, making cups of tea, cooking meals, firing the tail gun, tending to Lady's moorings at take-off and landing."

Maya nodded.

"May all of them rest in peace," Jack whispered.

"Amen," Maya said.

The drone then passed through the bulkhead into a section where it looked as if there had been some beds. Several broken fuel and bilge bumps, caught by the current from the drone's movements, drifted in slow motion just above the silt.

"No remains in this section," Jack said.

The drone manoeuvred through a second bulkhead. Two huge water tanks, both broken, had become detached from the sides of the fuselage. Once it had navigated its way past them, the images transmitted by the drone were as clear as they were concerning. The engineer had died here. His bones were broken, but the instrument panels he had used were preserved. Not one of them had been destroyed. The contrast between the durability of the machine and the fragility of the man were not lost on the professor.

The drone made its way through a third bulkhead. More remains. This time the wireless operator who was seated next to the ARB radio. Then another body in the same section. The navigator. He had his back to the bulkhead and was facing aft. His body was slumped forward, his rib cage fractured, confirming that he'd been subjected to a terrifying and sudden force. He lay beside two more large water tanks, in pieces like the two they had seen further aft.

Then, before they passed through the fourth bulkhead, they saw another body strapped to a seat. Sat beside the ANAPS 3 radar, it was clear this was the radar operator.

"The final section is ahead," Jack warned. "And it's the cockpit, the part of the plane manned by the two pilots and the forward gunner. This part bore the full impact of the crash."

Stone braced himself.

The drone passed through the bulkhead and turned left. Its lights, now trained on the remains of the Skipper, caused the second chair to be lost for a moment in the darkness.

The first pilot had, along with the bow gunner in front of him, received the most traumatic injuries. The bomb selector panel originally above and in front of him had been propelled backwards into his skull, slicing off the top of his head an inch below his scalp. The barrel of the machine gun in the front turret had been thrust backwards into his chest. Everyone in this forward section of the plane would have been killed in a split second.

Stone's heart sank.

The drone's camera pivoted right, its beacons illuminating the second pilot's chair.

Stone rubbed his eyes.

Maya gasped.

"It's empty!" she cried. "Where is he?"

Jack paused the media player.

"We've considered every possible scenario," he said, facing Maya. "We wondered at first whether he had somehow been hurled out of the plane, but we discounted that. The physics of the crash don't allow for it, and the fact that the other eight crewmembers stayed in their seats just supports our theory."

"What if he was taken back to the section where you said there were beds?" Maya asked. "Maybe he was wounded. Or sick. Maybe he was there rather than in the cockpit."

"We've considered that too. The bulkhead doors would have been closed for landing. Had anyone been in that compartment, their body would have been entombed in that space."

Maya continued to press. "Could his remains be underneath the wreckage of the plane?"

"We've run every possible scenario, but that's not our working hypothesis."

"So, what do you think happened to him?"

A pause, then, "We believe he wasn't on board."

"How can you believe that?" Maya asked.

"The main evidence is the absence of your grandfather's remains within the cockpit of the plane, or anywhere else within the fuselage. But there's also something else."

"What?"

"It's circumstantial, but at the same time consequential," Jack said. "I'm referring to the absence of a canine skeleton."

"You mean Scratch?"

"I do. The professor informed me in an email about your grandfather's little dog, and the fact that he flew with your grandfather on all the missions in the Atlantic. Even had his own dog tag. So, naturally, we've been looking for him."

"And you've found nothing..."

"Absolutely nothing. The drone has scanned the entire wreckage and the impact site. There are no signs of dog bones. And there's no sign of George Hailey's remains either."

"And you found all the other eight crewmembers besides George?" The professor asked.

Jack nodded. "Lady had a nine-man crew. The front gunner, first pilot, second pilot, navigator, radar operator, wireless operator, two air gunners, and a rigger."

Maya asked, "Could they have ended up in different parts of the plane before the crash?"

"The six crewmembers behind the cockpit had the training and the ability to swap roles, yes. All were expected to do wireless watches, gunnery rota, lookout duties on the A.S.V..."

"A.S.V?"

"Air to Surface Vessel Radar."

Jack took a sip of tea before continuing.

"The two pilots in the cockpit had only one task, to keep flying the Catalina and to bring her safely home. If the first pilot was wounded, the second one could take over. The only reason why either of them would have been further back is because they were wounded. The sleeping quarters were used as a sickbay."

"What about the communal toilet?" Maya asked. "That was right at the back, wasn't it?"

"It was, but no one would have been allowed to use it during landing or take-off."

Jack switched the lights back on, turned off the laptop and TV, and opened the curtains. The dull light of a grey, wet Fermanagh day filled the room.

Jack lit a candle on the mantlepiece, next to a small statue of Jesus with his hands clasped together in prayer. He stood and bowed for several seconds before he spoke.

"If you don't mind, I'd like to honour those who died on the Lady all those years ago. I'll mention your grandfather separately Maya, because we cannot be sure yet what happened to him."

"Thank you," Maya said.

Stone and Maya stood.

The room went quiet.

All Stone could think of was the photo of George Hailey

in the library back home.

"Find me," he said, over-and-over again, until at last Jack began to recite the names of the crew from memory.

"First pilot/Skipper, Flight Lieutenant Charlie Hobbs
Sgt Jonty Gowan
Sgt Freddy Quinn
Sgt Arthur Singer
Sgt Jonty Fleming
Flt/Sgt Norman Jones
Flt/Sgt Johnnie Rowe
WO Reggie Field."

Jack paused.

"And we remember Second pilot, F/Lt George Hailey, praying for a safe journey home."

Maya said, "Amen."

Stone mumbled.

As they looked at the flame struggling to be free from its wick, Maya shook her head and said, "How are we ever going to find out what happened to him?"

"You said you have some of George Hailey's letters," Jack said, looking at Stone.

"Twelve of them, from his arrival at Lough Erne in October 1943 until the day of his disappearance..."

"1944, March 15th," Maya interjected.

"There must be something in them that will give some semblance of a clue." He put his hand on Maya's shoulder. "And remember to keep your hope alive."

Stone, who was deep in thought, muttered some words. "Keep alive the dream; for as long as a man has a dream in his heart, he cannot lose the significance of living."

"What was that?" Jack asked.

"Something Howard Thurman said," he replied.

Jack turned and faced them both. "I need to insist on one thing, that you don't tell anyone about what you've seen. We'll get in very serious trouble with DAERA..."

"What's DAERA?" Maya asked.

"The Department of Agriculture, Environment and Rural Affairs here in Northern Ireland."

"Our lips are sealed," Stone said.

"What are you going to do now?" Jack asked.

Maya spoke first. "I've got to head back to the States and care for my father. He's very sick."

"I'm sorry to hear that," Jack said.

"I need somewhere near Lough Erne to do some of my research," Stone said. "I prefer, if I can, to be in a location connected with my studies. It grounds me."

"Birgit has offered you rooms in her place by lower Lough Erne," Jack said. "It's a most interesting estate."

Stone nodded.

"Sounds perfect," he said.

LETTER 6

December 10th, 1943

Dear Dad,

I'm going out with a girl. Yes! She's cute. A real sweetheart. I'm excited to tell you how we met.

I had come to the end of my fourth reading of *Native Son*, and I couldn't bring myself to read it again. I really needed a new book, so I set about looking for a library in one of the towns near Castle Archdale. I happened to mention this to the CO at our base and he told me that he'd opened a reading room in Irvinestown just a few months before. "There are lots of books you can borrow," he said. "Contemporary works as well as classics. You don't have to pay for them. They'll lend them to you, or you can read them there. Just make sure you give a small gift every time you go in to help cover their costs."

The next day I had some leave was in the week before Christmas. Off I went in a jeep to Irvinestown. I found the reading room after asking for directions. In I went.

The walls were covered in shelves, all filled with books – both hard covers and paperbacks. Many of them were recent. I found a copy of *For Whom the Bell Tolls*, and *The Grapes of Wrath*. I didn't select those but earmarked them for the future. Instead, I found *The Song of Bernadette* and sat down in an armchair next to a coal fire burning in a cast-iron grate. I started reading that. Franz Werfel wrote it after finding himself in Lourdes when he and his wife were on the run from the Nazis. He vowed he would write the novel if they escaped.

I must have become quite lost in wonder at the writing because the next thing I knew a young woman approached me. I had noticed her when I entered the building. She looked like Jennifer Jones, whose face I saw on a poster promoting the film version of *The Song of Bernadette*. This woman reminded me of her. She has striking dark eyes. Wavy hair the color of a raven. Beautiful pale skin. A coy smile. She's shy. Sweet-natured. Thoughtful.

"You look as if you're enjoying that," she said. Her Irish accent was strong. To my ears, it sounded like music.

"It's pretty good," I said.

"Would you like to borrow it?"

"Sure."

I stood and followed her to the desk. She has the finest figure. I had to look away towards the books on a table.

When I signed for the novel, she said I had a beautiful signature. She followed that by asking if I was based near the town. I told her I was a second pilot in the RCAF and based at Castle Archdale. She blushed a little and looked down.

Then she said, "You must be very brave."

"I'm blessed with a great crew, and a little dog called Scratch, my most loyal companion."

"I love dogs!" she cried. "Where is he?"

"He's back at the base."

"You must bring him next time," she said.

"Is he allowed?"

"I'll allow him. You can bring him in through the back. When will you return?" Then she caught herself. "Ach, look at me. I sound like I'm inviting you, so."

"You are," I said.

"Catch yourself on!" she cried.

"I will come back with Scratch."

"You'll have to warn me."

"What's your name?" I asked.

"Myra," she said. "Myra Coughlan."

"That's a pretty name."

"What's yours, airman?"

"You can call me George."

"Aye, I will. Well, George, you can telephone me here. I work most of the week. Mornings and afternoons. Then in the cinema some evenings. Here's the number." She passed a corner of a piece of paper which she had torn.

"Thank you, Mam."

"Myra," she insisted.

"Thank you, Myra."

Just then, I remembered that I had my copy of *Native Son* in the inside pocket of my coat. I took it out, presented it to Myra, and said, "Have you read this?"

She shook her head. "What's it about?"

Well, of course, I gave an enthusiastic synopsis. "That sounds tragic," she cried. "Is that how people like you are treated back home in the States?"

I nodded.

"Even though you're risking your life for your country?"

There was something in her eyes now, a mixture of sadness and anger. I have never seen anything like it.

"I'm a Catholic," she said. "We've been on the receiving end of brutal treatment too. The British government still looks down on us. Still makes our lives difficult."

"I didn't know that."

"There are so many examples, but you'll have to make do with one. Have you heard of Sir Basil Brooke?"

"Isn't he the Prime Minister of Northern Ireland?"

"Yes, appointed by the British."

"What about him?"

"Ten years ago, he said he'd never employ a Catholic worker on his estate because 99% of us are, apparently, disloyal."

"That's terrible!"

"May I borrow your book?" she asked, reaching for the cover. Her hand touched mine as she took it. I swear it was like a thousand multi-colored Christmas lights suddenly sprang to life in my brain. I thought I was going to stumble.

"Let me know what you think," I stuttered.

"I will," she said, her smile turning into a giggle.

She put *Native Son* into the pocket of the black coat she had just put on as she prepared to lock up the premises.

"I'll phone when I'm coming back," I said.

"Don't forget Scratch!"

"I won't."

And that's how we met. On my next day off, I returned to the reading room after letting Myra know. She allowed us both in through the back door. I sat with Scratch at my feet reading more of *The Song of Bernadette* which Myra had kept aside for me. As for Scratch, it was love at first sight when he and Myra set eyes on each other. The third time I visited, she insisted on taking care of Scratch in the back. I could hear him barking and her laughing at his antics.

It was after that we agreed that we would go out together. She and Scratch tend to walk either side of me. Scratch looks at her more than me as he trots along. Myra threads her arm through mine and leans her head on my shoulder when the urge catches her.

Tomorrow, she's taking me to meet her mother. Then we're going to see *Lassie Come Home* at the Irvinestown cinema where Myra works, although she's off duty. She says Nigel Bruce reminds her of her father. And then of course, she loves dogs, as I do.

Do I have feelings for Myra?

Yes.

Are those feelings strong?

Stronger every day.

Do I think about her when I'm not with her?

All the time.

Do I see myself with her in the future?

If the good Lord wills it.

Has she changed my heart?

When I'm flying, I am much more anxious to get back to base in one piece. And when I'm back at base, I'm no longer bored by the long hours and days between our sorties.

So, yes, she's changed everything.

Myra Coughlan has changed everything.

God bless you, Dad.

Your son,
George.
VV

11

THE FARM

Birgit's place, as it turned out, was far larger than Stone had anticipated. Situated about two hundred metres from the banks of Lower Lough Erne, the entire farmstead was enclosed by a wall of tall, impenetrable hedges and only entered by an electric double gate which Birgit activated using a remote from her vehicle. To Stone, it resembled the famous walls and houses at Hougoumont, the farmyard defended by the Coldstream Guards at the Battle of Waterloo.

Once past the curved gates, Stone cast his eyes over the buildings, the largest of which was a white-washed farmhouse in front of him. To his left, there was a garage, several storehouses, and some stables repurposed as offices, to his right, a hay-bale barn, open at the sides. Strewn around the spacious yard there was a retired tractor, an old tandem-disc harrow, two antique cultivators, a rusty plough, and four wrecked cars, each one an old red Firebird.

"Feel as if you're in your own home, Professor," Birgit

said as she turned off the ignition.

Birgit escorted Stone through the graveyard of vehicles to the front door of the farmhouse. On entering the kitchen, she assembled a basket of fresh bread, milk, butter, brown cheese, and red-berry jam before escorting him upstairs to a room whose front-facing windows overlooked the lough, and whose back-facing windows faced onto an enormous octagonal greenhouse that stood adjacent to the back wall of the estate. Row upon row of garden beds had been dug in front of this glasshouse. These long rectangular allotments were covered in nets to prevent birds from grazing on the vegetable seeds.

"This is some place," Stone said as he turned to Birgit. "Are you trying to be self-sufficient?"

"Not trying. Succeeding."

Stone walked over to a desk overlooking the lough. He unpacked his laptop and plugged it into a socket two feet away. He could feel himself beginning to relax.

"You have your own kitchenette across the way," Birgit said. "I'll put these supplies in there. The bathroom is also all yours. There's no one else staying in the house. You can use this as your base for as long as you need, Professor."

Stone thanked her, then asked, "Do you have a car I could borrow? I have a meeting with Jack."

"There's a working Firebird in the garage you can use. I'll leave the keys in the ignition. You probably noticed it's my favourite car. The other four are different 80s models, all decommissioned, but my existing one works just fine. Where are you meeting him?"

"The Catholic Church in Irvinestown. We're going to try and find out about George's young lady, Myra."

An hour later, Stone was shaking Jack's hand outside the Sacred Heart Church in the parish of Devenish. Devenish was a name familiar to Stone. He knew of the island of Devenish, also called Ox Island, the most famous of all the islands of Lough Erne. Situated at the south end of the lower lough, the most notable feature of its 70-plus acres was the church, the tower, and the abbey. Although much of the site had been ransacked by the Vikings in the twelfth century, the fortunes of Devenish and its sacred ruins were restored in the Middle Ages. Now, in the summer months, tourists from all over the world took boat trips from Enniskillen to its lush green fields and ancient ruins.

Stone followed Jack away from the church and across the road to the Garden of the Celtic Saints. "Saint Mo Laisse is something of a local hero," Jack said pointing to his effigy. "He had a gift, brought on by birdsong. He was able to travel through time."

"That would be a great superpower for a historian," Stone remarked. "I'd love to be able to go back and see what happened to this town at the start of World War 2."

"You can," Jack said. "... in your imagination. Just picture it. Before the Americans arrived, Irvinestown had nothing really going for it at all. But there were big changes when nearby Castle Archdale became a base for our visitors from across the pond."

"What changes?" Stone asked.

"For one thing, there were only a small number in work. A few families manufactured specialist farm equipment. Several couples ran eating and boarding houses. Another couple ran a restaurant. There were three hotels and no less than eleven pubs. Many wondered how these managed to keep their licenses and continue serving alcohol, given the rationing. There was talk of some of them crossing the border to the south to find alternative supplies."

"Sounds desperate," Stone muttered.

"Aye, it was, at least until Christmas Day in 1940 when a seaplane from 119 squadron flew over Lough Erne. I'm sure few people noticed it. The two pilots were on a reconnaissance mission, photographing the lower lough to see if it was fit to be an RAF base. They deemed it unsuitable, but Coastal Command disagreed. They chose Lough Erne without conducting a proper survey..."

Stone sighed, then muttered, "With tragic consequences for the Lady of the Night."

"Ach, right. It was only two years after the war that the waters were properly surveyed. Rocks were found just eighteen inches below the surface in the middle of the lough."

"The way you talk about 1941," Stone said, "it sounds like the war was, in a way, good news for the town."

"Aye, it was. The entire site over at Castle Archdale had to be developed very quickly to accommodate thousands of US, Canadian, and RAF personnel. Trees were cut down. Nissan huts were erected in the spaces where the trees had once grown. Old quarries had to be reopened to help make new roads. Local building firms were swamped with work. No one was unemployed anymore."

"All because of the Americans?" Stone asked.

"Mostly. There would have been hundreds of foreign service personnel descending on these streets from the Lough Erne area. Their jeeps had plenty of petrol. These men and women had cash to spend. Local hotels, pubs, and eateries were now so popular they had to turn customers away. The cinema was always full. A local drama club and a local band - both named after Saint Mo Laisse – held performances in the Town Hall. There wasn't enough room there either. The same was true for the dances held in the Orange Hall."

"Sounds like a revival," Stone said.

"Aye, you could say that. A lot of the airmen developed a strong religious faith during these years. The local Church of Ireland rector - called Heavener, appropriately - held Evensong services followed by supper in the houses nearby. These were very popular, partly because the meals involved meeting local lasses."

"Ah, yes," Stone said. "And that brings us to Myra, who won George Hailey's heart. She seems to have lived here. Worked in the cinema part-time, and in the reading room."

"Did you say the reading room?"

"I did."

"Ach, I know about that. It was on Pound Street, just a few minutes from here. People in the town donated their books. From what I recall, the most popular were detective stories and romance novels. The Americans loved them."

"When was it opened?"

"Sometime in March 1943. The commanding officer at Castle Archdale came and did the honours. He was a Group Captain. His name was Pearce if I remember right."

"All that fits perfectly with George's letters," Stone said. "He says he arrived at Castle Archdale in October 1943, which would have been just over seven months after the reading room opened. He met Myra there early December 1943."

"What was his girl's surname?" Jack asked as they walked

past Molly's Bar.

"Coughlan."

"What do you know about her?"

"She seems to have lived with her mother, Ruth."

"No sign of her Da?"

"According to one of George's letters, her father was killed in the Belfast docks during the blitz. Ruth and Myra were on their own, at least until George came on the scene."

Jack stopped outside a house on Pound Street. "I believe this was the reading room."

Stone gazed at the doorway to the house, imagining George walking over the threshold into a large room full of shelves, books, tables, and newspapers.

Stone said, "Someone around here must remember George Hailey and Myra Coughlan. Seeing them walking out together must have given the locals something to talk about."

Jack laughed. "In Northern Ireland, everybody knows everybody, and everybody is interested in everybody else's business. We're a small country, don't forget."

"That's my point. Is there anyone you know who might remember these two lovebirds?"

"Come with me," Jack said.

The next minute they were at the bar of an Irvinestown hotel ordering two pints of Guinness. The woman serving them was in her sixties. She had dark hair, hazel eyes, and a warm smile. When she laughed, there was the hint of a hack in her cackle.

"This is Jacqueline," Jack said after she had given him a hug. "Her late mother lived here during World War 2. She told many a story about those days. Jacqueline may know something."

As he wiped the cream from the bottom of his top lip, Stone addressed the woman behind the bar. "Do you happen to remember your mother saying anything about a black airman going out with a local girl called Myra Coughlan?"

Jacqueline nodded. "Of course. It was the talk of the town. The American was very popular with the children. He taught them how to play baseball. He was very good to Myra's mother. He brought her sugar, milk, meat, all sorts. He had the local children clean ruined with sweets. My own mother referred to him as the Candy Man." Jacqueline paused and stopped smiling. "It was terrible what happened," she said with a frown. "Truly terrible. Everyone was upset by it."

Stone placed his pint on a coaster.

"My mother said both incidents happened in the first half of 1944. The first was the American's disappearance. His aircraft must have crashed somewhere on Lough Erne. The plane was never found. None of the crew survived. Many people mourned, especially the children, when they heard the American was dead."

"And the other incident?" Stone asked.

"I suggest you head to Sacred Heart Church and look for her mother's grave. It's near those who fought in World War 2, and one for a soldier who died in the Great War."

Stone and Jack drained their pints and said thank you. Ten minutes later they were back where they had started their walk, at the Sacred Heart Church, this time standing in front of a gravestone. The memorial was for Ruth Coughlan who, the carved inscription read, died of a broken heart in May 1944.

Stone stared at his scuffed brogues. The grass beneath his

feet looked rain-soaked, neat, green. Dirty white petals lay strewn at the edge of the path several metres away. As he stared at the ground, he recalled words from his grandfather's funeral. "The grass withers and the flowers fall." He thought for a moment he was imagining their recitation. But he wasn't. He could hear them. They were being spoken out loud somewhere in the cemetery.

Looking over his shoulder, Stone saw a priest with a white surplus and a purple stole officiating at the interment of some ashes. There was one other person with him, a funeral director who had brought an inexpensive looking urn to the plot. The priest was the one speaking about the transience of human flesh.

As Stone stared at the grey-haired, balding cleric, the short service came to an end and the undertaker walked back to the church. The priest, seeing the two strangers in his graveyard, walked over to them, and introduced himself.

"Father John," he said.

Jack shook his hand.

Stone summoned a smile.

As Jack engaged in conversation, both men's Fermanagh accents became thick, their idioms unfamiliar and opaque. Jack said something about the priest being "clean foundered" in the grim weather. The word "craic" was uttered too. Stone could only feed on morsels of meaning. He caught one or two phrases.

As Stone tried to make sense of it all, his hopes for any kind of breakthrough became as bleak as the sky.

Until Jack turned to him.

"We're in luck," he said. "Father McNeil, who served here during World War 2, is still alive. He lives in the clergy house, in a room in the wing dedicated to 24-hour care. He's in his nineties, so it's not easy to understand what he's saying, but he might be able to help. Father John is going to speak with him this afternoon and see if he's happy and able to talk. He'll ring me when he knows, so."

Stone nodded. He asked the priest, "Do you think the Father's memory is still good?"

"His long-term memory is sound enough. He just can't remember what happened yesterday."

Jack chuckled. "Ach, I know the feeling."

"Please keep us posted," Stone said.

The priest turned back along the path and walked towards the door to his church.

Stone said goodbye to Jack and headed back towards Lough Erne. When he was no more than 100 yards from the black aluminium gates of Birgit's farm, they moved slowly inwards to allow him to drive into the grounds. As he proceeded towards the garage to the left of the house, he wondered how Birgit had known he was returning and to open the gate. The half-mile track leading to the farm entrance was flanked by lowering thickets like a more densely packed version of the Dark Hedges, one without any gaps either side.

Stone parked the Firebird in the garage and strode back across the mud towards the farmhouse. Its walls, washed in lime, were visible in the half light of the crescent moon. As he stepped along the path, the side of his shoe brushed one of the four Firebirds. He switched on the torch on his phone. As he examined the old vehicle, he couldn't help noticing the front headlamps. These were electronic and retractable, so he expected them to be in the closed position. But they were not. The lights were deployed, and the glass was not only unbroken; it was also unscarred. When he studied the other three cars, he found they were in the same position and condition.

Stone switched off his phone and was about to make his way to the front door when he glimpsed two large bats flying low towards him. They were darting this way and that, guided – he surmised - by echo sound. As they hurried past, Stone wondered if the waves emitted beyond his hearing had bounced from him to them.

Stone climbed the stairs to the top floor of the farmhouse and stood at the window. The silvery water of the lough seemed so tranquil, but Stone knew that this was an illusion. The waters may have been serene, but they hid their ancient traumas well. Below the surface, and not far below at that, men had fallen in battle, dying barbaric deaths, their bones buried in the mud. Some of these traumas were ancient, from the time of the Vikings. Some were more recent, from the time of the Lady of the Night. In Stone's mind, he could still hear the shouts and cries of men at the threshold of extinction.

As he watched the moonlight glistening on the water, the professor remembered the photograph of George Hailey in the archive room back at the university library. He imagined he heard the airman's words again and, as he did, he spoke under his breath.

"I *am* going to find you."

LETTER 7

December 15th, 1943

Dear Dad,

I've just returned from my first combat mission. Up until now, it's all been patrols. But I was awakened along with the rest of the boys at 0130 two nights ago. We were told to put on our flying gear – which was damp, of course. We headed to our respective messes where we were served steak, eggs, toast, and coffee. We were then handed a wicker basket with the rations for our 20-hour mission.

Two loaves of bread

A dozen eggs

Some meat

Potatoes and carrots.

They were all wrapped up neatly in packages as if we were going out for a picnic. Some picnic!

We were rowed out in a dinghy to Lady who was resting at anchor. The routine checks followed.

Engines.

Controls.

Ailerons.

Floats.

Radio.

Radar.

Guns.

After the depth charges were loaded, we took off.

I ought to explain something, Dad. Northern Ireland is part of Great Britain and therefore committed to the fight against the Nazis. The south is neutral. This can be a bit confusing, but if you look at a map of Northern Ireland there is a large stretch of territory along the North-West coast which belongs to the south. It's called Donegal. Normally, we wouldn't be allowed to fly over it because it's technically neutral territory. We'd have to fly north and then west to avoid it, adding over one hundred miles to our journey, and drastically reducing our range in the Atlantic. Fortunately, the two governments have come to an agreement. We are therefore permitted to fly directly west from Lough Erne to the Atlantic through something called 'The Donegal Corridor.' This has meant we can cover far more of the Atlantic, protecting the merchant ships travelling to and from the States, thereby saving many thousands of lives. So, now you'll know what I mean when I say that we flew west through this corridor out over the ocean.

The first three hours were the hardest. It takes a while for your ears to adjust to the constant vibrations and the cacophony, and for your body to get used to the cramped conditions. And then there's also the long wait before a second breakfast!

After bacon and eggs, we spent the next five hours of our

mission on a constant watch of the ocean. There are four beds further back, and the boys were allowed one hour off to sleep after every three hours on duty. Bully beef sandwiches would await us at lunchtime. I think all of us prayed our food wouldn't be delayed indefinitely by a call for help, or an encounter with the enemy.

Clearly, the crew and I weren't praying hard or well enough because that's precisely what happened. At midday, we approached a merchant navy fleet. We had signaled the commander to warn him we were friendly. This is vital. One of our seaplanes from Lough Erne – a Sunderland Short – was badly shot up recently by friendly fire. The destroyers can be very trigger happy.

The captain acknowledged our presence and we descended to about 800 feet. The Lady – a Catalina - is a slow aircraft designed to fly at a cruising speed of about 150mph at a height of between 400 and 1000 feet. That may seem very slow and low, but you can't see sailors swimming in the sea if you're flying at 20,000 feet and at 350mph. The Lady is a beautifully designed aircraft. Her endurance is a thing of wonder. She's basically a large boat with one single wing, which is why some people refer to the Cat as a Flying Plank. But it's so much more than that. The two Pratt and Whitney engines give us tremendous range. The four internal bulkheads are separated by watertight doors, making each section of the fuselage self-contained.

After an hour of anti-submarine patrol, I spotted something on the ocean below. It seemed to be no bigger than a cigar box from that height, well camouflaged against the waves with its light blue paint. Scratch, who had been in his makeshift bed behind my seat in the cockpit, started barking. He clearly thought it was a U-Boat. He must have sensed my heightened level of excitement.

During our first run, the U-Boat gunners opened on us. Their accuracy was as remarkable as their bravery. The cockpit was hit, and the Skipper cried in pain. He had taken several bullets to his right arm and shoulder. He lost a lot of blood before he lost consciousness. Once he had been carried back to the beds, where our medically trained crewmember took good care of him, I managed to move over to the first pilot's seat and take over the controls.

Grabbing the wheel, I maneuvered Lady up into the clouds where we found some cover from the anti-aircraft fire. There I had to think quickly. Either we headed home, or we dived down to the U-Boat and engaged with the enemy. Realizing that returning home would leave the fleet vulnerable, I told the boys to assume action stations. We were going to drop our depth charges on and around the sub.

What happened next was a blur. I seemed to go into a kind of trance where all that mattered was getting that rabid wolf away from the line of sheep headed for Londonderry. I was only barely aware of the flak around the aircraft and the tracers flying past the fuselage. My main memory was Scratch barking, as if cheering me on as I guided Lady towards the sleek grey killing machine below.

Billy, the bow gunner, opened fire on the deck of the sub as we descended. I was not happy with our approach, so I chose not to drop the depth charges. When we approached the sub again, the gunners had scurried below. The sub was beginning to submerge. By the time we reached the spot, it had gone beneath the surface.

I cursed my luck.

We dropped the depth charges. Reports came from the two gunners looking through the rear blisters that the bombs had detonated. I could imagine the huge plumes of water rising towards the grey sky. It must have been some sight.

When we returned for a final sweep, there was no sign of the U-Boat. No sign of debris either. I guess we will never know if we did serious, let alone catastrophic damage.

We started our journey back to the Irish coast, eating our lunch – Bully Beef sandwiches - over two hours late. They are a boring part of our diet, but that day they tasted like a king's feast. We were all starving, including Scratch. I gave the corners to him.

As we drew nearer to the Donegal Corridor, the crew reported good news about the Skipper. They had stemmed the flow of blood, cleaned his wounds, dressed them with bandages, and the Skipper had regained consciousness. He was in good spirits when he learned that we had given the U-Boat a chastening, maybe even worse. He even asked for a mug of tea. Eight sugars, not the normal six.

As we flew through the Donegal Corridor, I had the boys inspect the hull of the Catalina. Several of the men reported that there was damage from enemy flak – five holes, two large ones. I told them to patch things up as best as they could. I had our WO signal ahead to Castle Archdale to warn them we would need help.

When we landed, I took great care. I had done this many times in training, but this was different. We hadn't been damaged then, and the hull had not been porous, as ours was now. You need to be careful anyway on the lough. There are many challenges landing a Catalina or a Sunderland. There are hidden rocks, not marked on any map. If the hull strikes them on landing, that spells big trouble.

When we came to rest, there were boats at the ready to help prevent us from sinking. The Skipper was carried off first and taken to hospital. The rest of us were rowed back to base. In the Skipper's absence, I reported on the mission while the others went to the mess to celebrate. No one offered them a drink.

"All in a day's work."

That's the attitude here.

The Erks – the ground crews – set to work repairing Lady while the rest of us enjoyed some pancakes, bacon, and cocoa before heading to our beds for a well-earned sleep.

Scratch, having enjoyed several rounds of bacon, settled on my feet. He slept for eight hours straight before waking me up and telling me it was time for him to go outside.

It was morning when we did, but I wasn't sure which day it was. The mission had begun at 0200 hours, had lasted twenty hours, and I had slept for eight hours until 0800. The boys all started to rise and one by one patted me on the back for doing "what the Skipper would have done." Speaking of the Skipper, we went to see him in the hospital. He will be out of action for a few weeks while his wounds heal, but he will make a full recovery. He brightened when we walked in; we were told off by a ward sister for making too much noise!

So, that was my first combat mission. I thought about Myra a lot while I was in the air. I am even more careful now that I have her in my life. We want to be together forever.

Don't worry about me, though, Dad.

I'll be okay.
God bless you.

Your son,
George
VV

12

THE ASSASSIN

Agent Miller had not been spotted as he hid behind the wall of the graveyard, pointing a directional microphone at the three men. He smiled at the irony; he never became tired of seeing while not being seen. The sense of power that came with this had given him a rush for decades. He enjoyed observing others while they were unaware of his presence. It made him feel godlike. Miller, whose life had altogether departed from the religion of his youth, had enough residue theology to understand the complex paradox that lay in the very heart of the God believed by all three of the great faiths. In their credos, God could see everything and everyone while those being seen could not see him - except, like branches being blown by the wind, in the visible effects of what Miller regarded as his implausible interventions.

Miller shook himself out of his reflections. Maybe it was the mossy graves, the chipped crosses, or the frozen angels that were turning his thoughts to religion. Maybe it was repressed childhood memories. Whatever it was, the comment made by the officiating minister had struck him. There was an elderly priest, in his nineties, in a clergy house in Irvinestown. This priest had known George Hailey and his Irish girl, and her mother, Ruth. As he watched the three men leave the cemetery, Miller knew this was serious. It was already serious that these meddlers had discovered George Hailey was not on board the Catalina when it sank to the bottom of the lough. Now there was a chance they would find out why, and that could not be allowed to happen.

Miller rose from his almost genuflected state and walked to a spot under the boughs of a nearby tree. He took out his phone, worked out the time difference between Ireland and the States, then dialled the number of his handler at the Pentagon. When an automated response requested his identification details, he inserted a long number. He was asked for a code, which he also typed, followed by an extension number. After he had entered it, he waited.

A familiar woman's voice answered.

"We have a problem," Miller said. "Two in fact."

There was silence at the other end.

"Some local meddlers in Fermanagh have discovered the wreck of George Hailey's Catalina."

"How did they do that?"

They were in possession of an advanced sonar device." Miller paused. "But I'm afraid that's not all. They also had an underwater drone – former Royal Navy ordinance – and they guided it inside the wreck itself. Quite illegally, I should add."

"And what did it find?"

"Pretty strong evidence that George Hailey was not on board the Catalina when it crashed."

The woman cussed.

"There's more," Miller said. "Not only has the professor seen the film shot by the drone. He has also found someone here in Irvinestown who knew George Hailey during the war."

The woman cussed again.

Miller continued. "A retired priest, now in his nineties, knew Hailey and the Irish girl he was dating at the time of his death. This old priest knew the girl's mother as well."

Miller paused, waiting for another expletive from his handler. None came, so he continued.

"If this priest says something that arouses the professor's suspicions, if he provides any leads..."

The woman interjected. "Agent Miller, you must make sure that doesn't happen."

The line went dead.

It was Miller's turn to cuss now.

Returning to his car, he drove to the clergy house, a long two-storey Georgian building just outside Irvinestown. In addition to a central building fronted by a pillared porch, there were two wings either side of it, stretching towards neat lawns.

Parking away from the front entrance, Miller opened his laptop and accessed the architectural specs for the residence. He noted that there was a long corridor in the east wing of the house, with what looked like single-bedded rooms either side of it all the way to a fire door at the end of the hallway. He conjectured that the old priest occupied one of these cell-like spaces. Now all he needed to do was find out which room the man would be sleeping in that night.

Posing as a long-lost relative, he phoned the receptionist

and asked for the priest's full address so he could post him a card and a gift. The young woman on the line, who sounded like a local doing a holiday job, was so laidback her tone was soporific. But Miller smiled. The last thing he wanted was a strict and super-vigilant matron. A carefree temp was much more to his liking.

After securing the room number, he hung up and made his next decision - the disguise. He would wait until the shift changed that night, then arrive in the early hours pretending he was a local doctor responding very late to a call from the girl to whom he had just spoken. If the person on the next shift was anything like the girl, the ruse should work. All he needed to do was wear a wig and change his accent. Sporting a stethoscope like a clunky necklace was an old and familiar trope, but he couldn't help smiling at the thought of getting away with that too. The rest would be easy.

And he was right.

At 0200 hours he pressed the doorbell, gained entrance, submitted his story, explained that "Keely" from the previous shift had contacted him, informed the receptionist he knew where his patient was, told her it wasn't necessary to accompany him, and gained entrance to the old priest's room, all this while wearing a passable wig and employing an equally passable Northern Irish accent.

The old priest's bedroom was bare, save for a statue of the Virgin Mary in an ultramarine cloak. She was standing on a shelf on the wall at the foot of the single bed. The only other item of furniture was a crucifix made of darkened wood hanging above the priest's chaotic, silvery hair. Miller noted the face of Christ, turned downwards towards the aging, sleeping priest. There was a look of sadness in the carved eyes as they gazed at the snoring cleric.

Miller reached into his coat pocket and withdrew a small brown bottle half-filled with liquid. Withdrawing a glass dropper pipette, he used the sucker to draw some of the liquid. He looked around the room to doublecheck there were no surveillance cameras. Reassured, he allowed a solitary drop of the deadly solution to fall into the old man's half-opened mouth. Then, with meticulous care, he screwed up the top and returned the lethal phial to his coat pocket.

The old man stirred, as if he had been jolted awake by a coughing fit in the small hours.

His eyes opened.

Squinting at first.

Then wide.

There was a look of confusion.

Then a gasp.

His head fell back into his pillow.

His mouth opened as wide as his eyes.

His frosty chin protruded outwards and upwards.

Beneath the pinioned, wooden feet of his saviour.

Miller took a deep, long breath. He never felt more alive than he did at such moments. In his own eyes he seemed not only all seeing but all-powerful. He was Nietzsche's Übermensch; aware of the terrors of existence, he affirmed life without any bitterness.

Miller uncoiled the stethoscope from his throat and checked the priest's chest. He took a pulse and used a small cosmetic mirror to make sure the old man had uttered his last breath.

He replaced the instrument like a serpent around his neck and looked again at the face of Christ. Miller sneered. He despised him. This crucified man had promised so much when Miller was young, but he had delivered nothing except abandonment.

As he turned to the door, Miller remembered some favourite lines of Nietzsche. Passing the haloed Virgin, he knew he mistrusted those who spoke of otherworldly hopes. As far as he was concerned, he – Robert Miller - was the meaning of the earth itself.

He paused at the threshold and looked back at the crucifix above the dead priest's head. He withdrew his burner phone from his coat pocket and entered his boss's number. He typed a single sentence into the text message box.

"It is finished."

He closed the door and headed down the corridor to the desk where the ginger-haired receptionist had given up the ghost and fallen asleep. She was face-down in the visitor's book, her forehead resting on the two opened pages.

How easy it was for Miller to slip in and out of other people's worlds, acting as a silent angel of death. He took pride in such killings, even when the victim was a man in holy orders. But then, Miller had no qualms about killing a priest. The man could have shared vital intelligence. His chaffed lips had to be closed, his testimony silenced. Miller had done that without remorse. But then there was no regret at all when it came to the taking of this life. The death of the priest was for Miller like the death of God. There would be no tremors of guilt in his anaesthetized conscience.

As he left the building, Miller smiled. He had been ruthless, as he always was. That was an adjective he employed and even enjoyed when it came to what he called his 'work'. Ruth was the old English word for 'pity'. He had murdered without compassion. There had been no 'ruth' in his clinical termination of the priest, and, as a result, there would be no Ruth in what the professor was trying to reconstruct. Her story was stolen when the priest breathed his last breath.

Miller headed towards his car. On the way, he slid one of his tiny cameras into the trunk of a tree just off the circular drive before the clergy house. Several hours later, he watched what happened next on his laptop in a hotel room. A green-and-white-striped vehicle arrived. Two paramedics rushed from both front doors into the building. They were carrying resuscitation equipment. An hour later, they left just as a black hearse was arriving. Two undertakers entered the house with what looked to Miller like a collapsible gurney whose metal edges glinted in the moonlight. Ten minutes later, they wheeled out the body of the dead priest. Zipped in a body bag as black as a cassock, it was swallowed up in the rear of the limousine.

Miller changed the screen from the clergy house to the professor's apartment in Portsmouth. His plan was to access the four cameras he had planted and conduct a final sweep before laying his head on his pillow for a short, untroubled sleep. But what he saw did not bring the deep sense of rest he anticipated. Bret, the professor's young acolyte, was in the living room, watching TV. Miller supposed everything was normal and that the student was taking a break from his duties. But this impression did not last. The moment Miller accessed the camera in the professor's wall-mounted monitor, the young man's face registered shock. He had seen something. Something he wasn't expecting to see. Something, indeed, he wasn't supposed to see.

Bret stood and approached the monitor.

He waved his hand across it.

He shook his head.

He ran his hand through his thick hair.

Shook his head again.

"What the ....!" he cried.

Bret walked to one corner of the room.

He looked back at the screen.

He shook his mane again.

Uttered another expletive.

It was only when Bret hid behind the sofa, popped his head above the back of the furniture, then swore again, that Agent Miller felt a hot flush of anxiety. He knew what had happened. There was a glitch in the camera in the TV. Instead of the TV showing the Netflix stand-up show Bret had been watching, it was transmitting the images that Miller was seeing. And Bret could see them too. What was supposed to be a window had become a mirror.

Bret pointed his remote at the screen and switched off the TV. The young man knew something was wrong. He was shaking his head and stomping around the living room.

Miller rested his wigless head on a pillow worn thin by a multitude of other heads. Even though he tried, he could not shake off the anger. The technology had never let him down, not even during the Cold War. But it had now, and the frustration, morphing into rage, was acting in his body like caffeine.

From now on, Bret was a target too.

LETTER 8

December 20th, 1943

Dear Dad,

I'm sorry it's been a few weeks since I wrote. When I haven't been flying with the boys, I've been seeing Myra. She lives with her mother Ruth in a small house not far from my base. They have so little money. I give them some of my pay, as well as meat and other rations that I'm given by a friend of mine called Archie who's in the catering unit. He took a liking to Scratch and has been giving him bones. When I told him about Ruth and Myra, and the fact that Myra's father had been killed in one of the Belfast raids, he was happy to pass on some of our rations so that they can at least eat. Ruth is so grateful. When I visited yesterday, she hugged me when I gave her some beef wrapped in paper. When she released me, there were tears in her eyes.

Myra and I are getting along just fine. Last night we went to the movies where she works. They were showing *The Song of Bernadette*, the hit from Christmas a year ago.

There was great demand for it to be shown again. I'd missed it the first time around, what with my flight training in Canada, so I was eager to see it too, not least because the female lead looks so like Myra. It was very moving. I found myself captivated by the young girl's visions of the lady in white. When I returned to my bed late last night, I couldn't help thinking of the tension throughout the story between the scientists and the priests. I was very struck by the words on the screen at the beginning of the movie. "For those who believe in God, no explanation is necessary. For those who do not believe in God, no explanation is possible..."

Did this French girl, born into such poverty, afflicted with such suffering, really see Mary? Were people really healed by the water that flowed in the place of visitation?

Myra and I went for a drink at a nearby bar afterwards and talked a lot about the Catholic faith and their sincere veneration of Mary. I don't know where I stand on this. Sometimes I think religion swings like a pendulum too recklessly towards extremes. There are those who go too far in deifying her, and then there are those who go too far in dismissing her importance altogether. I prefer to come to rest somewhere in the middle. At the very least, Mary was a remarkable young mother. Myra, of course, thinks she is far more than that and longs, like Bernadette, to see her. She refers to her as 'Our Lady,' uttering these two words with the sweetness and adoration of Bernadette in the movie.

I drank my first pint of Guinness as we talked and liked it very much, telling her so. She smiled, saying that she was very glad I had a fondness for something Irish.

"It's not the only thing," I said, smiling back.

She blushed.

We finished our drinks and left for where my jeep was parked. I should tell you that some white GIs took exception to me going out with a local girl. They were about to do me some harm, when several of my fellow flyboys from Castle Archdale, who just happened to be passing by, saw what was happening and stood between them and us, telling them to back off or they'd be sorry. I thanked them. Then I drove them back to base, dropping Myra off at her mother's house on the way. The boys crammed into every part of the jeep and laughed about the way my assailants had slunk away in fear.

I was not so talkative or confident. My crew do not know what it's like to live as fearfully as I do. I am more in danger from some of my countrymen than I am from the German submariners. The last seven missions over the Atlantic have been uneventful. We have not been shot at by the enemy, nor have we seen any sign of them. There was some excitement when one of our planes sighted a U-Boat, but by the time they arrived at its position the wolf had fled the scene. No, it's here that the danger lies – from those who resent me outperforming them in my service for my country or showing them up in my courtship of a girl like Myra. I know I'll have to be more vigilant in the future. The friendliness of the Irish has made me relax a little too much. They have been nothing but hospitable and kind, so this is no comment on them. But I can forget that not everyone I move among is safe.

That night, as I laid my head to rest on my pillow in our hut, I remembered Bernadette. "I saw a lady, and she was all in white; and she wore a blue girdle and had a golden rose on each foot. I've never seen anything in my life so beautiful."

Part of me longed for such a sacred guardian in my own life.

I hope you're keeping safe as well, Dad. I would love one day for you to meet Myra. I think you two would get along. You would find her as interesting as she would you. Our stories are not that different, hers and ours. She has finished *Native Son* and is now rereading it. She says that even though Bigger Thomas was guilty of his crimes, she cannot help thinking that he started his race so much further back than white folks, and that if he had not been so steeped in poverty and powerlessness, he might have grown to become a very different man. In this, as in so many other ways, she shows such great wisdom and compassion. She seems to see it, although I should not really be surprised; our people and hers have been subjected to great injustices. If we ever marry, we would be a formidable pair of freedom fighters.

Victory at home, Dad, not just overseas.

VV until both are things of the past.

I love and miss you.

Your son,
George.

13

THE FRAGMENTS

"I'm afraid I've got bad news." It was Jack's voice at the other end of the phone. Stone was sitting at a small, round wooden table at the top of Birgit's farmhouse, eating a bacon sandwich and looking across the glinting surface of the lough.

"It's the old priest, Father McNeil." A sigh filled Stone's ears. As early warnings go, it was effective.

"He died in the night."

Stone lowered his sandwich.

"What happened?"

"We're waiting to hear, but it looks like he had a massive heart attack and died in his sleep."

"So, that's it. No more leads."

"I'm afraid so. Father McNeil was our only known link to George and Myra. Now he's gone, it's hard to know where else we can turn for reliable information."

"What about Father John?"

"He's too young to have known them."

"No, I mean maybe the old priest said something to him when they talked. You know... when Father John tried to arrange a meeting. Maybe Father McNeil shared some memories."

"That's possible. Father John had a long conversation with him yesterday evening."

"Why don't you ask him, Jack?"

Ten minutes later, Jack was back telling Stone that the younger priest had indeed heard some tales.

"He wants to meet us at the boatyard distillery in Enniskillen. Why don't I pick you up in an hour at the jetty?"

"I didn't know you had a boat."

"Ach, I'm hiring it."

"Let me pay for that," Stone said.

Stone cleared the table and washed his dirty plate and mug in the kitchenette. He was wondering if he was going to be safe in a boat driven by a man Jack's age when his thoughts were interrupted by his phone. The screen revealed the caller's ID.

"You okay, Bret?"

"I'm not sure, Professor... I can't say anything on the phone... We may have a problem... I mean, a *big* problem... Can't talk now. I'll come... come and find you tomorrow. Don't text me... Don't call me... I don't think it's safe. I'll explain ..."

"Bret!" Stone shouted. He fumbled a mug he was drying. It smashed on the metal draining board.

By the time he lifted the handset to his ear again, Bret had gone. As Stone brushed the shards of cheap pottery into a bowl and then into a flip-top bin, he wondered what had gotten into his apprentice. He had never heard him so agitated.

Stone put some items in a backpack, including waterproofs, before locking the front door and walking along a rudimentary track in the direction of a small wooden jetty half a mile away. How quiet it was compared to the bustling streets of Portsmouth. The only sound was the call of a heron standing on a small island on the lough. He watched as it launched itself into the bright sky with a lazy push and a languid flap of its grey wings. For a fleeting second, he saw in his mind's eye a seaplane taking off from the shimmering water, the floats on its wingtips retracting as it rose towards the heavens.

For the next quarter of a mile, Stone veered from the lough across a meadow adorned with bluebells before walking along a rough track through a thick forest of aspen and oak trees. The sweet smell of wild garlic and holy rope filled his nostrils as he emerged the other side of the wood. Finding himself in another meadow, he caught sight of two speckled deer moving out from under the lowering branches of a willow tree. When they saw him, they walked without any hint of alarm back into the cover they had just left. He, meanwhile, continued his slow march towards the jetty.

The path he trod took him towards the edge of the lough again, through a thick crop of reeds where he saw a black scooter resting in her nest and an otter slipping into the water, one eye watching his every step along the track. Two minutes later, he arrived at the old wooden jetty. It was deserted. Even so, he decided to make his way to the mooring posts at the far end of the walkway, its splintered planks creaking at the burden of his tall, lean frame.

When he reached the end of the tiny pier, Stone heard the low moo of a cow at the water's edge. He turned to see a small herd of cattle grazing at the lush grass on the banks of the lough. One of them had her front legs in the water and was bowing to the rivulets washing her shins. Under the morning sun, her form was reflected in the water in front of her. There was such a perfect symmetry between these two iterations of the same creature, one solid, the other liquid, that it seemed to Stone as if the separation between land and lough had all but been obliterated. They were bound together in a strange stillness in which the physical and the immaterial seemed to be one.

The professor, amused by the intrusion of such metaphysical thoughts, pulled himself together just as he heard the chugging of a motorboat. This brought him back to his mission with a jolt. No longer was he ruminating about the abundance of the wildlife and the fauna. He was worrying about what information, if any, could be gleaned from the conversation between the two priests. More concerning still, he was unsettled by the tremor in his young assistant's words. What was it that could not be said over the phone, but had to be conveyed in person, face to face? Why, in short, was Bret so afraid?

Stone stopped just as Jack pulled the sixteen-foot fishing boat alongside the jetty. The freshly painted bright white vessel had been refitted, like countless others, to carry the many tourists who flocked to the lough each year for day trips on the water.

Stone stepped over the gunwales and into the small cabin. He was silent as they slipped away from the jetty and out into the lough. Grateful that Jack seemed to sense his need for quiet, Stone stared out of the side window at the paddling mallards and the scudding greylag geese, envying their simple, untroubled focus. Jack only broke his fast when they passed a mansion on a hill.

"Portora School," he said.

"Where Oscar Wilde went," Stone added.

"Aye, and we mustn't forget Emily Valentine," Jack muttered, "the earliest female rugby player."

As the lower lough began to narrow, they approached the island town of Enniskillen, a bridge between the uninterrupted expanse of the lower lough, surrounded by fields and rolling hills, and the upper lough, a quilt of islands, waterways, inlets, and drumlins.

Seeing the high ramparts of Enniskillen Castle, Stone thought of its famous dragoons and began to hum the song they once sang as they left Erin's green isle for the sunny land of Spain. "Fare thee well, Enniskillen. Fare thee well for a while."

After mooring the motorboat at Tully Bay Marina, they headed to the boatyard distillery where Father John was waiting for them. He was seated on a stool, resting his elbows on a round table that stood on top of a refurbished liquor barrel. He had bought a round of sloe-boat gins, each one in a glass tumbler, with a wedge of orange resting on a floating cube of ice. When Stone and Jack approached, he greeted them by presenting a glass to each of his guests. Stone thanked the priest, then took a sip of the rich, ruby-red drink. It seemed to glow not only in the glass but in his throat and chest.

"I expect you want to hear what happened," the priest said.

Stone nodded.

"His death was a surprise. Although he was old, he was not in poor health. He just seems to have passed away in his sleep. Ach, sure, that's how we'd all want to go, so."

Jack agreed.

"The afternoon before he died, we had a conversation in the community lounge at the house."

Stone took a gulp of the sloe-boat gin.

"I explained about your research, Professor. The moment I mentioned George and Myra, his eyes lit up. It seemed to animate him. Fascinate him."

"Did he say anything?" Stone asked.

"Nothing coherent, mind, at least not in terms of a story. But he did share bits and pieces of interest."

"What, Father?" Jack asked.

"Well, he said that George Hailey was so in love with Myra that he had proposed to her. She had agreed but had set before him one condition, that he embrace her Catholic faith so they could both be one not only in body but in spirit. This was no small request for George. He had been brought up Pentecostal. But he agreed to it. The two then went to see Father McNeil at his church in Irvinestown, which is where he first met them properly."

"This is new information," Stone said, adding, "I have in my possession twelve letters that George wrote to his father back home in New England. He talks about his love for Myra, and the proposal. But he never mentions converting."

"Maybe he didn't want to upset his Da," Jack said.

"Was there anything else?" Stone asked.

"Aye. He mentioned that George enrolled to study the catechism when he wasn't flying. He had come to the first one, but then stopped when disaster struck."

"Is that the phrase he used?" Stone asked.

"Those were his exact words, yes."

"Did he explain what he meant?"

"I assumed at the time he was referring to the fatal crash of the Catalina, with all hands lost."

The priest drained his glass.

"But then I realised he couldn't have been."

Stone leaned forward.

"This is where it became a wee strange," the cleric continued. "I asked Father McNeil whether he had seen George before the American's Catalina and crew disappeared."

He drained his glass and waved to the barman.

"He replied that he had seen him before the fatal mission, yes. But he added he had heard about him after it too. A fellow priest told him he had visited a man answering George Hailey's name and description two weeks after Hailey's plane had disappeared."

Stone shook his head.

Three more sloe-boats dropped anchor at their table.

"I asked him where this was," the priest said, "but he was growing very weary and one of the nursing staff was being quite strict with me. She said I needed to go. But before I went, Father McNeil said one more thing that I feel I should pass onto you."

The priest sucked the gin from his orange slice.

"He said that there was someone who befriended George after the plane crash. Another American. Someone from a different part of the States from George. From the South. I think he mentioned Alabama, but he was mumbling badly by then."

"Maybe it was Tuskegee," Stone muttered.

"What's that, Professor?" the priest asked.

"George had trained as a pilot in Alabama. Maybe the man who was looking after him had been there too."

The priest nodded and said, "Father McNeil was compelled to promise that he would never say tell about seeing George, that he would keep it a secret from everyone, including Myra."

"Who made him do that?" Stone asked.

"He didn't say, but after he had told me he clearly felt guilty because he asked me to absolve him, which I did. He said that the prayer had lifted a weight from his shoulders."

Stone drained his gin. Seeing the priest making to order another round, he stopped him. "This has been helpful," he said, "but it's also an incoherent picture. Just fragments, really."

The priest's eyes brightened. He muttered, "Gather up the fragments that remain."

"What's that?" Stone asked.

"John Chapter 6 verse 12," the priest said. "The feeding of the five thousand. Jesus told his disciples to gather up all the pieces of bread that were left after the meal. They filled twelve baskets."

"I don't understand."

The priest, surprised by the professor's lack of comprehension, said, "Everyone wants the full loaf, but sometimes the full loaf is too much for a person to consume at one time. So, they must satisfy themselves with fragments. But fragments, like the breadcrumbs in the miracle, can be vessels of the grace of God."

"I'm not religious, I'm afraid," Stone said, placing his tumbler on the wooden table.

The priest smiled.

Fifteen minutes later, Stone and Jack were back on the motorboat heading to the jetty they'd left earlier that day. As they sped across the water, Stone's phone vibrated. Removing it from his coat pocket, he looked at the screen. It was Bret.

"Arriving, Belfast International, 9pm tonight. Please pick me up, Prof. I'll explain everything in the car."

Stone looked at his watch.

There was just enough time for him to get back to the farm and borrow the Firebird.

Stone typed a message back.

"On my way. Be safe. See you there."

Bret's answer came straight back.

Thumbs up.

Stone typed the word thanks. Before he pressed send, he watched the word turn into an emoji. Without thinking, he released the message as an image rather than a word.

Two hands pressed together.

As if in prayer.

14

THE TREE

Before Maya reached the door to the sideward, she heard strong familiar voices singing hymns she had loved since she was a child. She paused, knowing what this signified. Taking out her phone, she sent a text message to the professor.

How are things going in Ireland? Have you learned anything new? I'm about to see my father in hospital.

She paused before writing any more, weighing how to say what she wanted to type next.

Things are not looking good. It may not be long before he passes. Do you have anything encouraging I can share with him – anything that might lift his spirits?

She pressed send.

She waited, staring at a whiteboard with the names of patients written in non-permanent ink.

After five minutes, she could not tell whether the professor had seen her words or not. She strode to her father's private room. Peering through an oval window, she saw her mother and five brothers standing around his bed. Her brother

Robert, a huge bear of a man, was standing in her line of vision, obscuring the view of her father. She could see machines either side, their screens illuminated, numbers and shapes appearing and disappearing.

And then another song began.

The first verse of *Amazing Grace*.

In two-part harmony.

Tenors and baritones.

Until she entered, that is, when her soprano rose above the deeper tones of her brothers. Robert wrapped his huge arm around her shoulder as she entered the circle. All her brothers were standing there, along with three other suited men from church. Her mother was the only one sitting. She held her husband's hand, staring at his closed eyes. She shook her head and wept.

As Maya sang, she looked at the framed photographs that her mother had placed around the bed. Some were on a small bedside table. Others she had placed on shelves, a dresser, and a short cupboard. One stood out in Maya's eyes. Standing three feet from her father's face, it was a picture of the yard at her parent's house - the Boston townhouse they had lived in since he became a bishop. It showed the one tree in their garden, a sugar maple in the corner of a square of grass. Her father had set up a swing from a sturdy, low-hanging branch. She, aged six, was wearing a white dress and he was pushing her. She looked so carefree, with her wild smile and wondering eyes.

And he, how alive he looked. It was a blazing hot July day, and he was wearing a clean, sleeveless vest beneath the shade of the tree. The muscles in his arms and chest were flexing as he pushed and pulled. In the act of manoeuvring her slim and tiny frame, she could see his stomach muscles rippling like the inshore waters of a great lake. Everything about him seemed young, happy, and vibrant. But as she looked, she was struck by the contrast between her father and the tree. The tree, which was at least two hundred years old, seemed to be eternal, while he, in the light of the draining of his lifeforce in the here-and-now, appeared as transient as the deep red leaves that spontaneously combusted each fall. The tree, with its burning leaves, would outlive him. Another mother, one hundred years from now, would likely use its sap to make a syrup for her children's pancakes.

As her brothers began a new song, one from their ancient history in the Deep South, their bodies started rocking beside the bed, mimicking the motion she had sensed in her own body as she had relived the swinging from the old tree. Maybe it was the slow and restrained motion of their frames, or the hushed and mellow sound of their voices, but Maya now found herself lost in her photographic to-and-fro. It was as if she was back there, seated on the small piece of timber, holding onto the two black chains hanging from the low-hanging branch above. She was swinging as well as singing now, as she had been then, noticing again what she had seen at the time but long since forgotten – a monarch butterfly heading from a flower bed towards the alluring scent of the tree, resting for a heartbeat on her father's arm as he paused to let his daughter swing without his intervention. They had both stared at it with marvelling eyes. To Maya, it was like a coronation; her father was from that time on her king.

And then she was back in the ward.

Maya looked at a screen next to the head of the bed. A

line that had been jagged, like a range of sharp-topped mountains, had become flat. The singing stopped. The only sound now was the drawn-out whine of the flatlining on the monitor.

In unison with her father, Maya's heart stopped.

She turned as the door behind her opened and two nurses burst into the room. Her brothers and the other men stepped back to give them space to do their work. Maya seized her mother's arm and tried to pull her away from the bed, but she would not move. She buried her face in her father's side, shaking her head, uttering a cry unlike anything Maya had ever heard – a muted wailing that seemed to emerge more from her mother's womb than her mouth.

Maya knew what would happen next.

That which she had feared now came upon her.

Two more nurses entered wheeling resuscitation equipment to the side of the bed. Maya saw the paddles, followed by the rise-and-fall of her father's body in jerks and jolts. As her brothers prayed for their father's healing, Maya was already saying a hushed goodbye. She knew that this was the way of things. It was as unstoppable as the changing of the seasons. They could no more reverse their father's passing than prevent the fall or cancel spring.

A doctor entered. Maya recognized her from church. She sang in the choir every Sunday morning when she was off duty. Maya would smile at her as she watched her in her cobalt robe, joy radiating from her sweet, dark eyes. Tonight, it was all so very different. She was wearing a white lab coat, and her eyes were filled with a great sadness as she searched with fading hope for a pulse. She shook her head. The nurses holstered their paddles. She recorded the time of death, then took Maya's mother by the hand.

"I'm so sorry, Mother Rosa," she said. She bowed and added, "A great tree has fallen."

Maya's mother nodded, her eyes awash with tears.

"Thank you, Ebony," she whispered.

Her brothers began to sing the old song, "Jesus promised me a home over there." As they sang of mansions bright in the father's house, Maya stepped forward and looked at the man who had loved her every day of her life. She could not stop the tears now. She stooped, took her father's head in her hands, and kissed a brow no longer furrowed from the fight, but smooth and calm, like the crystal sea of heaven. As her brothers declared the promise of a home over there, she left the sideward and headed towards the foyer of the hospital. The cold night sobered her as she wandered into the parking lot and entered the shelter of her car. Driving home, her mind orbited around the moon of one regret, that she had not been able to tell her daddy what had happened to his own father. There had been no reveal, no twist, no epiphany to bring consolation. His mother had died at the time of his birth, his father not long after his conception. Daddy had died as he had lived, an orphan unsure of his roots, a wanderer looking for home.

Maya parked up at her father's house, a fine white wooden property in the New England style. She thought of how hard he had worked to buy it, then refurbish, and extend it, until it had reached the height, breadth, and length it was now. As she looked at a single light glowing above the porch, she realized she was staring at a million dollars, and yet she would, if she could, give every cent of it away for one more day with her beloved father.

She turned the key and entered the outer door of the porch. Hanging her hat, scarf, and coat, she proceeded to the kitchen and turned on the coffee machine.

It was then, through the kitchen window, that she saw it.

Out in the yard where her father had pushed and pulled her on the swing when she was young, out on the unyielding, snow-powdered ground, it lay.

The sweet maple tree.

Toppled.

Lying on its side.

Amputated.

Its roots showing like arteries.

Its base a severed stump.

Maya ran out of the back door and touched the wood, her hands jolting at the coldness.

She was not imagining it.

The tree had been uprooted. It had fallen upwards - lifted and released by a mighty force.

As she stood there in shock, some words began to surface from the trenches of her memory. Words of her namesake, Maya Angelou. Words that the wistful and lamenting author had penned in a poem about the death of a great soul. Words that vibrated with the sights and sounds of Africa, her primal home.

When great trees fall,
rocks on distant hills shudder,
lions hunker down
in tall grasses,
and even elephants
lumber after safety.

Maya remembered the words that followed too, about

great souls dying, and how grief brings a hurtful clarity, memory sharpened by the trauma of their passing.

The poet had given voice to it and Maya was now living it, inhaling the rare air of its coming, releasing cloudy exhalations towards the stars, watching them rise like incense.

Maya sought no rational explanation. She knew the old saying in Africa that a tree falls when a great man or woman of God passes away. Looking at the stump before her, she recognised that no natural force could have performed such a freakish surgery.

As she turned back to the house, she grabbed her phone. She found the professor's number and wrote him a text. She knew he would not understand what she had seen, so she settled on a short, prosaic line. "My father died at 8.17pm, EST."

With that, she entered the kitchen, poured herself some coffee, and sat in her father's favourite chair, waiting for her family to return, wondering how to tell them of the marvel in the yard.

LETTER 9

January 1st, 1944

Dear Dad,

Yesterday, on New Year's Eve, Myra and I rowed out to Lady in the afternoon. She told me it took some courage to come out onto the water. The locals, she said, are fearful of the lough. They believe that a lady walks the lake with wildflowers in her hand, gliding from island to island clothed in a garment of mist. Maybe this was the strange ghost I saw in the dream I shared with you. She said that many of her countrymen are too frightened to go anywhere near the water during winter. They don't take to the lough until after 'Whitsunday' (Pentecost).

She also told me about the saint who seems to have been an important figure in their history. He was called Mo Laisse. He brought Christianity to this part of Northern Ireland many centuries ago, displacing the older pagan deities and practices.

"The story goes like this," she said. "Mo Laisse built a

monastery on Devenish Island. He also created a library. He was a great lover of books and used to copy the sacred manuscripts of the faith, illuminating them with bright-colored paintings. He worked well into the night, painting the gold parts by candlelight."

Myra's eyes seemed to be aflame as she told the tale. I rowed across the water, keeping the strokes of the oars as smooth and serene as possible so I could hear every word.

"One night," she said, "the saint believed he could hear voices chattering down by the edge of the lough. At first, he thought it was the water washing against the stones and rocks on the beach. But then he heard words, phrases, bits of conversation. Either he was imagining it, he thought, or these were real voices."

Myra seemed to be far away now, while the island itself was within range of our dinghy.

"The voices grew so loud that his work copying the holy manuscripts began to suffer. He heard the voice of Searc, the woman he had once loved, and to whom he had been engaged before he became a monk. She had been heartbroken when he chose holy orders over the covenant of marriage and drowned herself in these very waters on the same day that he made his vows. She was one of those calling from the water, her wailing carried on the wind."

Myra seemed almost to be in tears. I stopped rowing and reached out to her, holding her in my arms.

"What did he do?"

Recomposing herself, she answered. "He decided to go down to the edge of the water and confront the voices from his past. Not just Searc's, but many others too."

I started rowing again.

"On the night of the shortest day of the year, he stood on Devenish beach and commanded the spirits to come and speak to him face to face. The water began to shiver as the spirits of the departed appeared, their eyes wide, their faces broad, their chins narrow. Mo Laisse made the sign of the cross. That stopped them. He considered now that he was confronting demons."

At this point, she beckoned to me to stop rowing. "This is the place," she muttered, drawing out a fishing rod. We had agreed to fish for our supper that night.

As she dropped her line, she continued her tale. "The saint asked the spirits what they wanted, and they replied that they wanted him to stop copying the sacred books, because every line was causing them enormous pain. At this, Mo Laisse was even more convinced that they were demons. They, however, sensed his suspicions, and told him they were not devils but the last of the Old Ones – the ancient people who worshipped the goddess Danu, many centuries before Jesus had been crucified. They asked him to cease his work because every color, every word, was hurting and destroying them."

Myra's rod twitched.

At just the right moment, she made a sudden jerk of her wrist and a few moments later, a large rainbow trout as colorful as an illuminated manuscript was flapping by her feet.

Setting the hook, she passed the rod to me. As I lowered the line, I asked her what happened to the Old Ones.

"Mo Laisse said that he was just a simple monk whose calling was to inscribe the Holy Gospel, whereupon the Old Ones began to descend into a pitiful state. They told him that they had once been the gods of Erin, known to all as the Shining Folk, but when Patrick came, they lost their power and lost the devotion of the people too."

Just then, I sensed a vibration at the end of my rod and struck the fish hard. But the line went slack. Myra reprimanded me for being too quick and rough. She said that women were better at fishing because they exercised a greater patience.

We laughed, but then she became serious again.

"The Old Ones begged him and the brown-robed ones to stop their work on that terrible book, by which they meant the Gospel, but Mo Laisse insisted that he could not. It was his life's calling. With that, a single figure appeared. A female spirit, coming to him out of the water. She told him that if he drowned that night, the work would stop because there was no one else who had the gift he had."

The line shook again.

This time I waited.

Then, when I knew the fish was hooked, I pulled the rod back towards my chest and reeled in a rainbow trout, which joined the other, now motionless, on the floor.

"Just when Mo Laisse thought the fierce-looking lady was about to drown him, he saw a thin streak of light appear in the dark sky. Dawn was breaking, and the monk began to clap and cheer, shouting that the light had come, and that she was defeated. She, feeling the piercing heat of the sun's rays, began to screech as the other spirits slipped back into the black depths of the lough. As she reached out towards him, her entire body turned grey and then became stone."

"And Mo Laisse, what happened to him?"

"He could not write or paint from that night on, and

devoted himself instead to sculpture, creating strange statues of the creatures he had seen the night that he and Erin met."

I handed the rod back to Myra, but she passed. We had enough fish. It was time to row to the Lady.

Once aboard, she filleted our catch and threw the heads and guts into the water. After we had eaten, she lay in my arms and whispered to me that she had reread *Native Son*.

"Poor Bigger Thomas," she said. "He was doomed from his first breath just because of the color of his skin."

"And the poverty to which that condemned him," I added.

She buried her head deeper into my arm.

"I can't bear the thought of you suffering such things," she whispered. "It's just so cruel."

"But you're not so different," I said. "You were promised a united Ireland by the British government before the last war with Germany. They lied. And see how you've suffered."

With that, she lifted her head and we turned towards each other, holding one another close.

"I don't know who you must be more afraid of," she whispered. "The Nazis or your own countrymen."

I sighed.

She wrapped herself around me and said, "Promise me you won't do anything foolish."

"What do you mean?"

"It's just something I read in your book."

"What?"

"Something about violence being a necessity for the oppressed. I'm not sure it's the answer."

I replied, "It's the deep, instinctive expression of a human being denied individuality."

She recognized the quotation.

"Don't be Bigger Thomas," she said.

I could tell there were tears in her eyes.

We knew each other that night, Dad.

We knew each other.

To know and be known, there is no greater thing.

The next day, as we were rowing back to Castle Archdale, she told me that she was still afraid, not that I would be harmed by the gunners on an enemy submarine. She said she was too confident of my courage and capabilities for that, which touched me. No, she was more afraid of those who claimed to fight alongside me but whose knives were out for me, not the enemy.

I'm afraid I deflected it, making some trivial comment about the Nissan Huts which we could now see from our boat, mumbling something about the Lady being warm and dry last night, unlike those makeshift dormitories.

She scolded me for changing the subject. Then she laughed as she saw the fishing rod propped up against the bow, saying how fine the two trout had tasted, and that hers was the bigger fish. We fought a little playfully before we said goodbye, after which I headed back to the mess to rejoin my comrades for the day's briefing.

I wish you could meet Myra.

She's sassy and fine.

I love you, Dad.

Write to me soon.

Your son,
George.
VV.

15

THE CRASH

Stone arrived at Belfast International Airport just as Bret appeared, a yellow bag slung over his left shoulder. Stone expected to see his customary flamboyant smile, but instead his apprentice's eyes darted left and right, then back to the canopied walkway from the terminal building. Dashing across the road, Bret arrived at the passenger door of the car that Birgit had lent – a fame-red Firebird that had been parked in one of the outhouses on her farm.

Bret threw his designer bag inside before casting a glance at the crowded pavement behind them.

As he slipped into the passenger seat, he lifted his index finger to his lips to prevent any conversation.

He drew out his phone.

The screen was on maximum brightness.

A first page appeared.

"SAY NOTHING."

Next page.

"WE'RE BEING FOLLOWED."

Stone was about to register his shock when Bret gestured once again for him to be quiet.

Next page.

"AND BUGGED."

Stone wanted to laugh but his reaction was halted by the gravity of his friend's face.

Next page.

"ARE YOU WEARING ANYTHING THAT YOU BROUGHT FROM YOUR APARTMENT?"

Stone was now beginning to feel like Ikea Knightley's character at the end of *Love Actually*.

"Only my blazer," he said.

Bret shook his head, his eyes frantic. Once again, he thrust his finger to his lips.

Stone uttered a deep sigh. He took his phone out of his pocket. As he did, he noticed Maya's message. His heart sank. Shaking his head, he typed his reply to Bret.

JUST THIS JACKET.

Bret typed, REMOVE IT!

Stone muted a laugh.

Bret presented the screen again, a look of grim determination on his pale face as he made his boss read the message.

Stone shook his head. Leaning forward, he shifted his body like a clumsy escapologist, manoeuvring the jacket from his arms and shoulders until it was lying on his lap.

Without asking, Bret seized the garment and ran his fingers behind and within the collars, arms, and cuffs. He took his time, using slow, methodical movements, checking every inch of the material. Having satisfied himself there was nothing there, he proceeded to the side and inside pockets.

Once again, the search was fruitless. Only when he forced his long fingers into the outside breast pocket did his expression change. Little by little, his hand began to emerge. When they were withdrawn from the cavity, Stone saw a tiny black shape - broad, long, and flat - in the first two fingers of his student's hand. Its dark colour and rounded head reminded him of a black sexton beetle. It was about the same size too – 20mm, Stone estimated. And there seemed to be something resembling the beginnings of a beetle's antennae – two stumps either side of its curved temple.

Bret placed the object on the dashboard in front of him. He then threw the blazer on the back seat of the car before returning to his phone. He typed again.

"LISTENING AND TRACKING DEVICE."

Stone shook his head.

He mouthed one word.

"WHY?"

Bret shrugged his shoulders.

Stone sat staring at the tiny gadget lying on the dashboard. What could have caused him to become the object of someone's surveillance? Was it something to do with George Hailey? And if it was, what was so important about Hailey's story that it made such acts of stealth a necessity in the first place?

He was about to move out of his parking space when Bret nudged him. He showed another page.

"YOUR APARTMENT IS BUGGED."

Stone mouthed a shocked NO.

Bret nodded.

YES, he mouthed.

His face was adamant.

A new page.

"I ASKED A FRIEND AT UNI TO SCAN IT. TECH GEEK. USED A BUG FINDER. FOUND FOUR."

Stone fought back the tremors of shock.

Next page.

A list.

"LAPTOP IN YOUR OFFICE.

TV IN THE LIVING ROOM.

ALEXA IN THE KITCHEN

GRANDFATHER'S PORTRAIT IN YOUR BEDROOM.

ALL BUGGED."

Reeling from the shock, Stone could not be sure whether he was more enraged by the violation of his home or by the desecration of his beloved grandfather's picture.

He swore.

Out loud.

This time, Bret did not attempt to silence him.

Stone pulled out from the curb. He was almost in a daze as he paid the parking fee using his credit card, even more so as he headed out beneath the raised barrier towards the airport road. He stayed in this state as he drove towards the M1 and then on towards County Fermanagh. He broke out of this trance only when he became aware of his friend looking in the passenger-door mirror. When Bret swivelled round in his seat and stared through the rear window, it was obvious he was checking to see if they were being followed.

It was now past 10.30pm and they had been travelling along the carriageway for twenty miles. The night was pitch black and the motorway almost deserted in both directions. Except for one set of lights. In the rear-view mirror, Stone saw someone driving about a quarter of a mile behind them.

Even in the darkness, the vehicle in question looked larger than the one he was driving. Its chassis was raised higher above the tarmac, like a jeep or pickup truck. The lights on the front were also larger and brighter than on a regular car.

Stone decided to accelerate from 70mph to 90mph. After two minutes, he looked in the mirror. The vehicle should have been out of sight, but it was the same distance away.

Stone slowed to a leisurely 50mph. Once again, the vehicle behind them remained the same distance away. Whoever they were, they were in pursuit, and they were being careful.

Bret, who had already sensed what was going on, reached for the beetle-shaped device, lowered the passenger-side window, and made to throw it into the darkness.

"No!" Stone shouted.

Bret, confused, relented.

Stone pushed the accelerator to the floor.

80mph.

95mph.

Until the needle was creeping over 100mph.

Stone had never driven this fast before, not even in his wilder days. Now it was his turn to be anxious. What if this was all a baseless fantasy? What if they were risking arrest for nothing? What if they were endangering their lives on a whim?

One moment, Stone was oscillating and unsure. The next, he was in no doubt.

The vehicle was just ten metres behind them.

Accelerating.

Two extra lights, situated above the cabin of the car, were now turned on, full-beam, dazzling them through the reflections in every rear-facing mirror.

Stone held his hand up to his eyes, trying to shield them from the blinding light. But it was no use. His vision was impaired. He could only just make out the lanes in front of them.

As he tried to keep control, he was distracted again, this time not by the light but by a violent jolt. The vehicle chasing them had just rammed the rear of their car. Stone gripped the steering wheel and tried to recover control of the Firebird. But the pursuer came at them again, the black bull bar in front of its grill crashing into their rear bumper, smashing the backlights.

"It's a Raptor!" Bret shouted. "We don't have a chance!" There was panic in his shrill voice.

As Stone fought to keep from crashing, he saw the headlights of a car approaching them on the other side of the carriageway. As it passed, he noticed the green-and-yellow patterns of a rapid-response vehicle. The paramedic in the driving seat glanced at him with a look of consternation and concern. He glanced at her across the central reservation, his eyes helpless and scared. If only she had been on the same side of the motorway.

As the view before them returned to thick darkness, the beams from behind increased and intensified until the interior of their car was saturated with a wash of white light.

Stone passed an illuminated blue board signalling the road to Enniskillen. He wanted to slow down as he approached the slip road, but another jolt forced the car to accelerate.

As he tried to navigate towards the turnoff, Stone knew deep down there was no chance of them making it. Their car was already out of control. In his final moments of consciousness, everything started to decelerate until it seemed as if they were heading down towards the centre of the earth.

His last thought was of the Lady of the Night, in a steep, sudden, and unexpected fall from the night sky, plunging towards the surface of the water, breaking up on impact, the one long wing snapping like a twig, the fuselage shooting like a torpedo to the depths of the lough below.

And then the lights went out.

16

THE FUGITIVES

When he returned to consciousness, Stone was in a hospital bed, a nurse standing over him, shining what looked like a small torch into his eyes. He turned off the handheld light and took out a biro. After writing some notes, he turned towards the door.

"You can see him now," the nurse said.

He was talking to Bret who had just entered.

"Are you okay?" Stone asked.

"Just a few bruises. Nothing serious. More importantly, how about you, Prof?"

"Have I been out long?"

"Couple of hours."

"How did I get here?"

"A paramedic saw the vehicle ramming us. She's the one who found us. She rescued us, bless her."

"I saw her."

"Who?"

"The paramedic. I was hoping she'd see we were in trouble.

Did she tell the police?"

"Yes. They want to take a statement."

"What time is it?"

"Two o'clock."

"Morning?"

Bret nodded. "I've told Birgit. Apologised for the Firebird too. Says she's coming to pick us up."

"When will that be?"

"After you've spoken to the police. I've already given my statement. Yours is just a formality."

"Let's get that over with, then."

"What, now?"

"Yes, now."

"One thing, Prof. In my interview, I restricted myself to the facts of the incident, not to any kind of explanation. I thought I'd leave it to you whether you said anything about what we are researching. That's your call - and Maya's - not mine."

Stone thanked him.

Bret left the room and returned five minutes later with a uniformed constable. The officer asked a raft of questions about the crash, recording the professor's answers on his phone, as well as taking notes on a pad. After an hour, Stone had had enough. His head was pounding, his lower back aching.

"Will that do?" he asked the officer.

"It will. Your answers are the same as your colleague's." The constable put down his pen. "Do you know why someone would want to harm you both?"

Just then the nurse entered with some painkillers. "That's enough questions for now," he said, handing his patient four pills and a small disposable cup full of cold water.

The constable rose, put on his hat, and turned to leave. Before he reached the door, he spoke to Bret in a voice loud enough for the professor to hear.

"I'll need a contact number," he said. "And the owner of your car will need to get in touch with the insurers. Tell them you've given us a statement. I'll text you the case number."

Bret waited till the officer had left before sitting beside the bed, producing the small black bug, and whispering in Stone's ear. "I kept this. You didn't want me to throw it out of the car window, remember?" He started playing a song on his phone. "When you're ready to leave," he typed, "our ride is nearby."

Stone beckoned to Bret to give him the listening device. He sat up in bed, pausing while he waited for the walls to stop moving, then withdrew the top drawer from his bedside table. Finding a tiny crevice, he secreted the bug and then put things back as they were. Winking at Bret, he pulled off his hospital gown and dressed in the clothes he had been wearing in the car. There was a thin stain of blood in a white space on the checked shirt just below his left shoulder. He covered this with his scarf. He turned and looked in a mirror to see if there were any other scars left by the crash. His complexion was pale and his right eye bloodshot, but other than these temporary indications of shock Stone looked fine and had got away unscathed. He was more concerned about the first hints of stubble on his bruised chin.

The main injury was invisible - a dreadful pain in his lower back. As Stone put on his trousers, he groaned. Never had he felt backpain like it. Every wrong move brought a fresh agony, as if the meat of his muscles was being seared.

To make matters worse, with each brutal stab in his back a blot of nausea spread like poison in the pit of his stomach. Bret, seeing his boss's distress, helped him with his socks and shoes. Stone nodded his thanks, managing a smile.

Stone's phone buzzed. Bret picked it up, read a text message, then typed a reply. He beckoned to the professor to follow him out of the sideward, down the corridor outside, through a set of swinging double doors, and off to the entrance to a stairwell at the end of another hallway, its shiny floor gleaming under the soft lights.

Bret pushed a movable steel bar fixed to the stairwell door and they were outside, climbing down a short flight of grey metal stairs onto a small service road. As several vents gushed steam into the night air, Stone looked up and down the rain-washed street. Two lights warned of a vehicle approaching. Whoever was driving had chosen not to use their headlights but navigate instead with their dimmer and less dazzling sidelights. Bret, seeing his boss's concern, put his hand on his arm and mouthed, "It's okay. They're with us."

As the vehicle stopped, Stone saw Jack looking at him from the passenger seat at the front of a grey Mercedes van. The driver, Birgit, waved to him and Bret, gesturing them to get into the back. Seconds later, he was being helped by Rory through the sliding side door. Looking left, he saw that the back half was separated by a closed door. The front section was designed like a motor home, with a movable table and cushioned seats positioned behind the two captain's chairs in the cabin. As Stone nestled into a seat opposite the habitation door, he winced again as he tried to get comfortable.

The van, which looked new, pulled away from the curb

and headed in the direction of the exit signs. Birgit kept looking out of the front and side windows, checking to see if there were any parked vehicles with shadowy observers sitting in them. But the roads were empty. Any cars in the vicinity were stationary.

As they drove away from motorways and out into the smaller roads in the countryside, Stone leaned forward, bowed his head, and reached round to the small of his back, pressing his fingers and palm into the throbbing, aching epicentre of pain.

Birgit noticed his discomfort in the rear-view mirror. "Are you in any discomfort?" she asked.

"It's my back. Whiplash, I think. The painkillers the nurse gave me aren't touching it."

Stone stared out of the side window next to him, watching as the dawn broke and a golden light appeared on the horizon. They were driving alongside the Erne which had reduced itself from a vast lough into a fast-flowing river.

Birgit turned to Jack. "Are you thinking what I'm thinking?"

Jack nodded.

They left the A46, crossed the border into Donegal, and headed along the N3 and then the N15 towards the coast. When they were within sight of the Atlantic, the sun began to rise. Stone could see the white main of the waves disappearing into the surf and sand. As he stared at the horizon, he thought again of the Lady of the Night, making its way back from a sortie in the Atlantic, heading towards the invisible corridor of Donegal, back to the cooked breakfast waiting for the crew in the mess at Castle Archdale. He thought of the long hours within the cramped bulkheads of the seaplane and, for a fleeting moment, felt guilty for grumbling about his back.

"Mullaghmore," Jack said as they made their way towards Sligo. "The Erne flows into the Atlantic just over there." Jack pointed towards the southern borders.

Minutes later, they were on a small peninsula, driving near a castle that stood tall in evergreen fields. A long and flat-topped mountain rose behind it in the distance.

"Ben Bulben," Jack said, nodding towards the rock formation, its ridge marked by what looked like the many vertical slashes of a giant's blade. "Yeats wrote a poem about the mountain," he said. "He's buried in Drumcliffe churchyard."

"Horseman pass by," Rory muttered.

"Aye, pass by," Jack said.

"Why are we here?" Stone asked.

"We're going to get your back fixed."

"How?"

"Have you heard of the cure?" Jack asked.

"Do you mean the rock band?"

Rory laughed.

"No," he said. "He means the charm."

"No, I haven't."

"There's an old man who lives near the white sands of Bunduff Strand. He has the cure for people with back pain. It's something he inherited. Many people have benefited from it. He used to be a monk. Left his order when he fell in love."

"Is this a natural remedy?"

"Not really," Jack answered.

Stone shook his head.

"Is this something to do with alternative medicine then – herbs, ointments, and the like?"

"People like the monk may sometimes use those things," Jack said, "but that's not all there is to it. This is something carried by their words and hands. Something more than what's normal or natural. The ability to heal specific pain and sickness."

"You mean it's supernatural."

"Ach, you sound sceptical, Professor."

"If I'm honest, I am known for being somewhat dismissive. But recently, I've had to have a bit of a rethink."

"What's done that?"

"A photograph."

Jack indicated to Birgit to stop the van.

"I had an experience I can't explain."

"Tell them..." Bret said.

Stone related the story of the old photo of George Hailey and his little white dog.

"Don't forget what happened at the awards," Bret said, even before his boss had finished.

"It happened again," Stone said. "While I was speaking..."

Bret did not interject this time.

"So, you're a believer," Jack said.

"No. I wouldn't say that. I lost my faith when my grandfather got cancer. He meant everything to me. I prayed, but nothing changed."

"So, how do you explain the photographs?"

"I can't."

"Doesn't that bother you?"

"Not really, I'm happy to live with ambiguity and uncertainty. Also, I think that what today we think of as paranormal we may one day regard as normal."

Bret interjected. "He's always banging on about science fiction writer Arthur C Clarke's third law."

"What's that?" Jack asked.

"Any sufficiently advanced technology is indistinguishable from magic," Bret answered.

"I don't know," Jack muttered. "I've seen some things..."

He paused, waiting for one of the two Englishmen to show some interest. Bret obliged.

"A lady called Dyan Tucker contacted Joe, an old friend of mine. She was keen for him to help her find out more details about her godfather, Maurice Vince Wareing. He was part of a twelve-man crew on board a Sunderland Short..."

"A what now?" Bret asked.

"There were two kinds of seaplane that took off from Lough Erne," Jack said. "One was the Catalina. The other the Sunderland Short. At the end of a long patrol, one of these was ordered to divert to Lough Erne. The weather had become too dangerous at Pembroke Dock where they normally landed. That was the first problem. The pilot was unfamiliar with the route to Lough Erne."

Jack paused to take a sip of coffee from a thermos flask. He offered some to his guests, but both declined.

"The second was that he had an unfamiliar aircraft. Unsure of his approach, he flew into the Donegal Corridor, continuing north, before turning east to Lough Erne. This took them over the mountains, and they crashed in the Blue Stack Range. Seven of the crew died, including Maurice Vince Wareing. Dyan Tucker was four years old at the time. She took the loss of her godfather very badly."

Rory and Jack, who were both wearing caps, removed

them and lowered their heads.

"Dyan Tucker decided to do some research into her godfather. She was living in New Zealand at the time and had just put her house on the market. A woman came round for a viewing. She and Dyan had never met. Here's where another photograph proved vital. When the viewer saw a photo of the flying officer, she mentioned 'the crew', as she called it. This total stranger gave details about the crash. She said they were near a lake, there was snow on the ground, and they were off course. She said that some had lived, adding, 'one survived the crash but died in the aircraft'. That was all true. The last thing she said was that the crew were pleased Dyan had found them all."

Rory crossed himself.

"Dyan shared all this with my friend Joe. He was most impressed with the report. He sensed that all the boys were happy in the hereafter. And he became convinced that some kind of spiritual influence was using people like him, Dyan, and her visitor as instruments of comfort to families who lost loved ones."

Jack turned and looked at Stone.

"What do you think, Professor?"

"I don't know what to make of it."

"Would you be curious enough to try the cure?" Jack asked.

"I think I would, yes."

"You may need to be more than that," Rory said.

"What do you mean?" Stone asked.

"If you're to benefit from the cure, you'll need to have more than a little curiosity. You'll need to believe."

"Will suspending my disbelief do?"

"Ach, I'm sure it will be better than nothing."

"The monk may prove helpful in other ways too," Jack said. "His sister married a Yank during the war."

The van pulled off the road onto a farmer's track. Every pothole brought Stone more pain until the vehicle stopped in front of a simple single-storeyed house at the top of a cliff.

Stone glanced in the rear-view mirror to make sure no one had followed them. He breathed a sigh of relief. The lane behind was deserted as far as the eye could see.

"I'm sorry about your Firebird," Stone said to Birgit.

"No worries, Professor. I'll have another in no time. And the most important thing is you're okay."

Stone thanked her and then pulled out his phone.

"Don't come over, Maya," he typed. "Someone's found out about our mission. It's dangerous. We're being followed and bugged. Even this message may be compromised. I'll be in touch when I can. Just stay put. I repeat, stay put."

As he made a slow and careful exit from the van, Stone heard the buzz of his phone.

It was a reply from Maya.

Just one word.

"No."

LETTER 10

February 2nd, 1944

Well, Dad, that was some day! It felt like two days and probably was. I'm talking about our latest mission. It was eventful right from the start. As we started the short boat ride to the Catalina, our Skipper began to vomit over the gunwales. I've never seen a man so sick. He would finish, sit back in the fishing boat, turn as white as a snow goose, then rush back to the side and start the entire cycle again. By the time we reached the Cat, he had made up his mind. "I'm sorry, boys. I'm just too rough. Second Lieutenant Hailey will be in charge. You can have every confidence in him." He promptly threw up again.

We wished him good luck and he, through a saliva-soaked handkerchief, muffled "Godspeed." After that, we took to our tasks with extra vigor, wanting the Skipper to be proud of us, even though he was absent. All the checks came up trumps, so we were able to stick with Lady rather than row to another Cat.

Take off was a breeze as was the flight down the Donegal

Corridor and out into the Atlantic. But then our sense of calm was ended by the bombardier in the nose.

"Enemy aircraft. Dead ahead."

Everyone assumed battle stations.

"Have they spotted us?"

"No, Skipper."

I relished the temporary promotion.

"I think it's a German reconnaissance aircraft. A Blohm and Voss. It's an ugly great beast!"

"Where's that come from?" The navigator shouted.

"All right. That's enough chat!" I barked.

I could not deny that the bombardier was right. The plane in front of us was indeed ugly. It had an asymmetrical gondola and the oddest tail you've ever seen.

I increased the speed and told the gunners to get ready. As I steered the Cat closer, I ordered the bow gunner to hold fire. I also instructed the gunners in the rear of the plane to wait until I was alongside the strange aircraft.

Ten seconds later, I ordered the bow gunner to open fire. As he pressed the trigger, I saw the three-man crew in the coffin-like gondola begin to panic. The rear gunner, who was in a prone position, didn't have time to respond before he was hit. The mid-turret gunner succeeded in letting off a few rounds, one of which hit our starboard wing, before he too was disabled by a mixture of bullets from our guns and the shards from the glass windows around him. Now it was just a case of strafing the single engine, so I steered the Lady until we were alongside the enemy. One of our rear gunners provided the coup de grace and the strange plane plummeted into the ocean.

After handshakes, there followed a discussion in the

cockpit between the bombardier and me.

"That was a Blohm Voss 141," he said. "They're using any old aircraft they can find now."

"Have you seen one before out here?"

"Never, Skipper. The only planes I've seen have been Condors. There have been no reports of the 141. I guess desperate times call for desperate measures."

"I heard their bases on the French coast were bombed recently," I said. "I think it's only a matter of days before the Nazis cease airborne operations in the Atlantic."

The bombardier nodded before grabbing a mug of tea from the wireless operator and heading into the nose. Once he was back at his post, I addressed the rest of the crew.

"Congratulations, boys. We are the first Cat to shoot down an enemy aircraft in the Atlantic." There were cheers. I added, "Don't get big-headed. We are not alone in this success. The first Japanese aircraft downed in the war was a Zero destroyed by a Cat in the Philippines. Our victim was no fighter, like theirs was. It was just a reconnaissance plane. Still, you did a good job."

More cheers.

Three hours later, we were cruising at an altitude of four hundred feet when we saw two U-Boats. The larger vessel was refueling the other. You may remember, Dad, we thought we'd seen two U-Boats before, but they turned out to be Blue Whales - a mother and baby. I was a bit doubtful at first. I thought we might be seeing the same thing, but Blue Whales don't have gunners on their backs. These did! So, when they opened fire, we dropped our depth charges on the subs. Both were destroyed. We saw no survivors.

It's hard to imagine how we felt as we travelled back to

the west coast of Ireland and then on to Lough Erne. After we had landed, there was a lot of excitement both about the aircraft we had shot down and the two U-Boats we'd sunk. The Skipper, who had recovered, joined in the fun. There were photographs in front of the castle, and the Group Captain bought us all a round of beer.

And here's the best news of all, Dad.

While he was talking to me in private, he indicated that he'd received a message from an American officer, a Tuskegee airman, high up in the chain of command. He'd heard about my exploits in the Cat and had asked my CO if he would be prepared to release me to fly in his squadron in Italy. I found it hard to contain myself, but I kept a lid on my feelings and asked him what he'd said. The CO told me that he'd replied that I was a fine airman and that he would miss me - that my crew would miss me even more - but he recognized that this had been my dream all along and so he said yes.

How about that, Dad!

I'm heading to Italy.

I'm not getting ahead of myself, though. The CO said it would be at least a month before all the paperwork could be completed and the transfer happen. Until then, I was to keep focused on the job and do my duty here at Lough Erne.

I was elated when I rejoined the boys and bought another round of beer for them all. One of them, our navigator, said that we'd enjoyed the kind of good fortune in one mission that most crews don't see in thirty. I agreed. He then asked why he thought we'd been blessed with such success. I said I didn't know.

"What about the cross you put in the cockpit?" he asked.

Then I remembered.

February 1st is Saint Bridget's feast day in Ireland. It's a very important day when people make crosses out of rushes and put them in the rafters of their cottages. Myra's mother made one for the crew of the Lady. She had given it to me the night before, on January 31st, and I'd thanked her by saying, "There's no rafters as high as the high un-trespassed sanctity of space." I was quoting the poem, 'High Flight.' She loved that and gave me a hug, telling me to be careful.

I said to the crew, "Our good fortune is the result of our Saint Bridget Cross. We should keep it with us."

I can't tell you how happy I am to have found Myra. It's an honor helping her mother too. I thought about them both on the long way home, and you too, Dad, and I gave thanks for my family as I stared out at the "footless halls of space."

I love you, Dad.

Write to me soon.

Your son,
George.
VV

17

THE CURE

The professor hobbled out of the van with the help of Bret's steadying hand. It took several metres before he was able to straighten his back. When he did, he saw the front door of a single-storeyed cottage. The name of the house, 'Saint Brigid's Well,' was painted in white letters on a piece of charcoal-coloured driftwood.

The door opened and a tall man with long silvery hair emerged. He looked at Jack and nodded, a smile breaking out on his grey face. His eyes then moved to the other three men, viewing each one in turn as if he was scanning them.

"You," he said, pointing to Stone. "What is your name?"

"Cameron Stone."

The old man tilted his head and said, "You have had a great shock. Your body is vibrating with it."

Stone was in too much pain to respond.

"Do you believe in the cure?"

Stone summoned the faintest nod.

"Come inside."

When the four men entered, their lean host walked into the main living room. It was only then Stone noticed that the man's enormous feet were bare. The host seemed to sense his curiosity and pointed to a picture on the wall. It contained a tapestry of a Bible verse, encompassed by a black frame. "Take off your shoes, for the ground on which you are standing is holy." Exodus 3:5.

Stone managed to sit on a wooden stool nearby. He beckoned to Bret to help him take off the trainers now scuffed with mud from the wet path outside.

As his apprentice inched the wet shoes and socks from his feet, Stone looked at his surroundings. They were in a spacious living room that led without wall or partition into a small kitchen area. Beyond that stood a closed door which Stone guessed led to the man's bathroom and sleeping quarters. There was a pleasant odour from the cabbage, potatoes, and bacon cooking in an iron skillet resting on a gas stove in the kitchen area. He could just make out the warm light beneath, offering a low heat for the Colcannon. If he had not been distracted by the pain, it would have tantalised his taste buds, but all he sensed was his growing nausea and his greening gills.

The man gestured to Stone. Bret helped him to his feet and took him by the arm. They headed past an unlit fireplace with yesterday's ash still in it and into the kitchen. They passed a basket of freshly picked leeks on the table.

"Just him," the old man said.

Bret turned back to the living room.

As soon as they were through the door, Stone saw that it led into another smaller room, this time carpeted, with another door at the end of it. This confined space had two armchairs in front of a fire whose burning coals brought an enveloping warmth to his entire body, from his hatless head to his shoeless feet.

The old monk beckoned to him to sit in the lefthand armchair. Stone eased himself into its cushioned seat while his host lifted his guest's feet onto what looked like an embroidered hassock from the pews of an ancient church.

The monk leant forward and poured something resembling tea from a China teapot covered in a hand-knitted, woollen cosy. There were two cups and saucers on a small table. The host filled both. There was no milk in either cup.

Stone frowned. "Were you expecting me?"

"Yes."

"How? We gave no word of our visit."

"I dreamed of it."

"I don't know," Stone said with a sigh.

"What don't you know?"

"A lot of things."

"That's good," the monk said.

"Why?"

"Because, my friend, it wouldn't do to lean too much on your own understanding right now."

"What do you mean?"

"I mean that you're used to relying on your analytical faculties for deciphering the mysteries of life. But in your own case, you may have to activate a different part of your brain."

"I'll try."

The monk passed him the cup and saucer and Stone lifted the lip of the cup to his nostrils. The hot concoction smelt like tea, but not any kind he could ever remember tasting. The liquid tasted as if it was composed of the purest, cleanest, natural water. As soon as he took a sip, Stone began to experience an overwhelming tranquillity. The liquid seemed to penetrate to the depths of his soul as well as his stomach, bringing warmth to both. Even the pain in his injured back was dulled by its permeating influence, causing him to sigh again, though this time with contentment, not confusion.

"Are you ready?" the old monk asked, taking the empty cup from Stone's hand.

"I'm ready."

The monk took a cross made of hand-pulled rushes from the rafters above.

"Hold this."

"What is it?"

"A cross from St Brigid's day two months ago. The healing that I am praying for comes from the holy cross of the Saviour. His wounds heal our wounds. I want you to remember that as I pray for the pain in your back to go."

Stone nodded. He was so desperate that he would have agreed to almost anything.

The monk stood in front of him and stretched out his hands. Laying them on Stone's head, he paused. As Stone waited, he became aware of a heat emanating from the monk's hands. It came in surges, like small and gentle waves of fire. With the breaking of each one, every neural pathway in his brain seemed to be ignited, every nerve in his spine aroused by a holy trembling, connecting his epicentre of pain to an energy he never knew existed.

Stone's breathing began to slow.

His eyes became heavy.

His questions ceased.

As the monk prayed, his voice seemed like a faraway ripple of thunder on the very edge of Stone's consciousness. The only thing remaining in the chamber of his mind was a picture from his childhood - his beloved grandfather reading to him from *The Lion, the Witch, and the Wardrobe*, as he perched on the old man's bony knee. Stone had been enchanted by one of the illustrations he was studying as he listened. It showed the children having tea and cake inside Mr and Mrs Beaver's house, and Mr Beaver announcing to all of them that Aslan was on the move.

Then, in the twinkling of an eye, Stone awakened from whatever altered state he had entered. The fire was out and the tea in the pot next to him was cold. Most unsettling of all, the lights in the room were out. As he tried to get his bearings, another picture from his childhood surfaced - Mister Tumnus sitting in an armchair beside a fire, offering tea and cakes to Lucy Pevensie. For a moment, his heart was troubled. Was this strange old monk a treacherous faun, seducing him into a comatose state to hand him over to some witch?

He stood.

And as he did, he became aware of two sensations. The first was the sound of laughter from the next-door room. The second was the complete absence of pain in his back.

As his vision returned, he headed towards the door and opened it. Moving past the kitchen table, he walked into the living room. The grate on his right was now filled with burning coals.

"Ah, there you are!" Jack cried, looking up from a white enamel bowl of hot Colcannon. "How are you feeling?"

"Remarkably, I'm pain free."

"Are you hungry?" the monk asked, without a hint of surprise in his deep voice.

Stone nodded.

The monk passed him a bowl.

"Help yourself," he said, pointing to the skillet.

"How long have I been asleep?"

"Six hours," the monk replied.

"What?"

"That's not long," the monk said. "Some have slept here for days when they've received the cure. The healing comes more quickly when a person abandons themselves to the process."

"Speaking of which, what did you do to me?"

"I prayed."

"There must be more to it than that? What about the tea? What was in that?"

"Ach, you can't ask that," Jack cried.

"It's all right, Jack," the monk said. "It was water from the well out the back of my house."

"What well?"

"We have many wells in our country blessed by Saint Brigid. The water in these is said to have healing properties. When my father administered the cure, he would dip a cloth in the water. The cloth was called a 'clootie.' I decided early on that it was better to drink it than have it wiped on the affected area."

"I also sensed something coming through your hands. A heat. What was that?"

"That was the gift," Jack said.

Stone nodded.

Feeling hungry, he now began to dig into the Colcannon. After four mouthfuls, he realised something strange was happening. Every muscle seemed to be relaxing into a state of unprecedented serenity. The shockwaves of his traumatic accident seemed to leave his body. The worry of being bugged and stalked disappeared. Whatever herbs the monk had added to this savoury dish had done their job. He had entered a state the Stoics talked about and longed for – *ataraxia*, freedom from care. It was a state he had championed in his lectures back home but which, until now, he had never experienced.

"I'm very grateful to you for your help," Stone said, his voice low, soft, and barely audible.

"He's not done helping you yet," Jack said.

Stone looked confused.

"While you were out of it, I took the liberty of sharing about you and Maya, your search for the black airman, the empty seat in the cockpit of the Lady, and the person or people intent on making sure you don't get any answers."

"And?"

"And our host has information."

Stone dragged himself back from the edge of another sleep and asked, "What do you know?"

The monk pulled a chair from the kitchen table and sat at the edge of the living room. As the fire continued to burn in the grate, he stared into the middle of the room, as if he was seeing events playing out in a different timeframe.

"During the war, my only sibling, my sister Clare, married an American stationed in Belfast barracks – a military policeman called Franky. His duties consisted of watching over prisoners in the cells. American prisoners."

The professor asked, "Do you remember what part of America Franky came from?"

"Alabama, near Tuskegee."

Stone could feel the bristling of a thousand tiny hairs on his arms. "You're sure of that?"

The monk nodded. "Franky passed away last year, but before he did, he told Clare about a black airman, one of his prisoners, who had trained at Tuskegee."

"Where does your sister live?"

"Near Trory Point, just outside Enniskillen, but you'll need the airman's granddaughter to be there. Clare won't share what she knows with anyone else but her."

Stone took out his phone and accessed his text messages. Maya had sent him a flight number and arrival time.

"She's on her way," he said.

LETTER 11

February 20th, 1944

Dear Dad,

I had my last day of leave for a while today. I thought I'd tell you about it before I go to sleep, while the memories are fresh and clear. Of course, I spent it with Myra. I had some petrol coupons which I took around to Myra's house, along with some sugar, meat, and butter. Butter is especially scarce, so Ruth was very grateful. While I waited in the kitchen for Myra to get ready upstairs, Ruth told me that before I arrived on the scene, she used to take the train down to Bundoran in the south. An elderly great aunt lives there, and she used to scrape together some supplies for Ruth to bring back home.

"It's called 'the Sugar Train'," Ruth explained. "When I left for Bundoran I was always skinny, like I am now. But when I returned, like many other girls, I had somehow become heavily pregnant. The bump, of course, was the sugar!"

She shared this after I handed over the rations that I found for her. She went on to say, "One time, I had too much to carry on the return journey. I spotted two priests sitting in one of the carriages on their own. I went to them, explained that I was a good Catholic girl, and asked them if they wouldn't mind carrying a large parcel for me. They thought I was close to giving birth, so they readily agreed."

"That was clever," I said.

"Ach, I never told them any word of a lie, Georgie." That's what she calls me, Dad. Georgie! "When the inspector came, he knew the two priests would never carry contraband, so he bid them good day and received a blessing for his good manners."

You'd like Ruth, Dad.

Her resilience reminds me of Mom.

And her ingenuity.

Myra eventually came downstairs, looking like a million dollars, and we headed off for a drive. On our way out of town, we were stopped at a checkpoint manned by some men of the Home Guard. There's khaki everywhere, but these guys seem to take a greater pride in what they wear than the rest of us put together.

Seeing that I was wearing RCAF uniform, the guardsman avoided me and walked around the back of the car, all the while peering through the windows. He arrived, after what seemed an unnecessarily long inspection, at Myra's window. He gestured to her to wind it down which she only did after sighing and then maneuvering the handle with slow motions, all the while staring out of the front window, never once making eye contact with the fellow.

"Name?" he barked.

Myra shook her head in disbelief.

I said, "Name!"

"Myra Coughlan," she said, enunciating each word as if the man was hard of hearing and soft in the head.

"Papers!"

Myra showed them her identification card.

"Proceed!" the man said with an extravagant and patronizing wave of his right arm.

One hundred yards down the road, Myra started venting her feelings, beginning with the word "eejit!" I think you can guess what that means. After she cooled off a bit, I asked her why she was so angry. "Because he knows exactly who I am and what my address is. He lives right across the street from me."

"Why's he so officious?"

"Because I'm Catholic and he's Protestant."

We approached a field bursting with snowdrops and the first snatch of primroses. The sun was out and the temperature warm, so we got out of the car, sat on an oblong rock, and drank some of the lemonade I had made. Mom's old recipe. We sipped out of two tin mugs I'd brought from the base and stared at the hills surrounding Lough Erne. To me they looked like the great waves of the Atlantic, frozen in time in the act of rising and falling.

"What's it like being a Catholic in the north?"

"Horrible," she said. After a long sigh, she reminded me yet again that the British government had promised before the beginning of the last war to let the whole of Ireland be united, but that they had not kept their word. They had divided the country into north and south. Most Catholics live in the south, and the few who don't – like her family –

must endure being talked to and treated like she was by the over-zealous guardsman at the checkpoint.

"It's enough to put your head away," she concluded.

I squeezed her hand. I couldn't say I understood. Our situations are similar, but they are not identical. I am no more a Catholic man in the north of Ireland than she is a black girl in the southern states of America. We are bound together by the fact that we have been, and continue to be, victims of historic prejudice, but our songs, while they share the same notes, have different tunes. We respect these things about each other. We therefore sympathize, but we never patronize – one of the many reasons I love her.

We left the snow-white field and drove back to town to Ma Bothwell's where we tucked into a meal of steak, onions, and fried potatoes. Before going to the cinema, we headed to the pub for a glass of cider. There Myra saw a woman being treated in an unwelcome manner. She was not accompanied by a man, and the publican, Mister Thompson, had taken exception to it. She explained to Myra that she was in the WAAF – the Women's Auxiliary Air Force. It was her day off and she wanted to go where she used to meet with her fiancé.

"What happened to him?" Myra asked.

We both feared the worst.

"Peter was killed three months ago." The woman, called Jane, spoke with an English accent.

Jane explained that she worked in signals in the operations room at RAF Castle Archdale. Like the other girls, she knew the boys who flew out into the Atlantic. She was on duty when Peter's plane was overdue. The base kept sending radio messages, but there was no answer. Jane waited long after her shift was over to see if the aircraft returned to base but it did not. Her heart sank with it, she said.

I remember the incident, Dad. It was a Sunderland Short seaplane. DD863. Lost off the coast of Donegal, not long after I arrived in Northern Ireland. It shook everybody.

"You sit with us," Myra said, pulling up a chair and giving the publican a rude stare. Jane wiped her tears and said that she was sorry. Myra put her hand on hers and told her not to be silly, and that it was only right to mourn the man she loved.

We invited Jane to come with us to Stuart's cinema to see *The Song of Bernadette* (we were watching it for the second time), but she said that she'd already been to see it. We guessed it had been with Peter, her love, so we did not press the matter. We said goodbye and walked through streets that were as crowded as they had been in the afternoon. It was Saturday, and we left the pub around 8.15pm. The shops were still open (they stay open until 9pm on Saturdays). There was also a line of people waiting to say confession prior to Mass on Sunday morning. Their bikes rested against the chapel wall.

We paid three shillings each (about $12) for the tickets and sat together arm in arm. *The Song of Bernadette* was every bit as powerful as it was the first time I saw it with Myra in December. Maybe more so. When the lady in white first appeared to Bernadette at the grotto in Lourdes, this time I found myself moved to tears. As a gust of wind caught Bernadette's hair in the cave, I felt a strange breeze. It made the hair on my neck stand up tall.

I don't know, Dad, maybe I just miss Mom and I'm comforted by the thought that this radiant mother is watching over me as I fly out on dark and dangerous missions over the Atlantic.

Maybe I was more spooked than I realized by the Lady of the Lake when I was on my own in the Cat that first night on guard duty, and I prefer the purity and safety of this holy woman.

Maybe I am turning towards the same light that burns in Myra's eyes and I want her flame and mine to join so that we are one in spirit, not just in mind and body.

We drove back to Myra's house afterwards where Ruth took some shirts of mine that she'd washed, then dried on a washing line outside. She ironed them while I went and sat in the sitting room and shared with Myra something I had wanted to say all day, but for which I had not found the moment. I told her what my CO had said, that my exploits flying over the Atlantic had brought me to the attention of the CO of the Tuskegee squadron. I shared that this CO wanted to see me, and that it would mean being enrolled in the United States Army Airforce.

"That's always been your dream," she cried, hugging me. Then she pulled away, a frown on her face. "But won't that mean you'll be transferred abroad?

"Italy, most likely," I said.

At first, she thumped my chest with her fists, devastated by the thought of me leaving the country, but then she just went quiet as I held her close, her arms by her side, her hands retaining the shape of the fists that had beaten my heart.

She was still like this when I took my shirts and left the house. I was already late getting away, and I couldn't stay any longer to see if Myra was okay. She didn't say a word. When I pressed my lips against hers, she did not respond.

It's as if she was in shock, staring out across the street, at the house of the man who had been so rude to her at the checkpoint earlier the same day.

Dad, I don't know what to do.

Please give me your advice.

Should I follow my dream and enroll?

Or should I stay here and marry Myra?

Maybe there's a way I can have both.

I'm mighty confused.

I really need to see Myra again, but my next leave isn't for at least a month. We are busy with night flight training, bombing practice at Gull Rock, and tactical operations in the Atlantic. For the first time since I met her, I'm terrified of losing her, and I'm tormented by the knowledge that I have made her so upset. It's now the early hours of Sunday morning and I can't sleep. That's why I thought I'd scribble a few thoughts to you and post them home.

Dad, please tell me what you think I should do.

I need your advice more than ever.

Write soon.

I love you.

Your son,

George.

VV.

18

THE DRAGONFLY

Cameron Stone was not the only one watching out for Maya Hailey at Belfast International Airport. At 1pm, Agent Miller had eyes on two positions at the same time. The first was a blue-grey Mercedes sprinter with blacked-out side windows - a 4x4 van conversion idling in a short-stay parking bay. The second was the entrance of the terminal. He was waiting for the emergence of one of his two targets, the woman who had travelled on the red eye from Logan.

Miller dialled his boss in the Pentagon.

"Update, Ma'am."

"Go."

"Maya Hailey booked a flight to the UK. I'm watching out for her outside Belfast International."

"What about Stone?"

"He survived the accident. He's also waiting for Miss Hailey. And he's not alone."

"Who's with him?"

"He's now working with two Irish men and a Norwegian

woman - the people responsible for locating and identifying the Catalina."

"How are they helping him?"

"I don't know."

"You don't know?"

"No, Ma'am." Miller cleared his throat as he kept watching the van and the entrance. "And worse still, I'm pretty sure the professor and Miss Hailey are on to us."

"Onto *you*, you mean."

"Onto me."

"How do you know?"

"The professor found one of my listening devices. Hid it in the bedside table at the hospital when he left in the middle of the night. He wanted to throw us... throw *me* off the scent."

"So, your cover is blown."

"Not exactly. They haven't seen me. They don't know what I look like. And that's the way I want to keep it."

"Even so," she said, "you're compromised."

"Not yet," Miller objected.

"You sure?"

Miller was about to insist that he was on course to complete his mission when he saw Maya Hailey walking out of the terminal pushing a trolley laden with three large suitcases.

"Target has arrived," he said.

"No more mistakes, Miller."

The line went dead.

Miller observed the professor as he jumped out of the side of the van and loaded Maya's baggage. Seconds later, the cargo was loaded, and the vehicle was heading out of the airport grounds back towards the A57 and thereafter to the motorway. Miller followed at a distance in his new replacement vehicle. When the van entered County Fermanagh, he had to be careful not to overtake on the country roads. With the skills he had learned from many years in the service, he managed to drive without drawing attention to himself until the van reached a track that led off the main road. Miller drove past his prey after it turned down the pot-holed lane. Looking out of his window, he noted his position near the banks of Lough Erne.

Parking in a layby, Miller opened his laptop and accessed satellite images of the area. He zoomed in on the van driving out of an avenue of trees and hedges before it passed through some sturdy electronic gates which closed behind the vehicle. Miller estimated that the farm was about half a mile from his position. Studying the grounds, he observed that this gate was the only entrance and exit point for cars. As for other points of ingress, the surrounding hedges looked too tall and thick to penetrate. Whoever this place belonged to, it appeared to Miller's trained eyes to be the perfect location and design for someone seeking a safe and secluded space – someone like the professor and his female colleague from the East Coast.

Miller exited his vehicle and walked to the rear. Opening the trunk, he drew up a black mat and pulled on a lever. Instead of a spare wheel, the space was occupied by a silver-grooved pilot case. He unlocked its aluminium top and accessed a vertical pouch. Closing the case, he walked to the front of the car, returned to the driver's seat, and opened a metallic-grey box.

Taking great care, he removed what looked like a large

insect from its container, followed by a controller. The black nano dragonfly now resting on his lap was a state-of-the-art drone designed in Scandinavia and purchased by the US for military and espionage purposes. It was called the Dragonfly Recon System - DRS for short. This drone, four inches long and less than one inch wide, weighed under half a pound. It possessed two cameras which transmitted HD pictures to his handheld terminal. This lightweight helicopter, already charged from a battery in the pilot case, was good to go. It had a 25-minute hovering time and its digital camera, with night-vision capability, had a transmission range of over a mile. This all meant that Miller was not going to have to drive or walk closer to the farm. As the rain began to pummel his hired car, he decided he was happy about that.

Miller now decided that he would launch the drone when what little sunlight he had seen that day disappeared altogether. Until then, he would use the time to charge the DRS's backup battery. Miller knew he needed the cover of darkness to get the drone within listening distance of his targets. The DRS was not just equipped with cameras designed to increase the user's situational awareness; it was also fitted with the latest audio technology programmed to listen in on a target's conversations. An earlier version had been used with great effect in Afghanistan. Soldiers had loved it for its almost silent electric motor and its ability to fly undetected around walls, providing a clear picture of enemy hideouts. The latest spec had the additional advantages of wind resistance and a collision-avoidance system.

For all these reasons, Miller loved it too; in fact, out of all the gadgets given by the quartermaster at Menwith Hill, the DRS was by far and away his favourite. To him, it was worth every cent of the $200,000 he now held in the palm of his hand.

An hour later, he set the giros in motion and opened the driver's window. Releasing the DRS, it ascended like a liberated bird with an almost inaudible whirring into the sky. Switching to his handheld terminal, Miller looked at the screen, guiding the tiny chopper back the way he had come and along the track traversed by the van. At a speed of just under 15mph, the dragonfly made its way about twenty feet above the track, avoiding the beach trees leaning in from each side of the road. At the end of this natural tunnel, Miller slowed the drone down and adjusted it to hover mode, guiding it a few feet above the ground towards the thick hedge that, like one of Wellington's squares, protected those huddled behind its bristling perimeters.

Miller put the drone into a measured vertical climb. At the top of the manicured hedge, he kept it airborne but stationary. In infrared mode, the camera at the nose of the DRS conducted a thorough scan of the grounds. It showed the disused Firebirds and harvesting relics. It scanned for signs of life, but the area was as quiet as an elephant's graveyard. Then it scoured the garage, offices, and storerooms. Plunged in a thick darkness, they were unoccupied. Next, it was the turn of the open-sided barn. Here there was stillness - except for a panicked rat in one corner scurrying away from the humming. Beyond that, the drone's examination of the allotments at the rear of the house revealed some twitches in the netting, but nothing more.

Before turning back to the farmhouse, the DRS found a cracked pane of glass and entered the octagonal greenhouse along the back wall. Once inside, it filmed plants and creepers climbing towards a glass ceiling that shimmered in the pale light of the moon. Wrapped around bamboo sticks, they seemed almost suspended in an invisible current. To Miller, it felt as if the drone was underwater, moving through rooted shallow-water plants that sought the light above.

The agent turned the DRS back to the broken window and sped through the night sky towards the farmhouse. The drone ascended the white wall at the rear, pausing at each window. There were lights on in the ground-floor rooms, but these were on the other side of the house. On the next floor, one bedroom had a tiny flicker of light which turned out to be Maya's phone. Someone was trying to ring her, but the phone was in silent running and its owner was in a deep sleep underneath an eiderdown in an old double bed. At the top of the house, the professor was sitting at a table next to the far wall. Even through the lens of the tiny camera, Miller could tell his target was googling something, although he could not make out what it was.

Miller activated climb mode and brought the drone over the roof. Hovering equidistant between the two working chimneys, one at each end, he looked down the slope of black tiles towards the muddy ground. Someone had just left the front door of the farmhouse and activated the motion-sensitive lights concealed beneath the black gutters running along the outside of the house. They were walking from the house to the open-sided barn. From the Nordic hand-knitted jumper, Miller guessed – rightly as it turned out – that this was Birgit, the owner of the house. He watched as she entered, training the camera on her movements. Just as he was about to manoeuvre the DRS to follow, the lights from the gutters cut out, leaving the screen dark and indefinable for several seconds. When the images became clear again, Birgit was not in the barn anymore, nor was she walking back to the house, or towards the greenhouse at the rear. She had disappeared.

Miller shook his head.

What was going on?

But he had no time to investigate.

His drone was not the only thing in the air.

Two large bats, perhaps sensing the vibrations from the drone's motors, were darting around the DRS. Miller pushed the lever on his handheld device and tried to lift the dragonfly above the creatures. He then steered the drone away from the house towards the gates, conducting evasive movements and accelerating to full speed. The DRS hurried away from the farm towards the avenue of trees. As it headed in the direction of his position, he saw the battery readout on the screen. It was in the red zone and flashing. The extra power required to escape had drained the dragonfly of its energy. As it darted down the forest track, the drone was now in danger of stalling. Miller had no choice. He had to switch to low-power mode.

And then the bats struck.

Tearing into the rotor blades, they disabled the drone and brought it down in a puddle beside the track. As the cameras started to fail, Miller cussed. The picture was hazy and spotty now, fracturing into moving horizontal lines. Two seconds later, the screen went blank, and the word "malfunction" – in bloodred capitals - replaced whatever semblance of a picture had been left.

The drone was gone.

$200,000 of equipment was lost.

Miller decided not to phone his boss at the Pentagon. Instead, he wrote her a terse text.

Discovered the farm where the professor and Ms Hailey are hiding out. It's secluded. Well-designed. Hard to penetrate. Just tried to acquire intel using the DRS.

He took a deep breath before relaying the bad news.

DRS attacked, brought down, lost in woodland. Presumed destroyed. Request replacement.

Miller paused and looked out of his front window.

Within seconds he had his reply.

No chance. Not a bottomless pit. I'm already under suspicion here because of costs. Just do your job.

Miller shook his head and frowned.

"Will do," he texted.

19

THE WIDOW

Even during breakfast, the jetlag was pulling at the blinds of Maya's eyes. The only thing keeping her from returning to bed was Birgit's strong, Nordic coffee which she referred to as her Scandi Noir – that and the possibility that a visit to the woman called Clare might yield fresh information about her grandfather.

"I suggest you two take the car," Birgit said, looking at Maya over a large plate of small slices of cheese – both brown and cream – and a selection of meats. As she poured Maya some more coffee, she added, "We will take the van and use it as a decoy."

"Why do we need to split up?" Maya asked.

"We had a visitor last night," Birgit said.

Maya shook her head. "I don't understand. I thought you told me this place is impenetrable."

"From the ground," Birgit said. "Not from the air."

Maya frowned.

"Let me summarise," Birgit continued. "Someone's

trying to prevent you two from acquiring intelligence about George Hailey. I suspect that whoever they are, they're working for a US government agency with access to military grade equipment."

"You're kidding!"

"I know you're sceptical," Birgit said, "but last night this place was invaded by a very sophisticated drone. One used by the military in your country. It's small, portable, hard to detect."

"How do you know?"

Birgit swivelled and picked up her laptop. Maya recognized it as the one Jack had used when they were viewing the footage of her grandfather's wrecked Catalina.

Birgit thrust it towards Maya with the screen activated.

"What do you see?"

"Looks like a large locust or grasshopper."

Even in the pretence of sounding confident, Maya was sceptical. Whatever this thing was, it was much bigger than any insect she had ever seen, even in the pinelands and hammocks of the Everglades she and her father had visited one summer. This frightening creature, whatever it was, seemed at least twice the size of the lubber grasshoppers in Florida. There were other marked differences too. The summer lubbers down south had emitted loud buzzing noises, but this creature was quiet. They had been daubed in bright orange and yellow streaks, but this thing was jet-black. They had been slow and cumbersome, unable to fly, but this was nimble, mobile, airborne, fast. No, this was different from anything she had ever seen except in the movies - *Dune*, to be precise, with its insect-shaped choppers.

They did share one thing in common, however – the

capacity to invade your property and cause a nuisance. When Maya and her father had stayed in the Everglades, he informed her that the locals were always vigilant during Spring, trying to spot the infant luggers before they grew. "You have to kill them while they're nymphs," he had told her. When she asked how, he replied, "You drown them in soapy water, otherwise you'll have trouble in the summer." Her father looked at her and added, "Black critters like these aren't popular." He laughed and laughed once he realised how the words sounded.

Forcing the grief down into her guts, Maya studied the screen. "You're saying this thing is spying on us?"

"It is," Birgit said, explaining the drone's provenance. As she concluded, she reached down to the floor and placed a beaten-up metal gadget on the table. It was the insect Maya was watching on the laptop, except its wings were fractured, its nose broken.

Birgit took the remains of the drone from the table and carried them over to a wood burner where a strong fire was raging behind its glass-paned door. She opened the two panels and thrust the wreckage into the flames. The five witnesses watched and listened as the dragonfly slumped, writhed, crackled, and whistled in the intense heat of the furnace. Maya continued to watch with fascination as the black skin of the drone evaporated, leaving only a metal, heat-resistant, endoskeleton, its steely outline cast into even sharper relief by the orange radiance of its surroundings.

"It cannot anymore hear or see," Birgit said.

"How did you get it?" Maya asked.

"It crashed."

"Did you make it crash?"

Rory interrupted. "We need to go."

"Right," Birgit said looking at Maya. "You and the professor will have to leave after us. We will head off in the van. As soon as we send you a text to say it's safe, you head for Franky's widow. The professor has the sat nav coordinates."

Maya took a final gulp of coffee. Even in the light of the laptop footage and the remains of the drone she was still struggling to comprehend everything that was going on, let alone believe it. If she had not been so exhausted, she might have expressed more reservations, but the disorientation and fatigue she was now feeling meant she knew that any further resistance to these plans was pointless.

Twenty minutes later, she was sitting next to the professor in the front of a replacement Firebird, travelling towards the house owned by the sister of the old monk with the cure.

"So, your back is better?" Maya asked.

The professor seemed reluctant to talk about it. He just nodded. Maya was not for relenting. "Jack told me last night that you had some sort of spiritual experience."

"I had an experience I cannot explain."

The professor described the bare bones of it, refusing to attribute any supernatural causation to his improvement, while at the same time expressing gratitude for being pain free.

"I'm surprised you're still sceptical," she said.

"I think you're being a little hypocritical," the professor answered. "I mean, you are presented with visible, tangible, physical evidence of something and you're still full of questions."

"What are you talking about?"

"I'm talking about the drone, which indicates with some

certainty that we are being followed."

"So?"

"So, you are reluctant to believe when you're confronted with things that are seen, yet you have a go at me for being reluctant to believe when I'm presented with things that are unseen. That, I think, is a bit hypocritical."

Maya laughed. Then she asked, "What are we expecting to learn from this widow?"

"I'm not sure, but I am guessing we'll find that your grandfather was indeed alive after his Catalina crashed and that something traumatic happened to him, something the authorities are determined we don't hear about it."

Maya sighed. "I'm sorry about your accident."

"It wasn't your fault."

"Even so, I feel responsible."

"Why?"

"If I hadn't written to you about my grandfather, you wouldn't have been with Bret in the car."

"That's probably not true, Maya. Your grandfather asked me to find him, remember? Whether you had contacted me or not, that's what I would have done. You were not to blame."

"Thank you," she said.

They drove in silence until Maya sighed and said, "I wish my daddy could have held out a bit longer. Maybe he would have been able to die with at least some answers."

"I'm sorry for your loss," the professor said, his voice soft, "But I should also add that what we are about to learn may not have brought him the peace you think."

Maya raised her eyes.

The professor, seeing her surprise, said, "Perhaps we

should just wait until we have the facts."

Half an hour later, they were in Trory Point near Enniskillen, sitting in the front room of Clare's cottage. She was pouring tea into her best China cups and saucers.

"I'm sorry to ask," she said, looking at Maya. "Do you have proof that you're George Hailey's granddaughter."

Maya withdrew a passport from her purse and passed it to Clare. She turned several of the pages then handed it back. "That's good," she said. Then her expression changed. "You poor wee thing. You have no idea what happened to your Granda, do you?"

Maya shook her head.

"Are you sure you want to know?"

"I am."

"Well, then, you need to hear about my late beloved husband first. He was a military policeman, part of an American unit based in Belfast. Sometimes, Maya, he found the work upsetting." The old woman caught herself on and asked, "May I call you Maya?"

"Of course."

"One evening I could tell he was lost in his own thoughts. I asked him what was on his mind. He told me that he had just met a black airman – an American who had trained in Tuskegee but then joined the Royal Canadian Airforce. He was a second pilot on board a Catalina at RAF Castle Archdale."

"Was that my grandfather?"

"It was. From what Franky told me, your Granda had always wanted to fly with the Tuskegee airmen. When he excelled himself, he was invited to enrol with the US Army Air Force and join up with the Red Tails in Italy. He duly received his wings and his uniform in a ceremony in Belfast, then went and had a drink or two to celebrate in a pub nearby. I believe he was alone."

Stone said, "I hope you don't mind me interrupting, but what date was this exactly?"

"March 15th, 1944."

Stone stared at Maya.

Clare poured some more tea.

"A unit of four M.P.s was on patrol in Belfast that night. Just after midnight, they stumbled on your grandfather coming out of an air-raid shelter. He was following a young woman who was fleeing the scene. Franky later heard that she had left her fur coat behind and was running in a white dress. He said she was a fine-looking girl."

"Who was she?" Maya asked.

"Franky wasn't allowed to talk about any of the cases at Belfast barracks, so I have no idea. All I know is that there was another man inside the shelter. He was dead. Your Granda was arrested, charged with murder, and held in one of the cells. Franky knew him. All he would say when he came home was that it was terrible what was happening to him. He repeated the word 'terrible'. He seemed very distressed about the way your Granda was treated."

"What do you mean 'treated'?"

"The honest answer is I don't know. Franky wouldn't talk about it. He seemed very reticent. In fact, he didn't mention it again until several months before he died."

Clare wiped a stray tear from her face.

"One evening, here in this room, Franky asked if I remembered the black airman. I said yes. He told me the man had been his prisoner, that he had written six letters during his time in the cells, and that he had given these to Franky to look after. He was to give them to the man's fiancée if it was safe to do so."

"Where are they?" Maya asked.

"Franky wanted to give them to her, but only when he felt it was safe. By the time he started making inquiries, she had sailed for America, and there was no one left from her family."

"Please don't tell me he destroyed them."

"No, he put them in a box."

Maya gasped.

"He wrote and sealed a letter with the location. And he gave specific instructions not to give it to anyone other than a close relative, stressing that I was to ask for proof."

"Which I've given you," Maya said.

"You have, but I have to confess that I'm more than a little nervous about divulging the details."

"Why?"

"Because Franky was nervous."

"I can understand why," the professor said. "He didn't want to put you in any danger. And nor do we. That's why we made very sure no one followed us here."

"Ach, I'm too old to worry about such things," Clare said. She walked to an old mahogany dresser on the far side of the room. "That's why I'm going to give you this letter from Franky. I hope you find everything you need in it."

Clare reached for a drawer and withdrew an old envelope with the letters GH written in red ink on it. She passed it to Maya who opened the seal. She drew out a single piece of blue letter-writing paper with a hand-drawn image of what looked like a cross.

Maya shook her head. "I literally have no idea where this might be," she said with a sigh.

"May I see?" the professor asked.

He confessed his ignorance too.

Maya passed it to Clare. The moment she saw the cross, tears began to fill her eyes.

"Where is it?" Maya asked.

"It's where Franky and I first held hands. A small island in lower Lough Erne. We stood in front of that cross when we visited it on a boat trip during the war. Franky remarked that it was probably twice as old as the United States. I told him true love stands after all the tests of time. That's when he held my hand."

Clare's voice was weaker now.

"My beloved must have buried the letters there," she whispered. "In the place marked in the drawing. The place you're looking for is just outside the fence that surrounds the church."

She sniffed the paper and closed her eyes, the faint scent of her husband carrying her to a thousand happy places. Then she remembered herself and handed the letter back to Maya.

"May the wind be at your back," she said.

LETTER 12

March 15th, 1944

Dear Dad,

Thank you for your advice about Myra. You're so right. I'm just going to have to be patient. I'm not good at that. I miss her so much. She's not sent any messages to me, and the thought that she's still so withdrawn fills me with sadness. But then you have been through this agony too. You had to be patient at times with Ma when you were courting. You said you were the gas pedal, and Ma the brakes.

Yes, I do remember the time we went to Pensacola, just the two of us. I'll never forget standing with you on the whitest sand I've ever seen. I can still recall the snow-white grains on the tops of my bare feet as we cast our lines into the sea. We waited for several hours before we even got a bite. You chastised me when I expressed frustration. "Patience is a fisherman," you said. I've never forgotten that. It was a few minutes later that I caught my first silver fish.

So, I'll make like a fisherman.

I'll practice patience!

In better news, I will be in Belfast later today receiving my wings from Colonel Benjamin Davis. I'm being enrolled in the USAAF, the United States Army Air Forces. I'm due to fly to Italy tomorrow, March 16th, to join up with the all-black 332nd Fighter Group. I'm getting the impression I'll be flying P39s to begin with and, in time, providing fighter escorts for the bombers. All this is a dream come true and I can't express how excited I am. My commanding officer from RAF Castle Archdale is coming with me to the ceremony. He is sad to lose me but excited for me too. He has been very kind, as is my new CO. I'm meeting him at a pub nearby at 9pm tonight to celebrate.

Last night, I said goodbye to the boys in my crew. They went to bed early at 6pm and left just after midnight for their briefing. I knew I'd be fast asleep when they left, so we had a farewell in the mess late yesterday afternoon. The Skipper said some kind words and all the boys wished me well. I will miss them. They have become a true band of brothers. They are flying a mission into the Atlantic today. Anti-submarine patrols. Protecting our ships from the wolfpacks, as always. Part of me wishes I was going too. The second pilot's chair has become a part of my life – and of course Scratch's little bed behind it.

And that brings me to my little white friend.

He slept on my feet throughout the night. He couldn't understand why I didn't get up and follow my crewmembers out of the Nissan Hut, with him in tow behind me. He uttered a lot of tiny, strange squeaks until early this morning. He seemed to know something was different. They have an inner sense, don't they, Dad? I found saying goodbye to

Scratch very tough. I don't mind admitting I shed some tears, comforted only by the Skipper's words.

"We'll look after him if he's still here when we get back. Although we'll understand if you have other plans."

Scratch pawed at the door of the hut just a few hours ago, when I closed it as I left with my bag for breakfast in the mess. I guess he lived up to his name. I'll miss him.

Anyway, that's where I am now. In the mess, eating breakfast, writing this letter before I go to Belfast for the ceremony. I fly to an airfield in Kent tomorrow before heading out to Italy to join the 301st squadron of the 332nd Fighter Group.

The thing that makes me saddest is Myra. I sent a letter to her asking to meet, but she didn't reply. I wanted to say goodbye in person and promise her I'd be back. It would have been so good to have her with me in Belfast at the ceremony. I was then going to ask one of the boys to give her Scratch to look after once I'd left. He would have been a comfort to her in my absence – a link connecting us while I'm away in Italy. I'm distraught that my plan has not worked.

There's one more thing that's going to make this all so much tougher, and it's something I need to share with you, Dad. Myra's pregnant. It must have been that night over New Year when we stayed in the Catalina. I think we just got so lost in each other's souls and bodies that we cast all caution to the Fermanagh wind. She told me during the last night we had together when we went again to see *The Song of Bernadette*. I've been meaning to tell you, but I allowed myself to get affected and distracted by the stigma. It's much worse in some ways here. Catholic girls like Myra are already treated like dirt. They have a reputation for sleeping with my

GI brothers. There's been quite a lot of talk in government about the dangers of "brown babies." Fortunately, this has been largely directed at Cookstown girls until now, but I'm concerned for Myra and our child.

"Our child!"

I can't believe I'm even thinking about that phrase, let alone writing it. *Myra and I are going to have a baby.* I had wanted to get down on one knee and propose to her tonight. I do want to make an honest woman out of her, although she is already more honest than any other woman I've ever met, apart from Mom, of course. That will now have to wait until I'm on leave from Italy, hopefully in the fall. That's if she's still speaking to me when I return.

This is harder still because of a disturbing dream I had last night. I saw Myra dressed like Bernadette. She was on a bed. At first, I thought it was a hospital and that she had just given birth to our child. But then it became quickly clear that this was a sad not a happy dream. The place was a hospital, yes, but the occasion was not one of birth, but death. Myra's death. I am shuddering while writing this. As I watched her, I saw the lady in white appear. She told Myra that she had once said to her, when Myra was a child, that she could not promise her happiness in this world, only in the next. What happened after she said that I don't know. I woke up in a sweat, with Scratch licking my forehead. He must have been awakened by my troubled state and crawled up the bed to comfort me. What a great pal he has been.

Dad, I know I'm very likely not making much sense. I am very conflicted if I'm honest. On the one hand, I'm hopeful and excited about being enrolled in the USAAF and heading out to Italy to join my new squadron. Over the moon, in fact. On the other, I'm grieving what feels like a double bereavement – with Myra and Scratch. What was it the novelist George Eliot once said? Something like "Every parting leaves an image of death." I think I know what she meant. Every temporary goodbye is a dress rehearsal for the final farewell. Except that in my case, I'm not even getting to say goodbye.

Oh well, I'll just have to stand in the sand. One day, Myra will take a hold of the line I've cast towards her. In the meantime, as you once said, patience truly is a fisherman.

I'll just wait.

But hopefully not for too long,

Right, Dad?

I'll write to you when I'm in Italy.

I love you.

Your Son,
George.
VV

20

THE CROSS

That night, back at the kitchen in Birgit's house, Maya was energised. The adrenalin generated by learning about the box had displaced every trace of her debilitating jetlag.

As she finished a glass of iced water, Jack walked into the kitchen. Rory had driven him back to the farm.

"Ask Jack about the island," Birgit said. "He's our expert on all things local. Even has an OBE..."

"O.B.E?"

"Order of the British Empire," Rory explained.

"You had me confused," Maya said. "In my world, OBE means something totally different."

She could sense them waiting for an explanation.

"Out of Body Experience," she said.

"And do you believe in that kind of thing?" The professor had now entered the room and the conversation. He was sitting at the island in the centre of the kitchen.

"Harriet Tubman had visions," Maya said, "ones in which she was taken out of her body and raised above unfamiliar terrain when she was rescuing slaves. She'd be given eyes to see what dangers lay there, and how to avoid them."

"Has that happened to you?" the professor asked.

"I have inherited some of Harriet's gifts."

"Inherited?"

"Tubman is my mother's maiden name."

The professor expressed surprise, then raised a tumbler of golden ale and took a sip.

"What did you learn from Clare?" Jack asked.

Maya related everything that Franky's widow had told them. There was an audible gasp from Birgit, Rory, and Jack as she produced the letter and revealed the drawing of the ancient cross, along with the arrows and measurements around it, highlighting the hiding place of the box. "The island where my grandfather's letters are hidden has a strange name. It's called Inishmacsaint."

"Ach, I know it well," Jack said. "It's a wee place on the western side of the lower lough. Ninnidh, the one-eyed saint, founded a monastery there. He was one of the Twelve Apostles of Ireland. Went to the same school as Saint Mo Laisse. Mo Laisse based himself at Devenish, Ninnidh at Inishmacsaint."

"What's on the island?" Maya asked.

"The ruins of an old church and..." Jack hesitated, before adding, "and the cross in Franky's drawing."

"It still stands?"

"It does."

"Then hadn't we better leave?"

Birgit looked at Rory, who nodded. She then glanced at Jack, who shook his head. "I'm getting too old for this craic," he said with a groan. "I'll hold the fort here."

Within half an hour, the four explorers were at the jetty a quarter of a mile away boarding the former fishing boat. A while later, they were drawing alongside another jetty, one that jutted out from the small island of Inishmacsaint. As Maya stepped onto its wooden boards, she swore she saw the blue sheen of a kingfisher shooting across the water. Wiping her eyes, she squinted at the coppice ahead of her, trying to make out any landmarks, but the island was cloaked in a habit as dusky as the ones worn by the monks who once prayed there.

Birgit moved ahead. In one hand she held what looked like a metal detector, in the other a torch. Rory was just behind her, carrying a small spade, some measuring tape, and a trowel.

"Follow me," Birgit said.

After leaving the wooden jetty, they made their way up an incline along a short path towards a clutch of trees. Thin lines of sporadic rain were now falling from the sky like liquid tracer fire, making the ground wet and clingy beneath their marching feet. As she made her way up the hill, Maya was grateful for the walking boots and waterproofs that Birgit had lent her back at the farm.

"Here we are", Birgit said, stopping at what looked like the edge of a perimeter fence.

She threw the light of her torch into the centre of the enclosure. There, in front of them, was a ruined church. Its roof had long since gone, but its stone-covered walls remained.

Birgit tried the gate, but it was locked.

"Barbed wire," she said, pointing to the fence.

"Do we need to enter?" the professor asked.

"Not according to this," Maya said, fetching the piece of paper with care out of her pocket. "See?" she said, sheltering the page from the rain. "The burial place is outside the fence."

Birgit nodded and cast the light onto the left side of the sacred ground. There was a path adjacent to the barbed wire fence on her left. She made her way along its course until she came to the corner of the field. As she shone the light on the old stone cross, Maya gasped. It was over a thousand years old, but it leant neither to the left nor the right, to the front or behind, but remained upright, planted deep into the soil of the island, its crossbeam and stake in a perfect and permanent symmetry, unmarred by the wind and the rain. The professor muttered that the shape of the cross was like the sword in the stone. "Aye, we're knights from King Arthur's table," Rory remarked.

Birgit now illuminated the space beyond the cross and the fence while Rory took the tape measure and marked the spot where the drawing indicated the box was buried. Birgit handed the torch to the professor and scanned the topsoil with the metal detector, pausing her sweep when the beeping, which had started out intermittent and soft, became louder and sustained.

"There," she whispered, pointing to a tiny patch no more than six inches from the tangled branches of a small hedge.

Rory began to dig. After a few minutes, he stopped. "There's something here."

The next moment, the professor was shining the beam on a rusty olive-green tin dappled by dark brown mud. The two colours made the box look camouflaged.

Maya clapped her hands. "Open it!"

"It's locked," Rory said.

"Can't you force it?"

"Don't do that!" Birgit interjected. "I have something at the farm. Besides, we mustn't expose the letters to the rain."

Maya switched on the torch on her phone and turned back towards the jetty. Minutes later, she was waiting next to the boat as Birgit started the engine and Rory set about untying two ropes, one at the bow, the other at the stern. As the diesel fumes filled her nostrils, Maya started to drift away in her mind. At first, she thought it was the jetlag, but then she remembered having a similar sensation when she was a girl. She knew she could not fight it. Her task was only to surrender to the strong current of its speed and direction.

Moving in what felt like an incorporeal, ghostly form, Maya rose above the boat and started to speed away from the jetty back towards Birgit's farm. This led her over an untended island a mile away, one no larger than Inishmacsaint. There was nothing there save a tonsuring of its grassy dome by matted hedges and tall reeds and rushes. She continued beyond the island towards the jetty not far from Birgit's home. She hurried over woods and meadows until she arrived at the avenue of trees leading to Birgit's farm. When she arrived at the gates, Maya proceeded to the back wall where the great octagonal greenhouse stood. What she saw made her gasp. There was a man dressed in a black outfit and black boots. He had a balaclava covering his face and eyes. He was using a small airborne drone to spy on the farmhouse and had spotted Jack sitting in the rocking chair by the fire in the kitchen. Maya shuddered. If the intruder could find a point of entry, Jack would stand no chance. He was fast asleep. As this dawned on her, a chilling wave of anxiety saturated her soul.

Maya's mind fell back into her body faster than a diving cormorant. Reorienting herself with her surroundings, she climbed over the gunwales into the open area at the stern of the former fishing vessel, then marched into the cabin.

"We need to hurry back," she said.

"What's up?" Rory asked.

"There's an intruder at the farmhouse. I can sense it."

"Who?"

"I don't know."

Birgit looked at her watch, pressed the screen, glanced at a camera view of her house, and frowned.

Rory began to steer the boat away from the single-file pier and out onto the lough. Maya watched as he and Birgit muttered to each other, figuring out a plan. Selecting the fastest route on the satellite navigation system, Rory adjusted the boat's front-facing lights to their highest setting. Birgit opened a laptop at a table and began typing on the keyboard, accessing more cameras back at the farm.

"What can you see?" Maya asked.

"Whoever it is, he's walking around the perimeter," she said. "He's now at the wall next to the barn."

"What's he doing?"

Birgit opened a laptop and accessed her security cameras. Both could now observe the intruder. He was still piloting his drone from a remote, directing it over the tall, thick wall of hedges and causing it to hover over the ground littered with old farm vehicles and wrecked cars. As he lowered the drone, Birgit became excited.

"Watch this!" she said.

As the drone touched the ground, the entire space was lit

up by what seemed like a thousand lights.

The intruder covered his goggles and cameras with his hand. Blinded by the sudden illumination, he seemed to stumble, only regaining his footing by steadying himself using the branches of the thickets next to him. This triggered a new reaction, this time the deafening sound of a World War 2 air-raid syren.

The son-et-lumière display was all too much for the uninvited guest. Imagining himself exposed and vulnerable, he hurried from the farm until he was halfway down the woodland avenue. There he took his remote and flew the drone over the trees to where the farmer's track joined the road. After he ran onto the tarmac, Birgit said, "He's beyond the reach of our cameras now."

Birgit typed on the keyboard. The bright lights on the farm went out and the old siren ceased. Switching views, she accessed a camera in the kitchen – one looking onto the old fireplace and the still glowing embers of the coals ignited before they had left. As the camera zoomed in on the rocking chair, Maya breathed a sigh of relief. Jack seemed to be fast asleep, oblivious to the sights and sounds that had ruptured the silence like a great fireball.

Birgit, who had one ear filled by the cup of a set of headphones, the other open to Maya, chuckled.

"What?" Maya asked.

Birgit passed her one of the speakers.

Maya heard something. At first, she thought it might be distant thunder. Then it hit her. She was listening to the throaty rumble of Jack snoring by the fire.

"I feel sorry for his wife," Maya said.

"Everybody does," Birgit replied. "In fact, I might give her these headphones."

Maya laughed.

As Birgit closed the laptop, Maya looked at her. "Why do you have all this high-tech stuff at the farm?"

"Always prepared," Birgit answered before walking to Rory and taking over the steering of the vessel. Maya sat down at a small table next to the port-side window, watching the outlines of the islands and hills rising and falling in the darkness. Her eyelids felt heavy now. She wanted to abandon herself to the seductive summons of a deep sleep. But then the boat slowed, and they were at the jetty not far from Birgit's place. Rory secured the boat to the small pier.

The four friends left the vessel, Maya cradling the box of letters in her arms like a rescued infant. When they reached the farm, Rory led them past the wreck of a tractor into the barn. He took out a remote and pressed a button. One of the haybales in the far-left corner opened like a secret trapdoor, revealing a staircase leading down beneath the ground. He beckoned to them to follow as he headed down the steps into a space illuminated by a soft light.

"What is this place?" Maya asked.

"An underground bunker," Rory whispered as they entered what looked like a control room.

Rory encouraged them to sit down at a long table while he went to fetch Jack from upstairs.

"There are surveillance cameras everywhere," Birgit said. "I've even got ones in the headlamps of my old Firebirds."

"This place is a fortress," Maya said.

Just then, Rory re-entered the underground chamber, holding onto his friend's arm. Jack was drowsy from his sleep and shuffling along the floor towards the table.

When he sat down, he turned and looked at Maya. "Is that the box of letters?"

"We haven't opened it yet," she replied.

"Ach, what are you waiting for?"

Rory walked over to Maya and stretched out his hands to receive the dirt-dotted box. He placed the treasured vessel on the table, then he opened what looked like a sleek black Swiss army knife, but which was in fact a set of lock picks of various sizes, all designed for covert entry into rooms and receptacles. There was a click. "There we are, now," Rory said, opening the lid and handing the box to the professor.

Stone put on a pair of white cotton gloves. Removing a small pouch from the inside pocket of his jacket, he withdrew a pair of clean silver tweezers. One by one, he removed what looked like old pages out of the box and laid them on the table. When the box was empty, he took out a small scope and began to examine the writing. He held some pages up to the light, examining paper, texture, ink, and signatures. Then he placed the letters in a brand-new storage box, taking care to separate each of the letters with a blank stencil sheet. When he had finished his examination, he looked up at Maya and smiled.

"These are, without any shadow of a doubt, your grandfather's missing letters."

LETTER 13

18th March 1944

My Darling Myra,

I am not sure whether you'll receive this in time to either reply or visit, but I am hopeful that you will. I need you so bad right now. I would give anything to be together, especially after we parted on such a sad note just three weeks ago. I am so sorry. Sorrier than I can ever say. If I could go back in time, knowing what I do now, I would never have said yes to enrolling with the USAAF. I would never have come to Belfast. Never have been in a pub waiting for my new CO. Never would have got into so much trouble for doing the right thing.

And that's why I'm writing. I need to tell you exactly what happened because you may one day get to hear a different story and I want you to know the whole truth about what brought me here to this Valley of Achor. That's important to me.

Anyway, this is the true story.

Three days ago, I received my wings and my new uniform from a USAAF Colonel in a short ceremony in Belfast at 7pm. He told me afterwards that he would meet me at a Belfast pub at 9pm and "buy me a drink or two" (his exact words). After a brief meal, I arrived alone at the Diamond Bar, North Queen Street, Belfast at 8.45pm. At 9.15pm, my new CO – the one who had just enrolled me - hadn't arrived, so I ordered a Guinness drink at the bar. While waiting for the cream to settle, I observed a man speaking in a disrespectful way to a girl who could not have been much older than eighteen. She was dressed in a fake fur coat. She also had a lot of makeup which, from my little time in Northern Ireland, I would say isn't common. You don't swear by it, nor do the other girls in Irvinestown. It seemed to me she had gone to great lengths to try to impress him but without success.

I could not tell what this bully was saying because of his very thick accent, but it was quite clear that she was upset by his words and their tone. At one point, she dried her eyes. This seemed to annoy him even more. He pulled her by the arm, forcing her to leave the pub. She was obviously in pain but trying also to hide it.

What happened next is what got me into so much trouble. I followed both until they reached an air-raid shelter at the top of Earl Street. By now, it was clear to me that the man was drunk and that he was intent on harming the poor girl. When he forced her into the shelter, I followed. As soon as I walked in, I could tell they were the only ones there. The girl's fur coat was on the ground, like a makeshift blanket, and the man was forcing her by her arms to lie on it on her back. He was about to unbutton his pants when he turned and saw me. He drew a pearl-handled jackknife from his pocket and charged me. I parried his blow using my left arm as a shield. The blade nicked my sleeve and drew blood. Fortunately, it was only a scratch.

With what I can only describe as a primal instinct, I took hold of the handle of his knife, turned it, and then in self-defense thrust the weapon back towards its bearer. The tip of the blade entered his throat. He collapsed to the floor where he began to make a very strange gurgling sound, as if drowning. I was about to try and help him when the girl ran past me. All I remember was the fact that she was wearing a long white dress and white shoes. Her face, as white as her clothes, stared at me for the briefest of moments. She frowned and said thank you. Then she looked forlorn and added, "Ach, you shouldn't have followed me. You'll get in terrible trouble now."

And she was right.

She ran from the shelter while I looked to see what the man was doing. He seemed to me to be unconscious. I walked out of the shelter in a state of shock and sat down on a stone step. I was on the edge of tears, Myra, when some M.P.s showed up. I called to them for help. Two of them held me while the other two inspected the shelter. When they came out, one of them said the man inside was dead and took from me what he described as the weapon responsible – the man's knife. The sergeant then said something that sent a chill down my spine. "I'm arresting you for violating the 92nd Article of War."

With that, I knew I was in deep trouble.

The M.P.s took me to Victoria Barracks, Belfast, where the Head Constable called for an ambulance to take the deceased man from the shelter to Mater Hospital. There a surgeon performed a post-mortem on the man and confirmed the cause of death as a stab to the throat. The Head Constable told me this news. He also said that the evidence against me looked very damning. However much I tried to convince him it had been an accident, he remained unmoved.

I was locked in a cell downstairs.

A staff sergeant from the criminal investigation division called Agent O'Connor took my clothes. He was interested in the tear in the forearm of my jacket and the cut on my lower arm, just above my wrist. He was followed by an M.P. who reminded me of my rights according to the Articles of War. He did this in the presence of a man from the Royal Ulster Constabulary. I signed a document acknowledging that I had heard and understood my rights.

The M.P. seemed to me to be a fair and kind gentleman. He is called Franky and comes from Tuskegee where I originally trained to be a pilot. He is the only companion here. It's thanks to him that I have these pages on which to write. He has also allowed me to borrow his pen for an hour each day. I am using the opportunity not only to prepare my case for trial but to write to you as well.

I have not slept well these past two nights. I'm aware that I am a Negro airman at the mercy of white army officers. I'm also aware of how tense the situation is right now between black and white US servicemen in Northern Ireland. I suspect that everything about my case may be hushed up and hidden, not just to keep whatever peace exists between white and colored Americans, but between the US military and our hosts here in your country. It's a terrible situation. I am deeply concerned that I may be sacrificed on the altar of political expediency rather than given a fair and public trial.

I'm therefore afraid, far more afraid than ever I have been flying over the Atlantic, taking enemy fire from a U-Boat recharging its batteries on the surface of the ocean. I have always said to you that my only fear is meeting my end by friendly fire. I never thought that might come not from over-exuberant gunners on an American escort vessel, but from military lawyers on dry land.

How I miss you, my darling. And little Scratch too. What I would do to be with you walking along the banks of Lough Erne or rowing out to the Lady for a night on the calm surface of the great lake. The water, the wind, and the rain of Fermanagh have never judged me. They act on you and me, on white and black, without favoritism. Oscar Wilde said this too. Franky has lent me a copy of *De Profundis*. There is one passage that struck me, one in which he says something so very similar, only so much better than I ever could. "Society, as we have constituted it," Wilde writes, "will have no place for me, has none to offer; but Nature, whose sweet rains fall on unjust and just alike, will have clefts in the rocks where I may hide, and secret valleys in whose silence I may weep undisturbed. She will hang the night with stars so that I may walk abroad in the darkness without stumbling and send the wind over my footprints so that none may track me to my hurt: she will cleanse me in great waters, and with bitter herbs make me whole." That is just beautiful. And Wilde was writing from prison too.

I have no idea what these coming days or weeks have in store for me. I just can't help thinking of Bigger Thomas and wondering whether truth is in some strange way imitating fiction. Maybe that's why his story has always affected me so deeply. I know it affected you too. You often said to me that you couldn't fathom how America could be so advanced with its planes but so backward with its politics. You were always right about that, except that now this is all not just an idea to discuss but a challenge to be met.

I hope with all my heart that somehow, some day, Franky will be able to get this letter to you, and others too, if I am able to write some more. I know it will be hard for him. He will be putting himself at risk with the authorities, but I can tell that he is a good man and that he will try his best to be a faithful go-between.

Know that I am not guilty of violating any article of war. I did not kill with premeditation. It was an accident. Self-defense. I was coming to the aid of a young woman in danger. All I could see while I was watching events unfold was you in that white dress, being abused by some cruel man, but with no one to come to your rescue.

Please know, also, that I love you with all my heart, and that I will never give up hope of being together with you and Scratch again and helping your wonderful Ma.

With all my love,

George.

21

THE SHOCK

That night, Maya slept in fits and starts. She would drop off for a while, then dream about the dark intruder who had tried to invade the farm. In her dream, he was wearing a hood and his eyes seemed to burn with fire. Scared by this lupine interloper, Maya would awaken in a sweat before floating away again, sinking into her subconscious where she would find the subliminal intruder waiting for her. She would calm herself by remembering Birgit's words, uttered just before they retired to their separate bedrooms in the bunker. "You are safe here. Nothing, no one, can touch you while you're underground, under my care." She would then pray for protection from all the perils of the night before the grim cycle reactivated. When the morning alarm went off on her watch, Maya felt like a wreck. When she stood in front of the wall-mounted mirror, she decided she looked like one too.

Even in this enervated state, however, Maya felt the revivifying power of an unrelenting curiosity concerning her grandfather's letters. This energised her for the single task of answering one simple question. What happened to the man who had loved Myra Coughlan, the man who had fathered her own late and beloved father? This exclusive focus now streamlined her priorities and harnessed her remaining reserves. She was interested in nothing else. She owed her very existence to George Hailey. If not for him, she would not be conscious of anything, including her own curiosity.

After a shower, Maya walked into the kitchen of the bunker and poured herself a mug of coffee. As she sat down at the table, the professor entered. He helped himself to some cold meat, cheese, pickled herring, and prawn salad from a Nordic smorgasbord resting on a work surface next to a large oven.

As Stone approached, Maya began to speak. "You read any of my granddaddy's letters?"

"Yes."

"What did you learn?"

"That the old priest was right about your grandfather not being on board the Lady when it crashed in March 1944. And that Clare's testimony about Franky guarding him in Belfast Barracks after the time of the crash is sound too."

The professor shovelled a mixture of prawns and eggs onto his upturned fork. As he lifted the food to his mouth, Maya thought the professor looked the antithesis of how she felt. His eyes were bright and brilliant, his skin fresh and smooth, his head of brown hair full and shiny. He was manifesting none of the exhaustion she had been feeling. The more he ate his breakfast, the more his tall, athletic frame seemed to be recharging itself.

Taking a break from his eating, Stone began to speak. "From the first letter I've studied, it seems that your grandfather had gone to Belfast on the night of March 15th to be officially admitted into the USAAF. He agreed to have a celebration drink at a pub afterwards. That all went tragically wrong."

"What happened?"

"The person he was supposed to be meeting – his new CO - didn't show up at the time agreed. While your grandfather was waiting, he saw a man bullying a young girl at the bar. He followed them outside and got into a fight in an air-raid shelter. It seems he was trying to help the girl, but in the process, he accidentally killed the other fellow. He was arrested by some American M.P.s."

"Surely the girl could have corroborated his story and helped him in his defence," Maya said.

"That's the problem. I haven't read all the letters yet, but from what I have read it seems clear to me that she disappeared from the scene, and that she went into hiding. Clearly, there was some good reason for her not handing herself in and helping your grandfather by confirming his story."

Maya sighed. "That's a real shame. But our story is still dynamite. I thought that my grandfather had been killed in a plane crash. Turns out he was a victim of criminal injustice by his own military – an injustice that appears to have been racially motivated."

Maya stood, turned towards the kitchen, and walked towards the cooker. Before serving herself some eggs she didn't want, she wiped her eyes while her back was to the professor, then returned to the table where she took a mouthful. The eggs were not as tasty as the ones she would have cooked on her own hob in New England. She always added cream and a little grated cheese.

As Maya was about to talk again, Birgit entered with some fresh pickings from the allotments.

"Is Jack up?" Maya asked.

"Been up for a while," Birgit answered. "He's been taking a walk next to the greenhouse."

On cue, Jack entered bearing a bunch of small, colourful flowers. Walking to the table, he offered them to Maya.

"I'm sorry about your grandfather," he said. "I thought these might cheer you up a wee bit."

"You shouldn't have, Jack."

"Aye, but I did."

Maya took the flowers. Somehow, she managed to say thank you. Birgit, who seemed to sense Maya's fragility, took them and placed them in a pottery vase after filling it with water. They were in front of Maya on the table in no time.

Birgit said, "We need a plan. We could sit tight here. We have everything we need. And this place is fully protected. However, doing nothing isn't really an option. I'm not keen on just waiting for our enemy to make his next move."

At the mention of the mysterious man who had been hunting them, the room fell quiet. Maya thought of the hooded figure in her dream. His eyes seemed to burn as she remembered him lurking in the dark, waiting to strike when she least expected it.

"I have a suggestion," Birgit said after a pause. "I think we should contact the Belfast Times. They have a US correspondent. She looks like just the right fit for a story like ours. Her track record is superb. Her reach is big. She has a passion for truth and justice."

"Won't we be putting her in danger?" Stone asked.

"Her hero was a journalist called Pauline Sullivan," Birgit said. "They were very close. Pauline was like a dog with a bone when it came to investigative journalism. In the end she was killed for it. Siobhan has the same spirit. She won't flinch at danger."

Rory brought out several sealed boxes containing brand-new mobile phones. "We can use burner phones and other safeguards if she's interested in pursuing the story," he said.

Birgit turned to Maya. "Could you record a plea for her help? We have a room we use as a studio here."

"Sure."

"Rory, could you film Maya?"

Rory nodded.

"Seeing as Bret's not with us yet, I'll start work on transcribing the letters," Stone said.

"I'm grateful to you for all you're doing," Maya said to Birgit. "I may not always say it, but I am."

"Ach, you don't need to thank her for anything," Jack said. "She absolutely loves this craic."

"Aye," Rory said. "She's been telling us for years that big brother's watching our every move. We've always humoured her, thinking she's one of those conspiracy ..."

"Oooph," Birgit said. "You know I hate that phrase. I'm not a conspiracy theorist. I'm a fact finder. And now you're seeing the facts with your own eyes, you may refer to me as such."

"We would do well to do as we're told," Jack said when the laughter had subsided. "Birgit is named after Saint Brigit, one of our greatest saints. A saint associated with fire.

There's something burning in our Birgit too. And I suspect her passion will not subside until this story has spread like wildfire across the world."

Just then, Stone's phone went. As he listened to the voice at the other end, his face turned white.

Maya's heart skipped a beat. "What's happened?" she asked as Stone put his phone back in his pocket.

"It's Bret."

"What about him?"

"There's been an accident."

22

THE EMERGENCY

The call had come from a friend of Bret's at Portsmouth University, a fellow postgraduate research student whom the professor was also supervising. Her name was Billie. A blonde and blue-eyed American, she had been Miss Texas in the state beauty pageant several years before. She was also one of the most sharp-witted and articulate students Stone had ever taught.

"Let's switch to FaceTime," Stone said.

When Billie's face appeared on the screen, it did not wear the normal bright-eyed and cheerful look to which the professor was accustomed. Her hair was not straightened but ruffled and untidy, as if she had tossed all notions of fashion to the wind and threaded her hands many times through her layered crown and shag-cut fringes. He could see the worry in her eyes and the creases in her forehead.

"What's happened, Billie?"

"Bret's been attacked." Billie had her hand over her mouth as she answered. Her eyes watered.

The professor winced as if he too had been assaulted. "Do you have any more details?"

"It was about an hour ago. He was walking back to your apartment. Along the seafront. Someone struck him on the back of the head, and he fell into the water."

Billie was stifling the tears.

"Take your time."

"He would have drowned if that man hadn't showed up ..."

"What man?"

"The guy who rescued Bret."

Stone waited while Billie composed herself.

"He was just passing when it happened. He shouted at the attacker, but he ran off. So, this rescuer guy jumped in the sea. Pulled him out. Gave him mouth to mouth and CPR. One of my friends arrived at the scene and phoned me straightaway. By the time I got there, Bret had been rushed to hospital in an ambulance."

"Is he going to be alright?"

"I'm at the intensive care unit waiting to hear. No one will tell me anything. I think he's in theatre."

"Can you stay with him?"

Billie nodded. Her face was now reddened by tears. Between sobs, she said, "The guy didn't steal anything. He just seems to have gone for Bret for no reason. I don't understand."

But Stone did. He knew who had assaulted his student. The assailant was either the same man that tried to run him and Bret off the road, or it was an accomplice. Either way, this was an attempt to stop Stone from telling Hailey's story.

"Bret and I are investigating something very important,

Billie. It's sensitive. Dynamite even."

"You're talking about the airman?"

"Bret told you, then."

"You know what he's like, Professor. He would never betray your confidence. He's devoted to you."

Stone nodded.

"You're sure you can stay there."

"I'll be here as long as it takes."

"Thank you, Billie."

"Do you need me to do anything else, Professor?"

"Do his parents know?"

"I've called them. They're on their way."

"How did you get their number?"

"Bret took me to visit them, remember?"

It was coming back to him now. Last Christmas, Billie needed to remain in the UK. Bret had invited her to his parent's house to experience his mother's cooking. Billie and Bret's mum had bonded over baking. When his two students returned to Uni at Epiphany, they came to the professor like the Magi bearing gifts - bread, cookies, and pie. Billie's cranberry pie had been out of this world. Even Bret's bold attempt to create a spiced gingerbread loaf had not been a total waste of time. As Stone recalled the glee in his eyes, he smiled.

"I remember," he said, his voice softer now.

Just then, Stone spotted a female police officer walking onto the ICU corridor and approaching Billie. Billie turned while keeping her camera trained on them both.

"Are you a friend of Bret's?"

"I am. Do you have any news?"

"Not yet."

The officer noticed the camera. "Are you recording?"

"No. I'm talking to Bret's boss, Professor Stone. He wants to know if Bret's okay."

"He's in theatre."

Billie shook her head.

The officer continued. "Did you witness the assault?"

"No. A friend of mine did."

Billie gave her the name and number.

"What did she tell you?"

"She said a man appeared, ran at Bret, struck him on the back of the head, and kicked him into the water."

"Did she give any description of the attacker?"

"No, to be honest, I was more concerned about Bret."

The officer continued taking notes. She looked up after finishing her scribbling. "How did Bret get out of the water?"

"Someone jumped in and rescued him."

"Any idea who?"

"He disappeared straightaway."

"Do you know any reason why someone would want to attack Bret in such as violent way?"

"You mean kill him?"

"We are keeping our minds open about that."

"No, I don't."

"So, your view is that your friend was a victim of an entirely random assault."

"I'm keeping my mind open about that, Mam."

The policewoman looked at her. If she had detected the irony, there was no hint of it in her expression.

The police officer asked for Billie's number and then walked off towards the reception of the ICU. Stone could see her leaning forward and asking a nurse for information.

"Save your battery, Billie. You can contact me anytime."

"Okay, Professor. As soon as I hear anything, I promise you'll be the first to know."

Stone thanked her and ended the call.

It was two hours later when the phone rang again. As Stone focused on the screen, he could see Billie's eyes. They seemed less anxious. More alive.

"I've got someone here who wants to say hello."

"Bret!" Stone exclaimed.

Others gathered around Stone's phone.

"Hello, Professor. Everyone."

"Are you okay?"

"Apart from a sore head and some stitches. I might need that monk who healed your back if it gets any worse."

Stone smiled.

"Here, show him this!" Bret was talking to Billie who responded by filming Bret in his full-length hospital gown. It had an opening at the back which Bret had only half managed to secure. His bottom was visible beyond the hole in the flimsy material.

Bret giggled. "Now you know why they call this place *I See You*!" he said, offering a half pirouette.

It took Stone a few seconds to get the joke, but when he did all the tension was released and he laughed, as did Billie who castigated Bret for playing the fool and not resting.

"I gather I was rescued by a tall, dark, and handsome stranger," Bret said, ignoring his friend's chastisement.

"I'm afraid we don't know his name," Stone said.

"Well, whoever he was, he was a complete darling. A Grace Darling, in fact. Pulled me from the sea, he did. Just like young Gracie did all those years ago."

Stone raised his voice. "You need to rest, Bret,"

"Alright Prof."

"One more thing," Stone said. "You can't travel back here. Do you have somewhere you can hide?"

"I do..."

Before Bret said where, Stone stopped him, putting his finger over his lips to warn him not to share the location.

Bret said, "You know the place, Prof."

Bret's parents had retired to a house they had owned for many years in North Norfolk, just outside a small village near the coast. Bret had often talked about it, reminiscing about the lapwings that nested in the eaves, and the trips in a motorboat out to Blakeney Point to see the seals basking on sandy islands and shingly shores. His dad, a keen sea fisherman, had bought a run-down cottage on a solid piece of land at the end of a single track that ran through the muddy Morston marshland. His clinker-built fishing boat was moored just beyond the house. Many times, Bret had pushed out from the shore with his father, dropping the lines beyond the estuaries and out at sea. They had pulled up mackerel and cod, returning to the cottage to gut and cook them in a cast-iron frying pan on a camping stove in the garden at the back. Bret loved to be near the sea, within range of the wind-instrumental music of boats shuddering in the breeze. He had chosen Portsmouth not just because he had set his heart on learning from Stone, but because he also needed the therapeutic power of the ocean.

"Promise me you'll lie low," Stone said.

Bret nodded.

"I'm sorry," Stone said, his voice almost inaudible.

"For what?"

"For putting you in danger."

"It was my choice, Prof. I could have said no."

"You never say no."

Bret smiled. "Not to you, Prof."

"Exactly. So, I'm not sure the university authorities will see things as kindly as you do."

"Well, they can kiss my ..." Bret did not finish his sentence. In an impressive display of Show Don't Tell, he swivelled around and thrust his backside out towards the camera.

Stone allowed himself a small smile while Billie dragged Bret off to his bed, apologizing as she left, blaming this unveiling of Bret's six o'clock on the sedative he had been given.

Once the screen went blank again, he looked up at Maya. "It's my fault this happened," he said.

"No, it's mine," she said.

Stone headed to the door and as he crossed the threshold, he said, "This is so, so wrong."

23

THE DAMBUSTER

Stone shut the door to his room and sat down on his bed. Like everyone else who had stayed up, the concerns around Bret had caused his brain to function at such a heightened level he was finding it hard to climb down to a place of calm conducive to sleep. Yes, the relief at knowing Bret was going to survive the attack brought a tranquilising relief, but at the same time there was something at work that was more powerful than the mood-altering chemical activated in his brain. While the good news had brought a measure of stillness to his racing heart, there was fear rising too, and this was proving a more potent force in the battle between waking and sleeping.

As Stone was trying to relax, he heard a knock on the door. He uttered a sigh. "Come in," he said.

Maya entered.

"We need to talk," she said.

"About what?"

"About what you said when you left the room."

"I didn't say anything."

"You did. You said this was wrong."

"I wasn't aware of that."

"Well, you said it, Professor."

"I don't know what I meant."

"I think you do."

Stone uttered another loud sigh.

Maya continued. "You're thinking of giving up and going back to your university, aren't you?"

Stone was silent.

"I'll quite understand if you wanted to do that. George Hailey isn't a relative. You have no personal or family reason for you to keep persevering with this. No one will blame you for going home after what's happened to Bret."

"You don't understand," Stone said.

"Then explain it to me."

"It's not easy to talk about."

"Let me help you then." Maya sat on the floor and looked up into Stone's eyes. There was concern there. Compassion too. "I can say what I'm about to say because I'm intimately acquainted with the subject I'm about to describe. So here goes. It's okay, Professor, to feel afraid, just so long as you admit it."

"What makes you think I'm afraid, Maya?"

"Everyone's afraid, deep down."

"So, what am I afraid of? Do you think I'm afraid of dying, or of death? Is that what you think?"

"No, Professor."

"Then what?"

"Listen, we both have something in common. We have lost our grandfathers. Mine was lost in a time of war. Yours in a time of peace. We share a comparable bereavement, although you were so much closer to yours than I was to mine."

"So?"

"In both our cases, these deaths resulted in us feeling afraid. Ever since your grandfather breathed his last breath, you've been afraid of losing someone you care about. That's made you distant and detached in your relationships..."

"Speak for yourself!" Stone interjected.

"Yes. I admit it!" Maya cried. "I'm afraid, and I keep my distance too. But my fear is different from yours, so we are not the same. You're scared of losing someone you know. I'm scared of knowing someone I've lost. That's the difference."

"What are you on about?"

"Unlike you, I never knew my grandfather. He's been a figure shrouded in mist. An unknown. My fear was that all this research we've been doing would reveal that he was a man I'd end up disrespecting, disliking even. And because I thought I'd be able to tell his story to my daddy, I was terrified that we would discover that he was a source of shame, not honour."

"I'm sorry, Maya. I didn't know."

"That's because I didn't tell you. But I'm telling you now. And what I want you to do is tell me about your fear too."

Stone frowned. "I'm not used to this kind of thing."

Maya waited, but Stone did not continue. "Tell me what you felt on the day your grandfather died," she said.

Stone did not want to answer.

But Maya waited.

"I felt what I'd felt twice before."

"When?"

"When my father left, and my mother died."

"Can you give a name to that feeling?"

"I felt abandoned."

"By your grandfather?"

"Yes, Maya. By my father and mother too. What is it you Americans say? Three strikes and you're out?"

Maya nodded.

"Well, I'd let abandonment take a swipe at me twice before, but when my grandfather died, that was the third and last time I was going to let it affect me."

"So, you decided to stop feeling."

"It's safer that way."

"And that's why you became a university academic and embraced a scientific mindset in your work, because it prioritizes detachment and frowns on attachments."

"In part, yes, although..."

Stone paused. He had never said what he was about to say to anybody else before.

"I also wanted to make him proud."

Stone wanted to say more, but he could not speak. He was overwhelmed by emotions he had not experienced in years. It was like Maya's questions were bombarding the defences he had built around his heart. One by one they struck the hard concrete walls of the dam. One by one, like the bouncing bombs of Barnes Wallace, their reverberations produced cracks in the walls.

If he let her continue, Stone knew that the tall, thick levy he had built would be breached and breached for good. Already he sensed the fissures increasing, widening, extending, tearing away the architecture of his cold indifference. If he allowed it to continue, the vast lough of sadness that he had held at bay for over twenty years would burst through the broadening apertures in his defences, flooding his heart, causing him to lose the one thing he had relied upon for many years to keep the wild tsunami at bay...

Control.

"This is why what happened to Bret has been a secret devastation," Maya said. "It's triggered the trauma of your grandfather's death and reactivated the lie you believed when you felt the agony of separation from his love, his wise and wonderful love."

Stone could not stop the tears now. The control was going. The walls of the dam were falling.

Stone knew that what Maya was saying was true. He had been living in abject and hidden fear since the day his grandfather had died. That first night without him, when Grandad had not come up the stairs and sat on his bed, when he had not read to him or prayed for him, when he had not held his hand or hugged him, Cameron Stone had not only switched off the light; he had switched off his emotions. He could not trust himself to care about someone he knew well ever again. To feel love for someone else meant opening himself up to the possibility... no, the probability... of living in the pitch-black agony of absence – a terrifying realm whose darkness was thicker than the peat-stained waters of Lough Erne, and whose currents were stronger and more deadly too. Never had he sensed the hollowness of life like he had that night – the chill of sensing that he was all alone not only in the house where he had felt so safe, but in the universe as well.

"And what was the lie you came to believe when you felt the pain of your grandfather's passing?"

Stone was unaware that Maya was sitting next to him now, her arm around his shoulders, her eyes upon his heart. So lost was he in the furious waters of his sadness that he was only aware of naming the lie. Somehow, above the of grief and rage, he said, "I believed that everyone I love will end up leaving me like Grandad did."

"And you made a promise, an inner vow, to yourself, Professor. What was that promise?"

"That I would never love anyone again."

Maya waited before she asked her next question. "I know this is hard, and I realise you may not want to do it, but can you find it in your heart to forgive your grandfather?"

Stone knew she was right. If he wanted to be whole, he had to let go of his resentment. He wanted to function not just with his trained intellect, but with a full range of healthy emotions. His wholeness was contingent upon his forgiveness.

So, one by one, he forgave them – first his father, then his mother, before finally turning to his grandfather. When he was done, Maya had one more question.

"If your grandfather was here, what would you want to tell him? You can speak as if he's in the room."

Stone paused, then said, "Granddad. I know you didn't mean to leave me. I know it wasn't your fault. I'm sorry that I've been angry with you. I miss you, Grandad. I miss you so much. I would do anything just to have one more goodnight hug from you."

Maya squeezed his shoulder. "Well done," she whispered, holding back her own tears now.

Without a word, she got up and left.

Stone did not bother changing into his pyjamas. He was

exhausted. He lay on his bed and closed his eyes. He could sense the serenity that had followed his deliverance. It had come upon him like a fresh golden dawn after a long night of turbulence and noise.

He opened his eyes and looked up at the ceiling,

"Goodnight Grandad," he whispered.

And then he slept.

LETTER 14

Monday March 20th, 1944

My Darling Myra,

I am growing more and more uncertain that you will ever receive any of these letters. My guard is a good man, a military policeman from Alabama; he tells me more than he probably should. He has given me some indications that my explanation of what happened on the 15th of March has been questioned and rejected. The authorities, it seems, don't believe my story. I am preparing now for a military trial conducted somewhere here in the barracks.

Yesterday, a young white American officer called Crosby visited me in my cell. He has no experience acting as a defense counsel, and no experience representing a black serviceman. Although he is well meaning and likeable, I fear he is out of his depth. I cannot help thinking this may be why he has been chosen for the task.

It does not fill me with hope.

One of the things he explained to me is that the charge

has now been fixed. I have been accused of violating the 92nd Article of War by killing a man – a man I was trying to prevent causing harm to a girl he was about to rape in an air-raid shelter. This means that my defense – that this was an accident, entirely unintended – now needs to be proven by my counsel. The prosecution is arguing that I killed him with "malice aforethought." I wrote to you in my previous letter what really happened. He came at me with a knife. I blocked his thrust with my arm. Then, instinctively, I hit back, reversing the knife. It struck him in the throat, and he died shortly afterwards. I acted in self-defense, but I am accused of premeditated murder.

I cannot describe how this has made me feel. I sense that those in authority - who I depend on for justice - have already made up their minds about my guilt, that they intend to deal with me severely, and that my case is going to be kept quiet so as not to fan the already existing flames of racial tension between white and black US servicemen. Add to this the fact that things are tense between the British government and the Irish population, and that the dead guy was a Catholic Irishman, and you can understand why I think these thoughts.

I asked my counsel if there had been any eyewitnesses. I told him I was sure I had heard doors closing on Earl Street and that there must have been someone out that night who saw what happened. He said that the M.P.s had been to all the houses within sight of the shelter and that their investigations had proved fruitless.

I then asked about the girl.

"It's as if she's disappeared into thin air," he said. "There's no trace of her. When the M.P.s went to the Diamond

Bar to question the barman, he said he had never seen her before. He also said he couldn't recall what her companion was like."

"I'm guessing he remembered me, though."

"You were rather conspicuous that night, Hailey."

"I was a black man in a white bar, sir."

"I was thinking more of your uniform."

"Then what about the dead guy, sir?"

"What about him?"

"Who was he?"

"His name and address are known, but not much else. I suspect he was a local pimp, that he was trying to entice the young woman into his employment, that she probably agreed because she was poor, and that he was forcing her to show him personally what she might be able to offer to men in search of gratification."

"You *suspect*, sir?"

"Yes, Hailey. I have no evidence at all, even though that's the picture I intend to paint. Unfortunately, it seems the two others in that shelter lived in the shadows."

"What about the M.P.s who arrested me?"

"They arrived after the event. They saw you appear from the shelter holding a knife covered in blood. They then found the deceased. They assumed you had murdered him."

I understood why they had done that. African American soldiers are known to carry Jack Knives on them, mainly for protection against attacks from white GIs. The fact that I never owned nor carried such a weapon doesn't seem to cut any ice with anybody.

"What about my uniform, sir?" I protested.

"What about it?"

"Don't you have the evidence of that technician, fourth grade, from the 12th Military Police – the Criminal Investigation Section. What was the guy called?"

Crosby looked at his notes. "Herbert Nash."

"Nash, yes."

"What about him?"

"He took my tunic and shirt. They had a tear from the knife. If the knife had been mine, why would I have a slash from it on my own clothes? That is important evidence."

"I've some bad news, Hailey."

My heart sank.

I could have told him what he was about to say.

"An agent took it off Nash to the 317th Station Hospital where it was to be subjected to a Benzidine blood test by a captain from the medical corps. Unfortunately, the agent says they were confused with another parcel of evidence to do with another case that night. The other materials yielded nothing, and the agent was told to dispose of it. Unfortunately, he burned yours instead."

I put my head in my hands.

Sighed.

Fought back the tears.

The captain changed the subject. "I've one more question, Hailey, to do with when you were charged."

"Sir?"

"I see here from my papers that you were warned of your rights under Article 24 of War at the headquarters of the 626th Ordinance Ammunition Company."

"Yes, sir."

"And that this warning was issued by Staff Sergeant O'Connor in the presence of a constable of the Royal Ulster

Constabulary, a Constable Ray. Is this correct?"

"Yes, sir. It is."

"And a statement was dictated by you to him about the events that transpired that night?"

"Yes, sir."

"And was this dictation done without force? Was what you said to them uttered voluntarily?"

"Yes, sir. Voluntarily."

"And you read it carefully before you signed it?"

"I did, sir."

The fresh-faced, boyish-looking officer looked disappointed. There was no hiding it.

"Is there a problem, sir?"

"Well, Hailey, if there had been coercion, that would have raised questions about due process."

"There was no coercion. I gave that statement and signed it freely. The staff sergeant told me he was from the States too. He put me at my ease. That's the truth, sir."

It was the counsel's turn to sigh.

"May I ask you something, sir?"

He nodded.

"Can you let my former skipper know what's happened to me? He will vouch for my good character as a man and my service as a second pilot with him on the Lady."

My counsel bowed his head.

"I'm afraid I have more bad news. Your crew went out on a mission on the night of March 15th. They never came back. It's assumed they crashed in Lough Erne."

My head began to spin.

I felt myself freefalling.

Without a parachute.

"I'll come back tomorrow," Crosby said as he placed his notes in a brown briefcase. "I'm so sorry for your loss. Truly. Your comrades served with distinction."

He placed his officer's cap on his head.

I somehow stood.

Saluted.

Then he was gone.

I was crushed and disoriented when the door of my cell slammed shut. I am all alone. My guard does what he can. My counsel too. But they are just small and powerless pieces in some larger landscape in which I, like a scapegoat, am being led out into the desert. How many of us will it take before a sufficiency of blood has been shed, before the ancient rage has been satisfied, before justice can come rolling on like the mighty Mississippi river in the Spring?

I am desperate.

Afraid.

I worry about Scratch.

Was he on the Lady when she crashed?

I worry for you.

Maybe you believe I'm dead too.

How anxious your heart must be.

I will continue writing in the hope that these letters will at last find their way into your hands, and that you will hold them to your heart and feel the beat of my undying love.

I promise I will tell you the truth. I will continue to write a faithful account of everything that happens to me, in the hope that one day every injustice and lie will be reversed, and that this stain of racial hatred will eventually be washed away in the blood of all those who have paid the supreme price for freedom.

Pray with me for that day, my beloved.

I know you feel the fire of it too.

It burns in us both.

It is unquenchable.

You and your mother have borne the brunt of many injustices from your oppressors.

We stand together, you and me.

We dream together too.

I love you.

Forever.

I am always yours.

Your beloved,

George.

24

THE JOURNALIST

Siobhan Lavery was not expecting to receive a special delivery at her office at the Belfast Times, but when she did, it was to change her life. Once across the threshold, the courier with the parcel took off a matt-black helmet to reveal a short pixie haircut - half blonde, half black. Having studied Siobhan's press pass, the rider asked in a southern accent for a signature and then left. Siobhan, impressed by the young rider's vibe, hoped that the contents of the package were striking too. Putting her cup of flat-white coffee on a coaster, she started to open the sandy coloured envelope. As she wrestled with the adhesive, Siobhan noticed that her fifty-year-old skin was showing the first shadowy indications of age spots, in stark contrast to the clear hands of the fine-looking rider who had just departed.

Siobhan emptied the Jiffy parcel onto a mousepad. In front of her lay a Farraday pouch containing a memory stick and a Motorola phone. Removing the stick from its casing, she inserted it into the dock of her laptop. A woman appeared on the screen. She had an East Coast accent. Around thirty years of age. She didn't use a script; she seemed comfortable speaking off-the-cuff.

"My name is Maya Hailey. I'm currently hiding here in Northern Ireland because there are certain people who don't want me to tell my story. I am the granddaughter of Second Lieutenant George Hailey, a courageous African American pilot based at RAF Castle Archdale, Lough Erne in World War 2. He flew missions through the Donegal Corridor into the Atlantic to counter the U-Boat threat.

When his Catalina crashed in 1944, March 15th, everyone assumed my grandfather had been on board, killed with the rest of his crew. He wasn't. His fate was perhaps even more traumatic. That same night, he was wrongfully arrested for murder in Belfast. His subsequent trial at a Belfast barracks was a terrible, racially motivated injustice. My grandfather was sentenced to death by hanging.

My family knew nothing of these events until a few days ago when the letters my grandfather wrote during his trial were discovered in a buried container on one of the small islands of Lough Erne. These letters provide evidence of what the US military authorities covered up at the time, and what government agencies are still covering up today – a lynching disguised as a legal execution.

I am in hiding with an English professor of history – a leading expert on the Tuskegee airmen, currently conducting research into African American service personnel in Northern Ireland in World War 2. Attempts have been made on his life, and his assistant. We have had to go underground to stay safe.

If you are interested in this story, in the package you'll

find a hacker burner phone that you can use without our conversations being traced. If you choose to help us, we will give you transcripts of the letters sent by my grandfather. There are eighteen in total - twelve while he was fighting in the Battle of the Atlantic, all addressed to his father in the States. The remaining six are to a Northern Irish Catholic girl, Myra. She was the love of his life and his fiancée. She was pregnant with their child while he was writing from prison, effectively from death row. That child was my father. He died just days ago.

We know you are the US correspondent for the Belfast Times, and that you have considerable experience when it comes to covering wars and helping whistleblowers.

We would appreciate your help."

End of clip.

Shiobhan picked up her desk phone and dialled for her assistant. "Hi Clarence, please add an item to the agenda for 10.00am. Something's come up and I'd like the team to see it."

"Sure."

Siobhan downloaded the film clip to her laptop and then placed both the phone and the memory stick in a small dark safe resembling a hotel minibar. Half an hour later, her boss – Richard O'Leary – was hosting their daily editorial meeting in the middle of a long wooden table in the boardroom. When the agenda reached A.O.B., he noticed Shiobhan's item and handed the room over to her. She linked her laptop to the wall-mounted screen and lowered the lights and blinds. Everyone adjusted their seats for an optimum view of the screen.

"This was brought by a courier earlier," she said.

Without any more introduction, Shiobhan pressed play and Maya Hailey began to speak.

A few minutes later, the clip finished, and Siobhan closed the lid of her laptop. There was a hush. She looked around the table at the five members of the team, and Clarence whom she had invited to come with her to the meeting.

"Thoughts?"

"Is Maya credible?"

The question came from Richard.

"It's too early to say. I only received this earlier. From the brief digging I've done, she seems legit. From the East Coast of the States. She's the daughter of a Pentecostal bishop, recently deceased, as she says. She herself is a former pastor. Divorced. I don't have any reasons to doubt her integrity."

"If you're satisfied at this stage," Richard said, "the key question is whether her story is true. If her grandfather really was subjected to a great wrong, as she claims, and if he was effectively lynched, then this could be a huge news story."

Clarence added, "Especially in the wake of George Floyd's murder, and the global reaction."

Richard nodded.

"This is why I wanted Clarence here," Shiobhan said, turning to her assistant. "Do you have any insights?"

"Other than the fact that she and I are African Americans, you mean?" Clarence's tone was respectful, but there was a hint of feistiness in it too. Shiobhan smiled. This is why she had voted for Clarence to be her apprentice when he was interviewed. Although he was half her age, he was not just conscientious, he also had the kind of wisdom forged from personal adversity – the kind of wisdom that she could never bring to the table. Scarred, yet luminous truth.

"Other than that, Clarence. Yes," she said.

"She has a Boston accent. And she's got fire in her bloodshot eyes. First impressions, she's genuine."

"Is that enough?" Richard asked.

"It may not be," Clarence answered.

"Why do you say that?"

"Let's say we are persuaded by George Hailey's letters that he was as innocent as he says. These, on their own, may not be sufficient. They may come across as the truth, but even in this post-Floyd world, black folks back home in the States can still be disbelieved, even when we are telling the truth."

"We need corroboration," Siobhan muttered.

Clarence nodded. "Precisely. It won't be enough to tell Maya's story. We'll need a credible eyewitness at the very least, and she's said nothing about that."

The room fell quiet.

It was several seconds before Clarence spoke again. This time his tone was softer. "Any of you folks seen the film, *Just Mercy*? There are two quotations I liked in it. The first was this, uttered by Jamie Fox on death row. 'You're guilty from the moment you're born.' In my country, people like me start life way behind white folks. It's just the way it is. George Hailey would have known that. He would also have known how much more would have been required of him evidentially if he was to stand any chance of acquittal."

He paused and took a sip of water.

"That's the bad news. The good news is another quote. 'It's not too late for justice.' If you want to know what I think, I think we should give Maya a chance to tell us everything she knows about her grandfather. And if her story crosses our evidentiary threshold, then we should tell

George Hailey's story to the world."

Richard asked, "Casting all personal views aside, are you sure this story is in the public interest?"

Clarence nodded. "I think we have a duty to expose crime and serious impropriety."

"But what if that violates our duty to protect public health and safety?" Richard countered.

"In what way?"

"What if telling this story inflames public protests in the States and elsewhere, leading to violence?"

Siobhan now spoke. "But isn't it more damaging for society if we fail to tell the truth? If this story turns out to be true and we suppress it, how damaging is that to our democracy?"

There was a murmur around the table, and several utterances of the word, "very."

"I agree," Richard said. He looked around the room. Everyone nodded. "One final thing. I have a duty of care to all of you, and everyone else working for the Times. If Maya and this professor are in danger, if they're having to stay underground, if an attempt has been made on at least one of their lives, then that means we may be putting ourselves at risk investigating this."

Richard ran his pale hand over his grey beard.

"If these threats are real, who's behind them? And if they find out we're covering this story, will that make us a target?"

There was silence in the room.

"For the time being, we keep this story a secret," Richard said. "What's been said in this room stays in this room."

After Richard had completed the remaining A.O.B. items on the staff agenda, Siobhan returned to her office with

Clarence. She beckoned to him to shut the door.

"Right, let's make a list. What do we need?"

"The eighteen letters," Clarence replied. "Or at least transcripts of them. These are our first-hand accounts."

Siobhan said, "We need one of the originals, at least, if we are to confirm the reliability of the documents. We'll also need to do some meticulous fact checking."

Clarence sighed.

"What's up?"

"We're still going to be faced with the challenge of corroborating George's story. We can't rely on a single source in a tale like this. But that's our problem. I mean, if this whole episode was as secret as Maya says, then finding people to verify and validate her grandfather's account is very likely going to be nearly impossible, especially eight decades after the events themselves."

"There must be someone out there," Siobhan said.

"Even if there is, you've got to remember how powerful fear can be in preventing people from coming forward. I mean, what kind of protection can we offer them?"

Siobhan nodded and said, "Maya's desperate, but we mustn't sacrifice accuracy on the altar of urgency."

Clarence sat down in an armchair. He stared at a row of books on media law. He said, "I suspect we're not going to find any court transcripts of George Hailey's trial."

"Even if they exist," Shiobhan said, "they're very likely going to be hidden in some vault somewhere."

"Do you believe she's telling the truth?" Clarence asked.

Siobhan answered, "Do you remember a story that broke here a few weeks ago about a World War 2 seaplane being discovered at the bottom of Lough Erne?"

"I do. It was the same kind George Hailey flew."

"Yes, and I don't think that's a coincidence."

"What do you mean?"

"Well, it could explain why, all of a sudden, certain parties are so interested in him."

"You believe Maya's story, then?"

Siobhan walked to the desk, picked up the burner, and turned to Clarence. "I'm going to phone her and arrange a private meeting. Want to come along?"

"Hell, yeah!"

She dialled the one number stored in the Motorola Moto G7 phone. After several rings, she heard a voice the other end of the phone. It was the same she had heard twice that same morning.

"Maya Hailey speaking."

"Maya, my name is Siobhan Lavery."

"Thanks for calling me back."

"That's okay. I thought I'd let you know that I showed your clip to a few of my colleagues. I'm keen to meet you as soon as possible."

"How about tomorrow afternoon?" Maya asked.

Siobhan turned to Clarence and gave him a knowing glance. He raised his eyebrows and shook his head.

"That should be fine. Could you bring copies of the letters?"

"Sure."

"And one of the originals, just for me to check?"

"Yes, Ma'am."

"Maya, I just need to say at this point that I can't give a guarantee that we will publish. This is just an exploratory meeting. But if we can make it happen, we will."

"I understand."

Siobhan heard some muttering on the other end of the phone before Maya spoke again. "How about a neutral, public venue? Say, Café Nero near your offices? 4pm tomorrow?"

"Perfect. I'll bring my assistant Clarence if that's okay."

"I'll have Professor Stone with me too."

"One more thing, Maya... May I call you Maya?"

"Sure."

"We are concerned for your safety, and the Professor's, but the problem is we cannot guarantee these things any more than we can our own. Are you able to take precautions?"

"The professor and I are being looked after by someone who's an expert at that."

Siobhan could hear a man speaking in the background. Next thing, he was speaking to Siobhan.

"My name's Rory. I just want to check if you're familiar with a burner and how to use it."

"I'm happy for you to talk me through it."

"Okay," Rory said. "You'll see that I've stripped most of the apps, reconfigured all your security settings, and changed your browser. There's now no way the phone can be traced back to you, unless of course you start entering your own email and social media. Don't forget to leave your regular phone at home when you're traveling with your burner. Keep the burner in the Farraday pouch I sent you."

Siobhan chuckled.

"What's up?" Rory asked.

"It's just that this is all a long way from the old Nokia brick I used to be given for undercover jobs."

Rory laughed too.

He handed the phone back to Maya.

"See you tomorrow at 4pm," Siobhan said. She waited for a reply but there was none.

"She did that thing you do," she said, turning to Clarence.

"What?"

"Ended the conversation without saying goodbye."

Clarence chuckled. "Keep it brief," he replied. "Wasn't it you who taught me that?"

This time it was Siobhan's turn to smile. But in her heart, she was not smiling. If the story they had been told was true, there would be attempts to suppress it. And those attempts might extend to suppressing them as well, and this would not be the first time a journalist had paid the supreme price.

Siobhan cast an eye towards a framed photo on the wall above her desk. It showed her and a friend called Pauline outside a Belfast restaurant just days before Pauline was murdered. Pauline had not only been a friend. She had been a fellow journalist.

As she stared at the two of them - arm in arm, carefree, laughing, hopeful – a tear began to form. Pauline seemed to be looking straight at her and smiling in her almost childlike way.

Siobhan made her decision. She would, of course, be careful, but right now, she wanted to be a truth seeker and a truthteller like her late friend. She wanted to make Pauline proud.

LETTER 15

Wednesday March 22nd, 1944

My Beloved Myra,

The trial began today. I was awakened early this morning and given a bowl of breakfast by my guard, Franky. He shut the cell door behind him when he entered, sat on my bed next to me while I was polishing my shoes, and shared that my counsel would be here within the hour to take me upstairs to the courtroom. He said, "I'm so very sorry what's happening to you, my brother." He put his hand on my shoulder before he rose and left the cell.

There are some good white folks in this world.

I should remember that.

When my counsel arrived, I had barely eaten. I had little appetite. Lieutenant Crosby led me out of the cell with an armed escort. It's hard to describe how humiliating this was. As a native son, I have given my all to defending my country. Now this.

When I ascended from the cells in the basement, I was

led to a door a few yards down the corridor. The top half of it was made of glass – the kind you cannot see through. Entering, I counted twenty people. They fell silent the moment I stepped over the threshold. All eyes were on me. Except mine. Mine were trained on the grey-haired man in military uniform sitting on a simple wooden chair behind a long table. He was at the front of the chamber. There were legal books with dusty covers in front of him. I could tell that he was a senior US army officer. I could see no one from RAF Archdale.

Franky led me to a chair at a smaller table and whispered for me to remain standing. As he checked my handcuffs, he shook part of my hand in a gesture of solidarity. I was resisting the overwhelming sense of isolation but doing it poorly, so I was grateful for that. When my counsel joined me, he sat down but told me to stay standing. Even within their metal restraints, my hands were trembling.

"The accused is charged with the violation of the 92nd Article of War." A court official was reading from a typed sheet of paper. The specification of the charge followed. "Second Lieutenant George Hailey, formerly of the Royal Canadian Airforce, serving at RAF Castle Archdale, but now a pilot in the United States American Air Force, did at Belfast, Northern Ireland, on the night of March 15th 1944 - with malice aforethought, willfully, deliberately, feloniously, unlawfully, and with premeditation - kill one Gerald O'Connolly, a human being, by stabbing him in the throat with a sharp instrument." He asked for my plea. "Not guilty," I replied. I was then invited to sit.

Crosby, my defense counsel, was asked by the judge if I had any previous convictions, to which he said no. After that, the prosecution – older than my counsel – set about proving my guilt in relation to both the charge and its specification.

The day passed in something of a blur, I found myself staring out of the one window near me, gazing at an oak tree in the center of the parade ground, watching a family of Linnets chasing each other around the branches. I couldn't help thinking of one of our favorite poems – 'The Lake Isle of Innisfree'. You introduced me to it when we were rowing over to the Lady one evening. Do you remember? How I long for the tranquil waters of Lough Erne. I long for it as Yeats's heart ached for the island of heather where peace dropped, oh so slowly, from the veils of the morning. I long to live with you in such a place, waking up to the low sound of the lapping water, watching the Linnets spread their wings and search for food in the branches of the trees. The longer the day went on, the more I found myself imagining my head on your lap, your soft marble hands stroking my hair, banishing my fears of marauding submarines and sinking ships.

By the time the day's proceedings had finished, sometime in the late afternoon, the prosecution had summarized their evidence and called all four of the M.P.s who arrested me outside the air-raid shelter. My counsel interrogated each of them too, seeking to call into question their presuppositions of my guilt. Try as he might, Crosby could not get any of them to admit that there might have been some truth in my version of events. They all remained convinced that the knife in my hand belonged to me, that I had used it to kill the victim, and that the act was deliberate, not accidental. I could not help thinking of some lines of T.S. Eliot, ones I read the last time I was with you in the reading room at Enniskillen. "Between the idea and the reality there falls a shadow." How deep is the shadow between the idea these men have of events and the reality of what transpired. If only someone could dispel the shadows of prejudice, ignorance, and misinterpretation. Crosby seems ill-fitted to direct some light into these cavernous minds.

After all this, I was returned to my cell where Crosby reviewed the first day's events. His account did not fill me with confidence. I asked him what his tactics are for tomorrow.

"At the moment, it's the prosecution's place to present their evidence for the charge and the specification. My task is to respond to their claims. After that, it will be our turn."

I did not have either the energy or the motivation to question him. After he had gone, and I had grazed on my evening meal, I lay on the bed and read the book by Oscar Wilde that Franky had leant me. I found myself saying the words of Psalm 130, "Out of the depths have I cried unto thee, O LORD. Lord, hear my voice: let thine ears be attentive to the voice of my supplications."

I succumbed to my exhaustion and dreamed that my prison cell had become the interior of a dimly lit submarine. I sensed the oppressive closeness of the walls, the suffocating lack of fresh air, the chilling atmosphere of constant peril. I woke with sudden and uninvited sensations of regret and guilt for my part in the Lady's assaults upon the U-Boats in the Atlantic. I thought of the men trapped beneath the waves in that confined and perilous space, unable to do anything other than wait for the inevitable caving in of the hull and the flooding of the metal tube they had inhabited. Maybe they were men like me, desperate to get back home, aching to fall into the arms of the one they loved. I am ashamed to say that until now I have not given these matters any proper thought but within my own place of grim restriction, I am overwhelmed with pity for them as I think of how they fought and scraped for just one more breath. Maybe my own incarceration and affliction are my punishment. Maybe this is the true charge of murder laid against me. Maybe all I can do is accept my fault, and the fate that accompanies it. Maybe this is justice after all.

I tried, on awakening, to read some more of Wilde's reflections from his time in prison, but our situations are not the same and there are only brief moments of enlightening consolation - like the striking of a match which releases a momentary flare, before burning the bearer as the flame dies between his fingers.

That is why I am writing this letter to you. I long to hear your voice, and your heart, my beloved. I have been writing about myself throughout this letter. But you are my true preoccupation. What must you be thinking, feeling, doing? You must believe that I perished with my crew when the Lady crashed into the lough. How you must be grieving – grieving not just the fact that I am no longer with you, but the way we parted the last time we saw each other. As I reflect on these things, the closeness of my own walls and the threat of my destruction become small indeed. You are my planet earth, my vast unfathomable universe. Without you, life is without form and void.

I wish I could see you.

That would be light indeed.

I love you always.

George.

25

THE NOOSE

Agent Miller had spent many years staking out houses during the Cold War, but keeping watch on the Fermanagh farm was proving to be an altogether different challenge. Maybe it was in part his awareness of the waning of his own faculties – ones that he had for so long taken for granted - but when the sun appeared, Miller uttered a long sigh. As the cloud of his breath made its way towards the windscreen, he wiped the sleep from his eyes, taking care to keep his focus on the laptop with its view of the farm, waiting for any signs of human life. There had been none during the watches of the night.

If Miller had underestimated his prey before this new dawn, there was no chance of him doing that again thereafter. He sensed there was far more to this farm and its grounds than met the eye. He had seen Hailey and Stone, and their new friends, entering, but now it was as if they had disappeared into thin air.

Where had they gone?

Having consumed an energy drink, Miller conducted some research on his laptop. The farm belonged to a woman called Birgit. A Norwegian by birth, she had lived alone in Northern Ireland for three decades. Delving some more, he learned that her father Hakon had been a businessman who had made his fortune drilling in the rich oilfields off the west coast of Norway. Opening two more windows, he discovered that Hakon and his wife Catherine had been killed when their private jet had lost control over Hardanger Fjord and plunged into the icy waters below. There had been no survivors.

Birgit, an only child, was in her twenties at the time. She had been working for her father but already decided to travel a different path. Miller watched a short TV interview in which she talked about her new direction after the tragedy.

"It was not so much that my loss caused me to go a different way. My grief simply put an end to any indecision I had about that. I am predisposed to be suspicious of powerful companies. I see quickly how they can be manipulated to serve political ideologies that oppress rather than liberate. My grief confirmed the need to leave this sphere. It did not cause it. From then on, I was in no doubt about replanting my soul in a land and lifestyle different from the one I'd known."

This last comment piqued Miller's curiosity. He typed away for a few more minutes before finding an interview with a reporter who was telling stories of people who had moved from other parts of the world to begin a new life on the Emerald Isle.

"But why Northern Ireland?" the reporter asked her.

"My mother came from Lough Erne," Birgit replied.

"But I thought your parents were Norwegian."

"My father was."

"Your mother was a Fermanagh girl?"

"She was."

"And you moved here to keep that connection alive?"

"Partly that. Partly also because I am inspired by the way the Irish saints saved this continent from a great darkness. I am intrigued by these maternal ancestors of mine."

The reporter asked, "Have you read Timothy Cahill's book, *How the Irish Saved Western Civilization*?"

"Maybe I have been influenced a little by the good things in it, but I had already come to my own conclusions during the many conversations I had with my mother about the Celtic Christian saints. We both admired their courage and their commitment."

"Is that why you're called Birgit?"

"My mother was the one who insisted I was named after one of the pioneering female saints. My father backed down in the end. I think he wanted to call me Freya."

The reporter chuckled and then grew serious again. "So, what is it you want to do here in Ireland?"

"I want to create an oasis of peace in a world of chaos."

"A kind of commune?"

"No. I'm not really a kibbutz person. My personality type is far too introspective. People annoy me quickly."

"Then what?"

"I have a dream to create a self-sufficient farm – somewhere that people who don't annoy me can share my resources in order to survive what I believe is coming."

"You mean the apocalypse?"

"Whatever it is, it will be something that requires ordinary people to do extraordinary things."

"Like what?"

"Like carve out a life that is not controlled by corrupt institutions and big corporations, a life more deeply connected to the land from which we have become so tragically alienated. A life in which the Nordic and the Irish in me can be combined."

"So, you're a survivalist."

Birgit laughed, then said, "According to Darwin, every human being is a survivalist."

"A prepper then?"

"We could all do with being more prepared," Birgit said, beginning to move away from the reporter. She turned before she left and said to him, "Everyone today talks about living for 'the moment'. But I believe we need to prepare for the future as well, otherwise there may not be any moments for us to live in."

Miller switched the heating on in the car, directing a stream of warm air to the windows, removing the fog and condensation that had accumulated during the interview.

He was clearer now.

Birgit's farm was much more than it appeared. According to his calculations, she had lived there for over two decades. Further research on his laptop revealed that she had not requested any planning permission for the existing buildings in the grounds. This meant that there had been no visible alterations to the farm. Everything was the same as it had been before she had bought the property. This could only mean one thing. If she had developed the site, she had gone underground. Everything that she had wanted to do to the place was invisible, not visible. As the sole inheritor of her parent's estate, she had the funds to do anything she liked. And such subterranean enhancements could be done in secret.

The more he thought about it, the more convinced Agent Miller became about his theory. The entire space was protected by an impressive array of lights at night – lights that were activated by touch. This touch had to be of a certain weight. Rodents or birds did not trigger the searchlights. Only something or someone with sufficient heft. A man. A woman. A child even.

And then there were the two large bats. Miller had sensed from their first attack that these were not real. His drone had been attacked by sophisticated robots. These formed part of the defensive array in and around the farm. They were nocturnal guardians, designed to intercept and destroy airborne intruders.

The evidence was conclusive.

Birgit was a dangerous adversary. She had a facility that even Miller found impressive, and she was protecting Hailey and Stone. These three were underground with the others – Rory, the sixty-year-old man with ginger hair and a ruddy face; Jack, the very elderly man whose mind was far more agile than his physique, and whose knowledge of Lough Erne during World War 2 was second to none. Only the young assistant called Brett was absent. Miller had so nearly managed to dispatch him. Bret was now somewhere in hiding.

But what were they planning?

Miller knew that they had made a covert trip several nights before to one of the islands. Accessing files from his own base at Menwith Hill, he found satellite footage for the night and the location in question. Sure enough, the targets had headed by boat for one of the many islands. They had alighted at a small jetty and walked along the wooden pathway to the banks at the bottom of a hill. They had walked up a thin track, through a thicket of trees, and stopped outside an enclosure with some ruins, including a tall, ancient cross.

As Miller stared at the grainy black-and-white footage, he saw the group move around the side of the enclosed, locked space until they were just beyond the cross. One of them, the ginger-haired man, began digging for something just outside the fence.

Minutes later, he lifted a box from the dirt.

He filled in the hole and the group returned to the boat.

They then motored back to Birgit's farm.

What was in that box?

Miller considered the options and, in the end, landed on two. The first was that it contained accounts of the court proceedings against George Hailey. Miller dismissed this. He knew there was only one record, and these papers were buried so far down in the deepest of restricted vaults that it would take an eternity for a stranger to find them. The second was that this box contained documents of a less formal nature, ones perhaps written by George Hailey during his time on trial, his time awaiting his execution. Maybe a journal. Maybe some scribbled notes. Maybe some poems. Maybe even letters.

As he considered the final possibility, he shuddered. If Hailey and Stone had discovered letters written by George Hailey – letters betraying details of the injustice to which he was subjected – the consequences would be catastrophic if the press were to hear of it.

As this thought dawned on him more and more, he realized that he had probably arrived, via some sound inferences, at something corresponding to the reality.

If that was the case, Hailey and Stone had one obvious and inevitable option – to approach a journalist with experience of this kind of story, a journalist working at a newspaper that would be respected around the world if it went to press.

That was it.

The next step.

Hailey and Stone would be talking to the media.

They might even have made first contact.

Miller accessed more files on his laptop. He was looking for any trace of emails or phone calls from the group to a media outlet. But there was none. The group had either not yet reached out to the press, or they had found ways of covering their tracks.

The more Miller thought about which one of these was the case, the more he had to force himself to respect the fact that these two, under the tutelage of the survivalist from Norway, had learned how to communicate off the grid.

Miller took out his phone and dialled the number of his boss at the Pentagon. He typed in his ID number and waited for her to answer. On and on the phone rang. Why was she not picking up? Miller let it ring for another thirty seconds. Still no answer. He cussed. What on earth was she playing at?

Miller was about to hang up when he heard the click of someone joining the line. When they spoke, the voice was not his boss's. It was a man. And he sounded angry.

"Who is this?"

"Agent Miller. Where's the boss?"

"She's been retired."

Miller reeled.

"Who's her replacement?" he asked.

"This department's been shut down."

"But I'm in the field."

"I don't doubt you are, but there's no record of any current, covert operations running from this desk. At least, not ones I know about, authorised by the company."

"I need resources, backup."

"What you need, Agent Miller, is to return to Menwith Hill and get ready to be retired."

"I'd like to speak to my boss."

"I'm the boss."

"I mean my old boss."

"I told you... she's no longer working here."

"Why not?"

"That's a need-to-know matter, and you don't need to know."

Miller sighed. "Why are you so angry, sir?"

The voice at the other end went quiet. To Miller, the answer felt so long in coming he thought maybe the man had ended the call. But he had not. When he did reply, his words were not framed in the form of an answer but a question.

"My name is Harper. Does that name ring any bells?"

"No, why should it?"

"I anticipated you would say that, so let me refresh your memory. Perhaps you'll be less forgetful when I inform you that I had checked into that motel room where you placed a hangman's noose outside the door. You must remember the incident, Miller. The shockwaves went through the whole service."

"I don't know what you're talking about."

"I think you do."

"Listen Agent Harper..."

"Director Harper ..."

Miller raised his eyes, "Are you really telling me to stop my surveillance and return to Menwith Hill?"

"I am."

"Is this conversation being recorded?"

"It is."

"Then I want this to be on the record. There are two people now in possession of a story that, if shared through the global media, would cause great unrest back home."

"What kind of a story?"

"Let's just say it's one in which the US military comes out very badly. Very badly indeed."

Miller convinced himself that he had said just enough to bait the hook. It was now up to Harper to take it.

"If the story is one that I suspect it is," Harper said, "why would I not want it to be on the record? And why would I ever want to help a man like you to suppress it?"

Miller could not answer.

"Stop this maverick mission and report to Menwith Hill. I expect to hear that you're back there tomorrow. Then we'll fly you back for a debriefing. After that, you'll be retired."

There was another click.

Harper had gone.

But Miller did not care. The call had unnerved him, yes, but it had also energised him. He would not head back to base. He would not abandon his mission. This operation was the fitting conclusion to his story. He was not retired. He was refired.

LETTER 16

Thursday March 22nd, 1944

My Darling Myra,

Before I tell what happened today, know this: I love you more than my weak words could ever express. The constant ache I have just to see you is so intense I think some moments it may devour me from the inside out. The desire to simply be in your presence is utterly overwhelming. The longing to hold you in my arms is driving me insane, as is the need to dispel all the confusion and doubts you must be harboring about where I am and what has happened to me. If only I could speak to you and tell you the truth. But even if I could, what would I say that might bring reassurance and comfort? You think I am dead; I am sure of it. I was supposed to be on the Lady that night. What if you were to discover I am alive, but then face the possibility of me being found guilty of the charge and specification against me in this trial? How cruel for you to grieve my second death.

And that is the prospect which I see ahead of me. The

trial today has not gone well. My counsel decided to focus on one line of reasoning and one alone – that the charge of violating Article 92 be changed. The court refused to countenance that, so then he tried to get the phrase "malice aforethought" removed instead, hoping to lessen the sentence and commute what is increasingly looking like the death penalty to a prison term. He argued as best as he could that I was responding to a damsel in distress and I had no intention of killing the man, simply preventing him from doing her harm. That argument was dismissed too, so "malice aforethought" remains.

In my heart of hearts, I knew it would come to this – not a battle between my innocence or guilt, but a battle between one kind of guilt (premeditated murder) and another (manslaughter). It has never seemingly entered anyone's heads that I might be telling the truth, and that I acted with the best intentions on the night of March 15th. I have not been presumed innocent until proven guilty. I have been presumed guilty all along. The question is, guilty of what? Murder or manslaughter? So, you see why I am in such mental torment, my love. Whatever happens from here, it is either prison or hanging. If hanging, it will be no more or less than a lynching.

I look at the black-robed judge at the front, sitting with such a stern face as he listens to and weighs up the evidence. He has no idea what it is like to be prejudged because of the color of one's skin - and all the assumptions that follow from that. He sits with an entitled sense of privilege which he takes for granted, not even imagining for a second what it might be like to have all his advantages removed from him and to start the race of life much further back than others, all because of an accident of pigmentation. Can he even begin to imagine what this is like for someone like me?

No, he cannot.

Ultimately, this, like everything else on the race issue, boils down to a failure of imagination. When I use my God-given faculty of imagination, I think myself into another person's shoes, travelling down the same road they tread, seeking to understand what it is to walk in a landscape more barren and perilous than my own. The failure to do this, to even attempt to do this, is the great darkness of our age. We do not have the capacity or the willingness to see with another man's eyes, to think another man's thoughts, to tell another man's story. We are condemned for the poverty of our imaginations. I am now very likely condemned because of the deficit of imaginative energy in the life of the man who sits in judgment over me, and in whose hands the future course of what is left of my life now rests. This judge is not some kind of white savior, any more than Crosby is. For me, there is no way out, no pathway to deliverance, no highway to safety.

As the day wore on, the court agreed to what is called the *corpus delicti*. They agreed, in other words, that the crime was committed in the way the prosecution portrayed, based on the eyewitness testimonies of the four M.P.s. The girl who I was trying to help has not been found. No one even knows her name. She is the only one that could prove my story is true. But she fled the scene. If there is a white savior, it is this girl. She has the information, and with it, the power to prevent this miscarriage of justice. But if I am true to my own principles, and imagine life in her shoes, how likely is it that she will come forward? If she is a young woman facing a life of desperate poverty, and the choice to follow the dead man's profession was her only way out of it, then I can also imagine the circumstances in which she would not want this known. Maybe she is an Irish Catholic girl, and her family regards this way of life as shameful. Maybe she is protecting herself.

See the trap that poverty creates.

This is as true for your people as mine.

The prosecution keeps referring to me as "the colored American soldier." I have only ever been known by the Irish as a Yank, or an American fighting man. Now, in this military courtroom, my color is the focus of attention. The prosecution counsel also keeps describing my conduct that night as "unlawful" and as "without legal justification or excuse." He has, as I have already shared, succeeded in persuading the court that I acted with "malice aforethought." He was, I admit, clever here. He used legal arguments to show that malice does not mean spite or hostility but "a wrongful intention". He also argued from law that this malice was not something harbored before the man's death, but during it. He cited precedent for this, stating that "it is sufficient that it exists at the time the act is committed." See how words are used to manipulate. In the hands of sophisticated lawyers, words are like submarines – covert vessels of destruction.

My counsel had no counterargument for any of this, and therefore the judge ruled that it stay in the specification. I tried to whisper to him as the prosecution counsel was speaking.

"Sir, I am being accused of malice, but this is being used to indicate a depraved nature. Ask them if they would even think of such a thing if I was white, not black."

He was so alarmed by this idea that he insisted that I remain quiet for the rest of the day and that I permit him the courtesy of acting on my behalf without interruption or distraction.

From then on, it was more semantics. The court agreed that my act was malicious, and therefore homicide, even though there was no design or intent on my part to kill the man before I did.

I shook my head when I heard that.

My counsel was seemingly lost at this point. I am not even sure he has the intellect to question the assumption. When the knife was added, he seemed all at sea without an escort. The prosecution maintained that the weapon was mine and that the inference or implication of malice could be drawn from my use of it.

The one reasonable attempt made by my counsel surrounded the idea of passion. The charge of murder can be changed to manslaughter if it can be proven that the intent to kill is formed both suddenly and under the influence of violent passion or emotion. If uncontrollable passion is aroused by what the court deems adequate provocation, then the person acting violently is seen to be incapable of reasoning and unable to control their actions. My counsel cited Wharton's Criminal Law, section 423, while proposing this argument.

The prosecution counsel turned to the jury at this point and in the most eloquent language admitted to the truth of his fellow counsel's reasoning, emphasizing that it is around the notion of malice that the thin line between murder and manslaughter is drawn. But he went on to say that two things would need to be proved by the defense for the charge to be changed to manslaughter. The first would be the heat of my passion, which the prosecution denied. The second would be adequate provocation, which the prosecution also refuted. The deceased had not provoked me to kill him. And just as importantly, my reason had not been dethroned by my passions.

As I watched the prosecution outsmart my counsel, and offer his counterarguments with such eloquence, I saw the judge at the front of the court. His mouth betrayed the hint of a smile as he watched from his elevated, almost perched position, observing the unfolding drama like a crow from the high bough of a tree. Can I trust him to be an impartial interpreter of these events?

My only hope now is the young lady in the white dress. What happened to her? If only someone could find her, persuade her to come and tell the story of what truly took place. I have asked Crosby, but he says he has already made inquiries, and these have come to nothing. But if he is using the same M.P.s who arrested me – and who are so invested in the credibility of their judgment – then what real chance have I of being helped by the one eyewitness who could reshape the bent arc of my story, redirecting it towards deliverance?

I am now underground again writing to you, while upstairs the judge, jury, court officials, and attorneys go back to their homes and eat pot-roast for dinner. Their world is above, where the sun shines on the righteous. Mine is here below, where the darkness envelopes sinners like a thick and slowly throttling cape. I just can't help thinking of what Bigger says in *Native Son*. "We live here, and they live there. We black and they white. They got things and we ain't. They do things and we can't. It's just like livin' in jail."

I agree.

Except that I would have used a metaphor, not a simile.

It's not *like* jail.

It is jail.

At least for me.

I began this letter by confessing my deep desire for you, my love. That desire from time to time articulates itself in sighs too deep for words, like prayer. I sigh for you to know the truth. I pine for you to be comforted. I groan for you to be with me. If this indeed is prayer, then I end this letter with a loud Amen.

I love you always.

George

26

THE STORY

Maya warmed to Clarence the moment she met him. Standing at six feet two inches tall, with inquisitive eyes, and a warm smile, Clarence reminded her of her younger brother Andy. At the coffee shop, when Clarence offered to sort out the drinks, she decided to join him. Maybe it was the unexpected comfort of finding someone from back home, but she felt at ease with him next to the tantalising traybakes.

"What's your story, Clarence?"

"Maya, it's your story that matters."

"I'm guessing you had a spell in the army," Maya said. "You have the physique for it. And you look like a guy who's been used to discipline. You carry yourself well."

Clarence said, "You're in the right ballpark."

Maya smiled and asked, "So, what brought you over here to work for the Times?"

"A few things, including *Just Mercy*. Have you seen it?"

"Of course. I can't get enough of Michael Jordan. I think

he's a beautiful man."

Clarence continued. "That film changed my life. I decided I wanted to be an agent of justice, so I started media studies. I met Siobhan when I was over here on a placement."

"She's very impressive," Maya said.

"She is. I've learned a lot. Still am."

Maya paid while Clarence walked to the end of the counter to wait for their order.

"And you, Maya, what's your backstory? I heard your father was a Pentecostal bishop, and that you were a pastor for a while. Are you still active in the religious world?"

"Not at the moment."

Clarence paused to see if Maya wanted to say more.

She did.

"I'm taking a break from church."

"Temporary or permanent?"

"Undecided."

"What's behind that?"

"Man, you really are a journalist!"

Clarence laughed.

"I had a very toxic marriage. He was a young pastor. Abusive. I'm still feeling the aftereffects of it all. It's like that book title says... *The Body Keeps the Score*. I am trying to figure out how the church, which should be the safest space on earth, can be the place where it's sometimes easiest to get hurt."

"I can't answer that," Clarence muttered as he took possession of a tray with four coffees and some fifteens.

"You're not a churchgoer, then."

"I'm interested in spiritual phenomena, in mystical experiences, but I'm just not a fan of institutions that set themselves up in the name of God. I prefer religion to be disorganised. When it gets organised, people get traumatized." Clarence chuckled as he spoke. "That would preach, wouldn't it?"

"I can feel a whooping coming!" Maya said.

Clarence smiled. "It's been a long time since I've been in a church where that happened."

Maya's expression shifted from sunny to cloudy. "My father did some whooping when he felt the anointing on his preaching. His great friend Matthew would be waiting on the keyboards, ready to improvise and synthesize - as he used to call it."

"You must miss your dad," Clarence said.

He carried the tray to a booth in the corner of the coffee shop. Siobhan and the professor were already deep in conversation. They stopped when Maya arrived.

Pleasantries over, Siobhan took a small laptop out of a bag and opened it. Having asked everyone's permission to take notes, she began asking questions about George Hailey.

"How did you find out about his letters?"

Stone shared about Clare and Franky, the military policeman who had befriended George in jail.

"Would Clare speak with us?" Siobhan asked.

"It's worth trying," Stone said, adding, "the more people who can corroborate the story the better. The letters on their own may not constitute sufficient evidence."

"Spoken like a true historian," Siobhan said.

Stone continued. "If I were to detach myself from this story, which I would now find difficult, and if I was looking to validate George Hailey's testimony as described in his letters, I would need to use what in the old days was called the principle of multiple attestation. In other words, the more witnesses, the better."

Maya could feel her heart sinking.

"You're absolutely right," Siobhan said. "Unless we can find people from the time who can verify this terrible miscarriage of justice, my boss won't press the publish button. We will need to find at least one authoritative witness."

"There's one that stands above them all," Stone said.

"The lady in the white dress," Maya muttered.

"What if she is still alive?" Stone asked.

"Even if she isn't," Clarence interjected, "she may have left some kind of account of what happened, in the hands of someone she trusted to do the right thing at the right time."

Maya could feel her eyes filling. "But how are we ever going to hear her side of the story? She didn't want to be found back then when my granddaddy needed her most. Why should she ever want to be found now? She's disappeared."

She wiped away a tear from her face.

Siobhan closed her laptop and reached across the table. Holding both of Maya's hands in hers, she said, "This is a challenge, yes, but I've seen many like this before now. Hurdles are designed to be overcome. Together we'll find a way to conquer it."

Maya thanked her, withdrew her hands, found a tissue in her purse, and wiped her eyes. "A phrase my mother uttered sums up the way I'm feeling right now."

"What was that?" Siobhan asked.

"Something Maya Angelo said in her book *I Know Why the Caged Bird Sings*."

"That's some book," Siobhan said.

"Mamma used to reference that book all the time," Maya continued. "And one of her favourite parts was this: 'there is no greater agony than bearing an untold story inside you.' That's what I'm feeling right now. Only it's my Granddaddy's story."

"It's your story too," Clarence said.

Maya nodded.

Stone said, "Well let's try and tell it. I'll spend the next few days accessing online sources using my university pass, see if there's anyone or anything that can help relieve the agony."

"We'll study the letters," Siobhan said.

"Speaking of which..." Stone muttered. He produced the transcripts and passed them to her. "There's a page from one of the originals in a separate folder. You can have your folks date the paper and authenticate the provenance."

Siobhan withdrew one of the letters and read several paragraphs. Her eyes started to fill.

"Here," she said, passing the page to Clarence.

During the next sixty seconds, Clarence's face resembled a typical Fermanagh day. It went from Spring to Summer, from Summer to Autumn, and from Autumn to Winter.

"Oh brother!" he said.

Siobhan put the letters in her bag. "Your grandfather must have gone through hell. I can't even begin to imagine the pain he felt being separated from Myra, his feelings of powerlessness in the face of what was happening to him. I just can't imagine..."

"But you can, Siobhan," Maya said, not allowing her to continue. "That's why we chose you. You *can* imagine."

Siobhan looked intrigued.

"My Granddaddy believed that the reason why

racial injustice thrives is because people don't use their imaginations. They have ceased trying to think themselves into other people's shoes and instead they take the lazy option of agreeing with the foolish prejudices that prevail in their culture. We chose you precisely because you have imagination. You have the capacity not just to wonder what it's like to be a victim of prejudice. You have the soul to feel it too."

Maya fixed her eyes on Siobhan.

"If my Granddaddy knew what you'd seen and reported," she said, her voice stronger now, "he would be applauding our decision to have you investigate and tell his story."

"I will do my very best," she said. "While we're following what leads we have, I'll start putting all this invaluable material together into a coherent and compelling story."

Maya said, "If you need my help..."

Siobhan reached across the table again. "I *want* you to help me. The most important thing for me as a journalist is that the world gets to hear your grandfather's voice. His authentic voice. Not some pale imitation concocted by someone like me. And for that, Maya, your help is going to be indispensable."

"To summarise, then," Stone said. "Maya and I will head back to the farm and continue doing what research we can. You two will do the same but from your base here at the *Times*. All of us have one common purpose – corroboration. We are looking for people who can confirm George's story, and any other discoveries that back up what we believe happened to him."

"In addition to Franky's wife, Clare, there's at least one other avenue of investigation," Siobhan said. "The people who lived at the end of the street where the air-raid shelter was situated. Families from areas like that tend to recall wartime events. Clarence and I will start knocking on some doors. We might get lucky."

"Good idea," Stone said.

"I'm curious," Clarence muttered as he finished his Florentine. "I can understand how you, Maya, became involved in this, but what about you, Professor? Was it your research?"

The professor shook his head and smiled. "I'm not sure you'd believe me." He paused, then added. "A few weeks ago, I wouldn't have believed me."

"Try us," Siobhan said, putting away her laptop.

"It was a photograph."

Moments later, Stone finished his story of the library, the archives, the mysterious image, and the mission given to him by the black airman with the little white dog.

"Find me!" the professor repeated.

Maya felt a shudder in her spine.

"You know what interests me about your story, besides the dead man talking from a photo?" Clarence asked.

"What?"

"The archivist."

"What about him?"

"He was the one that passed you the book of photographs. Did he know there was something strange about it?"

Stone answered, "When I asked him to look at the photo, he didn't seem to see what I was seeing."

"Did you ask him directly?"

"What do you mean?"

"Did you ask him if he saw a black airman talking and

laughing with his little dog?"

"Well, no, not directly."

"So, how do you know he couldn't see what you saw?"

"Because I asked him if he saw anything unusual."

"And that, right there, is your problem."

"Come again?"

"I mean, what was usual to you up to the moment of looking at that album was looking at photos of people who remain frozen in time and who don't talk. How do you know that was usual for the archivist? What if his normal was different?"

Siobhan laughed. "Clarence should be a paranormal investigator on one of those TV shows." She zipped up her bag and finished the last dregs of her coffee. Adopting a more serious tome, she said, "We all need to be careful. Whoever's trying to suppress this story has already shown what they're capable of doing."

Maya looked around the packed coffee shop. It was not so much the possibility that the other booths might conceal the presence of the person or people tracking them, it was more the fact that there was not a single person of colour in the room besides Clarence and herself. Their rarity just seemed to increase their visibility.

"You all right, Maya?" It was the professor's voice that awakened her from her worrying.

"I think we need to leave," she said.

The professor nodded. "Let's all keep in touch with each other using our burner phones," he said, taking his own device and sending a text message to Birgit and Rory.

"We're leaving," he typed.

"We'll do everything we can to lessen the agony," Siobhan

said as she shook Maya's hand.

"I appreciate that," Maya said.

Once outside, Birgit's van drew alongside the pavement. Haily and Stone slipped through the sliding door into the area behind the captain's chairs. As Rory drove the vehicle away from the curb, Birgit turned and asked how the meeting went.

Maya replied. "We're going to need more than my Granddaddy's letters. Siobhan's asking for corroborating witnesses."

"Do we have any?"

Maya replied, "There was the young woman my grandfather was trying to protect in that air-raid shelter." She paused before adding, "We've got to find her."

As the van accelerated, all Maya could think of was the lady in white. Was she still alive all these years after her vanishing? And if so, how were they ever going to find her?

27

THE BRIDE

That night, back in Birgit's bunker, Maya had a dream. She was in the air-raid shelter watching a replay of the tragedy. She saw the pimp throw the young girl's coat on the ground, push her down, and begin to unbuckle his belt. She saw the terror in the eyes of the girl as she started to manoeuvre her white dress, her long pale fingers snatching and clawing at the fabric, trying to procrastinate in the very act of making herself ready. She saw the commotion as her grandfather, young and vigorous in his uniform, charged into the dark, underground space. He uttered a command to the pimp and told the girl to leave. She saw the pimp withdraw a jackknife, open the sharp and shiny blade, before scowling at the American airman. And she saw the scuffle that followed. The thrust. The parry. The wound. The blood. The gagging. The desperate fight for life. The empty stare.

In the next instant, Maya found herself outside the shelter, standing twenty metres away, gazing at the entrance to the subterranean chamber. The irony did not escape her even in her dream, that a place designed as a refuge should have turned out to be a place of such peril, both for the young woman and her grandfather.

As she stood there, she saw something moving in the chiaroscuro beyond the threshold.

It was a girl.

Maya could see her white dress.

She was now emerging from the gloom.

Maya expected her to be running, like a startled hare in full flight, but she was walking with measured, elegant steps, as if attending a ceremony, not hurrying from the scene of a crime.

As she came into the warm wash of light from the streetlamps, Maya recognised her. It was the same girl who had been so petrified in the darkness, and yet she was not wearing the crinkled dress she had seen before in the shelter. She was now clothed from head to toe as a bride on her wedding day. Everything she wore was white, from the coifs and dimities on the covering of her head to the white shoes on her feet. Even though she wore a white veil, Maya could still make out the face of the girl whom her granddaddy had just saved. She was beautiful, but this beauty emanated from a purity that seemed out of place with the ugliness of what the pimp had planned. As the girl removed her veil to smile, Maya saw a childlike innocence in her dark eyes. Her high-necked bridal gown spoke of modesty. The only suggestion of a link between the violence of what had happened, and the almost angelic sanctity of her present state, were the roses in her white-gloved hands; they were a deep, dark red, like the pool of blood spreading beneath the pimp's nape as he lay dead in the dust of the shelter.

Maya looked for a groom, but there was none.

The girl, her face uncovered now, walked out onto the street. There was joy in her eyes, as if she had emerged from a place of shadows into a new world of flowers and lights.

As she made her way towards Maya, she slowed down until she was barely moving at all. As she passed Maya, she frowned, and her dark brown eyes filled with tears.

"Find me," she pleaded.

"Find me!"

As the words drifted into the night, Maya turned to see where the bride was heading, hoping even in her dream state for some kind of clue about where she might have gone.

But she had disappeared.

And Maya was awake.

She looked at her watch. It was just before dawn. Had she been in the farmhouse, she would have walked to the window and gazed at the first splash of colour on the horizon and listened to the birds trilling. Being beneath the ground there were no such scenes, so she headed for a shower and then to the canteen. There she found the professor, already up, his laptop on the table. He was typing away at breakneck speed, so focused on the task that he failed to even notice Maya until she asked if he would like some coffee, whereupon he smiled at her, nodded, and bade her good morning.

"I've just had the strangest dream," she said as she brought the coffees to the table.

Closing his laptop, Stone gestured to her to sit with him. She told him everything she had just seen.

"So strange," she said, her voice low. "She changed before my eyes. It was like a metamorphosis."

Maya took a gulp of coffee and looked at him. "What do

you think it means, Professor?"

"I was about to ask you the same question."

"Well, my first reaction is that the dream is symbolic, and that through its symbols it's telling us the girl got married. Maybe we'll find her when we discover the man she wed."

"And who is that man?"

"I have no idea."

"Do you think he's human?"

Maya shook her head in surprise. "What other kind of being could we be talking about?"

"Do you remember yesterday afternoon in the café?" Stone asked. "You were musing about the imagination with Siobhan. You said you liked her because she could imagine what it was like to be your grandfather. It was inspiring."

"So?"

"So, what about you imagining being the girl in the shelter? Have you thought of walking in her white shoes?"

Maya looked surprised.

"Listen, Maya. If you were that girl and you'd witnessed a man die in horrible circumstances, and you'd then been too scared to step forward and report what had happened, and then you'd somehow heard about, or simply guessed, what had befallen the other man present, your rescuer, what would you feel?"

"Guilt," Maya said.

"Exactly. Maybe this girl, very likely a Catholic, felt guilty about not speaking out on behalf of your grandfather."

"Damn right," Maya said.

"But why do you think she did that?"

"Maybe because she couldn't face the stigma of being outed as a prostitute, especially in those days."

"Precisely. I think there's a strong chance she kept her new profession a complete secret. Maybe she felt terrible inner anguish. On the one hand, she wanted to keep quiet. On the other, she wanted to speak out on behalf of her rescuer."

"That's plausible," Maya admitted.

"I think it is, but if we're to use our imaginations too, then we must ask one big and obvious question. What does this girl do when she realises your grandfather has died all because she did not have the courage to come forward and clear his name?"

Maya thought for several seconds, then said, "I guess in that culture, at that time, the guilt would have been overwhelming, and the only thing she could have done was find some future purpose and pathway that could help her atone..."

"And what kind of thing would that be?"

"I guess the religious life."

"Exactly!"

Stone drained his coffee cup before he continued. "You think you saw the girl emerging from the shelter to get married to a man. In a sense she was. But no ordinary man. Yes, this is the way a bride dresses when they marry a groom, but it is also the way a Catholic girl dresses when she's finished her six months as a postulant and is about to be received into the congregation in a convent."

Maya was now wide awake.

"What you saw in your dream was, I believe, the ceremony that a young postulant goes through on her reception day as she is received into the community as a novice."

"So, you're saying the girl became a nun."

"I'm saying that's what the dream may be implying. The

man she was marrying was no literal human man. He was Christ. She was becoming his bride. Maybe the girl is asking you to find her within some kind of religious institution."

Rory and Birgit had now entered and were sitting with coffees at the adjacent dining room table.

"Tell them what you've just told me," Stone said.

Maya recounted her dream.

"What do you think?" she asked them.

Rory, who had overheard the professor's words, said, "I have seen that kind of bridal outfit before."

"Where?" Stone asked.

Rory sat down at the table while Birgit headed into the kitchen to make breakfast. He fastened his gaze on Maya.

"When I was a boy. My mother had a framed photograph. It showed her sister going through a ceremony like the one you saw. She was dressed exactly like the girl in your dream. It was in the convent belonging to the Sisters of Mercy in Belfast."

Maya sensed her heart beating faster.

"It made a deep impression on me. I had never seen anything or anyone quite so stunning. I had been brought up on a rough estate in Belfast. I was only used to graffiti and grime. But in that photo, as the sun's rays poured through the stained-glass windows, it felt like a touch of heaven on earth."

"Is she still alive?" Stone asked.

"Aye. She's in a home now. One run by the Sisters of Mercy. She would be well into her nineties. I haven't visited her in a wee while. My sister mainly does that."

Birgit began placing food on the table.

When everyone was seated, Maya turned to Rory. "Would

it be worth visiting her? If the girl in the shelter became a sister in the same convent, she would have known her."

"Aye, I think it would," he said.

Rory took out his burner phone and found the number to the retirement home in Belfast. He waited as the call connected, then spoke to the sister on duty. Yes, his great aunt still lived there. Yes, he could visit her after lunch that day, around 2pm, so long as the visit was short. Yes, he could bring Maya with him.

Rory nodded to Maya as he finished the call.

"All set?" she asked.

"Aye. All set," he replied.

"While you're in Belfast, I've got something I want to explore too," Stone said, looking at Maya.

Maya waited for him to explain.

"We know, don't we, that your grandfather was executed on the 1st April 1944?"

She nodded. "We do."

"But what I'd like to find out is where exactly he died, and where exactly he is buried."

"Do you think you'll get anywhere?" Maya asked.

"My academic credentials give me access to lots of libraries, archives, files, and documents," he replied. "I think I've a good chance of finding some answers."

Maya thanked him as she stood. She took her breakfast tray into the kitchen, then turned to Rory.

"What time do you need me to be ready?"

"1pm. I'll meet you here."

Maya nodded.

She made her way down the corridor, past the shower room, and into her room. Lying on her bed, she opened the album on her phone. A picture appeared of her grandfather as a young RCAF pilot, holding Scratch. It was the same photo she had emailed to the professor what seemed like a lifetime ago. She stared into her grandfather's eyes. As she did, it was as if she could see the features and demeanour of her own father. Without any warning, she plummeted from her hope for what lay ahead into a deep dark trench of sadness about what lay behind. Once again, she grieved her father's passing. Clutching a pillow to her stomach, she groaned at the gnawing void created by his absence. As she lamented her lost granddaddy too, she sensed a burning anger rising from a hidden furnace in her heart.

"He was robbed of everything," she said, her voice and her sobs muted by the pillow.

A deeper rage burst from its burial site and surged within her chest and out of her mouth.

"*I* was robbed."

As her tears saturated the cotton cover, she recalled a sermon that her father had preached. It was just after Maya's husband had left her, taking every material asset she had, leaving her battered and destitute, like the poor bruised soul the Good Samaritan rescued. Her daddy had climbed the stairs to the stage the following Sunday morning with a fire in his soul-piercing eyes.

"My text this morning is Proverbs 6:31."

They could have heard a pin drop.

The bishop continued. "I have found the thief, and he must restore to me seven times what he stole."

Even this early, the shouts of "Amen" and "Hallelujah" were as vigorous as his delivery.

Her father explained every part of the proverb. He told

them that the thief was the enemy of their souls, and that he manifests his thieving ways through human beings whose consciences are seared and whose hearts are given over to greed. He talked about how the light can triumph over the darkness in such toxic human relationships, through the spiritual authority his flock possessed as the children of God, and he went on to talk about the sevenfold payback, which he said meant a full and complete restoration of what had been taken.

"This authority gives you the right and the might to rise above your misery, to pivot through the help of the Holy Ghost from destitution to restitution, from victimhood to victory."

The large crowd in Boston had begun cheering, praising, clapping, singing, speaking in tongues, declaring scripture. The place was on the very cusp of a good whooping.

But the bishop had raised his hand.

The place had fallen quiet.

Every eye was trained upon him.

What would he do next?

He stepped down from the stage and stood in front of Maya, who had been sitting on the front row with her mother throughout her father's passionate oration.

He had looked at her with the kind of agony that only true love generates. But then his eyes had turned from grief to hope. Something had come to him in sudden flight, like a hawk returning out of a morning mist to the gloved hand of its master.

"And for you, my beloved child, I prophesy this to you, that it will not be long before this great truth will be your decree and declaration. It's from Exodus 3:31. 'The favour of God in my life restores everything the enemy has stolen from me'."

The whole place erupted.

Everyone stood.

The next moment, every member of the congregation was dancing in the aisles and praising God, including Maya.

And as she remembered this, she pushed the pillow away from her abdomen and made the last words of her father's sermon a statement of authority and victory, just as he had urged. "The Lord will restore the years the locusts have eaten!"

With that, the tears ceased, and a peace enveloped her from the top of her head to the soles of her feet. It was time for triumph not for tragedy, and triumph – as her father used to say – was a combination of 'try' and 'oomph!'

LETTER 17

Monday March 27th, 1944

My Darling,

It has been a bleak and distressing day. I didn't have the heart to write to you before now; last Friday marked the end of both the prosecution and the defense's summations. Lieutenant Crosby articulated the case for my acquittal as well as he could, but the poor fellow looked nervous and several times stumbled, forgetting where he was in his argument. I watched each of the jury members throughout the entire course of his oration. I honestly think one or two may have felt sorry for him, but the majority looked irritated at his lack of fluency and clarity. I am not sure he has done me any favors. All I can say is that he did his best. It is not his fault that all twelve jurors are white and that his client is black. That fact, I suspect, will in the end be the defining issue, not whether he was sufficiently articulate and compelling.

Crosby made a mistake at one point – one that was picked

up and criticized by the judge. He tried to argue that the deceased was "a moral degenerate" – acting as a pimp and exploiting the lives of impoverished Irish girls in the city. The judge pulled Crosby up in the middle of his closing argument.

"Lieutenant Crosby, in what way have you offered the court concrete and compelling evidence for this portrayal of the deceased man's character and reputation?"

Crosby looked down at his briefcase, rummaged around inside, and then looked at the judge.

He shook his head.

"Then it is just conjecture and hearsay."

He nodded.

"I appreciate this is your first time defending a client in a military court..." that was news to me ... "but you should know the law sufficiently well by now to know that a depiction of the dead man as morally degenerate would not carry any legal weight."

The judge then opened one of the books before him. Turning to a page somewhere in the middle, he read, "A murderer is not excusable merely because the murdered person was a bad man." He added, "Underhill's Criminal Evidence, section 562, page 1111." He looked at the jury and said, "please strike this accusation from your minds. The deceased has suffered enough."

He then urged Crosby to complete his speech.

All this followed on from a bad Thursday when Crosby had tried, without warning me, to argue that I was sufficiently intoxicated from my time at the Diamond Bar not to be in full possession of my faculties, and therefore even more vulnerable to the kind of sudden passion that would qualify for manslaughter.

The barman at the pub in question was summoned as an eyewitness by the prosecution. He pointed out what I already knew, which is that I had consumed one Guinness drink. As you well know, I do not have a fondness for alcohol. I have seen too many young brothers back home take a liking to it and then do something they later regretted, sometimes at the cost of their lives. It has never been for me. This is not a matter of temperance but of taste.

The claim was dismissed.

Perhaps you can see now why I was concerned from the start about being given such an inexperienced counsel. This is one of the reasons I have not taken the stand. It's not that I don't trust myself to answer all the questions put to me, and to do so with honesty and credibility. It's more my counsel. I don't trust him to ask the right questions in the right way at the right time. He and I are on cordial enough terms, but I have reached the point where I tolerate him, that's all. He is not an adequate voice for one who has no voice. It is not that he is corrupt, like the judicial machinery in operation during this farce of a trial. He is incompetent, but the combination of incompetence and corruption can be lethal, as I fear it will be in my case.

After Crosby finished his closing argument, the judge adjourned the trial until this morning, advising the jury to keep themselves to themselves and only discuss the case with each other, and certainly not with anyone outside the courtroom. He was especially firm with them about the press. None of them was to speak at any time during or after the case with reporters. It was at this point that I realized that there had been no one in the court during the entire proceedings who was dressed as a civilian and writing notes of what was taking place. Everyone was in military uniform. With a crushing sense of doom, I understood what was going on all around me.

This has been a secret trial.

There has been nothing in the newspapers.

No one knows what's happening to me.

Including you.

I asked Crosby about this. He said, "There have been no reports in the newspapers. From the beginning, everyone has been told not to say anything to anyone about the trial. The tensions between black and white soldiers are at such a fever pitch right now that a case like this would cause widespread disorder."

When I checked this with Franky, he nodded his head, looked sad, and said, "This is why I have been so concerned for you from the start. You're not being treated fairly."

That was comfort, albeit cold, like my evening meal.

And there was even colder comfort this morning. The jury delivered their verdict. They found me guilty of murder. My counsel's attempts to prove my innocence have been futile. He couldn't even get the specification of my charge changed to manslaughter, so why would I expect anything else?

The judge then gave sentence.

There was no delay.

He asked me to stand.

He reminded me of the charge and specification.

He repeated the verdict given by the jury.

Finally, he sentenced me to be hanged by the neck until dead.

Somehow, I remained standing.

My counsel informed the judge of his decision to lodge an immediate appeal with the Board of Review. The judge replied that he would need to do that today. He had already spoken with the three judge advocates that would perform the review.

"They want to give their decision this Friday before the weekend. Make sure you get it sent tonight."

All I can think of now is his words.

"Hanged by the neck until dead."

I cannot write anymore.

All hope is gone.

It's lights out.

I love you.

Forever.

George.

28

THE WITNESS

After only one morning of research, Siobhan and Clarence had bad news as well as good. The street in North Belfast where the air-raid shelter had been situated had been destroyed by the developer's wrecking ball. That was the bad news. The good news was that they had managed to find the names of some residents who had lived within range of the shelter. Some of these had moved to residences close to the original street. Clarence had narrowed these to ten names and addresses.

As the two reporters set out, they decided they would approach each contact with the same tactic. Showing their press passes, Siobhan would say, "We're writing a story about something that occurred on Earl Street in World War 2. Did any of your family live there in March 1944?" If they received a positive answer, Clarence would follow up with a further statement. "We're investigating the fate of a black US airman who died under mysterious circumstances."

Whenever they knocked on the doors, the appearance of

the unusual duo was enough to elicit curiosity, but it was only after their sixth house that they made any headway. A woman in her early sixties opened the door of a small, red-bricked terraced house. Dressed in an apron, she was baking cakes in the kitchen.

Siobhan started with their agreed opening gambit, but she had not managed to finish her prepared line when the diminutive lady rubbed her hands together. Releasing a small cloud of flour, she bid them follow her into her two-up, two-down home.

"Would you like some tea and biscuits?" she asked.

Siobhan nodded.

Clarence muted a sigh.

As the kettle started to boil, Siobhan asked, "Did someone from your family live on Earl Street in World War 2?"

"Aye. My mother did. It was a cobblestoned street. She lived there all her life until we had to move. She went to school in Earl Street. Her father was a merchant seaman. My ma loved it there, as did I in the 60s and 70s. She often used to talk about playing on the swings with her friends when she was wee. Then they demolished much of the area in the late sixties and seventies."

"How old would your mother have been in 1944?"

"Twenty-one, I believe."

"Pardon me asking," Clarence said, his tone sensitive, "but is your mother still alive?"

"Aye, she is. Very much so."

"Can we speak to her?" Siobhan asked.

"When the doctor's finished?"

"Come again?" Clarence said.

"He's upstairs seeing her right now."

Siobhan looked at Clarence, trying to suppress her sudden fusion of surprise and excitement.

Just then, a man in a grey suit and carrying a glossy black briefcase descended the stairs and entered the kitchen.

"I've prescribed some antibiotics," he said. "Give it a few days and you should see an improvement in her cough."

"Thank you, doctor. Would you like a cup of tea?"

"I'd love to, but I'm flat out. I'll see myself out."

With that, he left.

After she had passed a cup of tea to each of her guests, Mrs Ryan said, "Let's see Ma before she falls asleep."

Carrying their tea, they trudged up a thin staircase into a bedroom full of nicknacks. In the centre of the one large double bed, a woman in her late eighties was lying on her back, her eyes open, her attention focused on the strangers entering the room.

"My ma," Mrs Ryan said. "You can call her Joan."

Joan gasped when she saw Clarence and started pointing at him. "Is it him?"

"Is it who, Ma?"

"The Yank."

"You're not making any sense."

Looking at her, Clarence said, "Something tragic happened in the air-raid shelter at the end of Earl Street in March 1944. You remember it, don't you, Joan?"

Her tired eyes began to fill.

Shiobhan pressed the record button on her phone.

"You saw him, didn't you?" Clarence continued.

Tears now.

Joan was nodding like a confronted child.

"I tried to tell them," Joan said between two bouts of

coughing. "The police. The military. I even went to Belfast Barracks. But no one would listen to me. No one believed me."

"What did you see?" Shiobhan asked, placing her phone on the portable table beneath Joan's furrowed chin.

"It was terrible," she said, her cough worsening.

They waited.

She looked away, staring out of the window at the grey skies above, lost somewhere in the sheets of rain.

"What was so terrible, Ma?"

Joan refocused on the room. "What happened to the Yank. I saw him. He was such a handsome man. Tall. Smooth black skin. Smart air force uniform. Boots that shone like stars."

She started to drift away again.

"What happened, Ma?"

"There was another lad, a very bad man. I knew what he was. One of those leery rats that preyed on young women during the war, promising them security in return for services."

"You mean prostitution?" Shiobhan asked, thinking of the need for clarity in the recording.

"Aye. And he was goading a young woman into the air-raid shelter. He was berating her as a farmer does his sheep. And she was scared. I watched it all from my doorstep. The sound of his shouts turned my head as I was returning from a meeting in church. It was clear what he wanted to do with her. I will never forget how pale she looked. Her eyes were desperate. So, so desperate."

A tear fell from each eye and ran down the soft surface of her irrigated cheeks.

"But then he arrived on the scene."

"The American airman?"

She nodded.

"What did he do?"

"He followed the man into the shelter. There were shouts. The young woman ran from the scene. Then the Yank walked out in a daze. He was holding both his hands out in front of him. There was blood on them. His legs seem to give way. He sat down on a stone step and burst into tears. He was clearly in shock."

"Was he holding a weapon?" Siobhan asked.

"He was not, no."

Shiobhan gave a knowing look to Clarence.

"He wasn't behaving like someone who had just committed a crime," Joan continued. "In fact, he saw a group of military policemen coming around the corner and called out to them to come and help. He was shouting that a man had attacked him in the shelter, and that he had been forced to defend himself."

Shiobhan scribbled in her notebook.

"The next thing I knew, two of the M.P.s had cuffed the Yank and were leading him from the scene. Another emerged from the shelter with what looked like a bloody knife wrapped in a white handkerchief. And then the fourth came out and started blowing his whistle. That's when all my neighbours started coming out of their front doors. But I was the only one who witnessed what had gone on."

Clarence shook his head. "What happened when you tried to provide a statement?"

"No one was interested. There was nothing I could do. I have had to live with that."

Mrs Ryan held her mother's hand.

Joan gestured to Clarence.

Clarence walked to her bedside and sat on the other side from Mrs Ryan. He held Joan's other hand.

"You are tall and handsome just like him," Joan said, her voice calmer now. "What is your name?"

"Clarence."

"And what was the airman's name?"

"George Hailey, Second Lieutenant,"

"What happened to him?"

"You don't know?"

"No one would tell me. They just hushed the whole thing up. After I had asked them five times, they told me I was a sickening dose and that I wasn't ever to come back. If I did, they threatened to put me in one of their cells and throw away the key."

"George Hailey was hanged," Clarence said.

"For saving that girl?"

"For saving that girl."

Joan shook her head.

Clarence asked, "Could you tell us what she looked like, the girl who ran out of the shelter?"

Joan's eyes looked wistful as she answered. "She was so pretty. Black hair. Dark eyes. She had lipstick. Yes, red. Dark against her pale face. As dark as the red stains on her white dress. She was thin. Young. No more than eighteen. Long legs. Lovely long legs that carried her quickly away from Earl Street."

"Did you see where she went?"

Joan shook her head.

"Did you ever find out her name?"

"I tried, but no one would tell me anything. They all

denied that anything had happened there."

"So, you don't know if she's still alive."

"No, I don't. To be honest, I was concerned for her safety when I found out that the whole thing was being hushed up. I thought someone might try to silence her too. But then I realised the authorities had no idea who she was, or where she had gone, and that I would very likely never find out either."

Clarence sighed. Turning to Siobhan, he said, "another dead end, I'm afraid."

"It is, and it isn't."

"What do you mean?"

"Joan's story corroborates George Hailey's, except in two very significant details. Firstly, he was not carrying the knife when he exited the shelter. And secondly, he appealed to the M.P.s for help. Neither of those details are mentioned in his letters as key arguments enlisted by his lawyer. But they are both revealing."

"They reveal the extent to which his lawyer was either incompetent or corrupt," Clarence said.

Siobhan nodded. She turned to Joan. "Would you mind if we came back to interview you on camera when you're feeling better? It would help restore George Hailey's name."

Joan looked at her daughter who smiled. "It's time for me to speak," she said. "I've been quiet for far too long ... and it has troubled me so... Yes... I will share my story..."

Siobhan handed Mrs Ryan a card with her number on it and asked her to phone when her mother was better. She then drained her cup of tea, ate a biscuit, and gestured to Clarence to do the same. She knew that Clarence disliked tea, and that he found the Irish predilection for offering large quantities of it to visitors more than a little irksome. So, there was a mischievous smile on her face as she did.

Clarence finished as much as he could, wiped his lips, and uttered a loud sigh as he placed the items of Mrs Ryan's best porcelain on the chest of drawers next to him.

"Another cup of tea?" Mrs Ryan said, picking up the receptacle with the half-empty and tepid drink.

"No, no, no," Clarence said. Judging that he had been a little too quick and forceful, he took Mrs Ryan by the arm and spoke in a quieter voice. "It was very nice, but no thank you."

Mrs Ryan smiled, the greater pleasure of his compliment masking the minor disappointment of his refusal.

"We look forward to seeing you in a few days," Siobhan said as she left Joan's bedroom and headed down the stairs. Once outside, Clarence said something about staging another Boston tea party and hurling as much British tea as he could find into the sea. Siobhan smiled, but then assumed a more serious demeanour.

Inside her car, Siobhan said, "Can you set things up for Joan's interview?"

"Sure." He looked at his notes and added, "Four more houses. Shall we get going?"

"Yes," Siobhan said. "We have to find someone who knew the girl in the white dress."

LETTER 18

Friday March 31st, 1944

My Darling,

This will be the last letter I write to you. The review board's three judge advocates – Ritter, Sargent, and Van Benschoten – have examined the evidence and the rulings of my trial. The Board of Review has upheld the findings against me, and my appeal has therefore failed. They have sent their findings to the Assistant Judge Advocate General in charge of the Branch Office of the Judge Advocate General with the European Theatre of Operations. This board has treated the findings of my trial presumptively correct and adjudicated that these findings are, in their view, supported in all essentials by competent substantial evidence. They uphold the charge of murder – that I killed the man with malice aforethought – and they have determined that the refusal to change the charge to manslaughter was proper.

Finally, they decreed that the court was legally constituted and had jurisdiction of myself and the offense. This may seem like a strange thing to say but you must remember that I was in the Royal Canadian Air Force until three hours or so before the incident. I became a member of the United States Army Air Force when I was enrolled as a Tuskegee pilot. The moment that happened, I passed over from British and Canadian to American jurisdiction. If I had gone to the bar in an RCAF rather than a USAAF uniform, I would not have been subjected to an American military trial, and most likely my case would have been subjected to far fairer scrutiny. These three hours now haunt me. If only I had delayed my enrolment into the USAAF none of this would have happened. If only I had done what you wanted, and stayed in the RCAF at Lough Erne, then I would not be under a sentence of death. Although it is also true that I would have been on board the Lady and therefore deceased. So, you see, fate has conspired against me. Whichever path I chose, the destination was the same.

Having determined that there were no errors in my trial – errors that could have injuriously affected my substantial rights – the Board of Review has therefore determined that my sentence is legal. General Eisenhower has signed my death warrant.

My counsel came into my cell an hour ago to tell me this. I am now, on completing this letter, preparing to leave for England on a night flight – presumably to keep me covered by a cloak of secrecy. I am being taken by transport to a military prison where sentence will be carried out at dawn tomorrow, April 1st, 1944. My body will then be buried among the dishonored dead.

So, my darling, this is goodbye. Please forgive me for causing you so much grief. I am truly, deeply sorry. My only dream has been to make you happy. I have failed in that, it seems, as well.

When our child grows up, and is old enough to understand, please show him, or her, these letters and explain that I was not guilty of murder. My only fault was trying to defend someone who was vulnerable from an opportunistic and depraved bully. If that is a sin in the eyes of Almighty God, then I shall be condemned in the court of heaven, not just the courts of this earth.

I deeply hope and pray that our child will grow to become a person who brings light into this dark world, and that our children's children will be champions of truth and justice for all people, no matter what the color of their skin or the contours of their beliefs.

Last night, I was thinking of the only words that the poor girl in the air-raid shelter uttered to me. "You shouldn't have followed me." I remembered the strange vision I had on the Lady. It was at dawn and the mist was rolling towards the Cat. A woman in white appeared. She told me not to follow her. I thought she was the Lady of the Lake, an ancient pagan goddess of the area, and that she was telling me not to follow the old gods of the islands and the lough. Now I understand that she was not saying that at all. She was telling me not to follow, not to pursue or run after, the girl dressed in white. In her own way, she was warning me. "Beware the ides of March."

Tell our child to listen to their dreams.

To their sacred intuitions.

To their conscience.

There is wisdom in weighing what we sense – in taking time to interpret what we see.

We could all do with learning from the example of Harriet Tubman, whose dreams and visions warned her what times and places she should avoid as she helped my ancestors escape to freedom along the underground railroad.

So, my love, this is it.

The end.

As the noose tightens, you will be my final thought.

Your name will be on my lips.

Your face, like a living photograph, before my covered eyes.

And then, who knows, maybe the lady who attended the passing of that humble girl at Lourdes will come to me as well.

I love you.

Always.

George.

29

THE SECRET

Lunchtime saw a small convoy of vehicles leaving Birgit's farm at the same time. Maya travelled with Rory in the van, heading for the retirement home in Belfast where his aunt now resided. The professor borrowed Birgit's Firebird and made his way towards the airport, setting his heart on the sad task of discovering the exact location where George Hailey's body had been buried. Birgit took off in a hired car towards the north coast, aiming to buy some items for Maya at the shop at the Bushmills Distillery. Maya had taken a liking to a sixteen-year-old single malt which she was now taking as a night cap.

"We'll depart simultaneously," Birgit had said after lunch. "That way, we will hopefully confuse our stalker." Draining her mug of broth, with vegetables from her allotment, she added, "I have spoken with Shiobhan and brought her up to speed. Please record your conversations, but don't forget to ask first."

Several hours later, Rory and Maya were sitting in the

lounge of a care home in Belfast occupied for the most part by the senior Sisters of Mercy. Opposite them was his aunt, a retired sister, sipping tea from a beaker. She was dressed in her black habit. A blotched plastic bib protected her white guimpe. A recording device stood good to go on the coffee table in front of her.

"I hope you don't mind me asking," Maya said pressing record. "Why did you choose to become a nun?"

Sister Mary placed her beaker on the table and wiped her mouth with a paper tissue.

"I was blessed with devout parents when I was a child," she answered. "I have fond memories of praying the family rosary in front of a picture of the Sacred Heart. It was during these early years I turned my heart towards God. I loved the flickering, tiny candles at church and the aroma of incense at benediction. I suppose you could say that my sense of vocation was forged in the home."

Maya nodded. She could almost hear the chiming church bells calling the child to mass.

"My favourite time was when we prepared our Saint Brigit's crosses. We made them out of reeds. Once they were sprinkled with holy water, I would take mine to school."

Sister Mary touched and then stroked the silver crucifix that hung from her neck.

"One thing led to another, and I found myself helping the sisters here in Belfast in the 1930s. During that time, they asked if I had ever considered joining them. My answer was that I had indeed. I made my final profession the same year war broke out. The first question Mother Magdalen put to me was, 'What do you ask?' I replied, 'The Mercy of God.' I was very soon to need that."

"Why?" Maya asked.

"Because of the bombs."

"I don't understand."

"When the Germans hit Belfast docks," the sister said, "there was a terrible loss of life and destruction of property, and because of that, it was decided that children living in the city should be evacuated to safer places in the countryside. Along with a group of other sisters, I was entrusted with the task of making sure that some of these evacuees were given good homes and a continuing education."

Maya took this mention of the war as her cue.

"In 1944," Maya said, "my grandfather, a US airman, was in Belfast. He saved a young girl when she was being abused by a pimp in an air-raid shelter at the end of Earl Street."

As she mentioned the shelter, the sister turned her face away towards the wall where a carved, wooden Christ was hanging on a cross. Her eyes seemed to be awash with sadness.

Maya continued. "As far as we know, the girl, who was wearing a white dress, disappeared. She has never been identified. Did you, by any chance, hear about her ... meet her even?"

The sister turned her face back towards Maya and looked at her. Her fading eyes were pensive, as if she was weighing up what she should say and how she should say it.

"It would mean the world to my family if you were able to share any information with us," Maya said. "We are desperate to right a wrong done to George Hailey, my grandfather."

The sister took another sip from her beaker, and then returned it to her table. "Ach, I can help you, yes. Her name was Deidre McVeigh, and she was my closest friend in the convent at the end of the war, and in the decades after the war ended."

Maya could not contain herself. "You did know her!" she cried. "I can't believe it!"

"I did know her, yes."

"But how?"

"She became a helper in a group of us that were told to take child evacuees from our school in Belfast to another school in Bessbrook. No one loved the children like Deirdre did. And they loved her back. Mother Magdalen encouraged her to join the convent as a sister. Her name was changed to Sister Catherine, in honour of Catherine McCauley, the founder of our order."

"Did Sister Catherine ever talk about what happened in the air-raid shelter that night in 1944?"

"Only once, and only to me."

Maya waited for her to explain.

"It was after the war. She told me what had happened. She was so sad about the injustice done to your grandfather. The tears were streaming down her face. She said she wished she could go back in time and make better choices..."

Rory interjected. "Did she not share this story with her seniors when she was preparing to join the convent?"

"We all have secrets," the sister said, her voice almost a whisper. "They're a part of us, like a broken bone that's never fully healed. We disguise it well, but the shame still makes us wince whenever we allow pressure to be applied to the wound."

Rory nodded.

"What did she say about my grandfather?"

"That he entered the shelter just as the other man was

threatening her with his jackknife. She said she'd never forget that weapon. It had a handle that looked like marble."

"Do you think he was going to rape her?"

"She was certainly unwilling. Terrified too. So, yes, I would call it rape. He was forcing himself on her."

"So, my grandfather was in fact trying to prevent a terrible crime from taking place."

"That's the way she saw it, yes."

"So, what did my granddaddy do?"

"He stood between the man and the girl. He turned to tell her to run when the man lunged at him. The blade cut your grandfather's arm. Deirdre tried to help. Your grandfather grabbed the man's hand – the one holding the knife. A struggle followed in which the knife, intended for your grandfather, pierced the man's neck."

"It was self-defence, then."

"By your grandfather and Deirdre, yes. She was pushing his arm as he fended the blow."

Maya sighed. "Why didn't any of this come out in the trial? Surely the lawyer should have shared this with the court. It would have shown that my grandaddy didn't commit premediated murder."

"They wouldn't have believed him," the sister said. "I'm afraid they had already made up their minds. In their eyes, the knife belonged to your grandfather, and he was guilty."

"Yes, because he was black."

The sister nodded. She shook her head and said, "I'm so sorry. It was a terrible way to treat such a good soul."

Maya wiped a tear before she spoke again. "Did she ever share with you why she never told the police?"

"She said she was too ashamed."

"About becoming a prostitute?"

The sister nodded.

"So, joining your order as one of the sisters was in her mind an act of atonement."

"Maybe not an atonement, for Christ alone atones. Penance might be a better word."

Maya sat back in her chair. As she pondered in her heart all that had been said, it dawned on her that they had been speaking of the girl in the white dress in the past tense. The realisation forced itself upon her mind like a cold compress.

"Is Sister Catherine... is she still alive?"

The sister looked down then up again.

"It's a tragic story," she whispered. Her eyes began to glisten as she shuffled in her chair.

Rory grasped the cushion that had slipped down his aunt's back and pulled it up to support her head and neck.

"Ach, that's much better. Thank you, Rory."

The sister straightened her posture.

"Our history as an order has had its shameful moments. A few of our sisters behaved in a very cruel way towards unmarried mothers and babies in some of the laundries in the south."

She paused, as if the words were too hard to utter.

"Sister Catherine was sent to one of these institutions. She made a stand against the bullying and acted as a whistleblower. For that, she was marginalised and then ostracised."

"Did she renounce her vows?" Maya asked.

"No, she was sent to work in Africa. I'll never forget saying goodbye to her at the docks. We held each other tight and wept into each other's cloaks. That's when she whispered something in my ear. Something for which I'm sure you'll be grateful."

Maya waited.

"She told me that if anyone from your grandfather's family ever found me, I was to tell them her name and her story. If not, I was to take her secret to the grave."

Maya sighed. "Sounds to me like she didn't think she was ever coming back to Ireland."

"God told her she wouldn't."

"She stayed in Africa?"

The sister wiped her eyes with a tissue. "She died in a terrible accident in Uganda twenty years ago."

Maya gasped.

"She was with a group of her school children, all of them orphans, in a circular raft. They were spinning down part of the Nile when a King Cobra dropped from the branch of an overhanging tree right into the middle of the raft."

Maya shuddered.

"My friend, seeing the snake raise its hood to spit venom into one of the children's eyes, quickly unbuckled herself, shouted at the serpent to distract it, then threw her body over its long black coils. She threw it into the rapids, but it was too late. It had bitten her in the neck. By the time the raft settled at the end of the ride, she was dead, and the poor children were beside themselves."

Maya uttered a silent "no!"

"My beloved friend is buried out there," she said, her voice quiet and wavering. "I went just once to her humble grave. I have wept every night since. Out there, she is still a hero. Back here, she is yet to be honoured for her stand against the few among us who forget their calling to love mercy and walk humbly before our God."

"So, she was robbed too, just like my Grandaddy."

"And just like you too, my child."

Rory reached for the recorder and pressed the stop button. "Thank you," he said.

The sister looked at Maya, a look of concern written on her face. "May I pray for you?" she asked.

Maya, close to tears now, nodded.

The sister stretched out her hands and laid them on Maya's head. The moment they rested on her braided hair Maya sensed an unexpected warmth. As it made its way from her scalp to her soles, Maya became aware of the paradox. The energy that flowed into her body was revivifying – so much so that she felt, in the words of the prophet, that her youth was being renewed like the eagle's. Yet, at the same time, this mysterious power was passing through a conduit that was old, debilitated, and frail. How could one whose life force was waning be the conduit of such rejuvenating potency? Maya could not answer that except to say that what she was experiencing in those fleeting and sacred moments was something numinous, ineffable, and divine. In the words of Howard Thurman, it was if she had been brushed by the wing of an angel.

And then came the old woman's words. There were only a few, but when Maya heard them, they acted as a levy against the dark tsunami of despair that had threatened to overwhelm her soul. "The Lord will restore the years that the locusts have eaten."

"Thank you," Maya said.

"God bless you, my child."

"I receive that. God bless you too."

The sister smiled. "Don't be leaving it so long next time," she said to Rory, who smiled and nodded.

As Maya stood, her burner phone vibrated. It was a text message from Professor Stone.

At Belfast International. Through security. Have a very good idea where your grandfather is buried. Boarding soon for a flight to Charles de Gaule. About 3-hour train ride to Dormans. Then taxi to war cemetery. I'll keep you posted.

Maya replied. *We've just seen Rory's aunt. She knew the lady in white. Sister Catherine. Originally Deirdre McVeigh. Died in Africa twenty years ago. Rory's aunt knows what happened in the bunker and her testimony is recorded. I'll have it transcribed.*

Stone replied with a thumbs up.

As Rory drove her back towards Birgit's farm, she sent another text to the professor.

I'm disappointed, if I'm honest. It sucks that she's dead. I know that she told her story to Rory's aunt, but it's not going to have the same evidential pulling power that her own voice would provide. It's like one step forward, two steps back.

Maya pressed send.

She waited for the two ticks that signalled Stone had read the message, but there was only one.

The professor must have boarded the flight.

He was on his way to find her grandfather's grave.

30

THE CEMETERY

Agent Robert Miller had an impressive record in the service of his country. He had always sought to keep within his mission parameters. He had never gone maverick in the line of duty, and he had always respected the chain of command.

Until now.

Miller's latest orders from the Pentagon had been to head back to his base in North Yorkshire and to contact his new director back home. That call was meant to have been made three days ago, but Miller had not returned to Menwith Hill, nor had he contacted his new boss. In fact, he had just this minute exited an EasyJet plane in Paris. He was now following in the jet stream of his quarry, Professor Stone, who had just boarded a train heading east.

Miller sat in a seat a safe distance away from his subject, watching him through the gap in two headrests in front of him. Stone was sipping from a carry-on coffee and typing fast into his mobile phone. Miller conducted a quick sweep of the carriage. Apart from a young couple canoodling at four o'clock, his car was empty. If he kept low, he could surveil his target without being seen.

Using a company pocket monocular, Miller peered through the scope and focused on the small screen of the professor's smartphone. Stone was studying an online brochure about the military cemetery and memorial at Oise-Aisne. Miller knew what that meant. Stone had discovered where George Hailey had been buried after his execution. If Stone was heading there, Miller would need to arrive first and prevent him from acquiring sensitive information.

Miller pocketed his monocular, took out his phone, and organized a taxi to be waiting for him at the first available stop. On arriving two hours later, he found his ride just outside the station. Looking back towards the platform, he noticed that Stone had not left the train at the same station. If the taxi driver pushed the peddle to the metal, the agent would be at the cemetery well before his target.

Twenty minutes later, Miller stepped out of the taxi at Oise-Aisne and walked down an avenue flanked by oriental trees, boxed hedges, and polyantha roses. To the left were two green fields studded with white crosses, the same on his right. Each of these four plots was identified by a capital letter – A, B, C, D. Together, they formed the resting place for over 6000 US soldiers who died in World War 1.

As Miller approached the memorial at the end of the avenue, he looked up at the curved Romanesque wall made of pink sandstone, and then paused at the rectangular marble altar. He turned back to look at the blood-red roses lining the avenue.

He withdrew his cap and bowed.

Realizing that he needed directions, Miller walked to

the supervisor's office and knocked on the door. A short American man in his late fifties emerged. He had a full head of grey hair and was wearing a jacket, shirt, and tie over a well-ironed pair of chinos.

"I'm looking for Plot E."

"May I ask why, sir?"

"I need to visit a grave."

"You a family member, sir."

"No."

Miller could sense his impatience growing.

"I'm here on official business."

"Well then, Plot E is over the road back there. You'll find a large oval space with small white plaques in the ground. They each have a number written on them, but that's all. If you know the name of the person, I can give you the number of his grave."

"Second Lieutenant George Hailey."

The superintendent frowned.

"Information about that grave is classified."

Miller drew out his NSA identity card.

After he had looked at it, the superintendent said, "You'd better come with me."

"Can't you just give me directions?"

"Even if I told you the number, you'd not find it."

Miller followed the superintendent out of his office, across a small road, through a gap in a thick hedge that surrounded an oval lawn devoted to the dishonoured dead of World War 2. Unlike the main cemetery, there was no American flag flying here. The only memorial was a pale granite cross.

Miller scanned the plot as well as the area they had just left behind. There was no one else about. It was an overcast, midweek day out of season and Miller had not seen any sign of tourists, service personnel, or gardeners. For once, lady luck seemed to be smiling on his endeavours. Eyewitnesses would not be a problem.

"Do you notice something unusual about these tiny plaques?" the superintendent asked as they stepped between the numbered plates planted in the damp grass.

"Only that they don't have their names on them, unlike the crosses in the other four plots."

The superintendent smiled. "That's true. But there's another detail that isn't immediately obvious. The soldiers buried here all have their backs to the four plots across the road."

"That's the way it should be," Miller muttered.

"I agree," the superintendent said. "I resent having to mow the grass and trim the hedges here. This part of the cemetery is a field of shame. I'd rather it was left wild. But then I guess you'd never have found where George Hailey is buried."

"I guess so."

The superintendent walked to a spot away from the rest of the 94 plaques and swept aside the low branches of a small tree. There, in the dirt and the sticks, was a faded white plate with the number 95 printed on it. As soon as the plate was visible, Miller decided to act. He grabbed hold of the superintendent and held him in a lock. When the man passed out, Miller took a small black case from his raincoat, removed a syringe and injected the man in his arm. When he was sure his victim was incapacitated, he dragged his limp body into the undergrowth and covered it with branches. The man could stay with the dishonoured dead until he awakened 24 hours later.

Miller hurried back to the office and closed the back door providing sole access to Plot E. He rifled through the cabinet and found George Hailey's file. Sitting at the table, he began reading details of the airman's execution and burial in Shepton Mallet prison. As he read the report of the hanging, he came across words written by the British executioner, a man called Albert Pierrepoint.

"When it came to the hanging of Second Lieutenant George Hailey, I couldn't help feeling sorry for him. With condemned British prisoners I was allowed to proceed with haste. In fact, it was a matter of seconds between entering the execution cell and pulling the lever that propelled the man to his death. With our American prisoners, I had to stand with them while their charge sheet was read. They were then invited to say some last words. George Hailey said just four. They were more of a whisper than a declaration. 'I love you, Myra.' But this statement was preceded by seven minutes of a US army officer reading out the summary of his case and three further minutes of the Roman Catholic chaplain, whom Hailey had requested, praying for his soul. By the time all this ended, the poor man was more angry than afraid when he fell through the trapdoor. I was grateful that his neck snapped straight away and that he did not have to suffer further agony. All this left me with the conviction that there is a cruelty and inefficiency in the American way of dispatching their prisoners. I was so upset that I visited his grave in the prison cemetery and apologised."

Miller smirked at the sentiment of superiority he discerned in the executioner's words. He always resented what he considered an air of privilege and an attitude of arrogance in Englishmen. He would have indulged this anger, even permitted it to grow, if it had not been for the fact that there was someone knocking at the office door - an Englishman, no less, Professor Cameron Stone.

Miller placed the papers back in the filing cabinet before answering. Standing close to his prey for the first time, Miller was surprised by how commanding the man was. He was at least three inches taller than Miller, who measured just under six feet. He was also struck by the professor's hair. Unlike Miller, who would not have been able to spot a single follicle on his own scalp, Stone boasted a full head of swept-back chestnut hair. Most striking of all were the professor's eyes. In marked contrast to his dark locks and pale skin, Stone's eyes were a bright ocean blue – almost bioluminescent, like the sparkling, florescent waters around the coast of North and South California. It was hard not to be impressed. He may have been an academic by profession, but his face and physique were more like those of a celluloid celebrity – someone as dashing and refined as Tom Hiddleston.

The visitor stretched out his hand. "Professor Cameron Stone. Portsmouth University. I'm here to find a grave in Plot E. I'm conducting research into one of the dishonoured dead."

Miller, who had taken the proffered hand, introduced himself as the superintendent of the cemetery.

"Who are you looking for?" Miller asked.

"Second Lieutenant George Hailey. United States Army Air Force. Executed by hanging on April 1st 1944. His body was transferred here from Shepton Mallet jail in 1949."

"Are you a relative??"

"I am here on behalf of his granddaughter, Maya Hailey.

She and I want to tell his story."

"In that case, I will need to see your credentials."

Stone nodded and withdrew a black leather wallet from his blazer pocket. He presented his Portsmouth University ID. Miller studied the photo before handing it back to him.

"I don't know why you want to tell the story of a man like Hailey," Miller said. "He murdered an Irishman in cold blood. As far as I'm concerned, he got what was coming to him."

"I'm not so sure. If I may speak candidly, my new project is to do with the presence of African American service personnel in Northern Ireland during the Second World War. From my studies, I'd say that they were at a very serious disadvantage when it came to criminal proceedings by the military."

"And why was that?" Miller asked, ushering Stone to sit in the chair opposite his desk.

"African American soldiers faced extreme prejudice and stiffer penalties when it came to military justice. This was true in all theatres of conflict, not just in Northern Ireland. You can see this in the statistics. Only ten percent of the United States military was black, and yet out of the nineteen US soldiers executed in the United Kingdom during World War 2, including George Hailey, ten were black, that's about 60%. I would say that was disproportionate, wouldn't you?"

Miller said nothing.

"My research confirms that men like George Hailey were already condemned because of the colour of their skin. They were given unequal justice. Poorly defended by legal counsel. Victims of systemic racism. Vulnerable to foolish myths about black criminality, especially in relation to white women."

"I'm sure he had a fair trial," Miller said, his southern accent surfacing as he became more heated.

"Really? Many whites at that time believed the lie that African American men were over-sexed, and that they had a particular proclivity for white women. We call it the 'rape myth'. Some black servicemen were clearly victims of this southern fantasy."

"If what you're saying is true, then how do you explain the fact that Private Leroy Henry, a black man, was reprieved and cleared of the charge of rape during World War 2."

"He is the exception that proves the rule. His case confirms my point. It highlights the institutional racism that most other African Americans had to face, a racism that led in some cases, such as George Hailey's, to what was effectively lynch law."

"So, you think this Hailey was innocent?"

"I am convinced of it. I have eighteen letters written by him in my possession, six of which were composed during his trial and smuggled out by an M.P. who guarded and befriended him. My colleagues also now have the testimonies of people alive at the time of the alleged crime – testimonies that confirm that a terrible miscarriage of justice was carried out against him."

Miller was finding it hard not to erupt.

"Why do you want to see his grave?"

"I want to pay my respects. But I also want to mark the site in my head, so that when he's publicly exonerated, he can be brought back home with full honours."

Miller gritted his teeth.

"He was denied his rights," Stone continued. "He was

tried in March of 1944, but four months earlier the US military issued a command that all African American soldiers were to have a black officer present. Hailey had no such representation."

"There may have been a reason for that."

"What might that have been?"

"The memorandum was only circulated in March 1944, and it had to be passed on by word of mouth. It was not to be written down on paper. Maybe they just hadn't heard in Belfast."

Stone looked puzzled. "How do you know so much about this case?"

Miller turned to the filing cabinet. "There are 95 files in there. One of them is Hailey's. It's my business to know about all the prisoners, especially when people ask questions."

"May I see it?"

"See what?"

"His file."

Miller leaned over and pulled open the middle of three drawers. In the section marked 'H', he took out a fat file of papers and handed them over the desk to the professor.

"Would you like a coffee?"

Stone nodded.

Miller got up and left the room. The office building was small but had enough space for a kitchenette on his left as he walked into a small corridor. He switched on an old kettle. As the sound of the boiling began to grow, he glanced through the door at the professor who was using his phone to photograph sheets from the file. Miller's blood began to boil at the same speed and ferocity as the water in the kettle. Who did this man think he was? The whiff of English entitlement was pungent, and his patience was all but gone.

Using the whistling as cover, he tiptoed through the door. On Miller's left, there was a bookcase with volumes and pamphlets about the battles of World War 1 and the American cemeteries in Europe. On top of the shelves, there was a single object – a snow globe with a solitary American infantryman standing in an attitude of prayer, his head bowed, his rifle over his shoulder. His uniform was from the Great War. The globe was made of glass, the base – about eighty millimetres wide and fifty millimetres tall – was metal.

Grasping it by the dome, Miller raised the snow globe above Stone's head. The professor seemed to catch a glimpse of something in the framed picture above the desk on the wall in front of him. He looked up towards the strange movements reflected in the glass. Perhaps he had a momentary awareness of something raised, something descending, both at high speed. Perhaps it was all intuition more than observation. If it was, the professor had no time to react to it. The metal base of the snow globe hit the back of his head with a dull but sonorous thud, causing the man to lurch forward and fall on the papers, his long thin arms stretched out to the edges of the desk.

Miller put the snow globe down on the bookcase. He was surprised that the object was unbroken, although some of the glass above the base was now stained with patches of the professor's blood, giving the scene inside – set in No Man's Land – an eerie crimson hue as the tiny snowflakes fell upon the mud.

Miller checked the professor's pulse.

He was still alive.

Locking both doors, he pulled the man's body off the desk and chair. Dragging him over the threshold, he proceeded past the kitchen and the restroom to a door at the far end. The key was in the lock. He turned it. A wall of cold air greeted him. In front of him there was a staircase leading down to what he presumed was a cellar. Without any concern for the professor, Miller shoved him down the stairs until he tumbled onto the cold stone floor at the bottom.

Miller scanned his surroundings.

Brick walls.

Broken crosses.

Carving implements.

And rope.

Along the end wall Miller saw a led pipe running about half a metre from the ceiling. He lugged the Englishman to the wall and left him there. Running up the staircase, he darted back into the office, cleared up the papers, put them in the file, which he then placed in the grate of a fireplace. He checked to see if the flue was operational. Sensing a draft up the chimney, he took a cigar lighter and set the file on fire. While the papers burst into flame, he wiped and cleaned the desk, leaving no visible trace of his assault. Before he returned to the staircase, he took the wooden chair that the professor had been sitting on and brought it with him into the cellar. Placing it under the lead pipe, he pulled the professor's body upright until he was slumped in the chair, his back leaning against the bricks. Using one rope, he fastened him to his seat. Using another rope, he created a noose, fed the long end of the rope behind and over the led pipe, and strung it around Stone's neck. He pulled the two ends of the rope until they were taut, then climbed back up the stairs. Making his way to the kitchen, he made a mug of coffee and located some eclairs in the fridge. These he brought with him into the subterranean prison he had created, locking the door behind him, smiling as he bit into the chocolate.

He would now wait until the professor wakened. He would then interrogate him. When he had all the answers he needed, he would pull the free end of the rope, yanking the man so hard that he would end up standing on his toes on the seat of the chair.

Then it would be time for another execution.

31

THE INTERROGATION

When Stone regained consciousness, he groaned as he felt the throbbing pain in the back of his head. He had never suffered from migraines, but he imagined that this was what one must be like. Intense. Constant. Unrelenting. Severe. The kind of agony that brings a person right to the very edge of despair.

Stone opened his eyes and tried to wipe them, but he could not move his hands. Looking down, he saw they were bound by duct tape. Someone had wrapped them so tight his fingers had gone a blue-grey colour. He pulled against the adhesive but to no avail. He tried to stand, but his feet were strapped together too. It was then that it dawned him that he was someone's prisoner.

He moaned again at the pounding pain in his head.

It was only as he calmed his breathing that Stone understood the dire nature of his plight. There was a noose around his neck and the rope had been fed around a pipe running just beneath the ceiling. Someone had lassoed the tube in such a way that if Stone attempted to leave the chair, the noose would tighten, and he would experience a slow and terrifying asphyxiation. The only course of action was no course of action at all. The alternatives were too perilous.

As Stone sized up the cellar, an ice-cold fear began to infiltrate every major organ in his body. It took all his self-discipline to master it, to use the rational rather than the feelings part of his brain in response to the threat he was facing. As he began to render his emotions submissive to reason, he remembered how he had been sitting at a desk studying papers from a file about George Hailey. He had just managed to read a letter written by a high-ranking American officer dated 16th March 1944. It had said something about George Hailey's arrest on the charge of murder. There were comments expressing relief that the case was subject to US military rather than British civil law, in accordance with the Visiting Forces Act – an Act that had been rushed into law in 1942. "We should try George Hailey in secret, making sure no one from outside our military – especially Irish journalists – is present." The letter had proceeded to identify the reasons why this subterfuge was necessary. From the perspective of the US military, there were signs of growing resistance by black servicemen to the actions of their white comrades. If George Hailey's story became known, he could become a catalyst for increased hostility within the ranks. From a Northern Irish perspective, if the press got hold of the story, it could cause trouble between the local Irish population and the US Army. The writer had added, "There is even the possibility of Irish protesters resorting to acts of terror as a way of inciting hatred towards us."

This letter was incendiary, and Stone knew it. If he

could free himself from his bonds and escape from this subterranean prison, he could email the photos he had taken of the incriminating evidence from George Hailey's file. These pictures, in Siobhan's hands, would give her the corroboration she needed to go to press and, in the process, relieve the agony of an untold story.

Remembering these documents, Stone engaged in slow, measured movements to see if his phone was in any of his pockets. It was then that he spotted a wooden workbench standing against the wall on his left. On the top, his mobile phone was lying face down on his jacket, along with various other items that had been in his pockets – his wallet, ID, keys, and a small notebook.

Stone cursed under his breath.

He shifted in the chair, trying to get more comfortable. Whoever had assaulted him had tied the rope around his neck in such a way that the hemp was rubbing against his skin, causing a mild burning sensation every time he changed his position.

As he looked beneath his chin, a movement that caused an immediate and increased pressure on his windpipe, he saw that whoever had incapacitated him had tied a perfect hangman's knot, or what the Elizabethans called a 'collar'. Stone allowed himself to be impressed. The kidnapper knew his nooses.

But then the cold fear slipped back into every vein in his sore body. This noose was not a topic of academic study. It was a threat to his very existence. He was trapped in an execution cell, waiting as George Hailey had waited, for his sentence, confused and in shock to the very last, desperate for an improbable intervention and deliverance from the callous strangulation that awaited.

This time, the fear was not so easy to control.

As Stone considered his mortality, he noticed that there were seven white stone crosses lining the wall opposite the workbench. On six of these, the wording had faded to the extent that the names of those they were commemorated had all but disappeared. The hammers and chisels on the ground indicated the purpose of the cellar; it was dedicated to the restoration of weather-beaten memorials.

As Stone studied the crosses, he saw a seventh on which the letters were well worn. He could make out the inscription.

JOYCE KILMER
SERGT. 165 INF. 12 DIV
NEW YORK JULY 30 1915

Stone knew the name. The sergeant in question had been shot by a German sniper not far from the grounds of the cemetery. His loss had been keenly felt, not just because he was a popular soldier, but also a popular poet. Stone's favourite poem was almost childlike in tone. It was called 'Trees' – a simple meditation about how a tree is more beautiful than even the finest poem. It had contained a couplet about a tree spending its time gazing up at God, stretching its leafy arms upwards in an attitude of prayer. Although he could not remember the exact words, he could recall the metaphor.

As Stone remembered the poet and the poem, his thoughts turned to his beloved grandfather, the one man who had known how to console him when death came knocking at his door. When Stone's mother died, his adoptive granddad had taken him into his heart and his home, soothing his aching grief, offering him hope and healing, creating a calm eye in the storm of extreme sadness. This man was the nearest thing he had ever known to a father, and right now he missed the serenity that had flowed like ointment from the old man's life. How he longed for his granddad's arms and glowing eyes.

A memory fired in his brain like a scene from an old black-and-white movie. Stone, aged ten, was waiting for his granddad to say goodnight at bedtime. The boy wanted him to stay longer, so when granddad was done telling a story from his childhood in Jamaica, Stone asked him to do something he knew his granddad would not be able to refuse – to say a prayer for him.

"Let me teach you a prayer composed by Pastor Howard Thurman," his grandfather said.

Open unto me - light for my darkness.
Open unto me - courage for my fear.
Open unto me - hope for my despair.
Open unto me - peace for my turmoil.
Open unto me - joy for my sorrow.
Open unto me - strength for my weakness.
Open unto me - wisdom for my confusion.
Open unto me - forgiveness for my sins.
Open unto me - love for my hates.
Open unto me - thy Self for myself.
Lord, Lord, open unto me. Amen."

The words sounded like music – the music of the soul. From that night on, they said the prayer. The last time Stone uttered it was when his grandfather died – the night the lights went out forever. He had refused to believe that there was any point in asking for help from someone or something whose reality was at best a matter of speculation. Right now, however, he felt different. Was it not significant that these words had surfaced from the deep places of his heart, that these were the words his soul had decided he needed in his outward plight and inward desperation? Maybe he needed to be like Kilmer's tree. Maybe he needed to look up to God, not down at the noose.

In that instant of desperation, Stone began to recite the words of Thurman's prayer, and as he did, the child within spoke again - not the sophisticated academic nor the cynical adult, but the part of him that once enjoyed a naïve and unfettered trust in things he had, until recent times, regarded as impossible. Now, in this predicament, his mind submitted to his spirit as the imminence of death apprehended him. What benefit did all his scepticism bring him now, at the hour of his passing? What value did his anger over the loss of first his mother and then his grandfather bring to his life *in extremis*? In the weeks just passed, he had come to see that the raw material of enchantment was not just the product of a childish mind. It was real. Tangible. Part of ordinary life. Experiential. He had seen with his own eyes and sensed with his own body that the gnarled hands of old monks can become the frail conduits of powerful, supernatural healing - that long-dead men in photographs can come alive again and even speak. No person's thinking could remain in stasis after such startling interactions with the mystical world that Howard Thurman, his beloved grandfather' hero, inhabited. Grandad saw that world as real. At the hour of his death,

Stone would suspend his belief as well. Was this not what most of the soldiers buried nearby would have done? Was not 'Jesus' the name above all names that the dying soldiers called out in the trenches?

Closing his eyes, Stone continued the prayer as if his grandfather was sitting beside him, and as if the God to whom they prayed was not a product of his imagination but one who heard the cries of human souls and acted in the world, not always in the manner sought, but in opaque, surprising, and mysterious ways.

As Stone said 'Amen', he heard a key turning in the door at the top of the stairs and someone descending. As they reached the final step, he recognised who it was.

"Why are you holding me here?" Stone was surprised by the indignation in his own words.

"I see you are awake, Professor."

Stone repeated his question. Once again, the assailant refused to answer him.

"You're the agent who's been stalking us, aren't you?"

The man removed his cap, revealing his bald dome, and walked to Stone's chair. Like a skilled hangman, he adjusted the rope, increasing the pressure on Stone's throat.

"I'll ask the questions," the agent said. "If you stick to answering them, I'll loosen the rope."

The noose relaxed a little.

"How many people know George Hailey's story?"

Stone paused.

The noose contracted.

Stone managed to mumble, "Eight."

The noose slackened.

"Are they all hiding in the bunker beneath the farm?"

"Four are. Two work away from the farm. Two have left."

"Who are the two who left?"

"My assistant, and an old man."

"Why did they go?"

"Safety reasons."

"What about the two who work away?"

Stone did not answer.

The noose nibbled at his flesh.

Stone yelped.

"I'll ... tell ... you..."

The constriction eased.

"They're journalists."

The bald man cussed.

"Who do they work for?"

Stone did not want to answer. He was sure it would be signing their death warrants. But right at that moment, he could not keep silent. The rope was a reticulated python, and his bruised head was about to enter its four swinging jaws, trapped forever by the angle of its two rows of sharp, backward curved teeth.

"They're with the Belfast Times. They have everything."

The noose relaxed.

"And what is everything?"

"The letters Hailey wrote, first to his father, then to his fiancée, an Irish Catholic girl called Myra."

"How many?"

"Twelve to his father back in the States, six to Myra in County Fermanagh. All between 1943-44"

"Where are these letters?"

"I've locked the originals away in a safe. Copies are with the Times reporters in Belfast."

"Where is the safe?"

"In the bunker."

"Who are the four people in the bunker?"

"Up until yesterday, Maya, Birgit, Rory, and me."

"Are they there now?"

"No, they left when I did."

"Where for?"

"Birgit went to a store to buy some provisions. Rory and Maya went to a nursing home to interview someone who knew the young woman whom George Hailey rescued."

"Who is she?"

"A retired nun. I don't know her name."

The kidnapper let go of the rope and headed to the workbench. He removed the professor's phone and accessed the photograph album. Switching to video mode, he pointed the camera at his captive. As he was lining up the picture, he said, "I'm going to film you. You're going to answer my questions. Then I will send the video to your colleagues in Northern Ireland. If they agree to suppress Hailey's story, I'll set you free. If they publish it, you will die."

Stone knew the man would most likely kill him once he had answered the questions, but the thought of grasping a few more minutes of life was impossible to resist. What was it Dr Samuel Johnson once said? Something about when a person knows they're about to be hanged, it concentrates their mind wonderfully. Stone was concentrating. Whether it was wonderful or not, he could not decide.

Just then, Stone heard movement beyond the door at the top of the stairs. He also heard words. Something about their being fire in the hold. A deafening bang followed. Smoke. Darkness. Footsteps. Shouting. Torches. Shadows.

A sensation of relief in his hands and feet. Freedom from the noose.

Stone felt himself being lifted by firm hands and arms beneath his shoulders. Whoever these people were, they were fit and strong – very strong. In their grip, he felt as light as the fabric of the fluttering American flag in the cemetery.

Seconds later, he was in the superintendent's office where visibility was restored. He saw an army medic attending to a man with mud and grass stains on his clothes. The injured man looked startled and afraid. He was pointing to the bald man being dragged by two black-clad operatives through the door.

"That's him! Bastard knocked me out!"

The two special ops captors cuffed their prisoner.

Just then, a tall man entered through the front door. He was wearing an olive-green military uniform with a light blue shirt and black tie. The golden buttons on his jacket were like small, polished shields glinting in the sun before battle.

One of the operatives brought the rope that had been on the point of killing Stone and showed it to the officer. The officer took one look at it and shook his head.

"What is your obsession with nooses?" he asked.

The bald man said nothing. His face was still, but there was a sneer in his eyes which Stone thought was either because the speaker held a higher rank, or more likely because he was black.

"I'm being rude, Professor," he said, turning with indifference from the arrested agent's scorn. "I should introduce myself. I'm a director with the NSA. My name is Harper."

Harper helped Stone to his feet.

"I'm sorry this man has been abusing you, Professor," the officer said. "He's gone rogue. We're taking him back to the States. He won't trouble you again."

"Thank God," Stone said. "Thank God."

32

THE EVIDENCE

Stone stared out of the window as his train sped west towards Paris. He leaned back, avoiding the stitches in the back of his head provided by an army medic at the cemetery. As he gazed at the fields and woodlands of France, now manifesting the luxurious colours of Spring, he reflected on the opportunity he had just been given. He had come so close to death by hanging but had been rescued in the nick of time by a man he had never met before. Director Harper of the NSA had been tracking his stalker, the rogue agent, and followed him to the cemetery. He and his team had arrived as his kidnapper had been about to hoist him up onto his chair. Without Harper's intervention, and that of his men, Stone would likely have ended up in a hidden grave somewhere near the dishonoured dead. That thought made him shudder. He owed everything to the NSA Director. And not just his life either.

Stone reached down to the brown, vintage, goat-leather briefcase at his feet, not just checking that it was still there, but that it was tangible, material, real. Harper had passed it to him when he had dropped him off at the railway station.

"There are seven files in there," he said. "Each one has been buried in the NSA archives since World War 2. Very few people have seen them since then. But now, in a little while, you will too. Everything you need in terms of documentary evidence is there – everything supporting yours and Maya's thesis about George Hailey. When you show Maya, please be sure to say how sorry I am."

Stone said thank you. "Why are you doing this for us?" he then asked. "Won't you get into trouble?"

"My reputation is secondary. The reputation of Second Lieutenant George Hailey is the only thing that matters here. If I'm retired early, I'll go home to Atlanta and sit on my deck and drink bourbon. At least I'll be able to lay my head on my pillow at night and go to sleep with a clear conscience. There's a lot to be said for that."

Stone smiled.

Back in the railway carriage, he fought with his own conscience. When he boarded, he promised himself that he would not open the briefcase and examine the documents until he was back at the farm by Lough Erne. He considered it only fair that he should not read the evidence that Harper had furnished without Maya by his side, studying it with him. But now that he had several hours to fill on the train, he was finding it hard to resist the temptation to examine the treasure he was carrying. In the end, he decided to keep his word and distract himself by downloading a book onto his phone – a phone with which he had been reunited thanks to Harper. He chose the novel Maya had been reading, *The Man who Lived Underground.*

As the train passed a field full of cherry blossoms, their white and pink hues so vivid against the arable land, Stone decided it was time to send a text to Maya.

Breakthrough at the cemetery. On my way back. Lots to show you. Assemble the others. Got in a bit of difficulty, but I'm okay. Stitches. Nasty bump, just like Bret's. Don't be alarmed when you see the damage! Eta 7pm at airport.

The answer came within seconds.

What breakthrough?!!!!

Then a second one hot on its heels.

Are you okay? So sorry you got hurt.

Stone replied with emojis. A winking face for the first message. A thumbs up for the second.

As Stone immersed himself in Richard Wright's story of the black fugitive living underground, the minutes seemed to accelerate. In what felt like no time at all, Stone was stepping out of the carriage in Paris and stepping onto the EasyJet plane back to Belfast International airport. When Rory escorted him to the van, Maya and Birgit were waiting for him along with Siobhan and Clarence. All were shocked to see the ligature marks on his neck and the bandage around his head. When they asked how he was, he recounted what had occurred in the office of the superintendent who looked after the war graves. This narrative evoked a mixture of compassion and anger, with Birgit evincing the latter when she expressed the desire to hurt the man who had hurt him, and 'hurt him bad.' Stone explained that no act of Viking revenge, however much he appreciated the thought behind it, was unnecessary. The agent in question, the wayward man called Miller, was now under arrest and most likely on a private NSA jet back to Washington DC where he would face justice for his crimes.

"What happened to the superintendent?" Maya asked.

"He was discovered alive under a tree in the plot where your grandfather is buried. He's going to be okay."

"You found Grandaddy's grave?"

"I did. It had been separated from the others and concealed over time by the grass. But the superintendent knew which number it was and where to locate it, so all's well."

"You said you'd show us what Harper gave you," Maya said, her tone insistent, her voice shaking.

"I did."

Stone opened the briefcase. There were seven folders, just as Harper promised, each with TOP SECRET written in bold red capitals across the front covers.

"The first one has letters between high-ranking members of the military. Dated March 1944. Even a cursory glance shows there was a coverup, just as we suspected."

Stone put the folder back in the briefcase.

"The second is a document that we would now call a non-disclosure agreement. It seems to have been signed by all the men involved in George's arrest."

Stone put these away in the case.

He drew out a third file, much fuller than the previous two. "The third has the court proceedings from George's trial. There's a summary of the proceedings and then the full transcript."

Stone repeated the procedure.

"The fourth is the letter to the authorities after sentencing, requesting that the death sentence is authorised quickly, spelling out reasons to do with social unrest."

Stone sighed when he scanned the fifth folder.

"Next is the account of George's transfer to Shepton Mallet prison, his execution, his burial in the prison graveyard, and the exhumation and relocation of his body in France." Stone turned to Maya. "I read this in the superintendent's office. He had the same file and let me see it. You'll need to be in a safe place when you read it. It's very distressing. Harrowing stuff, I'm afraid."

Maya nodded.

"The sixth file is the equivalent of a non-disclosure agreement signed by all those who attended George's trial, including a promise not to share any details of the proceedings, including even George's name, with anyone, even spouses. The file includes an official press embargo document, preventing the story from being released to the Irish news media in 1944."

When Stone saw the seventh file, he gasped. "Bloody hell!" he exclaimed as he skim-read the four pages covered in single-space paragraphs in unfaded black, typewriter ink. "This is the most damning of all, in many ways."

"What is it?" Maya asked.

"It's a report about what happened to the woman in white. The military clearly knew who she was. She was placed under surveillance until she became a nun. At that point, they ceased spying on her, deeming her to no longer be a threat."

Siobhan said, "They spared no effort in suppressing the truth and committing these crimes."

"Do you think we have enough now?" Maya asked.

"We sure do," Clarence exclaimed.

Siobhan leaned forward and placed her hand on Maya's shoulder. "Your grandfather's story is going to be told at last. I hope you'll help us do it justice."

Stone said, "Harper, the NSA director, he told me to tell you how sorry he is about everything that's happened to you and your family. He's a good man, Maya. He's sincere."

Maya nodded before daubing her eyes.

Half an hour later, the van pulled into the avenue of trees leading to Birgit's farmstead. As they decanted themselves from the vehicle, Birgit walked towards the entrance of the bunker.

"Why are you going that way?" Stone asked. "We're not being followed anymore. We don't need to hide like rabbits underground. We can return to the house."

Birgit smiled. She uttered something in Norwegian that sounded to Stone like "shemper bra."

As they entered the kitchen, Siobhan, Clarence, and Maya sat at the island examining and photographing the documents in the briefcase while Birgit prepared some coffee.

Stone, meanwhile, walked into the sitting room, sank into a deep armchair, and retrieved the novel he had been reading on his phone. He returned to the page he had dogeared and began to read. "And again, he was overwhelmed with that inescapable emotion that always cut down to the foundations of life here in the underground, that emotion that told him that, though he was innocent, he was guilty; though blameless, he was accused; though living, he must die..."

Stone got no further than that. A deep sleep overwhelmed him, and in the dream that followed, he found himself climbing up a small steel ladder in a tube-shaped shaft. As he approached the top, he could see a manhole cover above him. Pushing with all his might, he forced the lid to move to one side. He emerged from what he presumed to be the sewers expecting to see a busy street bustling with cars and people, alive with the sound of horns and chatter.

Instead, he found himself in a garden walking on an untrodden way flanked by rank upon rank of cherry blossom trees. Never in his life had Stone seen such a place. The flowers blooming in the garden beds each side of the track – from narcissi to vibrant tulips - displayed a rainbow of colours. Even in his dream, Stone could smell the fragrance above, below, behind, and beside him.

When he reached the end of the path, he found himself standing on an oval lawn, its grass both like and unlike the grass of this earth. It seemed brighter and lusher than anything he had ever seen, as if each blade had been resurrected from the dead and infused with spiritual not just biological life. Each leaf seemed in Stone's eyes to tremble and vibrate like the strings of a musical instrument, releasing a hum that rose from the earth like a subterranean chant.

As Stone stood at the edge of the lawn, he could see in the distance a small iron gate on the latch. Someone beyond was approaching it. Stone tried to make out who it was, but they seemed more of a sheen than a shape.

The gate opened.

The visitor passed through it.

As they drew closer, Stone saw that it was a tall and vigorous looking man with smooth ebony skin and piercing dark eyes. When he was just ten metres away, he stopped and smiled. He said something in a low and lyrical voice. When he had finished, another shape appeared from behind him, that of a bounding, happy, bright-eyed dog, with fur as white and fluffy as a cloud.

It was George.

And little Scratch.

Both, in their own way, were smiling.

"You found us," George said.

Scratch barked and barked with joy.

"Thank you," he said, before turning with his dog and heading back to the gate and returning to the place beyond.

Stone was about to turn, when he saw another person enter and cross the lawn. They stopped ten metres away. And then their face, which had until then been like a shimmering mirage, opaque and lustrous, became clear.

It was his grandfather.

Stone fell to his knees. The tears that he had denied himself as a boy came pouring down his face.

"I have never stopped watching over you," his Grandad said. "I'm so proud of you. And so is George."

Stone tried to speak but could not.

"It's time to right a great wrong," he said, turning to the gate through which George and Scratch had disappeared. "Don't hold back, my son. Go tell the world!"

As his grandfather walked back towards the hazy vista beyond the gate, Stone wanted to run after him, but his knees seemed to be stuck in the earth and his legs unable to move. Instead, he found himself waking with a start and catching his phone as it fell.

Stone wiped his eyes and took careful steps from the living room to the kitchen. Everyone was drinking Birgit's coffee and exchanging animated thoughts about the documents strewn across the island. When they saw him, they stopped.

"How are you feeling?" Maya said.

"Better for a nap."

"Good," Siobhan said. "We've been talking. We have everything we need to put together and publish George Hailey's story, including the corroboration we were asked to find."

"So, what are we waiting for?" Maya asked.

"The recognition of what this all means for us."

"Say what?"

"Listen. Once we press send, once this story is in the public domain, there'll be no going back. The repercussions will be like shockwaves, spreading out from our little offices at the Times to the very ends of the earth. All our lives will change."

Shiobhan paused before she concluded.

"I need you to think about that for a moment and consider whether you're okay with it."

"I've thought about it for a moment," Maya said. "And I'm okay with it. Very okay!"

"Me too," Stone said.

"And me," Rory added.

"I'm in," Birgit said.

"Clarence?" Shiobhan asked, turning to her assistant.

"You bet!"

Stone smiled and left the kitchen. He walked up the stairs to the top floor and looked out of the window onto the glinting water and verdant islands of Lough Erne. He recalled the page of the photograph album with the picture of the Lady resting on the lough and the crew standing in front of the mansion. He remembered Hailey coming alive before his eyes and saying, "Find me!" Now he had found him, it was not the end of the matter. There were important and testing tasks to come – some involving exhumation, others exoneration. But before that, the most important thing of all was for them to do what his grandfather had told him in the dream.

"Go tell the world!"

33

THE PLAN

At the headquarters of the *Belfast Times*, Siobhan assembled her team. In addition to Clarence, she now had a lawyer and a photographer in her crew. Maya and Stone were present too.

"I'd like to divide our story of George Hailey into five parts," Shiobhan said as she opened the meeting. Pressing a key on her laptop, words appeared on the screen.

Part 1: The Courageous Airman.

"Let's discuss the broad outline of George's wartime experiences. Maya, Professor, we need your help here."

Maya began. "Granddaddy wanted to fly with the African American pilots he trained with at Tuskegee, but there wasn't enough space, so he enrolled with the Royal Canadian Airforce."

"That's why he ended up flying with a Canadian crew," Stone said, apologizing for adding some detail.

Maya continued. "In Ontario, he trained to be a Catalina pilot and was then sent to Lough Erne, where there was an airbase at RAF Castle Archdale. He became second pilot in a crew of nine, flying over the Atlantic, looking for U-Boats."

Stone joined in again. "There's a couple of things to note here. The first is that George Hailey took part in the Battle of the Atlantic. Most people have no real knowledge of the epic struggle this involved. For example, how many of you know that this was by far and away the longest battle of World War 2?"

No one raised their hand.

"And the second?" Shiobhan asked.

"The second is that most people think of the Battle of Britain when they think of courageous airmen in the 1940s. They think of Spitfires. Hurricanes. BF109s. Heinkel bombers. I can guarantee that no one thinks of Catalinas and their pilots. Yet the Catalina was a remarkable plane. And their crews were heroic too."

"You mean people don't think of them as glamorous, like the few that Churchill talked about," Shiobhan said.

"Until now," Stone said. "But there is something different about George too. He was adopted by a Westie called Scratch. Scratch went everywhere with him, including on his sorties to the Atlantic. The crew constructed a small berth for the little feller just behind the second pilot's chair, where George sat."

"That's a great story!" Jimmy exclaimed.

"Let's not get distracted by minutiae at this stage," Shiobhan said. "Even canine ones." She smiled at Maya, giving her the all-clear to continue her synopsis.

"In the next stage of my grandfather's story we find him flying through the Donegal Corridor and risking his life to protect the merchant navy. He and his crew sank two

U-Boats in a single day. That will be worth including."

Siobhan turned to Jimmy. "We'll need photos, old and new, of Lough Erne and Castle Archdale."

"And presumably some sort of digitally designed map showing the route of the Donegal Corridor," Jimmy said.

"Yes, exactly."

Maya continued. "Then comes the mystery at the heart of the story. Granddaddy's Catalina crashed into Lough Erne when it returned from a mission on March 15th 1944. For decades, my family thought he'd died in the accident, but drone footage from a few weeks ago revealed he was not in the second pilot's seat."

"Question!"

Sally, the suited lawyer, had spoken.

Siobhan nodded at her.

"How did you manage to get pictures of the inside of a designated war grave? Isn't that guarded by law?"

"It is, but I think we'll need to protect our source, if you don't mind," Stone answered.

"I don't mind at all, but DAERA will," Sally said. "We'll need to find a way around that."

Sally wrote some notes while Maya continued. She recounted how they had discovered her grandfather's true whereabouts on the 15th March 1944, learned of his arrest and charge, and his imprisonment. When she recounted the trial, the transfer to Shepton Mallet, and the execution, there was silence in the room.

Siobhan waited a few moments.

"Journalism is really storytelling," she said after a respectful pause. "What we have in Maya's summary is a story with a very shocking twist, one that has been kept as buried as that sunken seaplane for generations, one that needs to be told."

"On that," Clarence said, "I think this first report should be told from Maya's point of view. The story will be much more compelling and emotive if it's her voice."

"I agree," Siobhan said. "I also think this is a Northern Irish story. Yes, it's about George. He's the protagonist. The hero. But it's also one that takes place in this country, so we need to make sure that the voice of Lough Erne is heard too."

"I can help you do that visually," Jimmy said.

"Good. Let's now proceed to the second report. This will focus on racial discrimination."

Siobhan pressed a key on her laptop. On the screen, they all read the heading Shiobhan had created.

Part 2: The Dusky Doughboys.

"Our readers will need to understand what larger social issues contributed to this injustice."

"I'm working on this during my current sabbatical," Stone said. "I've found some disturbing facts."

"Can you give us some bullet points?"

"I can indeed, but I'll keep the focus on George Hailey. What would he have walked into when he arrived on the shores of this country in 1944? The first thing was the welcome from the local population. Unlike his white brothers in arms, the population of Northern Ireland treated him as a Yank, not a coloured man, or worse. He was astounded at the difference between the way the Irish embraced him and the way his own people excluded him."

"We should underscore this feature of the story," Siobhan said, "not least to highlight the difference between Irish attitudes towards people of colour then and now."

"You shouldn't be too idealistic about that," Stone said. "There was Irish prejudice. I can cite a unionist politician guilty of stereotyping black GIs and local Catholic girls. Others issued private warnings about 'brown babies' being born to such couples."

Siobhan shook her head.

"I can elaborate on these next bullet points later," Stone said, "but just to say that George was arrested by four American M.P.s. These were simply soldiers given armbands and batons. *White* soldiers. There were no black M.P.s in Northern Ireland. And when it came to the trial, George was supposed to have a black officer present, yet none were asked to sit through the proceedings and protect George's civil rights. The courtroom was a whites-only zone."

"Jim Crow," Clarence muttered.

"Precisely. George Hailey was in far greater danger from white American GIs than he was from the German gunners on the U-Boats – a fact confirmed by his trial."

"Did that mean he was scared of his own crew on the Catalina?" It was Jimmy who asked the question.

"No," Maya answered. "Granddaddy's crew was made up of a mixture of Canadian and British air force personnel. He was part of the RAF at least until March 15th 1944."

"What happened then?" Jimmy asked.

"He was enrolled as a pilot in the US Army Air Force so that he could head to Italy and join the Red Tails. That had always been his dream. He joined the USAAF at about 8pm on 15th March. Several hours later he was arrested by US M.P.s."

"I presume that is why he was tried in an American military court, not a British one," Sally said.

Maya nodded.

"I think it's going to be vital to emphasise just how agonising all this was for George," Siobhan said. "He was fighting all the time on two fronts. He sought victory away from the USA against the Nazi fascists. Victory back home against racists inspired by Jim Crow."

"I'd like to take a lead on this one," Clarence said.

Siobhan smiled, nodded, then put up the next page on the screen in the board room.

Part 3. A Doomed Romance.

"This will be devoted to the relationship between George and Myra. Maya, could you summarise?"

Maya shared about the meeting of the two lovers in the reading room at Irvinestown, their mutual love for books, their courting, their visits to the movies, their shared experience of oppression by colonial overlords, their final argument, their mutual agony – George's at not knowing what Myra was suffering, Myra's at not knowing what George was enduring in prison. "We have all this from my grandfather's letters, which you can use in your report."

After a short silence, Jimmy asked, "Is the reading room in Irvinestown still there?"

"No," Stone said. "But I can put you in touch with Jack. He knows more than anyone about this period in Irish history. If anyone can help you find pictures, he will."

"Again," Siobhan said. "It will be important to stress some of the similarities and differences between the black experience of oppression that was part of George's story, and the oppression felt by Myra and people of her faith and background."

"You'll need to tread quite sensitively there," Sally

interjected. "You don't want to aggravate relations between Catholics and Protestants, especially after Pauline's murder."

Siobhan winced. It took all her resolve to push back the tears. "I agree. Let's keep the focus on what things were like in 1944. Perhaps, Sally, you can recommend a sensitivity reader to check the drafts of all five parts of our reporting of George's story."

"We have one in our team," Sally said.

Siobhan thanked her before shifting to the next page.

Part 4: The Lynching.

"I'll be brief," Shiobhan said. "The priority here is to give George Hailey what he was denied during his trial. Namely, daily reporting on the proceedings by the Irish press of the day. We now have both a summary of what happened and the transcript of everything that took place and was said in that courtroom."

"We'll have to make this visually appealing," Jimmy said. "I'll need help finding photos from the era of Victoria Barracks in Belfast and the main players in the trial."

"I can do that," Stone said.

"Just take care not to be defamatory," Sally said. "Some of these men, however evil their behaviour, will have descendants in the United States. We don't want them suing us."

"That's good and sound advice," Shiobhan said. "Let's stick to factual details that suggest a lot while saying little. Remember Hemingway's iceberg theory. Show the reader a small tip of the iceberg when it comes to describing the main players in this trial. But do so in such a way that the reader can infer the 7/8th of the mass below the surface. And remember, Hemingway devised this while he was working as a reporter for the Toronto Star."

"That's helpful," Sally said. "But I'll still need to check the 1/8th of the iceberg you do reveal."

Siobhan smiled.

It was time now for the final visual on the screen.

Part 5. Burying the Evidence.

"We will need to read what we have of George's execution and burial," Shiobhan said. "And we will need to visit Shepton Mallet prison and see his original execution cell and gravesite. Jimmy, I'll be asking you to come with us to do some filming."

"Is there anything still there?"

"A lot," Stone said.

"I'd like to be part of that," Maya remarked.

"Of course," Shiobhan said. "And you might also like to be part of the second leg of our journey, which will be to the cemetery in France where your grandfather is buried."

Maya nodded.

"This part of the reporting is not going to be easy, I'm afraid. We are going to have to show that this whole story was buried, covered up, kept from public view, a bit like George was."

"Good metaphor," Stone remarked.

"Please make sure that everything you say is backed up by solid evidence," Sally said. "There are large institutions with big stakes in this story. You're opening Pandora's box here."

"I'd like to say something," Stone said. "I had a reassuring conversation with the NSA director who rescued me in France. He has, in that one decisive action, removed the threat to the Times, its employees, and us. I cannot divulge what his motivation is for supporting us but suffice it to say we are not going to have to live underground or look in our rear mirrors."

The sigh of relief was almost audible.

"Who's the culprit, institutionally speaking?" Sally asked.

"There are at least two. The US military back in 1944, and the NSA today," Stone replied.

"And what would be your charge against them?"

"That racial prejudice caused them to send an innocent man to a horrible and ignoble death. If you want me to put it another way, in more emotive language, then I will evoke another black victim called George and say that what they did to Maya's grandfather was to choke him to death with indifference and cruelty."

"That's a good segue to the final matter," Shiobhan said. "What do we want to gain from publishing this story?"

"I want the truth told and justice done," Maya said.

"Me too!" Clarence exclaimed.

Stone was next. "I want to see George Hailey given a complete pardon by the President and his remains buried in the States. It's time he was moved from among the dishonoured dead. He never belonged there. He was an honourable man."

"I want to see the trial and the sentence exposed for what they really were," Sally said, adding, "Lynch law."

Siobhan chimed in. "I'd like to see the awful agony of an untold story alleviated at last."

"And what about you?" Shiobhan asked, turning to Jimmy.

"You mentioned about George's little dog."

"Scratch," Maya interjected.

"Yes, that's him."

"What about it?" Shiobhan asked.

"Well, I'm a dog lover. I know it sounds trivial in comparison, but I'd like to know what happened to him."

"Trust you, Jimmy!" Shiobhan cried.

"I'm sorry!"

"Don't be," Maya said. "Scratch had a very special... no, a unique bond with my grandfather. They went everywhere together, even on the Catalina. Scratch was absolutely devoted to him. The boys on the Lady even gave him his own..."

"Dog tag?" Clarence asked with a smile.

"Yes, dog tag."

"So, what happened to him?" Jimmy asked, his tone insistent, his expression serious.

"Honestly, we don't know yet," Stone said.

Maya said, "If we can find his remains too, then I'd like to have his ashes buried with my grandfather's. In death, as in life, they can be together again."

Jimmy tried to hide the tears in his eyes.

"Right!" Shiobhan said, regaining control of the room. "We have two weeks. Today is Monday. In a fortnight's time, if it's a slow news day, I want to publish the first story. The second on Tuesday. Third on Wednesday, and so on. By the end of that week, I want George Hailey to be the name on everyone's lips. And, Jimmy, I want George and his dog to be the picture in everyone's heart."

Jimmy's sad eyes brightened, and a smile began to spread across his kind, unshaven face.

"Two weeks today," Shiobhan concluded, "I'm going to press publish. Let's make sure we're ready."

34

THE REMEMBRANCE

No sooner had she stepped out of the taxi in Shepton Mallet than Maya was struck by the towering height of the rubble limestone walls of the prison. When the guide appeared, an elegant and well-spoken English woman, she explained both the dimensions and age of the edifice. Although there had been an original gaol built in 1610, what Maya was looking at now, along with Clarence and Jimmy, was the enormous renovation and development conducted in the first decades of the 1800s and completed in 1848. Once new wings were added, this created a quadrangle effect with a courtyard at the centre and a classical gatehouse for access. By the time this house of correction was closed in 2013, it was the oldest prison in the world. Now it was a location for tourists, ghosthunters, and thrill seekers. Visitors could even pay to spend a night as pretend inmates behind its austere walls.

Eizabeth led Maya and her colleagues down a corridor between two cell blocks until they arrived at the execution chamber where Maya's grandfather spent his final minutes.

"Eighteen American soldiers were executed in this prison during World War 2," Elizabeth said. "Two of them by firing squad in the yard outside. The other sixteen by hanging."

"Nineteen," Maya muttered.

"I'm sorry?"

"My grandfather's time here wasn't recorded in the prison logs, nor was his execution. He was hanged. So, that makes seventeen deaths by hanging, two by firing squad, nineteen in total."

"Are you sure?"

"We're about to break the story in the *Belfast Times*," Clarence said. "I'm a reporter there and I can assure you that what Maya is saying is correct. She is the granddaughter of the nineteenth man, whose story has been covered up until now."

"I'd love you to tell me more when you can. Perhaps you could send me some details."

Clarence nodded. "I'll send you the links."

The guide stopped outside a room designated "the executioner's chamber." It was sparse and basic. There was a desk opposite the door with a lantern and an old clock. To the right of the desk was a single bed with its head next to the whitewashed wall. It had a grey military blanket. Maya could almost feel the coarse material. Above it, there was a small shelf with a *Book of Common Prayer*.

Two things caught Maya's attention. The first was something on the desk. Next to the executioner's leather notebook, there was a full-sized hangman's noose made of rope.

Maya shuddered.

Further to her right, she saw another room. This was

where the condemned prisoner would stay for ten days before his execution. A bookcase covered a secret door onto the execution chamber. Guards would remove this bookcase on the morning of the hanging. In this adjoining room, there was a black cutout of a condemned man sitting at the end of the bed, his head in his hands.

Maya shuddered again.

Elizabeth explained. "The executioner would arrive at 4pm the day before the execution took place. He would remain in this room until the time came for the prisoner to be taken to the execution chamber. He would not be aware that this was right next door."

After Jimmy had finished filming, Elizabeth led them into a room with what looked like an enormous wooden playpen. Only it was not for play, and it was too big for any child. It was designed for adults, and it was not built for recreation but for hanging. Maya could see two footprints on the floor. This was where her grandfather had stood before he was hanged. The soles of his feet would have been pressed upon these spaces, until the trapdoor opened, and his body dropped below, the noose snapping his neck.

Maya shuddered a third time.

Without warning, she was seized by a disorienting dizziness. The four walls of the execution chamber seemed to be closing in on her and the entire room shifting in and out of focus.

"Do you need to sit down?" the guide asked.

Clarence took hold of her arm and led her back to the condemned man's cell where she sat on the bed. She put her head as close to her knees as she could. Moments later, her vision was restored, and the building ceased its unnatural motions.

"I'm sorry," she said.

"Would you like a few minutes on your own?" the guide asked, passing her a glass of water.

Maya nodded and the three others left the old cell, closing the door behind them. She shifted her body so that her back was now leaning against the wall. Looking around her, she took in the size and shape of the room, committing all its dimensions and features to memory. She thought of her grandfather arriving at the prison gates on the last night of March 1944, sitting and lying on a bed just like this – simple, cast-iron, too short for his tall body, and, above all, itchy. Did he sleep that night after the executioner in the next-door room had informed him that he was there to oversee his hanging before first light? How did he endure these final hours with no one to comfort or reassure him? What crushing loneliness did he feel?

Maya shook her head. She railed in silence against the injustice of it all. How could her own nation have treated a man like her grandfather like this? He had fought for his country with courage and great skill. He had been instrumental in destroying U-Boats and had saved the lives of many sailors in peril on the sea. He had piloted his Catalina with dexterity and flown his comrades safely home when called upon to do so. He had lost none of those the air force had given him. How could the land of the free been so callous and ungrateful? How could it have allowed someone as beautiful and brilliant as her grandfather to be hanged by the neck from the ceiling of the chamber she had just left? What kind of terrible insanity was this?

"I'm so sorry, Granddaddy," she said. "I'm sorry they did

this to you. I'm so sorry you were all alone."

When she had finished her lament, she recalled what the professor had shown her among the files that Director Harper had given them - the report of the executioner, Albert Pierrepoint.

She thought of her granddaddy standing in the wooden pen, listening to the charges that had been manufactured against him, astounded by how they had been fabricated to bring his life to an end. As she closed her eyes in the cell, it was as if the past and the present fused, as if the grandfather and the granddaughter became one. So alive was this connection with the dead it was as if Maya herself was standing with the noose around her neck listening to the summary of the legal proceedings from Victoria Barracks in Belfast. She joined at that moment with every oppressed soul in her ancestral family who had borne the biting wounds of the bond and the chain, the whip and the noose. She stepped into this communion of broken saints, sensing both the soul-destroying sights of white victimization and their counterpoint, the life-enhancing songs of black victory. Maybe one day all these sights and sounds deep within her DNA would bear much fruit, fruit that lasts, fruit that would blossom in the deep dark soil of adversity and injustice. Perhaps her grandfather's death would not have been in vain, and in some mystical and numinous reversal of the earth's stark wrongs, his death would help to change the world.

She thought of the chaplain, dressed in suit and stole, trying to bring hope to her grandfather from his book and rosary. She caught a glimpse of her grandfather mouthing these liturgical words that were, up until his intimacy with

Myra, something altogether foreign to his spiritual history. Perhaps, in their desperate utterance, these words had brought his mind to focus not on the man of sorrows who had saved him from his sins but on the girl who had saved him from the enervating loneliness of being in an alien land far away from his beloved father and from the community that had cradled him. His last words, Maya had read, were this: "I love you, Myra!" It was Myra's face he had held fast before his tear-stained eyes.

Maya heard the lever being pulled.

The floorboards retracting.

The dull thud of another lynching.

She imagined the noose being removed from her grandfather's bruised neck and his lifeless body placed on a gurney. She imagined his body being inspected by a physician with a stethoscope. She walked in procession with the padre and the guards to the prison morgue and stood at her grandfather's side while a white bedsheet was laid over his limp frame and lifeless eyes.

She watched as an officer walked into the darkened room and told the three men involved that they must be sworn forever to secrecy. Even her grandfather's name must now be forgotten. When he was buried in an unmarked grave outside, while the prison was at its quietest, all trace of him was erased just before the dawn broke. A small cross marked the site, but it did not bear his name.

As she lived all these moments with her granddaddy, Maya remembered the last time she preached, two years before, on Easter Sunday. She had spoken about the women who appeared early in the morning at the tomb of Jesus. They had gone there to anoint his body with aromatic oils, but when they arrived the heavy stone that shut him in had somehow been removed, even though the Roman seal had been upon it. Only celestial beings could have put their shoulders to so great a weight. They had removed the boulder. They had penetrated the dark cavity of the cave beyond with the majestic brilliance of another world. They had stood guard as the intense light of recreation and resurrection had manifested like a blinding singularity, one in which the power of heaven came to earth in what Maya said were the first seconds of a new creation in which all things were made anew. She had stood with the women at the empty tomb and marvelled at it all.

Maya found herself back in her pulpit in Boston on Easter Sunday, declaring these things with a passion that surprised even her. She had been going through hell, and everything within her weary mind told her that she would not be blamed for questioning every detail of the ancient narrative. But when it came to the recitation of it, the flickering candle of faith within her battered soul had grown into a forceful and ferocious flame until, by the time she finished, it was as if she was like the prophet Jeremiah, and her heart had become a furnace. "His word is in my heart like a fire, a fire shut up in my bones."

A few hours later, Maya and her companions were in a hired car proceeding from Paris to the war cemetery the professor had visited several days before.

"I heard something interesting in the prison." It was Clarence who broke the silence. "Something the guide told me. Do you mind if I share it? Or do you just want to be quiet?"

"Go right ahead," Maya said.

"She told me about one of the black soldiers imprisoned there during World War 2. A private called Leroy Henry. He had been twice with an English girl, a prostitute. Both times she charged him £1. But when he went a third time, she asked for £2 when they were done, saying that the price had now doubled."

"Nice of her to tell him afterwards," Jimmy muttered.

"Well, in a way, that was the point. She wasn't very nice, and the people in her town knew it. When she kicked up a storm and had him arrested for rape, he was sentenced to death. Almost certainly, he would have been hanged in Shepton Mallet prison. Except that something very unusual happened."

"What?" Maya asked.

"A petition was created by local English folks and sent to General Eisenhower. It was signed by over 33,000 people, all clamouring against the injustice of the sentence, asking the General to exercise clemency. The General ordered a review and the prosecution's case was overturned. It was an extraordinary thing the English did."

"What do you think motivated them?" Jimmy asked.

"It could have been any number of things. But one thing that stood out to me was what a local leader where the alleged offence had occurred, a village called Combe Down, said as the petition was being formed. It was so moving I thought I'd write it down."

Clarence withdrew his phone.

"We feel that if this coloured soldier is considered man enough to come over here to fight for freedom alongside the white man, he should be afforded the same rights of a white man, a full enquiry and every witness in his favour brought forward."

"Wow!" Jimmy exclaimed.

Maya said nothing.

Jimmy parked the car and they all sat for a moment looking at an American flag fluttering in the wind nearby.

"What do you make of that story?" Clarence asked, turning to Maya, his eyes glistening.

"I'm happy for Private Henry but sad for my grandfather. I honestly believe that if his case had been made known to the good people of Northern Ireland, there would have been an outcry greater than the one you've just described. My granddaddy would have been spared the noose. I am sure of it."

Clarence nodded.

Just then, a man in a long military coat appeared. Maya and her colleagues stepped out of the car.

"I'm the superintendent," he said, offering his hand. "I met your friend, Professor Stone the other day. Let's just say the circumstances were a bit different." Maya managed a smile. "It's this way," he said. "Over the road and through a hedge."

When they arrived at the oval lawn of plot E, Maya noticed the cross that the professor had mentioned. She also heard the flapping of an American flag in the wind.

"Usually, we don't allow a flag to be raised here," the superintendent said. "But the story I've been told about Second Lieutenant George Hailey convinced me that he does not belong here among the dishonoured dead. He does not belong here at all." Turning to Maya, he said, "I am sorry for your loss, Miss Hailey. And I'd like to thank you for your grandfather's service."

Maya wiped away a tear.

Maya stared down at the small white plaque in the damp green grass with the number 95 painted in black. Somehow, out of the secret places of her heart, she dredged and raised the same words sung at her daddy's bedside in hospital. She had little faith when she began; the suffering of recent years had diminished her capacity to believe in the way she once had. But as she sang, her faith began to grow again just as the sun broke through the heavy clouds.

Jesus, He, promised me a home over there;
Jesus promised me a home over there.
No more sickness, sorrow, pain or cares,
Jesus promised me a home over there.

35

THE INVITATION

Siobhan placed her phone on the boardroom table. All eyes were on her. Stone, Maya, Rory, Birgit, Clarence, Bret, and Jack. This was the moment they had been building towards for two weeks.

"Well?" Maya asked.

"That was Richard. My boss," Siobhan said. "He's read the five pieces over the weekend. The lawyers have poured over everything. The digital guys have formatted the series."

"And?" Maya asked.

"And I can now do *this*."

Siobhan's laptop screen synced with the board room screen. She positioned the cursor over a button with the word PUBLISH. She clicked on it, and the first document uploaded to the world.

In the twinkling of an eye, Siobhan's quiet voice was drowned by applause. Clarence, who had come prepared, filled seven flutes with champagne and passed the glasses.

"To George Hailey!" Stone proposed, and everyone

repeated the airman's name.

When the room was quiet again, Siobhan spoke. "It's 2pm here. People will be waking up in many parts of the USA. They'll be awake in a quite different sense very soon."

Siobhan watched as the story began to gain traction with other media outlets across the pond, garnering attention on social media platforms. It was only the first article, but Maya's account of her father's brave service for his country, and his country's brutal treatment of him in return, was already making waves.

By the end of Day 4, the whole world seemed to be talking about George Hailey's story. On TikTok, Gen Z influencers were using it to address the crisis in army, navy, and air force recruitment. The numbers were way down for people of their age group. Part of the reason, these influencers argued, was the suspicion of institutions felt by millions of their viewers. This included a profound mistrust of the military. In high-impact videos, young people were commenting on George Hailey, stating that the terrible injustice he endured, even though it was over eighty years ago, had fuelled their cynicism.

On X, film stars and famous authors started punching out pithy statements about George Hailey being a forefather of victims like Breonna Taylor. One claimed that George Hailey was a John the Baptist to George Floyd's Jesus. Siobhan pointed to the like button for that claim. Everyone in the room watched with amazement as it sped from hundreds to thousands, from tens of thousands to hundreds of thousands, and then to over a million.

"This is what we need," Siobhan said. "If George is to get the justice he deserves, we need his story to go viral."

At 6pm Thursday, the professor, who was following feeds on his phone, spoke up. "Interesting reactions from members of the US military." Siobhan leaned over and clocked the account he was studying. Within seconds, a senior-ranking African American airman was on the big screen. He was in full ceremonial uniform with a chest full of medals. The words, "US Air Force, Chief of Staff" were written beneath his distinguished and aging face.

"George Hailey's story should shock us all to the core," General Brown said, his voice trembling. "It's all too easy to think this was decades ago in World War 2 and not true of POC in the US forces today. But that would be wrong."

Another black officer, this time retired and wearing a polo shirt, appeared from his own home in a study flooded with sunlight. He had achieved the rank of Major General in the US Army but was pointing out in his interview how hard it was for officers of colour to progress beyond the rank of captain. "Even today," he said, "there's an implicit bias in many units towards white service personnel. When officers of colour try to progress, they see their white competitors, and the white senior ranking officers who decide who gets promoted, and they come very quickly to realise that they will have to put in double the work and double the effort if they're to progress further up the chain of command. The odds are stacked firmly against them."

Other servicemen and women of colour were now interviewed. They shared stories of their own attempts to rise through the ranks, attesting to obstacles not faced by white colleagues.

The news channel then shared some startling statistics about systemic racism in the army.

"Approximately 17% of US troops identify as black. Over 50% state that they have witnessed white nationalism or racism in the military during their service."

Maya shook her head when the next stats were revealed.

"In the US military justice system, black service members are approximately twice as likely as white service members to be tried in general and to be subject to special courts martials."

"That's what we've been waiting for," Siobhan said. "No one can use the that-was-then, this-is-now argument. The need for reform is still urgent. The judicial system still discriminates..."

A young African American lieutenant appeared on the screen. She was more upbeat. "There's still a way to go, but joining the army gave me great opportunities I wouldn't normally have, and it has cemented in my mind the importance of the power of diversity when it comes to working on a task as a united team."

Another mid-ranking army officer said he had been the victim of racial discrimination, but that it was increasingly rare. "I heard people using the 'N' word about me years ago when I was training, but I don't hear it today," he said. He added that it was common earlier in his career to see Confederate flags in army bases in the south but that this too was a thing of the past in his experience. He concluded by saying that senior officers had instilled a policy of zero tolerance for racism and that this was beginning to permeate the system. "We're like an aircraft carrier, not a patrol boat. It's easy to turn a patrol boat quickly. It takes time to change the course of an aircraft carrier."

A final POC officer appeared on screen to say that she felt

safer in the army than she did driving outside the US bases where she served. "Even though I'm serving my country, I still live in fear of seeing blue lights in the rear-view mirror."

Siobhan shut down the news feed on the board-room screen. Maya, who had been conducting her own search on a tablet, exclaimed, "This to me is interesting."

Siobhan asked for a link. As she was setting it up on the screen, Maya explained that the man they were about to see speaking to camera was a well-known bishop and civil rights activist.

The video ran from the beginning, "When George Floyd was murdered by a white police officer, one of his close friends saw the news spread across the world like wildfire. He was grieving and guilty, but even in his pain he experienced a moment of heavenly clarity. 'Is George the sacrifice?' he asked."

The bishop stroked his short, white goatee beard. He stared into the lens with the sternness of an old prophet.

"If you're black, and you go to church, you'll know what he meant. He was referring to vicarious sacrifice, to what Jesus experienced two thousand years ago - dying so that others might live, taking the punishment so that others don't have to, receiving the worst that an evil social system can throw at you in order that that same social system can pivot from violence to peace."

He paused again.

He was into his groove now.

"George Floyd's death was like that. A sacrifice. And like all sacrificial deaths, it was an invitation. It was a great wrong inviting us all to put things right. In my opinion, George Hailey's death is just the same. It's a sacrifice. An invitation. Not just an invitation given to the military here in America, but to the peoples of the world. We can either let this gesture pass us by, or we can use it as the wellspring for global transformation, for the eradication of racism and other ways of thinking that divide us and make us less than human."

The bishop sighed and then leaned forward.

"I went to the theatre the other night," he continued. "A friend of mine has been directing George Bernard Shaw's play *Saint Joan*, about the martyrdom of Joan of Arc. That too is about sacrifice. That too is an invitation. An invitation to the characters within the story, and an invitation to the audience watching it."

The bishop took a copy of the paperback of the play and turned to a dog-eared page.

"After watching her die, two characters get to talking about the meaning of her sacrifice. One is a bishop. The other is a chaplain. The chaplain is talking about what a huge impact Joan's death has had on him. He says that it has redeemed and saved him because its effects have changed his life."

The bishop put on his spectacles.

"The other man objects to this, saying that the chaplain should have experienced that kind of impact from examining the death of Jesus, not from looking at the death of Joan. The chaplain replies that he has tried to imagine Jesus's sacrifice many times, but that it hasn't touched him as Joan's sufferings have."

The bishop turned a page.

"This is what the cleric says. 'Must a Christ perish in torment in every age to save those who have no imagination?'"

He placed the book on a table and took off his glasses.

"That is a question that I, as a bishop, ask all the time. Must someone die a Christ-like death in every generation for those who have lost the capacity to imagine the sacrifice of Jesus? Must a Dr King, a George Floyd, or a George Hailey die a dreadful death to awaken in us the same need for redemption that we should be recognising as we look at the face of the crucified Messiah?"

Pictures began to appear on the screen, replacing the headshot of the bishop. Pictures of George Hailey in his flight jacket, of a Catalina flying over the Atlantic, of a noose, an unmarked grave, a little white dog howling at the night sky, and finally the cover of Harper Lee's novel, *To Kill a Mockingbird*."

"In the end, what we all tend to be guilty of what Shaw identified. A lack of imagination. White people fail to imagine what life is like for some black people. Black people fail to imagine what like is like for some white people too. We refuse to allow ourselves the time to walk in another person's shoes. Someone different from us. Someone we have othered. And when someone does try to do that, as Harper Lee did, people denigrate them for their act of misappropriation rather than celebrate them for their exercise in imagination." He paused before saying, "How lost we are. All of us."

Maya dabbed at her eyes with a handkerchief.

"Let me give you an example of this failure of the imagination."

Maya uttered a muted yelping sound.

"The failure by white Christians in America to even begin

to see the full spiritual significance of the lynching tree. To any black person, it is the most natural thing in the world to connect this with the Cross. Jesus, our Friend and Saviour, died for our sins on the tree at Calvary. The New Testament uses the word 'tree.' What is it that white supremacists used to torture and kill us in times past? The lynching tree. The lynching tree is the most blatant reminder of this failure of imagination on the part of white nationalists and white racists. George Hailey's death was an atrocious act of legalised lynching. His body was asphyxiated and suspended just like that of Jesus."

The bishop paused to take another volume.

A book of poetry by Countee Cullen.

"See here what the Harlem poet says. Jesus hanging on the Cross... are you ready for it? Jesus hanging on the tree at Calvary is, I quote, 'but the first leaf in a line of trees on which a Man should swing."

He put the book back down.

"Why do you think it's the poets that connect the tree of Christ with the lynching tree? It's because they have imagination. Remember the poet, Gwendolyn Brooks? She was the first black winner of the Pulitzer Prize. She said, 'the loveliest lynchee was our Lord.' Only someone with imagination can say that."

The bishop took hold of a paperback of *To Kill a Mockingbird*. He turned to another dog-eared page.

"Remember what Atticus Finch tells his young daughter, Scout. He says, 'You never really understand a person until you consider things from his point of view ... Until you climb inside of his skin and walk around in it.' That's imagination! And imagination is what leads a person to the experience of empathy. And empathy is love. And love, in the end, is justice, just as justice, in the end, is love."

The bishop set the book down on his lap.

"The world is dying for a lack of imagination," the bishop said. "George Hailey was a Christ figure, not by choice, but by compulsion. George Hailey's death, if the depths of its full meaning are to be plumbed, should be seen as an invitation. It is an invitation to activate our imaginations. Let's not allow another Christ to perish in torment to save those who have no imagination."

The end credits rolled.

Maya wiped her eyes.

"My granddaddy believed that too," she said. "He was very influenced by Richard Wright, the novelist. He said the same thing, that the world is dying for lack of imagination."

She blew her nose and composed herself.

"I'm sorry," Siobhan said. "We can have very little idea what it was like for George Hailey, and so many others, to live between the desire for dignity and the longing for survival."

Maya looked up at her and their eyes met. "But you do, Siobhan. Only someone with imagination could have articulated what you just have. That's how my ancestors lived. That's how most young black men in America live today. Between survival and dignity. Not many white people have the empathy to see that."

Siobhan nodded. "Maybe something in our Northern Irish experience has helped a little, although, like George's beloved Myra, I understand the differences too."

Just then, Stone retrieved his phone from a pocket. It was vibrating. "May I answer this?" he asked.

Siobhan nodded.

"General Brown, good to hear from you. Of course. When would you like to see us?" Stone looked at Maya. She smiled. "The Pentagon. Your office. 1700 hours. Yes, of course."

Stone wrote some notes on his phone.

"What was that?" Maya asked.

Stone replied, "An invitation."

36

THE SIGNATURES

The next day, Stone and Hailey were driven from Dulles Airport to the White House. Two suited agents escorted them from a well-guarded side gate through several crowded corridors to the office of General Brown, the highest-ranking officer in the US military. When they entered, the General, bespectacled and entirely bald, walked towards them and proffered his hand. Stone noticed the silver wings on the General's chest just above a block of colourful ribbons – a reminder of his former role as the chief of staff for the United States Air Force. He was the first African American to hold such a senior position. Having been promoted from that role in October 2023, he was now the chairman of the Joint Chiefs of Staff and the military advisor to the President of the United States. No one in the military had more authority than he did. As far as Stone was concerned, no one had more power to right the wrongs done to Second Lieutenant George Hailey in 1944.

After they were invited to take a seat, the General chose

not to return to his desk but to sit with them in a space designed as a small living room flanked by tall bookcases. These were filled not just with military volumes but with some of the great classics of African American literature, from the poetry of Phyllis Wheatley to the novels of Octavia Bulter, many of them first and Folio editions.

"My condolences, Ms Hailey," the General said, looking into her eyes, his face etched with an empathy that derived not from a disciplined imagination but from racial solidarity. "What happened to your grandfather was wrong. On behalf of the United States military, I'm deeply sorry. We are deeply sorry."

Maya nodded her thanks.

"What can I do for you both?" he asked.

Stone turned to Maya, checking if he could answer first. She was still recovering her poise after the General's apology, so she indicated for him to go right ahead.

"We have two requests, General. I will speak to the first. I am sure Maya will want to address the second."

"Of course," the General said.

"I have conducted a lot of research in previous years into the Tuskegee airmen."

The General interjected, "I have read your book. I am a great fan of your work, Professor."

He pointed to a small mahogany table under a window whose white blinds were half open. It was a hardback first edition. There was a sheafed fountain pen next to it.

"I would love it if you signed it for me before you leave later. I consider it one of the most important works not just of World War 2 history, but also of the civil rights movement."

"I'd be delighted," Stone said. "And thank you." He inhaled before continuing. "As you will know, one of the three men arrested at Freeman was Second Lieutenant Roger 'Bill' Terry. He was the only one to be severely punished. He was stripped of his rank, fined, and court martialled. The charge was jostling."

The General poured all three of them a glass of bottled still water and passed a crystal tumbler to each.

"Thurgood Marshall, who was one day to become a supreme court justice, represented him, but he still couldn't prevent Bill Terry from being dishonourably discharged in 1945."

The General muttered, "Another shameful racial stain on our military history."

"Yes, but in Bill Terry's case, there was a good outcome. Thanks to people petitioning on his behalf, he was exonerated by President Bill Clinton in 1995. His rank was restored. His fine paid back to him. And the letters penned by General Hunter were removed from the files of all those who participated in the Freeman Field mutiny, including the one he wrote condemning Bill Terry."

"That was a good day," the General remarked.

Stone turned to Maya, looked at her, readied himself, then turned back to the General. "We are here to ask you to do for George Hailey what President Clinton did for Bill Terry. We would like George Hailey to be granted a full pardon."

The General walked to a bookshelf and pulled out a large, hardback book about World War 2 aircraft. He turned to a dog-eared page. When he placed it on the coffee table between them, Stone could see that it contained a large oil painting of a Catalina flying towards a U-Boat in the

Atlantic. The lookout was shouting to his Captain below, warning of the impending danger.

"He flew one of these, didn't he?"

"He did," Stone said.

"Two things impress me most," the General said. "The dedication it took for your grandfather to train with the Canadian Air Force, and then fly with the Royal Airforce. He clearly wasn't one to take no for an answer, at least as far as enrolling at Tuskegee was concerned. And the other thing is the courage it must have taken to fly these seaplanes in battle conditions. I was a command pilot with F-16s. They are fast. But flying in a seaplane at such slow speeds, and into the face of enemy fire from the deck of a submarine, that required an almost superhuman level of discipline and bravery."

Stone nodded. "And yet, speaking as an historian, no one seems to know about that. How many books or films have focused on Catalina crews and their missions?"

"Well, I guess the only one I know of recently is *Greyhound* with Tom Hanks, but that's really about battleships, although a Catalina does make an appearance towards the end."

"That's really the exception that proves the rule," Stone quipped. He took a sip from his water. "And then there's the Northern Ireland factor. That's played a part."

The General looked quizzical.

"I mean, the fact that the Catalinas were not based in the south of England but in part of the United Kingdom that most Brits outside that territory barely think or care about."

"I see," the General said.

"We would respectfully ask that you exonerate George

Hailey. It will forever remind the world of the extraordinary sacrifices and enormous skills that were exhibited by the crews of these Catalinas, especially in the Emerald Isle."

The General smiled. "You put the case with typical eloquence and cogency, Professor."

He poured some more water for Stone, whose mouth was now dry not just from his speech but his nerves.

"And the other request?"

Maya took the reins. "General, as you know, my granddaddy is buried among the dishonoured dead in a hidden part of a war cemetery in France. He was transferred there after his execution in Shepton Mallet prison. That execution was a legalised lynching."

The General frowned.

"He was, at the time, in love with an Irish Catholic girl called Myra. She was pregnant with their child. When her mother died, she had no one in the world to support her. Thinking that her soulmate had died when his Catalina crashed, she boarded a ship for the US and went to visit my great grandfather. He looked after her until she gave birth to my father, after which... tragically ... she died."

"I'm sorry," the General said.

After thanking him, Maya continued. "My great grandfather paid for her to have a Catholic funeral and had her buried with other members of our family in a plot outside Boston, in a small-town cemetery. He brought up my father."

Maya took a deep breath.

"My request is that the remains of my granddaddy are taken from among the dishonoured dead in the cemetery in France and buried with Myra's, his sweetheart, in the same family plot here in the States. And I ask that this be done at a ceremony attended by my family and a detail of US Air Force personnel in full uniform who can act as the firing party. I'd like a bugler and for the flag to be placed on his coffin too. I want my granddaddy to be one of the honoured dead."

Maya turned to Stone, indicating it was his turn.

"I'm sure you know that there is precedent for this request, General. Private Eddie Slovik was buried in Plot E after deserting. He was the first soldier to be shot for desertion since the American Civil War, and the only one in World War 2."

"Another tragic story," the General said.

"But in some ways, it ended well," Stone replied. "Eddie's case was presented to President Ronald Reagan. Reagan ordered Eddie's remains to be transferred to a cemetery in Detroit. In 1987 he was reburied there, next to his wife. So, there is a precedent."

"The stories are not identical though," the General said. "Eddie was, I'm afraid, never pardoned."

"Maybe you should look into that one too," Maya said.

The General smiled. Then he rose, walked to his oak desk, and fetched two documents. Bringing them to the table, he presented them to Maya. Both were official orders on military-headed paper. The first was an order for Second Lieutenant George Hailey to receive a full pardon, and for his family to receive compensation in full for all losses he incurred because of his trauma, and theirs. The second, also an order, was for the exhumation of Second Lieutenant George Hailey's remains in the cemetery in France, and for his careful transfer to a place of the family's choosing, where he might be reburied with full military honours. On both documents, there was a space for a signature and a record of the date - the day of their meeting.

Maya gasped. "How did you know?" she asked.

Stone chose to answer. "The task of a great leader is to anticipate other people's moves and to pre-empt them. The General is showing why he's in the position he is. Mediocre leaders are prone to reactivity. Great leaders specialize in proactivity."

The General smiled.

"Are you going to sign it now?" Maya asked.

"It's not for me to do that," he said, his voice soft. Returning to his desk, he picked up the receiver of his telephone. "We're ready," he said, before replacing the receiver in the dock.

The door opened.

It was Stone's turn to gasp.

In walked the President of the United States. He had a kind and genuine smile as he stretched out his hand.

"Ms Hailey. On behalf of the United States, I offer my full and unreserved apology for the terrible wrongs done by unscrupulous people in our country to your beloved grandfather. He served his country well. Our country treated him terribly. I'm truly sorry."

Maya's tears were falling.

"I'm here to sign the two documents that General Brown has presented to you. It is my pleasure to put my signature to both, to order the full pardon of your grandfather and the removal of his remains from among the dishonoured dead."

Maya nodded her thanks.

The President sat behind the desk. He was handed a

fountain pen while a White House photographer entered and set up her camera. The President signed both orders and confirmed the date while the photographer took pictures of him from three different angles. When the President was ready to stand, he shook Maya's hand once again and the professor's before leaving the room.

Stone was the first to speak. "I am very surprised."

"He wanted to be here," the General said.

"Not so much by that," Stone said, "but by the fact he didn't ask Maya to be photographed with him."

"He's a man of integrity," the General replied. "He didn't want to be seen to be making any kind of political capital out of this sacred moment. As far as he's concerned, this is about George Hailey, it's not about his own popularity. The photos are for you to use as you see fit, and for our White House archives."

The General walked over to the small table where the professor's book was lying. He took it, opened the front cover, presented a pen to Stone, and said, "Your turn, if you don't mind."

Stone signed the book and returned it.

The General thanked them both and then led them to the door. "My security detail will take you back to the airport. I trust you enjoyed the private jet."

They both nodded.

"Well, you're about to enjoy it again."

Stone paused. "I have one question before we leave."

"Sure."

"The NSA agent who tortured me..."

The General walked back to his desk. He produced another document. It looked like another official order.

"I've just signed this," he said. "It's my order for Agent Miller to be stripped of his rank, and all the rights and privileges thereof, and to be dishonourably discharged with immediate effect. I think you'll both appreciate the appropriateness of that punishment."

The General turned to the professor. "I know about your new research concerning African Americans in Northern Ireland during World War 2. You are welcome anytime to see our military files relating to your studies. Let me just say, I have access to archives that would make even Indiana Jones envious!"

"Thank you, General."

"Don't thank me. It's my way of making amends."

Minutes later, Stone was sitting with Maya in the back of a yellow taxicab heading for Dulles.

"How do you feel?" he asked her.

"I'm still reeling, if I'm honest."

"Good reeling, or bad reeling?"

"Good. I'm shocked it went so well."

"I agree, but General Brown's a fine man. I had an inkling he might do what he did. I don't know if you've seen his speech after George Floyd's murder. It's a very personal, vulnerable, heartfelt testimony of his experience of racism in the Air Force, as well as a plea for racial unity. It's inspiring."

"I'm glad you benefited too, Professor."

"What do you mean?"

"I mean you've done so much for me and my family. You've had your life threatened twice. I'm just glad that you have that connection with the General, a door into the White House, and access to the archives he was talking about."

"I'm glad too."

"Speaking of archives," Maya continued. "I have a favour to ask. When we have done what we need to do, I'd like you to take me to the archives room in your university library?"

"Why?"

"You've met my granddaddy. Seen him play with Scratch. Heard him speak too. I'd like to have the same experience. All I have is some letters and photos – letters in which his voice is inaudible, photos in which his body is immovable."

"But I can't guarantee he'll do again what he did before. I was not in control of that at all."

"I appreciate that, Professor. But we could at least give it a try. I don't want to finish this project together without you showing me the album. Promise me you'll do it."

"I promise, Maya."

Stone settled back into his seat and leaned his forehead against the car window. He watched as planes took off from the airport they were now approaching, rising into the jet-black night with only their flickering lights to reveal their steady ascent. Once again, he found himself thinking of the many missions flown by Maya's grandfather and his crew. His mind was again in County Fermanagh. More than that, his *heart* was there. For all his academic objectivity, the mystical lough and its timeless tales had shifted the centre of gravity in his life. It might only have been a little, but it was now as if he thought from the feeling not just the rational part of his brain. He knew, from that moment of reflection on, that whatever writing he did about Northern Ireland in the future, whatever lectures he gave as well, would come as much from his reignited limbic system as from his well-used neocortex. He would, in short, be a scholar on fire.

37

THE HUNCH

Siobhan just could not shake the impression that she had seen something – something that had masqueraded as trivial, but which was, in truth, a key that would unlock the one remaining mystery in George Hailey's story. Never one to dismiss the role of intuition in her investigative endeavours, she resisted the temptation to rationalise and chose instead to follow her instincts.

"Jimmy, I'd like you to come with me today. Clarence, you stay here and let me know about any developments."

"Where are we going?" Jimmy asked.

"Back to Clare's house."

Jimmy did not need any elaboration. In the two weeks running up to the publication of the story, they had visited Clare's bungalow and interviewed her about her late husband Franky – the American M.P. who had guarded and befriended George Hailey.

"Did we miss something last time?" Jimmy asked.

"I just want to check."

After half an hour, Siobhan and Jimmy were approaching Clare's house when the phone rang.

"I've got you on speaker, Clarence."

"That's okay. You can both hear this."

"What's up?"

"Well, you asked me to keep you updated. I've just seen a very powerful interview with the Sergeant Major of the US Army. He's seen a lot of racism directed towards him and others. We could use one of the stories he shared. It highlights the issues."

"We're just arriving," Shiobhan said. "Give us a synopsis."

"It's about a colleague in the army. African American. The short version is that this guy took off his uniform, put on his civilian clothes, and headed home from his base. As soon as he reached his front door, he was arrested by the police for breaking and entering."

Siobhan's gasp was audible.

Clarence continued. "So, when leaders who are steeped in white privilege say that we don't have a problem with racism in the States, this might be a good story to tell."

"Totally," Siobhan said. She added, "We're pulling up at Clare's drive. I'll be in touch."

Siobhan exited the car and knocked on Clare's front door. Seconds later they were in the kitchen being invited to have a cup of tea and some traybakes. Siobhan and Jimmy accepted and sat down at a circular table topped by a lace cloth.

"You said you had a question you wanted to ask me." Clare said. "And that you'd need to ask in person."

"That's right. But we'll need to move from the kitchen."

Clare looked surprised.

Siobhan rose to her feet and headed out of the kitchen

into a long corridor. The front door was at the end of a short corridor on her right. Also on her right was the door to the sitting room where they had filmed the interview. But Siobhan did not turn right. She kept going down the long corridor towards the bathroom.

"Last time I was here, I asked if I could use your toilet. I walked down here and passed the snug on my right and the dining room on my left. When I had used your bathroom on the left, I came out and paused. The door opposite was open. It seemed to be a smaller room than the others. I didn't stand here for long because it felt like I was being a wee nosey, if I'm honest."

Siobhan looked at Clare. There was a hint of sadness in her face.

Putting her hand out towards the handle of the closed door, Siobhan asked, "May I?"

Clare looked even sadder.

The door opened.

"There!" Siobhan said, pointing to something on a mantle shelf a few metres to her left.

"What?" Jimmy asked.

"The China dog above the old fireplace."

When Jimmy saw it, he uttered a quiet expletive. Looking around the room, he cried, "They're everywhere!"

And they were. There were little models and effigies of the same breed of dog, all in the same colour - a white Westie. And in the hidden part of the room to the right, beyond what was visible when Siobhan had been looking in from the outside, there was one framed black-and-white photograph on the wall. A young Franky, in his military police uniform, was kneeling in his garden.

He was not alone.

There was a white Westie sitting between his knees, looking up at him, licking his chin.

"It's Scratch, isn't it?" Siobhan asked.

Clare burst into tears.

Siobhan passed her a tissue and she began to recover. When she was composed again, Clare said, "I wanted to tell you, but I just couldn't bring myself to do it. I was scared you might take him away from me. Ach, I was being selfish, I know."

"I don't understand," Siobhan said.

"Come with me."

Clare took them out of the kitchen door into the tarmacked drive that ran along the back of the bungalow. When she reached the end of the stretch of garden next to the drive, she passed through a gap in the hedge and entered a tiny grotto. There, in the grass in front of them, was a granite cross planted in the soil. It had one solitary word on it, and a date. 'Scratch. 15th March 1945."

"We buried him there," Clare said.

"Do you mind?" Jimmy asked, pointing to his camera.

Clare shook her head.

"What happened?" Siobhan asked.

"Come inside and I'll tell you."

Once in the sitting room, Clare brought in a tray, and they began to drink tea from her best cups and saucers.

"My Franky was very upset when George Hailey was transferred for his execution. Eventually, he went looking for George's fiancée, Myra, but by then she had left the country. I think it's fair to say that he delayed that visit, putting it off on purpose."

"Because of Scratch?" Siobhan asked.

"George Hailey had told my husband about his little dog, how much he loved and missed him. George was worried about Scratch being left all alone. So, Franky wanted to find him. He went to Castle Archdale and asked around. Eventually, a gardener told him he'd seen a dog answering that description, but that the dog wouldn't let anyone near him. When Franky saw him, he called out to Scratch. Scratch seemed to know he was friendly. He walked towards Franky slowly, then accelerated. I think he must have picked up traces of his master on my husband's clothes. Scratch went mad, licking and barking, snuggling and jumping. The gardener couldn't believe it. From that moment on, Franky became very attached to him."

"So, Franky brought him home with him," Jimmy said, trying to control the tremor in his voice.

Clare put her teacup back in its saucer and set both on the table beside her armchair.

"Aye, he did. He always wanted to take him back to Myra. 'I'll do it tomorrow,' he would say. But every time tomorrow came, he just couldn't bring himself to do it. If I'm honest, in the end, I think he regretted not returning him to her."

"Why?"

"Scratch loved Franky, but he was never really settled. Not completely. We could tell he was restless. Whenever Scratch heard a car drawing up outside, he would get very excited, thinking maybe it was his master coming to fetch him. When he saw that it wasn't, he would go into the room where his photograph is and just lie down in his bed, his wee nose tucked between his front paws, his ears pricked, his sad eyes scanning the room."

Jimmy wiped away a tear.

"Airplanes were the worst," Clare muttered.

"What do you mean?"

"Every time Scratch heard a plane flying overhead, he would bark at the door. We would let him out and he would look up into the sky. When he realised it wasn't his master's plane, back he would go into his bed, lie down, and wait for the next time."

"That's heartbreaking," Jimmy stuttered.

"How long did he live with you?" Siobhan asked.

"Just over a year. He wasn't old, but he died in 1945, one year to the day after his master was executed. I think, in the end, it was a broken heart. The poor wee pet just went to sleep one night and never woke up. Franky was beside himself with grief. I think maybe some of his tears were for George Hailey too. I'll never know, though. Like most men, he kept things buried."

"And Scratch is buried under the cross outside?"

Clare nodded. She took a sip of tea, and then said, "I know why you're here, Siobhan. I know it's not just for information. You want to bury him with his master."

Siobhan smiled and nodded. She said, "Two days ago, George Hailey's granddaughter visited the White House and met with the President of the United States. He signed two documents. The first was a full pardon for her grandfather. The second was for his body to be transferred from a cemetery in France to one just outside Boston, Massachusetts, so that he could be buried alongside Myra, his beloved Fermanagh girl."

"So, you want Scratch to be transferred too."

Siobhan did not answer.

Clare looked out of the window. She stared at the ploughed fields and the rolling green hills beyond, far away in her thoughts until she caught herself on and brought herself back.

"I'm very old," She said, her voice soft, "And I have no children or grandchildren to leave all this. I'll be reunited with my Franky before long. And it's only right that Scratch should be reunited too. Not with us, but with George and Myra, where he belongs."

"Thank you," Siobhan said. "I'll be in touch with details."

When they were back on the road, Jimmy asked, "Shouldn't we tell Maya that we've found Scratch?"

Siobhan looked at her watch.

"They should be back at Birgit's farm by now," he said. "Probably awake too. I'll try her."

Ten minutes later, Siobhan had told Maya what had just happened. Maya was in tears while Siobhan was speaking, as was Jimmy while he was driving. Even Shiobhan found it difficult to maintain a semblance of journalistic objectivity and detachment.

When the time came for Scratch to be exhumed, the gravediggers refused to take any payment and the funeral director donated the white coffin with its gilded gold handles.

When the time came for the little coffin to be transported to the airport, the limo company would not take a penny. Word also got out, and the streets of the town near Clare's home were lined with well-wishers, many of whom threw garlands at the hearse as they saw the name SCRATCH formed out of a huge and ornate display of white orchids. They were given for free as well.

And when the time came for Scratch to be taken on

board a passenger jet bound for Logan International, he was flanked all the way home by two attendants with immaculate hair and just as immaculate red dresses. And once again, the transport was free, thanks to the kindness of the dog-loving CEO of the airline – a kindness that was repeated every step of the way Stateside too.

When Siobhan wrote up the story for the *Belfast Times*, she said that she had never seen such an outpouring for an animal in her life. Even Scratch's dog tag was turned into a framed adornment for the top of his coffin, shaped and engraved by a man called Sam, the most brilliant young jewellery designer in Britain. He loved dogs too and gave his time and skills for free.

Siobhan had tears in her eyes when she came to the end of her piece. She decided to finish with a poem by Jimmy Stewart, the greatest American actor of the World War 2 era. He had been an airman in the war. He had suffered too, the terrifying ordeal of piloting B24s over Europe, facing flak and loss with his typical gravitas and old-school dignity. Jimmy loved a dog too, and in his own old age wrote a poem when his dog called Beau passed away. When Siobhan wrapped up her article with the final lines, she was glad of the privacy of her office and the blinds that separated her from those beyond.

There are nights when I think I feel him
Climb upon our bed and lie between us,
And I pat his head.

And there are nights when I think
I feel that stare

And I reach out my hand to stroke his hair,
But he's not there.

Oh, how I wish that wasn't so,
I'll always love a dog named Beau.

38

THE CLOSURE

When the day of the burial arrived, Maya was happy that it was under cloudless skies. She had been to too many funerals where the heavens were heavy with rain. Today, in the grounds of a white-wood church in the New England style, she was glad that a place so steeped in death was alive with photosynthesizing light.

Myra's grave stood beneath a row of sycamore trees in one corner of the lush, green-grassed cemetery. It was marked by a marble headstone with her name and date of birth. Next to it, a new headstone had been planted. It gave George Hailey's name and rank, the dates of his birth and death. It stated that he had fought bravely in the Battle of the Atlantic, and that he was Myra's beloved fiancé. Between these two graves stood a smaller stone for Scratch, saying that he was the beloved companion of both. On all three stones, the engraver had inscribed the words, 'separated on earth, united in heaven.'

Maya inhaled the warm, revivifying summer air and

waited at the foot of her grandfather's grave. She stared into the two hollow cavities in front of her, one wide and long, the other narrow and short. Ranks of foldup chairs had been placed beneath the shady boughs of the trees. Maya walked over to them and sat on the front row in the centre. She waited as members of her family joined her. She nodded at Professor Stone when he came to stand beside the grave, along with the others in the small group of guests. Birgit, Rory, Bret, Clarence, Siobhan, and Jack had all given their apologies.

A soldier with a strong voice issued his orders and a unit of seven USAF personnel appeared in their uncreased honour-guard uniforms. This ceremonial team was made of men and women of diverse ethnicities, just as Maya had requested. They looked resplendent in their white gloves and ascots, their silver belts and aiguillettes. Six of them were carrying her granddaddy's coffin, marching in slow, measured steps. Their timing was as well-rehearsed as their air of solemnity. In front of them, a seventh man wearing sergeant's stripes bore the tiny coffin containing Scratch's remains.

The airmen placed the coffins above the graves and then walked back to their vehicle while Maya stood to say some prayers. When she finished, she took her seat again. The sergeant issued an order to his team, and they marched to a space beneath the shade of the sycamore trees. Another order followed. Four volleys sounded from their rifles, each fired in perfect unison. Then they shouldered arms and stood guard over Maya, her family, and the graves.

One of the airmen stepped forward with a bugle and played 'taps', a haunting 24-note melody first used in the Civil War at the extinguishing of lights at the end of each day, and then in 2012 designated the National Song of Remembrance.

The sergeant bellowed another order and the six members of his unit stepped out of the shadows and headed to the two coffins that were resting on trestles above the graves. Four men folded the Stars and Stripes designated for George Hailey, followed by the one for Scratch. When they had finished the elaborate procedure, the sergeant presented both to Maya, offering words of gratitude for the service of the brave airman and his canine companion.

One of Maya's brothers stepped forward along with her aunt and stood by the graveside. Her brother Andy read the sonnet 'High Flight' and then returned to his seat. Aunt Bernice, the finest singer in the church choir, took a deep breath. Maya had asked her to sing a song that she had always loved - Billie Holliday's rendition of "Strange Fruit," said to be the saddest jazz song ever written. She knew that its words would be as haunting as its melody, and she was not wrong. Everyone bowed their heads as Aunt Bernice sang.

Southern trees bear a strange fruit
Blood on the leaves and blood at the root
Black bodies swinging in the Southern breeze
Strange fruit hanging from the poplar trees

Pastoral scene of the gallant south
The bulging eyes and the twisted mouth
Scent of magnolias, sweet and fresh
Then the sudden smell of burning flesh

Here is a fruit for the crows to pluck
For the rain to gather, for the wind to suck
For the sun to rot, for the tree to drop
Here is a strange and bitter crop

When Bernice released the last note, a sacred quietude descended on the chiaroscuro where they sheltered. No one moved. No one remained unmoved. Every mourner heard the call to end the vile and vicious hatred that had sundered the two dead lovers beneath their feet. How could anyone remain contaminated by abject hate when the world still bore such strange and rotten fruit? How could anyone not fail to rage against the blood on the leaves?

As Maya pondered these things, she looked up at the branches of the sycamore trees reaching up towards the blazing sun. As she gazed at their twisting boughs, she remembered her dad pushing her on the swing in their yard. She smiled as she recalled how the breeze kissed her dark, soft skin. But then her mind turned to those who had hung from the end of a lynch-mob's rope. She trembled at the thought of it and, as she did, a gust of wind caught the branches above her head, causing them to tremble too. Maybe, like the rood of Christ, the tree felt the depraved misuse of its trunk and arms. Maybe the boughs sighed at the gross, grotesque conscription of their sturdy limbs.

Maya's eyes fell on Cameron Stone. He had risked his life for truth and justice. He had not patronised her with patriarchal tropes. He had never tried to embrace some white and privileged saviour role. He had been there for her throughout their journey, just as he was there for her now, not as someone blinded by superiority but as her equal, her comrade, her brother in arms. He was the only white-skinned guest, and yet she knew that afterwards, back at the family home in Boston, he would be embraced by her mother, her siblings, her cousins, and her church members with a joyful, warm, and genuine humanity as everyone partook of her mother's famous southern, deep-fried chicken around the stump of the maple tree. This gesture might be as tiny as a seed, but a seed buried in the earth could bear much fruit.

Not strange fruit.

Good fruit.

Maya asked everyone to stand, and as they did, it seemed that the earth began to shake. Somewhere from behind them, a great sound began to cause their bodies to vibrate. Whatever it was, it was above them, drawing nearer and nearer to the sycamore trees. Mourners stepped out of the shade, some removed their hats, and peered up at the blue sky through their sunglasses.

That was when they all saw it.

A PBY Catalina in the striking dark blue colour used in the Pacific Theatre of Operations, a World War 2 treasure, its two loud Pratt and Whitney engines causing a rush of adrenalin in Maya's body. It flew past and over the cemetery while every witness gasped. Some clapped. Others lifted their black hats and cheered. Maya shook her head. She had no idea that this was about to happen.

"CQ fixed this," the Professor whispered to her, using the name by which General Brown was more commonly known to those who worked with him. "He asked me yesterday if it was appropriate, and if you'd appreciate it. I said I thought so."

"I do," Maya said. "I truly do."

The professor passed her his handkerchief. She patted at her eyes and tried to give it back, but he insisted that she keep it. "Just in case," he said, his voice rising above the din.

"Why?" she asked. "Have you anything else planned?"

The professor smiled. "I don't."

When the Catalina had disappeared beyond their sight and hearing, Maya called them around the grave. She invited Aunt Bernice to lead the mourners in an acapella rendition of Amazing Grace. While the honour guard departed, the mourners sang.

As the hymn progressed towards its conclusion, Maya recalled the story her father once told of the man who composed the timeless words. The author, John Henry Newman, had been the captain of a ship tasked with the transportation of slaves to the colonies. He had, by his own admission, been steeped in a catastrophic darkness – not just his own, but that of the wicked, oppressive, dehumanizing trade to which he had given his nautical gifts. Slowly but surely, Newman had come to see the light, to the point where he could at last declare that once he had been blind, but now he could see, once he had been lost, but now was found. So great and deep was the transformation of his soul that he became a supporter of William Wilberforce, the most influential abolitionist in the world at the time. Thanks to Newman's counsel, Wilberforce had decided not to become a clergyman – where his influence would have been diminished – and resolved instead to be a voice for the slaves in Parliament where his impact could be far greater. Newman's enlightenment had led to the emancipation of countless victims of the foul, pernicious sin of slavery.

By the time Maya came to the final stanza of the hymn –

'When we've been there ten thousand years, bright shining as the sun' – she sensed a surge of hope in her heart. She had lost so much of her previous confidence, thanks to her former husband's degradations and her desperate yet unanswered prayers, but now, under the sycamore trees, she felt a frisson of that overarching love she had known when she was a child. Standing next to her granddaddy's grave, celebrating with her family this final vindication, she trembled at the current of 'perhaps' that flowed through her body and soul. Perhaps, after all, there is a force at work, a force of good, that bends the arc of history towards justice. Perhaps it just takes longer than impatient human beings want and takes routes that seem incomprehensible.

As Aunt Bernice invited a repetition of the final couplet, Maya thought of her father too. How she had wanted to see him healed, at least long and real enough to stand with her there and feel the bright serenity that follows in the wake of righted wrongs. How he would have loved to sing these rousing words, here where the searing heat of unjust shame had at long last morphed into a cool, refreshing sense of righteous honour and respect. She had prayed for his healing, but his life had ebbed away before he ever knew how the story of his father's life had taken such a strange but therapeutic route. And when it had, Maya had been crushed by disappointment once again. Where was the divine love when her husband, a so-called pastor of the flock, was wounding her? Where was it when her father breathed his final breath in the hospital? Where was it when her granddaddy's neck was constricted and crushed by the deadly coils of the executioner's noose? Maya had known so much despair, and yet, underneath the sycamore trees, she found a tiny mustard seed of faith again. Opening her mouth, she made the words of Isaiah chapter 24 her declaration, her voice growing like the throaty roar of a lioness against her enemies.

Thou hast been a strength to the poor, a strength to the needy in his distress, a refuge from the storm, a shadow from the heat, when the blast of the terrible ones is as a storm against the wall.

Thou shalt bring down the noise of strangers, as the heat in a dry place; even the heat with the shadow of a cloud: the branch of the terrible ones shall be brought low.

And in this mountain shall the Lord of hosts make unto all people a feast of fat things, a feast of wines on the lees, of fat things full of marrow, of wines on the lees well refined.

And he will destroy in this mountain the face of the covering cast over all people, and the vail that is spread over all nations.

He will swallow up death in victory; and the Lord God will wipe away tears from off all faces; and the rebuke of his people shall he take away from off all the earth: for the Lord hath spoken it.

When she had done, the mourners began to depart from the graves. As they did, Maya's phone buzzed. It was a video from their friends in Northern Ireland. She could see Jack and his wife Orla, Birgit and Rory, standing with a small crowd on the top of a hill on an island next to the stretch of water where her grandfather's Catalina had crashed. Jack was reading out the names of the dead who lay in the war grave at the bottom of the lake. When he had done, a bugler played, and a priest gave a benediction. A plaque carved into the highest rock above the lough was unveiled. It had the number of the Catalina, its moniker – Lady of the Night – and the names of the crew - everyone bar Second Lieutenant George Hailey and of course Scratch.

As Maya walked back towards the hearse, she smiled. The professor, catching her up, asked her what was on her mind. She showed him the video clip from Lough Erne.

"It's worked out well," she said. "They had their little service just as we were having ours. It kind of reminds me of something they used to say on the A-Team, one of my favourite TV shows when I was a little girl. I used to watch it with my father. He used to say it all the time in church. People always cheered when he did."

"What was that?"

"I love it when a plan comes together."

39

THE BEGINNING

Stone had made a promise to Maya, and he intended to keep it. That promise involved a walk to the university library in Portsmouth and a look at the photograph album which had marked the beginning of it all. Maya had travelled over from the States a few days earlier. Instead of staying at the Marriott, Stone had invited her to occupy the ensuite guest bedroom in his apartment. He had also asked Bret to look after her and to take her out to visit shops and historic sites. Having adjusted to the different time zone, Maya was now ready to visit the archives room and look at the picture of her grandfather and his dog.

Stone contacted the library using the same email address as before, organizing the visit for the evening of Maya's third day in the UK. At 8.45pm, they walked from his apartment to the library and headed upstairs to the archives room.

"Good to see you again, Professor."

The voice came from the same smart, suited man in his early sixties. He was carrying the album under one arm, using his other to offer his hand to Stone.

"And you must be Miss Hailey," the man said in that same mid-Atlantic accent Stone remembered.

"I'll leave this with you."

Stone sat at the one large reading table in the centre of the small room, gesturing to Maya to join him in the second chair next to him. There was a third chair opposite, but Stone figured that if the strange phenomenon occurred again, it would be better if they shared the same angle of vision.

"I don't mind admitting," Maya said with a tremor in her voice, "I'm a little nervous."

Stone said, "We don't have to do this."

Maya shook her head. "I want to."

Stone waited for her to compose herself before opening the cover of the album. He turned the pages, revealing pictures of the people and places of County Fermanagh during World War 2. There were images of GIs and airmen, farmers and policemen, parents and children, all preserved by the black-and-white film. There were images of towns and fields, lakes and rivers, hills and mountains. Stone was captivated for a moment by the rocky summits, mindful of their sturdy and stubborn resistance to the march of time, in stark contrast to the faces of those captured by the camera, vulnerable and docile to the forces of mortality and transience. Stone knew from her sighs that Maya was moved by the pictures too. Both had been impressed by the inhabitants of Northern Ireland. Both had found themselves enchanted by its thin places, soaked as much by stories as by rain.

Stone turned the page.

There, in the top half, was the white Catalina resting

at anchor - the Lady of the Night floating on the tranquil surface of Lough Erne. There, in the bottom half of the page, was the crew of the Lady, posing for the cameraman in front of the façade of the castle where so many service personnel were billeted.

Stone took a deep breath.

Seconds passed.

Maybe the image of Maya's grandfather and his bright white dog would remain like all the others, in a perpetual state of stasis. Maybe, now that Second Lieutenant George Hailey and his companion Scratch had been laid to rest, they would not come alive again and speak to them. Even though Maya needed this momentary resurrection, they might not sense the same need. The airman's mission, summed up in the two words, 'Find me,' had been fulfilled. What need was there for him to bridge the great expanse of years with some new utterance? The call he had issued had been heard, the quest achieved. What new task could there be for Maya or for Stone?

But then the airman moved.

The dog barked.

And Maya gasped.

The airman spoke, this time not a word of commission but of recognition.

"Maya," he said.

Scratch barked, as if he too was speaking her name.

Maya, whose hand was over her mouth, spoke just one word back. "My granddaddy!"

The airman smiled.

The Westie barked again.

Before they returned to their pictorial repose, the airman

took his right hand and placed it over his heart. He nodded his head and smiled, signalling his solidarity with the descendant he was studying, marvelling at her, startled by the mysteries of time, that he could be younger than her while at the same time being her grandfather.

The airman and his dog took one brief look at Stone. There was a shining in their eyes as they peered into Stone's soul. He knew what the airman was conveying, even though his communication involved no utterance, just a wordless nod of gratitude.

As Stone smiled back, the airman and his dog became still again in a perpetual and peaceful rest.

Maya wiped her eyes.

"Thank you," she said, her voice tremulous.

Stone was about to speak when the archivist appeared at his left shoulder. Stone had not heard the man enter or approach, but now he was in the room he walked to the chair opposite them. Taking the album, he closed it and then placed both his hands on the cover. Stone noticed for the first time the golden signet ring he was wearing on the little finger of his right hand. It had the engraving of a golden compass on it, raised towards what looked like the stars.

"You two have done well," he said.

"Excuse me," Maya said.

"We have been watching you both," he continued. "You work together very effectively. There's a synergy here. You've impressed us with your methods and results."

"Say what?" Maya said.

"I said we're impressed."

"Who's impressed?" Stone asked.

The archivist tapped his nose.

"That won't do," Stone said. "Who are you? And what's this collective you're referring to?"

"I can't give you details."

"Then this conversation's over," Maya said. She got up to leave, adding a sarcastic, "Bye Felicia," as she turned.

"Wait!" the man said.

Maya looked back at him.

"What if I told you there are other cases like the one concerning your grandfather. Other cases that need to be investigated. Mysteries that need to be solved. Ones for which your respective gifts, both intellectual and, shall we say, *spiritual*, are suited?"

Maya paused.

"What if I told you that there's a group of us who have devoted our lives to solving cases that require hearts that are open to the transcendent and minds capable of high levels of reasoning and analysis? What if I told you that we are caretakers and guardians of a collection of archives that the conventional authorities cannot or even will not investigate? What if we wanted to pay you handsomely to open these supernatural files and bring to bear the same considerable expertise you have shown thus far?"

"You're still not making sense," Maya said.

"I think I'm speaking quite plainly."

"She means you still haven't said who or what this group is," Stone objected, his voice rising.

"Nor your purpose," Maya added.

"Our purpose is exploration," he said. "And the landscape we explore is the largely undiscovered land between life and death, between the finite brain and infinite consciousness."

"Oh," Stone cried. "You're parapsychologists."

"We have several eminent parapsychologists in our group, yes. But we also have theologians, a neuroscientist, two former intelligence chiefs, an astrophysicist, a detective..."

"And are they all white, like you?" Maya asked.

"No, we are a diverse group ethnically, and we're not just males either. We are united by our common curiosity, by our shared desire, in the words of *High Flight* to travel to the untravelled sanctity of space and time, put out our hands ..."

"And touch the face of God," Stone said.

"Precisely." The archivist looked up into Maya's eyes. "We believe, Miss Hailey, that you possess great knowledge in this field. Knowledge that is not just rational, but spiritual." He turned to Stone. "And you, Professor. You are more sceptical yes, but scepticism is necessary in adventures such as these. And in any case, your scepticism is less dismissive than it used to be."

Stone ignored the comment. Instead, he pointed at the album. "The photograph. Is it a magic trick, an illusion? Or is it, for want of a better word, 'real'?"

The archivist smiled.

"Why do people indulge in this great dichotomy between the magical and real?" he asked. "The categories are far more blurred than that. There are many things that people designate as real which are truly magical, and vice versa."

"Explain," Stone said.

"Well, the fact that the sun rises every morning is part of our everyday reality."

"Except in Northern Ireland," Maya quipped.

The archivist chuckled. "True," he said, "but the point I'm making is that what we call real is quite magical."

Stone shook his head.

"I know that you're a fan of Arthur C Clarke, Professor, and that you believe what today we refer to as magic will one day be explainable as technology. But I am not talking about that."

"What are you talking about, then?"

"I'm saying that it's quite possible to find magic in the fact that the sun comes up, that we have air to breathe, and that we can look at places like Lough Erne and be overawed by the mystical, magical, and even miraculous nature of it all."

"If that's true," Stone said, "why are you so interested in exploring metaphysical more than physical phenomena?"

"Because of the reverse side of the coin."

Stone shook his head again.

"What I'm trying to tell you is this: not only is the real much more magical than people - especially those prone to sensationalism – realise. It's also true that the magical is more real than people – especially those prone to materialism – realise."

"You're talking about wonder, aren't you?" Maya said.

The archivist smiled.

"I am."

"In that case," Stone said, his voice betraying a note of impatience, "let me repeat the question. Is that photograph of Maya's grandfather something real or something magical?"

"There you go again," the archivist said. "You're stuck in a false dichotomy, in the either-or of real versus magical. What if something like this photograph can be both? What if the photo is real, in the sense that it can be studied as any material object can, and in the sense that the picture it records corresponds to something that really occurred? But what if, at the same time..."

"It's something infused with the supernatural, the spiritual, the mystical," Maya interjected.

The archivist nodded.

"But that's contradictory," Stone said.

"Is it?" the archivist retorted. "Who was it that said that the test of a first-rate intelligence is the ability to hold two opposing ideas at the same time without losing the ability to function?"

"F. Scott Fitzgerald," Maya answered.

"Exactly. We're looking for people like you who can navigate the landscape of paradox. We think Hailey and Stone would make a great team for a task such as this."

"You haven't even told us your name," Stone said. "Why should I commit my time to someone I don't even know?"

"You can refer to me as the archivist."

"That's not a name," the professor cried.

"But it is my job title."

"What's the name of your group?"

"I can't tell you that."

"Then how are we supposed to trust you?"

"Professor, do you remember just before you were run off the road by Agent Miller? You saw a paramedic on the other side of the carriageway. She saved your life. She works for us."

Stone laughed. "I suppose you're going to tell me Director Harper works for you too!"

The archivist smiled.

"You're kidding!"

The archivist shook his head. "I'm not. Why don't you

call him and ask him now. Use my phone."

The archivist found the number and presented his phone.

"That won't be necessary."

Stone was shaken.

"There are others," the archivist said. "Some of them you have met, although in passing. They are like the angels that people are said to encounter unawares. Bret met one, the night he was viciously attacked by Agent Miller. That angel saved his life."

Maya sat down again. "So, you're saying that all along you've been observing us, protecting us when you could?"

The archivist nodded. "We had to. Agent Miller was a very clear and present danger to you and to our plans."

Stone sighed. "Thank goodness he's in custody."

"Ah, there's a problem there."

"Don't tell me he's escaped."

"His former boss managed to get him out. We are going to have to have eyes on them in the future. Miller has an axe to grind. And you two are not in his good books."

"That's hardly an incentive!" Stone exclaimed.

"But I know something that is," the archivist retorted.

"What?"

"We have access to intelligence and information that the world's best espionage agencies would give anything to see. And I know that within everything we have there will be vital data about someone you have secretly longed to know about."

"Who?"

"Your father."

Stone's mouth opened wide. He stared at the man opposite and shook his head.

"If you two work for us, I'm sure we can dig deep into our files and tell you what you want to know."

The archivist stood. He handed them a business card. The same sexton's compass formed the basis for the logo in the centre. On the back there was an email address and a phone number.

"Contact me if you decide to join us."

He gathered up the album under his arm.

"There are other cases besides the one in this book. Cases that you two could investigate and solve."

He left the room.

"Fancy a drink?" Stone asked.

"After that, I think I need one," Maya replied.

40

THE DECISION

Stone ordered a double shot of Bourbon for Maya and a Guinness for himself. When he had paid, he carried the drinks to a secluded alcove in a quieter room in his local pub. He smiled and said 'Cheers" as he sat at the small wooden table.

"What do you think of the archivist's offer?"

"I'm conflicted," Maya replied.

Stone took a gulp of Guinness. As he licked the cream from his lips, he waited for her to elaborate. They had been working together long enough for him to know when she had begun a reply but not yet completed it. Sure enough, she continued.

"I won't lie to you. I'm fascinated by cases like Granddaddy's. Seeing him speak to us out of that old photograph has shown me how much I don't know about the supernatural."

Stone took another gulp.

"I've always seen supernatural phenomena as events that

occur within Pentecostal communities. I have never really thought of them happening beyond the walls of churches such as the one my father led. It's a huge shift in my thinking to see that people who don't go to church can witness genuine marvels."

"People like me, you mean," Stone said. He smiled as he answered. The white foam from the top of his Guinness spread around his lips, making his mouth look like a clown's.

"Yes, people like you, Professor."

"I don't see anything contradictory here," Stone said. "If a person believes in God, I assume that means they sign up for the belief that this divine being is present everywhere, not just in churches. Indeed, if I was God, I would demand to be anywhere else but in church services. They can be so excruciatingly dull."

Maya chuckled.

"You may laugh, Maya, but I think if a person is going to believe in God, then their God should be big, not small. Their deity should be involved in all human lives, not just some religious lives. To be restricted to speaking and acting in the lives of the religious alone would be my idea of hell on earth."

Maya was laughing so hard now that she almost choked on her Jack Daniels.

"Surely, this God would want to speak to people outside the church as much as those within it."

Maya's face became more serious. "You'll have no argument from me on that front," she said. "But what if the supernatural phenomena I'm talking about are not from God?"

"You mean the dark side."

"Yes, I do. My daddy brought me up to condemn such phenomena. When I was a teenager, he often quoted Isaiah 8:19 when I talked about Ouija boards and other things at school."

"What did Isaiah say?"

"A modern version of it goes like this. 'When people tell you, "Try out the fortune tellers. Consult the spiritualists. Why not tap into the spirit-world, get in touch with the dead?" Tell them, "No, we're going to study the Scriptures." People who try the other ways get nowhere - a dead end!' That' quite direct, isn't it, Professor?"

"It's very binary."

"What do you mean?"

"I mean, the verse you just cited makes it sound like the spirit world – I think that's what the text called it – is made up of either good phenomena or evil phenomena. It's binary. Dualistic. Either or. But what if this world, if it exists, is more complex than that? What if there are grey areas where the phenomena the archivist is talking about are neither obviously and straightforwardly from the light nor from the dark in origin and nature?"

"But that's not what Daddy believed!"

"I know this is hard, Maya, but maybe it's time for you to grow from a parental to a personal philosophy. Maybe there's more to this so-called spirit world than you've understood."

"It's your turn to explain, Professor."

Stone took another drink.

"Let's take the photograph. When I first saw it, your grandfather came alive and spoke to me. Was there anything evil about this? Was there anything good for that matter? To use slightly Medieval terminology, there was nothing angelic about your grandfather, but there was nothing demonic about him either."

Maya nodded.

"When he asked me to find him, I was not blinded by the light as Saul was on the Damascus Road, but I wasn't taken over by the darkness, as Jack Torrance was in *The Shining*."

"What were you, then?"

"Sorry?"

"What happened to you, Professor?"

"I had an experience that I'm still trying to explain. If it was supernatural, then it struck me then as it strikes me now that it certainly wasn't evil. As we discussed in a restaurant when we first met, I was not consulting with a medium, nor was I seeking a message from the dead. The desire, the motivation, came from your grandfather, not from me. He sought me. I didn't seek him."

Maya drained her Bourbon and offered to pay for a fresh round of drinks. Several minutes later, she was back at the table, passing a full pint of Guinness to the Professor.

"Would that it was that simple," she muttered.

"Come again?"

"This separation between light and darkness." She pointed at the cream resting on the surface of the liquid – a liquid as black as the peatlands of Fermanagh.

Stone smiled before he tipped the glass, causing the cream and the stout to blend into each other.

"Is that better?" he asked.

Maya smiled.

"What are you going to do, Maya?"

"My little trip to the bar gave me a few minutes to reflect on what you've been saying, Professor. I think I'd like to give the archivist a try. I think I'd like to say yes to his invitation."

She took a sip of golden liquid.

"What about you?" she asked.

"I'm technically free for a year."

"On sabbatical, you mean."

"That's right."

"Aren't you supposed to be writing a book?"

"I was going to ask you about that, Maya. Feel free to say no to this, especially if you want to do it yourself, but what if I wrote up the story of your grandfather?"

"You go right ahead," Maya said.

"Are you sure?"

"Yes, I'm no writer. And I'd rather you did it than someone we don't know. In fact, I was going to ask you."

"That will free up a lot of time this year," Stone said. "I could then say yes to the archivist too."

Stone and Hailey lifted their glasses and brought them together to toast the agreement.

"One more thing," Stone said.

"What's that?"

"The royalties. I'm not comfortable keeping them. I think you should decide where the money will go."

"That's a great idea, Professor."

"Good."

They drained the dregs of their drinks and headed out of the pub into the night. As they walked back towards Stone's apartment, Maya took hold of Stone's arm and pulled him to a halt. She gazed out across the calm sea. As swallow-tailed flags fluttered in the breeze, she turned away from the marina to look at Stone. "I'm excited about working together in the future. Are you?"

"I feel invigorated," he replied.

"Your grandfather will be smiling, Professor."

"Why do you say that?"

"He loved Howard Thurman."

"He did indeed."

Maya continued. "Thurman said, 'Don't ask yourself what the world needs. Ask yourself what makes you come alive and go do that.' I think you should *go do that*, Professor."

A strong wind shook the burgees and ensigns in the mastheads of the anchored yachts. Hailey kept her arm in Stone's as they walked towards the cobbled street and his apartment.

"Thank you for everything, Cameron," she said.

Stone replied, "My friends call me Cam."

"Thank you for everything, Cam."

And they both laughed.

AUTHOR'S NOTE

When I'm leading workshops or coaching sessions for writers, I'm often asked where people find strong ideas for stories. For some, it's an exciting *premise* – an idea that becomes luminous in the writer's mind and which then forms the big theme for the entire story. For others it's an interesting *protagonist* – a character that jumps like Aslan into their dreams. For others it is a compelling *plot* – events that lead through twists and turns to a surprising resolution. For me, it is none of the above. The genesis of all my stories is an enchanting *place* – a cottage, house, village, or lake that mesmerises me so deeply that it digs up the soil of my imagination and plants the seeds of the other three elements above – premise, protagonist, plot. The Celtic saints called such locations 'thin places.' By that they meant settings in which the membrane between the ordinary world we inhabit (often characterised by the noun 'realism') and some otherworldly dimension (often characterised by the adjective 'magical') is permeable.

When I look back at the novel writing I have done since 2012, I can trace the genesis of each of my stories to a place that became thin, at least to my senses. *King of Hearts* started with me visiting a tiny village on Christmas Eve – a village that became the location for the beginning and end of my story. *The Fate of Kings* began with a visit to the smuggler's museum in the basement of Bleak House in Broadstairs, Kent – the house in which Charles Dickens wrote some of his novels at a desk overlooking the ocean. *A Book in Time* owes its origin to a tiny cottage owned by two elderly women – both literary geniuses – who used to wine and dine me when I was in my late teens and early twenties. *House of Dreams* began when my wife and I stayed in an old rectory in Dorset – a house that was originally a hunting lodge given as a wedding gift to Queen Catherine Parr by King Henry VIII. Each of these locations became 'thin places' in my soul. They triggered stories with interesting premises, protagonists, and plots.

In the case of *Dead Man Talking*, everything began with a wedding. I ought to explain that I am very fortunate to be married to a stunning, red-headed Northern Irish girl. Her closest family and friends, by and large, live in the Emerald Isle. This means that I get to visit Northern Ireland with her quite often. On one of those visits, we found ourselves at the wedding of one of her oldest friends. The location? The Lough Erne Resort in County Fermanagh. The moment we arrived I could sense the allure of the place. Lough Erne, as you'll see in my story, is a huge lake made up of two parts (upper and lower) and over one hundred small islands. To travellers in the eighteenth century, it was deemed one of the wonders of the world. Its natural beauty, combined with its rich mystical history, proved to be an enticing lure to those who wanted to explore the world. Many authors have praised it. I am simply another doing the same.

What captivated me most was not the stories of the ancient deities worshipped on and around Lough Erne, nor those of the brave Celtic saints whose faith displaced them. It was the more recent history from World War 2. I learned that the RAF had spotted the lough and decided it would make an ideal liquid runway for seaplanes venturing into the Atlantic. Winston Churchill said there was only one thing he really feared during the war - the deadly, lupine submarines that hunted and sank the merchant navy vessels bringing vital supplies from the USA to Europe. The Catalina and Sunderland Short seaplanes that flew through the Donegal Corridor were every bit as courageous as the Spitfire pilots who flew from the airfields where I live and write in Kent. Until *Dead Man Talking*, these Catalina and Sunderland crews have not been remembered and honoured in either novel or film. When we remember that the Battle of the Atlantic was by far the longest battle of World War 2, it should give us pause.

On the night of the wedding, my imagination was ignited as I gazed out of the windows onto the lough. I knew there was a story incubating in my soul, but I needed help learning about the history of these seaplanes, especially the greatly under-appreciated Catalinas. That help came in the form of a wonderful Northern Irishman called Joe O'Loughlin. In his nineties, he possessed a wealth of information about the war years at Lough Erne. He had been a teenager at the time and had seen and heard the Catalinas and other aircraft taking off and landing on the lough. He shared his memories with me in emails, calls, and over one memorable cup of coffee in Belleek. His books, along with one by Breege

McCusker (*Castle Archdale and Fermanagh in World War 2*) provided much of the anecdotal history I needed for *Dead Man Talking*. I owe a great deal to them both, but especially to Joe, who gave me permission to use anything he had shared.

Then I discovered Dr Simon Topping, a professor of history at Plymouth University. No one to my knowledge knows more than Simon does about the history of black service personnel in Northern Ireland during World War 2. Simon is a Northern Irishman with a generous spirit; he replied straightaway when I wrote to him. He shared the fruits of his research during zoom conversations and email correspondence. He sent me PDFs of his rigorous and eminently readable research into the experiences of American soldiers in Northern Ireland. He is one of the finest historians in the British Isles. I have been very blessed to have him as a guide, especially during the early months when I had to be brought up to speed quickly on the complexities of a socio-political context in which black GIs were fighting two battles – the Nazis in Europe and the racists in their own ranks – and in which Irish Catholics were fighting against political persecution in their own country while trying to play their part in the war against Germany.

The breakthrough for me came when I read Simon's disturbing account of what happened to a black soldier called Wiley Harris. He was arrested for murdering a pimp and tried at the Victoria Barracks in Belfast. Simon pointed out that if he had been tried in a British rather than a military court, he would likely have been sentenced for manslaughter. Harris would therefore have received a prison sentence. He would not have been hanged. This stirred my imagination and led me to base Second Lieutenant George Hailey – the black airman in my novel – very loosely on Wiley Harris. Those who are knowledgeable about Harris's grim fate will notice some of the broad parallels while also being alert to the differences that fiction writing demands. Those who read African American literature will recognise other narrative echo effects. They may also see how white authors like Harper Lee and John Grisham have likewise influenced me.

The biggest influence of all, however, has been Lough Erne. My brief exposure to its history and mystery at the wedding sparked something in my soul. I was struck by the raw realism of what men and women experienced there during World War 2. But I was equally enticed by the sense of mysticism that hung like a morning mist all over the lake and its many islands. This is why I am less inclined to use 'magical realism' as a generic descriptor for my fiction writing, and more inclined now to talk about 'mystical realism.' Mysticism is really a word reserved for the human experience of communion with God. Although it is the province of deep thinkers, it is more a spirituality of the heart than the head. This preference for the affective over the cognitive, the experiential over the cerebral, the intimate over the intellectual, is one of the defining qualities and identification markers of mysticism. Such encounters with the transcendent do not have to be religious – in the sense of Christian, Jewish, or Islamic – to qualify as mysticism. Poets who value spirituality but eschew religion can have mystical encounters. In truth, anyone who is docile to the spiritual realm can have them too.

I like to think of my novels as examples of Mystical

Realism. They are written for anyone who enjoys stories that take place in real rather than fantastical worlds, but where the realism is enlarged by the phenomena of mysticism rather than diminished by the prejudices of materialism. Lough Erne of all places lends itself to such a perspective because the borders between the sacred and the mundane, between the spiritual and the material, between the unseen and seen, are more flimsy than fixed. These boundaries are not like stone-walled levies that keep the two worlds apart. They are more liquid than solid, more fluid than concrete. Lough Erne is simply one of those thin places where your sleeves are brushed by angel's wings. I am forever grateful for being introduced to it during the wedding celebrations.

Another time, my wife and I visited Lough Erne and stayed in a much smaller place than the big resort we had stayed at for the wedding. After a good night's sleep, I got up and sat outside in the sun drinking a mug of coffee. I watched swans floating on the water and a heron soaring effortlessly into the sky. After several minutes, I became aware of men walking down to the edge of the lough. They were dressed in fishermen's gear and heading towards a flotilla of small boats with big motors. They carried fishing rods and nets. I soon discovered that I had woken up on the morning of an international pike fishing tournament that takes place every year at Lough Erne. I stared with fascination at these men and women in galoshes speeding out to the deepest, darkest parts of the vast lough, eager to set their hooks and lines, waiting to catch the huge pike for which the lough is famed.

As I watched these eager and excited anglers, I thought of all the men who had once ventured out in boats to their Catalinas resting on the water. I saw them in my mind's eye clambering aboard, unloading their food and equipment, and checking all the systems on their aircraft. I heard the Pratt and Whitney engines bursting into life and the seaplanes moving like swans on the water until they rose into the sky with majestic ease and headed off towards the ocean.

Whenever I am asked, I always say it is *places*, especially *thin places*, that spawn the stories I feel compelled to form and write - places like Lough Erne in Northern Ireland. While there are people like Joe and Simon I want to thank, the greatest debt I owe is to the great lakes of County Fermanagh, to the glorious waters of upper and lower Lough Erne. To this vast and liquid expanse, with all its many inlets and islands, I offer my heartfelt thanks.

Mark Stibbe, July 2024.

ACKNOWLEDGEMENTS

I am so grateful to my two expert readers, Rachel Wilkinson and Renée Heywood, especially for their invaluable input on issues related to Northern Irish issues and African American culture. I'm deeply thankful to those who have offered advice about Second World War history, in particular events to do with Northern Ireland's part in the Battle of the Atlantic. Dr Simon Topping at Plymouth University has been an invaluable help, especially concerning the experiences of African American service personnel in Northern Ireland during this fraught and volatile time in history. Joe O'Loughlin has also been a great help. Having someone to talk to who grew up in the Lough Erne area during WW2, and who saw with his own eyes some of the things I describe in this novel, has been of priceless value. Joe's permission to use anything in his books was an act of supreme generosity.

I would also like to thank theologian James H. Cone for his exceptional book, *The Cross and the Lynching tree* – in my view, the most important book on the Cross written this century. Some of you will recognise his voice and views in the bishop's oration after the story of George Hailey is published. It is my homage to a great work of theology.

I also want to thank those who have helped me get this book into print and get it out into the marketplace, especially the wonderful Esther Kotecha (cover design, typesetting, formatting etc) and the equally wonderful Kelly Lacy (Love Book Tours) and her great team of booklovers and reviewers.

I have been blessed by my many visits to the USA and the many opportunities these have afforded to give talks in African American conferences and seminars and to speak with close African American friends. More importantly, this has given me many opportunities to listen. I have learned so much from your stories, both sacred and earthy. Some of you have adopted me as not only a brother but a father. You know who you are. I love you dearly.

Above all, I've been blessed by my marriage to a Northern Irish beauty, Cherith Stibbe. Marrying her was the best decision I ever made. If it had been her alone, that would have been amazing. But I have also been richly blessed by her family and friends in Northern Ireland who have embraced me as a member of the family. I have fallen in love with Northern Ireland and the Irish – a people whom I now regard as the finest on earth. It is to these dear ones that I joyfully dedicate this story – the first in a series of supernatural investigations for the unlikely duo of Hailey and Stone.

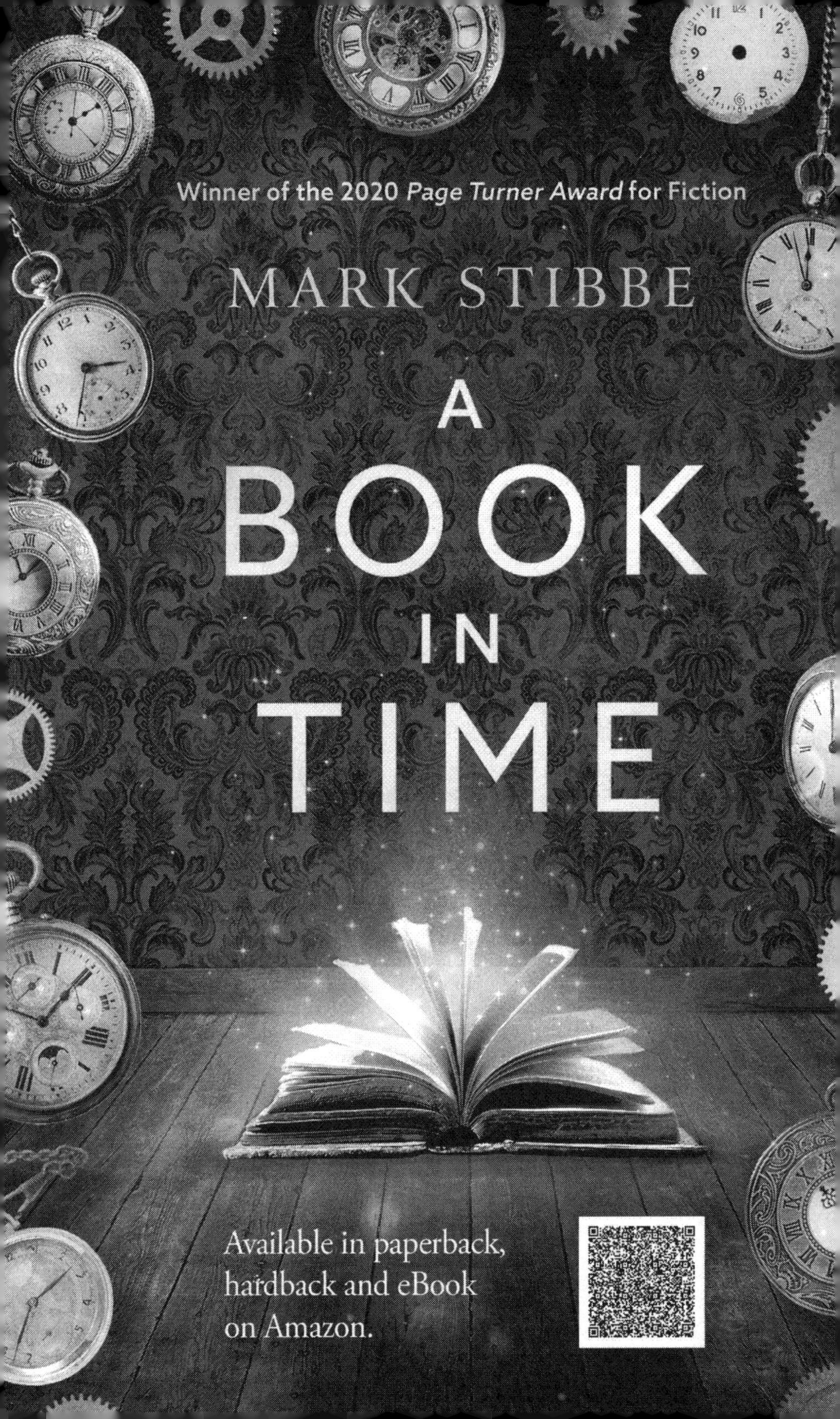
Winner of the 2020 *Page Turner Award* for Fiction
MARK STIBBE
A BOOK IN TIME
Available in paperback, hardback and eBook on Amazon.

Printed in Great Britain
by Amazon

0ced67e2-2e9c-4b0f-9704-f6af96f11180R01